Beneath THE Haunting Sea

Beneath
THE
Haunting
Sea

JOANNA
RUTH MEYER

PAGE STREET
PUBLISHING CO.

PAGE STREET
PUBLISHING CO.

Copyright © 2018 Joanna Ruth Meyer

First published in 2018 by
Page Street Publishing Co.
27 Congress Street, Suite 105
Salem, MA 01970
www.pagestreetpublishing.com

Distributed by Macmillan, sales in Canada by The Canadian Manda Group.

22   21   20   19   18   1   2   3   4   5

ISBN-13: 978-1-62414-534-6
ISBN-10: 1-62414-534-5

Library of Congress Control Number: 2017947935

Cover and book design by Page Street Publishing Co.
Cover photo by Laura Ferreira
Author photo by Gary D. Smith

Printed and bound in the United States

To Jenny–you'll always be the Lewis to my Tolkien and for Aaron, my Faramir (they wouldn't dare cut *our* scenes out of the movie).

Part One:

GODS AND MEN

But the gods thought them small and without knowledge, and did not like that mankind had been given love and they had not.

Chapter One

T ALIA THUNDERED ACROSS THE PLAIN, HER HEAD bent low over her mount's neck, the world a blur of dust and wind and exhilarating speed. The sun was just slipping above the peaks of the northern mountains, bathing the desert in liquid gold—already it burned blistering hot on her shoulders. She'd have to go back to Eddenahr soon, but she couldn't shake the feeling that if she rode just a little faster she could leap into the sky, race the goddess of the air herself, and *win*.

But her mare couldn't run forever. Talia pulled her to a walk and peered back toward Eddenahr, breathing hard. The city sprawled white and silver across the desert, a maze of blue-tiled roofs and white walls; the heat made it shimmer. Even from this distance the light refracted blindingly from the domes of the spired towers, and she had to squint, shading her eyes with one hand. Bells clamored in the dawn hush, calling up the sun.

She really needed to go back. *Now.*

Talia nudged her mare toward the city, wishing she could stay out here forever between the boundless earth and sky. Wind tugged her hair loose from its careless braid, whipping long black strands into her face. Sweat prickled at the back of her neck. She wouldn't have time for a bath if she didn't hurry, and appearing before the Emperor of half the world smelling of horse was probably not the best plan. Her stomach wrenched nervously as she touched her heels to the mare's flanks.

Halfway back to the city, she spotted another rider coming toward her across the plain. She gritted her teeth, afraid it might be a palace attendant sent out to collect her—or worse, her mother.

But as she and the other rider drew near each other and reined in their mounts, Talia was surprised to see a young woman, elegantly dressed in flowing gold silk trousers and a sleeveless top studded with sapphires. The top was cropped short to show off her midriff, brown skin gleaming with sandalwood oil. Her black hair was pinned elaborately on top of her head and woven through with strands of gold. Her lashes were lined with kohl, her eyelids dusted with shimmering gold powder. Her beauty was unmistakable, untouchable—like a goddess of old.

"Eda," said Talia at last, forcing herself to speak civilly, though everything in her wanted to wheel the mare around and gallop away. "What are you doing out here so early?"

Eda brushed a stray curl out of her face with one elegant hand, eyes narrowing. "Why has the Emperor asked you to breakfast?"

Talia's mare fidgeted beneath her, "That's none of your concern."

"Isn't it?" Danger lurked beneath her words, a thunderstorm about to break.

Talia couldn't help but remember the first time she'd met Eda, half a lifetime ago when Talia's parents had brought her to visit Eddenahr from their estate in mountainous Irsa. A peacock had gotten loose in the palace corridors and Talia had chased after it, laughing, losing one of her new silk slippers and tearing her too-long, brightly embroidered skirt. She'd bumped into Eda after an attendant scooped up the miscreant bird to return it to the garden. The other girl stood there frowning like an old lady, even though she was a gangly girl of eleven.

"It's unseemly to run in the Emperor's halls," Eda had told her. "You disrespect His Imperial Majesty."

Talia stammered an apology, but it didn't seem to be enough.

"Who are you?" Eda demanded.

"Talia Dahl-Saida of Irsa. Who are you?"

"I'm the Countess of Evalla," Eda said coldly. "Didn't you ever learn to show deference to your superiors?"

Talia didn't know what to say. She was the daughter of a countess—which made them equals as far as she could tell—and she hadn't known then that this girl, barely older than herself, was Governor of the entire province of Evalla. So she'd dropped a confused curtsy and run back to her parents as quick as she could, hoping her path would never again cross with the severe child Countess.

But it did, and far more frequently than Talia could have imagined. Her parents were on the Emperor's Council, and their visits to the capital of Enduena increased exponentially until they were in Eddenahr a vast deal more than they were in Irsa. Talia had to attend lessons with a dozen other courtiers' children, spending nearly every day shut up inside, working through mathematical equations or memorizing historical facts or learning to dance, sew, draw. Eda was at every lesson, as she was considered too young to live in Evalla and govern the province on her own without a proper education—a fact that she deeply resented. She'd become Countess at the age of nine, when both of her parents had died of a vicious fever, but had been living in the palace ever since.

She was also rumored to be the Emperor's bastard daughter. Talia had asked her father what that meant, and his answer both embarrassed and fascinated her; Eda's mother had grown up in the palace and was a favorite of the Emperor. Her hasty marriage

to the Count of Evalla and Eda's birth barely nine months later
had caused more than one raised brow. Whether it was true or not,
Eda certainly considered herself royalty. And her opinion of Talia
had never improved since that day with the peacock.

Out on the plain, the sun burning hotter and hotter with
every degree it rose into the sky, Talia tried not to squirm under
Eda's scrutiny. The other girl always made her feel so small.
"What do you want, Eda?"

"I want to know what the Emperor could possibly have to
say to you."

"Why do you care? Still waiting for him to admit he's your
father so you can feel like you have some worth in the world?"

Eda's eyes burned with cold fire. "You will fall very low, Talia
of Irsa. Then we will see how quick your tongue is."

A fierce wind whipped up between them, hot and stinging
with dust, and Talia had the sudden, horrible feeling that Eda's
threats were every bit as menacing. She shuddered; Eda smiled.

"I have to go," Talia snapped. "I'll be late."

Eda made a little mocking half bow from her saddle. "Then
go, and gods keep you."

Talia nudged her mare on toward Eddenahr. But she couldn't
quite shake her sense of foreboding as she rode through the gate
and the white city swallowed her up.

Talia followed an attendant down the long white corridors to the
royal wing of the palace, her bare feet slapping over the white-
and-gold marble floor. She hadn't had time to call an attendant to
fix her hair or line her eyes with kohl, but at least she'd managed
a hasty bath.

She'd never been in the royal wing before. Pillars carved with
lattice work soared to high domed ceilings, and the walls were

covered in mosaics, the brightly colored pieces of glass depicting scenes from mythology. She glimpsed the god of the earth and the god of the sea holding two shining Stars; she saw the Immortal Tree laying on its side as all mankind wept over it.

Talia's heart belonged in Irsa on her parents' mountain estate, but she had grown to love Eddenahr too. Maybe it was because her father had always seen adventure around every corner, or because she could feel the weight of history whispering in the corridors of the two-thousand-year-old palace. The royal wing seemed even older than the rest of it.

"This way, Miss Dahl-Saida." The attendant opened a carved ivory door and ushered her into a small inner courtyard.

For a moment she stood there, blinking, as her eyes adjusted to the sunlight. And then she saw the Emperor of Enduena.

He was sitting at a low ebony table, propped up against a dozen pillows, his brown hand shaking as he raised a goblet of wine to his lips. He was not an old man, certainly not above sixty, but he looked as ancient as the earth itself. His eyes were sunken into his face, his skin sagging about him like an oversized shirt. He looked impossibly frail, vastly more ill than the last time Talia had seen him at a court dinner about a week ago.

Tamping down her anxiety, she stepped toward the table and curtsied very low.

It was only then she became aware of her mother, kneeling on a cushion to the Emperor's left. Her eyes pierced through Talia, instantly disapproving of her unkempt state but just as equally resigned to it. She wore a deep-green sleeveless top and matching mirror-embroidered skirt, with a gauzy blue sash draped over her shoulder and gold threads wound into her beautiful black hair.

"Sit down, my dear," came the Emperor's voice, wispy and small and sounding far away.

Talia sank onto a cushion opposite the Emperor, glancing to her mother. Her mother gave her an encouraging smile, but Talia didn't miss the way she was fidgeting with her glass. Talia had never known her mother to be nervous.

Sunlight poured into the open courtyard, and a pair of attendants pulled an awning from wall to wall, tying the ends onto waiting hooks. A fountain burbled in the back corner and jasmine vines crawled up the stones, their white star-shaped flowers closed tight until the evening. Talia glimpsed a peacock pecking for bugs by the fountain and wondered idly if it was a descendant of the one she'd chased around the palace.

Attendants poured cardamom tea and spread breakfast onto the table: mangoes and flatbread drizzled with honey, rice cakes and fried bananas, poached duck eggs and spicy lentils. Talia heaped everything onto her plate. She was ravenous from her long ride, but it was disconcerting to be stared at by the Emperor at such a close range, and her anxiety quickly smothered her hunger. She found she could barely touch her food and just sipped her tea, the spicy sweetness sparking on her tongue.

"Well," said Talia's mother after a few minutes of agonizing silence, "I suppose it's time to discuss why we asked you here. Your Imperial Majesty?"

The Emperor blinked at her mother and then turned his gaze to Talia. Spittle clung to the corner of his mouth and dripped in his patchy beard. His hand shook as he set his goblet back on the table, red wine sloshing over the edge. "My health is failing," he said in that far-away voice. "I must choose an heir."

He was seized by a coughing fit. He couldn't seem to stop. An attendant appeared with an etched metal cup and put it to his lips. The Emperor drank, slowly, and his coughing subsided.

Tears leaked from his eyes, and Talia bowed her head, ashamed for him. Once, this man had been young and strong—a war hero, a fearless leader. He'd been the one to abolish the slave trade and unite the mainland provinces, to claim the island of Ryn for the Enduenan Empire, to strengthen relations with the colonies on Od, to demand tribute from Halda, and to establish trade with Ita. He'd defended Enduena from the warriors of Denlahn and driven them back across the sea to their own land. He'd launched countless ships after the Denlahn, determined to absorb them too into the Empire, but the long voyage weakened his soldiers and the Denlahn slaughtered them. It was considered his only failure.

But that was decades ago, long before Talia was born. Now the Emperor was a wasted shell. The Empress had died ten years ago, her health never recovered from bringing a son into the world. The teenage prince had been killed last year in a hunting accident, and the Emperor fell ill shortly afterward. The court pinned silver mourning tokens to their sleeves, whispering that their heartbroken Emperor would never be the same. And they were right.

"You come of age next week," said her mother, causing Talia to look up again. "His Imperial Majesty will make the announcement at your party."

Talia glanced from the Emperor to her mother and back again, a confused suspicion darting into her mind. "What announcement?"

The Emperor's watery eyes focused on Talia's. "The gods saw fit to give me a daughter," he whispered, "to keep her safe when my son was gone. An heir to the Empire."

Talia's heart raced, thinking of her encounter on the plain. "Do you mean Eda, Your Imperial Majesty?"

A frown pressed between his eyes, and he slowly shook his head. "I mean *you*, Talia Dahl-Saida. You are my daughter. My heir. A gift from the gods. You will be Empress of Enduena when I am gone."

Talia started shaking violently, her body understanding the Emperor's words before her mind did. Before her heart did. A hot wind curled under the awning and whispered across her neck. She sucked in a sharp breath and jerked up from her seat, knocking over her tea. Milky-brown liquid leaked across the ebony table and dripped onto the ground. Her head spun. She forced herself to focus on the Emperor, on her mother, forced the words past her lips: "I don't understand."

Her mother's hand trembled where she gripped her own cup; but for that, she was still. "The Emperor is your father, Talia. You will be the next Empress of Enduena, and at your party he will announce it to the court."

She couldn't breathe, couldn't think. A rift opened inside of her, a chasm spiraling into yawning dark. Everything narrowed to the Emperor, his sagging face and hollow frame. "I have a father," she whispered, voice cracking.

Her mother rose from her cushion and attempted to lay a hand on Talia's arm.

Talia shook her off, seizing onto the one emotion she understood: anger. "I. Have. A *father*."

"Talia—"

But she was already gone, bolting from the courtyard and back down the corridors the way she had come.

She ran until her lungs burned and sharp pains shot through her sides. She ran until she reached her rooms, dashing out onto her balcony and hoisting herself onto the roof. She curled up underneath an overhang of blue tiles, jasmine and honeysuckle twining up to meet her, and allowed the sun to sear her toes, the scent of hot stone to overwhelm her.

Talia had always divided her life into two halves: before her father died, and after.

Almost everything she dearly loved belonged to the first half: long winter nights on her parents' estate in Irsa; learning to ride;

learning to read outside on a grassy hill with the wildflowers dancing and the bees keeping time. Every summer she traveled with her parents to Eddenahr, and her father was the one who taught her to love the ancient city, its white walls and tiled roofs, its gleaming spired towers. The two of them went on adventures in the Emperor's gardens when Talia didn't have lessons to attend. Together, they explored the stables and the hound runs and the aviary. He held her hand as they visited the tiger pits, and would climb up with her onto the palace roof. They'd sit there with their legs dangling and eat sherbet that melted rapidly into colorful sweet soup in the hot sun.

But the year she turned eleven, he died in an accident on the road and the second half of her life began.

His scent faded from the book room in Irsa, and her mother packed their bags and moved them to Eddenahr for good. Talia was left with a raw, aching emptiness where her father had been. Her days were consumed with countless lessons and Eda's never-ending derision. She lived for the moments she could steal to herself: riding on the plain or climbing about on the maze of palace roofs like a monkey escaped from the Emperor's menagerie.

She thought about her father as she sat tucked under the roof tiles, hugging her knees to her chin and trying to understand what her mother had told her. What the Emperor had told her.

Talia wasn't like Eda, desperate for any sign of affection from the Emperor, straining to see echoes of her own features in that wasted man. The thought that *Talia* might be the Emperor's illegitimate daughter had never even entered her head.

It wasn't possible. It couldn't be.

And yet—

"Talia?"

She jerked her head up to see her mother hauling herself onto the roof, then coming gingerly toward her across the slippery tiles. Her mother sat down beside her and peered at her with dark eyes.

Talia turned away, rubbing her thumb over the jagged edge of a broken roof tile. The tile cut into her skin and she flinched. "I don't have anything to say to you."

"Let me explain."

"What is there to explain?" Talia wiped her bleeding thumb on her skirt and faced her mother. "You couldn't have spared even a *second* of your time in the last sixteen years to tell me that my father was *the Emperor of Enduena*?" Her shout echoed among the roof tiles, and her mother winced.

"I didn't want to hurt you. Especially after Celdahn died. And I didn't think it mattered. Not when the prince was alive and well."

Bile burned in the back of Talia's throat. "And now that he's dead you find you have use for me."

"*Talia.*"

"I loved my father! How can you take that away from me?" Tears nearly choked her.

Her mother bit her lip, moisture gleaming in her own eyes. "Celdahn loved you dearly. But he wasn't your father."

"How could you do this to me? To my father? Were you the Emperor's *mistress*?"

"No."

The fierceness in her mother's tone refocused her, and Talia angrily scrubbed the tears from her eyes. "What then?"

Her mother squared her jaw, and for the first time in her life Talia realized her mother might not be the impenetrable marble queen Talia had always thought she was.

"The Emperor is not to be denied. What he asks for . . . he receives." Her mother lifted her shoulders and let them drop again, the careless gesture belied by the shake in her voice.

"Did my father know?"

"Of course he knew."

She let out a breath—she couldn't have borne it if her father had only loved her because he thought she was his.

"Talia, you have to listen. Perhaps I should have told you a long time ago, but the Emperor and I wanted to protect you. No one else knows, and no one *can* know until the Emperor makes the announcement. You can't tell anyone—not even Ayah. It's too dangerous. Courtiers will try to manipulate you, maybe even try to harm you. Promise me, Talia."

She felt blank and dull and numb. She didn't understand how that even mattered. "Were there others like you? Is Eda my sister?"

Her mother frowned at the unexpected question. "Perhaps, but that doesn't matter now. You have to promise me. If anyone asks about your party, it is only to celebrate your coming-of-age. Do you understand?"

Talia stared out beyond the rooftop. Heat rose in waves from the sprawling city below her. A crane winged its way across the sky, glinting silver in the sunlight.

"Talia. Will you promise me?"

She attempted to gather the shattered remains of herself, and turned her eyes to her mother. "I promise."

Chapter Two

TALIA PRACTICED HER SPEECH IN FRONT OF her dressing table mirror while her parrot chattered from its perch and the fountains laughed just below her window. Her eyes were hot and itchy from too many sleepless nights, and she gave up trying to hold onto the formal words she was expected to say in a little less than six hours.

She collapsed onto the floor and lay flat on her back, staring up at the white dome of her ceiling, at the curls of vines and blue orchids painted on the marble. A hot breeze blew through her balcony and she screwed her eyes tight.

Tonight, the Emperor would announce that Talia was his heir, and her life would never be the same again. Already she felt like she didn't belong to herself—she'd been passed about between seamstresses and dance masters and an ancient librarian who kept insisting she recite a passage from a dense religious text for the occasion. Her head had been measured for a crown. She'd been asked what she requested from the Emperor for a birthday present by a very stern steward. Talia had stammered something about a new saddle for her horse; the steward had blinked at her with amusement and said her father would supply her with an entire stable if she wished.

She still couldn't think of the Emperor as her father. She didn't think she ever would.

Tomorrow, she would move into the royal wing of the palace, into the prince's old suite.

Tomorrow, she would be someone else: heir to half the known world.

"Talia Dahl-Saida, *what* are you doing?"

She opened her eyes and jerked guiltily to a sitting position. Her friend Ayah Inoll stood there with her pale hands on her hips, curls of startling orange hair tumbling into her face. "Are you feeling sorry for yourself?"

Talia stood up and walked over to her parrot's perch, stroking the bird's bright feathers as she avoided her friend's question.

"You're not even dressed yet," Ayah admonished.

"I wanted some time to myself. I sent the attendants away."

"You are entirely too dramatic."

Talia glanced back to see Ayah grinning at her.

"It's not going to be that bad."

Talia forced a smile, trying to ignore the wrench in her stomach. She'd promised her mother to keep her true identity hidden, even though every last servant seemed to know. "I have to give a *speech*!"

Ayah grabbed her hands and spun her around in a circle. "*And* be presented to the court as an eligible woman, and eat mountains of food, and dance with every handsome man in Enduena. I don't know what you're worried about."

"I might not get to see you as much."

"Huen's bones. Of course you will."

Ayah's oath made Talia smile in earnest—her friend's religious inclinations made her curse all the more amusing. It wasn't popular to believe in the gods anymore—religion had scarcely been practiced at all in the last half-century, and it was rare to even find a working temple these days. The Emperor frowned upon belief in the old gods, and most people only used them to swear by. But Ayah hailed from one of the Empire's colonies on Od, where the old myths were more generally accepted, and she had apprenticed with a palace librarian. Od supposedly had the greatest university in the world, but Eddenahr still boasted the best library—even though, according to Ayah, they were still trying to recover texts lost in a fire several centuries back. Talia didn't like the library. It was huge and oppressively ancient and too easy to get lost in. If she believed in ghosts—which she didn't—she was sure that's where they would all live. Ayah was always nagging her to go in there anyway, quoting from her dusty religious books and trying to convince her that the gods were as real as the palace stones. Talia liked to tease her that if the gods did exist, it was awfully cruel of them to have made her hair so very *orange*.

"What would I do without you, Ay?"

Ayah grinned again. "Allow yourself to be very miserable. Now come on, I'll help you get dressed."

Talia showed her the gown that had arrived that morning from the seamstress, and had to laugh as Ayah punched her in the shoulder and cursed again. "What on gods' green Endahr are you miserable about, you ridiculous mongoose? Arriving at your coming-of-age ball dressed like a goddess?"

The gown *was* beautiful. It was a delicate yellow silk so pale it looked like starlight, and its accompanying air-light sash was sewn with gold thread and glints of diamonds.

"We don't do anything for coming-of-age in Od," said Ayah wistfully.

"What do you miss most?" This was a question Talia had asked frequently, ever since she'd found a very homesick Ayah sobbing in the corridor outside the library four years ago. It seemed to help Ayah to talk about Od, and Talia loved hearing her stories. Sometimes Talia imagined visiting her friend's homeland, but it was hard to wish to be somewhere else when she already lived in one of the wonders of the world, "the Jewel of Endahr." *Endahr* was an ancient word that meant "the earth," and Eddenahr's name was derived from it, which seemed appropriate to Talia. Eddenahr really did seem like it contained the whole world.

"The forests," said Ayah. "Starlight through the trees. Winter."

Talia slipped into the yellow gown, and Ayah started fastening the back. "We have winter in northern Irsa."

"Not like in Od. Snow so high you can't leave your cottage for days. Cold so sharp you feel it in your bones."

"Sounds miserable."

Ayah punched her in the arm again. "No disrespecting my homeland!"

They both dissolved into laughter.

There came a knock on Talia's door and she went to answer it. An army of attendants flooded in, propelling her to her dressing table and wrapping a sheet around her neck so her dress wouldn't get dirty as they applied her cosmetics.

Talia tried to sit as still as possible while the attendants went to work. Ayah hovered nearby, chattering about the latest mythological text she'd been copying in the library all week, but Talia couldn't pay attention. The words of her speech tumbled about with the memory of her father's laughter, the image of the Emperor in the courtyard, spittle running down his beard.

The attendants twisted her hair into elaborate braids and pinned them on top of her head, crowning her with fresh lilies that filled the whole room with their sweet scent. Over the balcony, the sun began to sink below the city and Talia's anxiety sharpened. It was nearly time. Soon Ayah and everyone else would *know*. Would Ayah treat her differently?

The attendants brushed gold powder across her eyelids and painted her lashes with kohl. They stained her lips a deep blood red. They rubbed her arms and neck and shoulders with citrus-scented oil. They hung sapphires in her ears and slipped calfskin sandals onto her feet. Then they drew the sheet away.

Talia stood from her dressing table and Ayah appraised her with wide eyes. "Caida's teeth," she whispered. "Beautiful."

They went into the corridor together, where Talia's mother was waiting. She wore a red gown that cascaded like water to the floor, with a shimmering, gold sash. Her black hair was bound up with diamonds, her brown skin glimmering with that same citrus-scented oil. "Are you ready?" A question deeper than the one she'd asked hung in her dark eyes.

Talia sucked in a deep breath. "I'm ready," she lied.

When she stepped into the ballroom, bells resounded in the city below to call up the moon—Talia could just glimpse its silver edge through the gauzy curtains adorning the open balcony. Thousands of candles in iron stands and glittering chandeliers cast flickering shadows over the white-and-gold inlaid marble floor. People were already dancing, to the music of harps, flutes, tuned cymbals, and the resounding pulse of a booming drum that echoed in the huge domed chamber.

The attendant in the doorway announced Talia and her mother as they stepped through: "The esteemed Countess Aria Dahl-Saida, Governor of Irsa, and her daughter, Talia Dahl-Saida."

Talia tried not to think of the "Imperial Highness" that would be added to her name after tonight. She shuddered.

Ayah didn't get an introduction. She slipped in behind them and gave Talia a wave as she pushed her way through the dancers to the refreshment table at the back of the room. As much as she'd teased Talia about it, Ayah didn't care to be the center of attention either. Her bright hair and pale skin already made her stand out.

Talia glanced at the raised dais a few feet from the refreshment table where two carved-ivory thrones stood empty. "I thought the Emperor would be here already," she whispered to her mother.

Her mother frowned. "So did I, but I'm sure he'll be here soon." She grasped Talia's shoulders. "I'm so proud of you. I hope you know that. Your father would be, too."

She knew her mother didn't mean the Emperor, and her eyes started to tear.

Her mother smiled. "Don't cry, my dear girl."

For the first time in years, Talia pressed her face into her mother's shoulder and hugged her tight. She wasn't alone in this. Her mother would be beside her, guiding her, helping her. And once Ayah got over her anger at Talia for keeping such a huge thing from her, Talia knew she could count on her friend's help too.

Her mother kissed her cheek. "Happy birthday, Talia."

They drew apart, and Talia turned to see a young man sweeping an elegant bow in her direction. He was startlingly handsome, with midnight-black hair and skin a few shades darker than hers. Diamonds gleamed in his ears, matching the crystals sewn into his cobalt and black silk jacket. "Lord Rone Hohd-Lorne at your service, my lady. Would you care for a dance?"

Talia had never met Rone before, but she already disliked him. He was the son of the Baron of Tyst and she'd seen him beat a hound once. But it was her duty to dance with anyone who asked at her coming-of-age ball, so she put her hand in his and allowed him to lead her onto the floor.

They danced, Rone's hand pressed against the small of her back, his warm breath too close to her cheek and smelling of spiced wine. She had the sudden, horrifying realization that because she was now the Emperor's heir, she might be made to marry someone like Rone. Marrying for love was not a luxury an Empress could afford. The Emperor's marriage had been political—hers would be, too.

"Are you enjoying yourself, Lady Dahl-Saida?"

Rone's words startled her out of her thoughts and she lost track of the dance, tripping over her own feet and causing her partner to stumble as well.

Irritation flashed across his handsome face. "I had expected the future Countess of Irsa to be a more accomplished dancer—you'll have to work on that if you want to catch a husband." He had the gall to wink at her.

She wanted to smack him—she didn't have the mental fortitude to deal with this right now. "And here I expected a man who beats his own dogs to have beautiful manners. Excuse me."

Talia left him standing stupidly in the middle of the dancers and stalked over to the refreshment table, ears burning. Ayah wasn't there anymore. Talia glimpsed her out on the dance floor, whirling about in the arms of a gawky marquis.

Talia resisted the urge to slip out to the balcony and scramble onto the roof. Ayah would follow her eventually, with a stolen jar of wine and a skirt full of cakes. They'd drink until they got dizzy and lick cake-sugar off their fingers and not come down until the party was over.

But she couldn't do that anymore. Future empresses didn't do that.

"Dance, my lady?"

Talia cast a regretful look at the refreshments—squares of lamb glazed with honey, sugared cakes and mango sweetmeats, iced wine and spiced tea—and turned to accept the outstretched hand of a courtier's sweaty son who was just straightening up from a bow.

She danced for what felt like hours, the heat in the ballroom barely broken by the jasmine-drenched night air blowing in from the balcony. She thought the lilies in her hair must be wilting already. Every so often she glanced at the empty ivory thrones and felt a fresh wave of panic. *Where* was the Emperor?

And what about Eda? She wasn't here either.

Her absence was probably purposeful—it would make a statement. The court would notice that Talia did not have the support of the Countess of Evalla when she was announced as the Emperor's heir, which was politically disastrous. Evalla was the most powerful province in Enduena, boasting its own private army and navy, and it was one of the largest trading hubs in the world. Without Eda on her side—

Gods above, did Eda already know about the Emperor's announcement? Was *that* the reason she'd failed to come?

Talia excused herself from her latest partner and went to find her mother, who was standing near the balcony with a cup of wine in her hand, speaking to an attendant. Whatever the attendant was saying made her mother's face smooth over into that courtier's mask that meant she didn't care to broadcast her feelings. The attendant bowed and slipped away, and Talia stepped up to her mother.

"Is the Emperor coming?"

Her mother shook her head, a hardness coming into her eyes. "He's very ill and can't leave his rooms. You'll have to make the announcement yourself."

"What?" Talia hissed. Her stomach turned over, and she suddenly regretted every single bite of food she'd ever eaten.

Her mother's mouth pressed into a firm line. "You'll be fine. Just give your speech like you've been practicing, and explain at the end that the Emperor couldn't be here."

"I'm not telling the entire Enduenan court I'm their next Empress. I can't announce *myself.*"

"You have to. The Emperor's already signed the necessary documents to prove your claim. We'll show them to the court tomorrow."

"Mama—"

But her mother had already grabbed her arm and was steering her toward the dais.

She felt like the walls were closing in around her, squeezing all the breath out of her lungs. "Please," she whispered. "Don't make me do this."

But then they were standing on the dais, just in front of the thrones, and her mother was smiling brilliantly at the mass of courtiers and calling for quiet.

Talia swallowed, fixed in that spot on the dais and blinking out at the crowd, her speech skittering through her mind in the wrong order. She searched for Ayah but couldn't find her.

"It is my great honor to present to you my daughter, Talia Dahl-Saida."

That was her cue. But every word she had ever known had gone completely from her head.

The courtiers waited, a sea of whispering skirts and silk sashes and elegant jackets. They shifted where they stood, wine glasses in their hands. They would toast her health when she finished speaking. If she spoke at all.

"Talia?"

What was she supposed to say? Why wasn't the Emperor here to do it for her?

She finally found Ayah in the mass of courtiers, and her bright smile gave Talia enough courage to begin.

"Friends and—friends and honored guests." She bunched her skirt in one hand, crushing the delicate material, and went on: "It is—it is my great privilege to accept the—the responsibility that—"

Away down in the city she heard bells, clamoring suddenly from the spired towers, all of them ringing at once: alarm bells. It couldn't be a storm coming—it wasn't the season, and the night had been clear.

Talia shot a panicked look at her mother, who nodded tensely for her to continue. But she'd lost her place and had to start over.

"Friends and honored guests. It is my great privilege to accept the responsibility of—of the Emperor's heir and future—future Empress of Enduena. I—I swear to—"

The bells grew louder and louder as the wind blew their jangling music into the ballroom.

She fought to go on: "I swear to uphold the honor of the Empire, enforce its laws, and serve it to the best of my ability, as long as—"

Another gust of wind tore through the room, so strong it ripped a lily loose from Talia's braids. The flower fell, quiet and spinning, to the gold-and-white marble floor. She stared at it, feeling strangely outside of herself.

"As long as—as long as I draw breath," she finished, still looking at the fallen lily.

There was no applause, no toasting—the courtiers were confused by her speech. The bells rang on and on, until Talia thought the world might be swallowed up in their noise.

And then, as suddenly as they'd begun, they stopped.

The ballroom doors burst open, and the Emperor's personal guard marched in: twelve helmed soldiers with blue sashes slung across their bare chests. Half carried sabers, blades naked and ready in their hands, the other half spears. Talia gaped, not understanding.

Until she saw, striding behind them with a tiger-sharp smile, Eda Mairin-Draive.

Chapter Three

SILENCE ECHOED AS EDA STOOD THERE, SMILING, her glance
sweeping over the glittering courtiers. She was dressed in
a simple, old-fashioned gown the color of pomegranates,
with gold clasps at both shoulders and an embroidered, blue belt.
Lilies crafted in delicate gold leaf crowned her head and oils
gleamed on her skin. Talia recognized both dress and crown as
exact replicas of those worn by the goddess Raiva in a mural in
the old palace temple. Talia wondered faintly if equating oneself
with a goddess was profoundly arrogant or just blasphemous.

Eda spoke, her voice echoing sharply through the deathly
quiet hall: "His Imperial Majesty Scain Dahned-Aer, Emperor
of Enduena, Lord of Ryn, and Ruler of Od, is dead, claimed this
hour by his long illness."

The crowd gasped, and Talia stared numbly at Eda. Her
heart beat too fast, too hard.

Eda's smile sharpened. "*I* am His Imperial Majesty's heir.
For proof, I present to you these documents"—she snapped
her fingers and a pair of attendants stepped forward, unfolding
cream-colored pages affixed with the Emperor's seal—"and His
Imperial Majesty's ring, which he bequeathed to me before he
died." She lifted her left hand high for all to see: a heavy gold

ring in the shape of a tiger chasing its tail, with rubies for eyes.

And then Eda's own eyes found Talia's. "This girl is an imposter, and a traitor to Enduena."

Talia stepped down from the dais almost without realizing it. "No."

"Evidence has been found detailing her long correspondence with Denlahn, and her plot to seize the throne."

"*No!*" Talia stood frozen on the dance floor, staring into the sea of courtiers who just moments before had meant to toast her health. They glared at her now, murmuring angrily. Some of them cursed and a few spat at her. She found Ayah in the crowd, her friend's face wracked with confusion and betrayal.

"Seize the traitor!" Eda commanded.

Two guards came forward and clapped their hands on Talia's shoulders, their fingers biting like stones into her skin.

"No!" she cried. "I haven't done anything, there's been a *mistake—*"

But they were already dragging her away, across the dance floor and past Eda, who didn't even look at her as she went by.

"Arrest her mother, too," said Eda calmly.

"No!" Talia screamed, writhing in the guards' grasp. "Eda, you *can't!*"

Eda glanced back at her, one eyebrow arched upward. "That's what you've never understood, my poor, *dear* Talia." She smiled. "I can do anything I want."

Talia woke to the noise of bells and the choking scent of moldering stone pressed up against her cheek. She jerked upright, heart stuttering.

Images of her own beheading had haunted her through the night.

She was shocked she'd slept at all.

Where was her mother? What was Eda planning to do to her? To both of them?

And she couldn't stop thinking about the look of betrayal on Ayah's face. Did her friend really believe her capable of treason?

She hugged her knees tight to her chin.

The hours spooled slowly away, one thread at a time. Talia got up and paced the confines of the tiny cell: five steps from one wall to the other, just three between the hardwood door and the bare stone sleeping ledge.

After a long while she heard bells again, distant cheering, the brash ringing of trumpets.

She sat back down on the stone ledge, folded her hands in her skirt. Waited.

Waited.

Waited.

Perhaps that's all Eda intended for her—to waste away into nothing and fade into the stone, turn to dust for the wind to scatter.

The day was at least half gone by the time she heard footsteps on the stone outside her cell.

She went over to the door, heart pounding. There came the jangle of keys, the creak of wood, and the door opened, the sudden blur of orange torchlight making her eyes tear. She blinked rapidly, trying to adjust to the light.

Eda stood there, two guards at her back, that same gold-lily crown from last night circling her black hair. She was dressed in a deep-green gown, clasped again at the shoulders in gold. Her bare arms gleamed with scented oils and she wore a dagger at her waist. "Didn't you ever learn to show deference to your superiors?" she said coolly. "You will *bow* before your Empress."

Talia sank to her knees on the hard stone floor, hating that she shook, hating that Eda saw it.

"You tried to take everything from me. My birthright, my crown. You dared imagine you could be Empress, and now you grovel at my feet."

Talia jerked upright, staring Eda directly in her kohl-rimmed eyes. "I never wanted to be Empress—I never wanted any of this. I certainly didn't try to take anything from you. You always thought you were so neglected and miserable, soliciting sympathy while putting yourself above the rest of us. You—the Governor of Evalla!"

Eda's eyes glinted. "The regent never thought me capable of ruling Evalla, Talia. I decided to take the Empire instead."

"You told the court I conspired with Denlahn!"

"Denlahn is easy to hate. Easy to blame." Eda shrugged. "I did what I had to, fought for every scrap of power I possess. It was just handed to you, and you squandered it. That's why this morning I bathed in the sacred pool and was crowned Empress of Enduena, while you cowered in a cell like the miserable rat you are."

Talia studied Eda in the torchlight. "What do you want with me?"

Eda smiled, sharp and humorless. "I want to pluck your heart out and use your sinews for harp strings."

Talia took an involuntary step backward, but Eda caught hold of her chin, fingers digging deep, forcing her to be still. She squared her jaw, despising her own terror.

"But death is quick. Living is not. I want you to feel the depth of your own insignificance."

Her nails pressed even harder, cutting into Talia's skin. "I'm banishing you from Enduena, little sister. On pain of death if you ever return. I don't recollect which of my supporters I promised Irsa to, but I expect they're already rearranging the furniture."

Without warning, she let go of Talia's face and shoved her backward; Talia stumbled and fell, jamming her elbow hard against the stone.

"You thought you would be Empress of half the world. Now you will see how far you will fall." Eda turned to the guards. "Get her out of my sight."

"What about my mother?" Talia demanded as the guards hoisted her upward.

Eda swept away without answering, and the guards dragged Talia through the prison, out into a bare stone courtyard. The sun was just vanishing over the western horizon, but there was enough light to see the executioner's block in the center of the courtyard, the dark stains on the stones around it.

Where was Eda sending her that was a fate worse than death? And what had she done to her mother?

The guards brought her through a gate in the wall and down a hill to the outer edge of the city. The last gleam of sunlight disappeared, and one cold star awoke in the twilight.

A carriage was waiting there. The guards shoved Talia unceremoniously into it.

"Wait," she said as they shut the door and latched it from the outside. The windows were nailed shut, making the air inside stifling and hot. "Wait, *please*—"

But outside she heard the driver crack his whip. The carriage lurched into motion.

She hurtled into the unknown, the white city and Ayah and everything she had ever understood fading fast away behind her.

Chapter Four

I T WAS NIGHT WHEN THEY REACHED THE sea. She could
smell it through the rough sacking a guard had shoved over
her head as he yanked her from the carriage. She could hear
it, crashing against creaking wood, feel its sudden cold spray
against her bare legs.

She'd spent five days rattling onward in that awful carriage,
with little food and nothing but her own dark imaginings to
keep her company. Worry for her mother ate her up, dwarfing
even her dread for her own uncertain future.

And now she'd come to the sea.

The long days of immobility made her unsteady on her feet.
She tripped as her guard hauled her along, his grip too rough just
under her armpit. She tried to shake him off, but his fingers dug
deeper. Salt-drenched wind whispered underneath the sack, and
a chill ran down her spine.

The harsh cries of birds and shouting men tangled with
clanging bells and snapping ropes. Wooden planks swayed back
and forth beneath her, scraping her feet through the holes in her
ruined calfskin sandals. The wind stank of salt and fish and tar.
Her free hand scrabbled to pull the sack off her head, and she
caught a brief glimpse of stars and dark water stretching out to

meet the moon, before the guard jerked her across a deck and shoved her through a low door.

She nearly collided with a brown-skinned man in a naval uniform and blue cap, who caught her by the shoulders and steadied her. He looked about forty and had a captain's sigil pinned to his collar—she recognized both uniform and sigil from the envoys who reported regularly to Eddenahr with shipping reports for the Emperor, though she didn't remember seeing this particular captain before.

"Hey, now!" he said, peering behind Talia to frown at her guard. "There's no cause to be discourteous to a lady."

"You have your orders, Captain, and I have mine. She's your responsibility now." And then her guard was gone, his boots creaking back across the deck the way they'd come.

She was on a ship, Talia realized belatedly, staring through the doorway at huge white sails that billowed full in the light of the moon. Men clambered on the rigging, hauling ropes and shouting to each other. The sea shimmered black beyond the rail.

It was only then that she understood the true scope of Eda's words. *I'm banishing you from Enduena, little sister.*

"Welcome aboard, Miss Dahl-Saida."

She turned back to the captain, who gave her a polite bow. "I'm Captain Oblaine Al-Tesh, at your service. I believe you know my other passenger."

He stepped aside so she had a clear view of what had to be the ship's great cabin. In the center of the low chamber, lit by a green glass lamp swaying from the ceiling, stood a wooden table ringed with chairs. Behind it, square-paned windows, tall as grown men, were set into the side of the ship, winking out into the night.

A woman crouched on one of the windowsills, the dirty red silk of her dress pooling in tatters to the floor, black hair hanging in knots on her shoulders. She lifted her head, remnants of kohl and gold powder smeared across her cheeks.

"Mama!" Talia cried out, lunging across the tilting cabin and into her mother's arms. "I thought I'd lost you—I thought you were dead!"

Her mother kissed her hair and hugged her fiercely. "My dear, dear girl. I thought I'd lost you too." She sounded more tired than Talia had ever heard her, and dark circles sagged under her eyes. But her smile was bright. "It seems the gods are watching out for us."

Talia flinched. She wished her mother wouldn't bring the gods into this—sometimes she was as bad as Ayah. "How can you say that, when everything went so wrong?"

Her mother's smile vanished; she seemed suddenly listless and ill. "The gods saved us, Talia. Don't blame them for what Eda did. I think she's been planning this for a very, very long time, no doubt bribing supporters with her parents' fortune. And I suspect the timing of the Emperor's death was no accident."

"Before I hear any other treasonous remarks," said Captain Oblaine behind them, "Her Imperial Majesty commanded me to give you this." He held out a letter, sealed in red wax. "For you, Miss Dahl-Saida."

She took it, breaking the seal with her thumb and squinting at the elegantly penned words in the dim light. Beneath her the ship creaked and swayed, and water slapped up against the hull.

Aria Dahl-Saida, formerly the Countess of Irsa, and her daughter, Talia Dahl-Saida, are hereby stripped of land and titles, and banished to the imperial province of Ryn for the duration of their lifetimes, under pain of death if they should ever attempt to return to Enduena, by order of Her Imperial Majesty Eda Mairin-Draive, gods-blessed Empress of Enduena, Queen of Ryn, and Ruler of Od.

Talia felt numb, seeing her fate inscribed before her eyes in stark ink. She passed the letter to her mother without a word.

Ryn was the most remote part of the Empire that Eda could possibly send them to. Besides Od, it was the only other non-mainland province, located thousands of miles northeast across the sea, and was little more than a large island. The Emperor had conquered Ryn on one of his first campaigns, shortly after ascending to the throne some forty years ago. Ryn's only export was fish, and by all reports, its people were uneducated and boorish.

They might as well be going to the ends of the earth.

There was a knock on the door, and a sailor stepped in with a laden tray, which he balanced expertly against the roll of the ship.

"I expect you're hungry," said Captain Oblaine with a kind smile as the sailor set three places at the table and then left again.

Oblaine sat at the head of the table and poured tea, while Talia took a seat next to her mother. The two of them piled their plates high with biscuits and salted fish. A week ago, Talia would have sneered at such fare—now it seemed a feast fit for the Emperor himself. She'd had nothing but dust-dry bread and stale water since her party, and she found it horrendously difficult to not devour everything in sight like a starving hound.

"Where are we?" she asked between mouthfuls.

The captain took a swig from his mug, which Talia suspected contained something stronger than tea. "Just leaving the main port in Evalla. If we catch a steady wind we should reach Ryn before autumn."

Talia nearly choked on a biscuit. "That's half a year from now!"

"It's a long way. But I've made the journey many times, and perhaps the wind gods will favor us."

"And the sea goddess too," said Talia's mother unexpectedly.

Oblaine laughed. "The sea goddess favors no one but herself, if the stories are to be believed."

"They're just stories," Talia snapped.

"Right you are." He took another drink. "Seafaring men tend more toward religion than most, but I only care about a safe journey and a ship in one piece at the end of it. My men can sort out which of the gods to thank. Ryn, now *there's* a place filled with superstitious people. They're always going on about the Tree— supposedly that's where it fell, when the gods tore it out of the ground."

Her mother was eating at a much slower pace, trembling as she lifted her fork. "All stories have at least a grain of truth in them. One ought to think carefully before dismissing them out of hand."

Talia frowned. Her mother hadn't gone on about the old myths in years—what was wrong with her? "Do you know where Eda's sending us once we get to Ryn?" she asked the Captain.

"You're to be wards of Baron Graimed Dacien-Tuer, the Governor. Used to be a prince before Ryn became part of the Empire."

So Eda was shutting them away with other forgotten royalty. Talia would have no life to speak of, no future. She stared at her plate, her appetite gone.

"I'll endeavor to make your journey as comfortable as possible. You'll have to stay belowdecks during storms and keep out of my men's way, but other than that you're free to go where you please."

Her mother drooped in her chair, and Talia laid a hand on her arm.

"We need to rest now," she said to the Captain.

Oblaine nodded. "I'll have one of my men show you to your quarters at once." He scraped back his chair and stood, eyeing them with a distant sort of pity as he left the cabin.

Her mother's shoulders shook and tears leaked from her eyes. She seemed like a wholly different person from the impenetrable woman Talia had known all her life, and it scared her. "What's wrong, Mama? We're together now. Everything is going to be all right."

"Can't you hear it?" her mother whispered.

The only sound was the water, slapping the sides of the ship. "Hear what?"

"The waves. They're singing."

Chapter Five

T ALIA WOKE IN A CRAMPED BUNK TO the motion of the ship beneath her, sunlight slanting in through the porthole. The quarters she shared with her mother were hardly bigger than the prison cell back in Eddenahr—nothing but two narrow bunks opposite each other, with a scant bit of floor between, and a chipped porcelain chamber pot shoved up against the wall. There wasn't room for luggage, even if they'd had any.

She lay quiet for a few minutes, listening to the creak of wood and the grasping waves, hoping her mother would be back to her normal self after a good night's sleep. She glimpsed sky and sea through the porthole, merging on the horizon into an endless stretch of gray.

There was a knock at the door and she slipped from her bunk to answer it. An older Enduenan sailor with silvering hair smiled at her over the bucket of water and slab of soap he was carrying.

"Captain thought you and your mother would like a wash, and something clean to change into. This was all we could scrounge up, I fear." He nodded at the assortment of clothes draped over one arm. "I'm Hanid, first mate."

His friendliness cheered her. "Thank you, Hanid."

"Sure thing, Miss." He set the bucket on the floor before handing her the soap and the bundle of clothes. "Let me know if there's anything else I can do for you."

And then he ducked back out of the cabin.

Her mother stirred and climbed out of her bunk, looking bewildered. "Where are we?" Her voice was rough with sleep.

"On a ship, headed to Ryn, Mama. Don't you remember?"

Her mother gave her a vacant smile. "Of course I remember."

They washed awkwardly in the tiny space between the bunks, scrubbing away as much dirt as possible and drying off with empty flour sacks. It was a far cry from Talia's private marble bath back in Eddenahr, with its perfumed hair oils and stone-warmed towels, but it was definitely better than nothing.

When she was finished, Talia cinched a sash around a pair of too-big trousers and slipped into a shapeless blue shirt that had clearly seen better days—though at least it was clean. She thought about her wardrobe in the palace, filled to the brim with gowns and sashes and elegant shoes. Already, it seemed so far away it might as well have been a dream.

Talia helped her mother button up the back of a garish purple dress that must have come from Ryn, or perhaps Od, with its dropped waist and full, burdensome skirt. No Enduenan courtier would have been caught dead in it, but somehow it seemed to suit her. No matter where she was or what she wore, her mother would always look like a queen.

Hanid had thoughtfully tucked a few combs into the pile of clothes, and the two of them worked the knots from their hair when they'd dressed. Talia braided her hair into a single plait down her back, while her mother wound hers into a shiny black coronet on the top of her head, fastening it with pins that had miraculously made the journey from Eddenahr.

That's all they had to their name now. A handful of hairpins.

"What happened to you after my party?"

Weariness dragged on her mother's face. "Guards shoved me into a carriage. I was given water, once or twice, but nothing else. I've been on the ship since yesterday morning, not knowing what became of you. The Captain gave me food, but I wasn't hungry."

"Mama, you have to eat something! You're in shock."

"All my hopes for you—for your future. Gone forever." Her voice cracked.

For a moment, Talia imagined herself in Eda's place—Empress of Enduena, a lifetime of luxury, arranging the world to align with her every desire. But that's not what she really wanted.

She wanted her father to be alive and well again; she wanted to inherit Irsa, like she'd always planned. To visit Od with Ayah one day, and see all the things her friend described in such wistful detail. Maybe marry, maybe not, so long as the choice was hers.

But that future had vanished the moment she sat down for breakfast with the Emperor. That future had never truly existed.

Talia clenched her jaw. "We'll carve out a new life together on Ryn. You'll see."

Her mother stared out through the porthole, a crease in her forehead that Talia never remembered seeing before. "We shouldn't be here. We should never have set foot on this ship. The sea listens. The sea *knows.*"

"The sea is just the sea, Mama." Talia took her arm, tugging her gently away from the porthole. "Come on. Let's find some breakfast."

They ate belowdecks in the crew's mess, nothing more than another small cabin crammed with a rough oak table and a pair of sagging benches. There wasn't even a porthole here, which made Talia unaccountably anxious—she didn't like being shut away from the sunlight and the sea. The cook, a grumbling Odan with fierce black brows who looked as though he'd never smiled in his life, served them more tea and fish and biscuits. To Talia's relief, her mother finished her whole plate and seemed to perk up a little.

Talia tugged her mother up from the bench when they were done, fighting off the feeling that the ship was squeezing all the breath from her body. The two of them climbed the narrow steps leading from the hold up to the main deck, Talia shoving open the hatch at the top. Sunlight hit her full in the face, and the sea air assailed her senses: salt and fish and a wild tangy freedom that made her skin prick. She could breathe again. She tilted her head back, staring up at the main mast, canvas sails billowing full. Sailors scaled the rigging, hauling lines and shouting to each other. They looked like gangly spiders, climbing silk ropes up into the wind god's domain.

Her mother laughed and rushed over to the port side rail. She had eyes only for the sea.

Talia followed at a slower pace, adapting her stride to the continual rolling of the ship. She stood beside her mother, curling her hands around the wooden railing as she stared out into the fathomless waves. They stretched forever into the horizon, all blue and green and gray, glinting gold where the sunlight touched them. A longing she didn't have a name for rushed up to swallow her. She felt full for the first time in her life, when she'd never known she was empty.

"Have you ever seen the sea before, Mama?"

Her mother was leaning her elbows on the railing, the wind teasing strands of hair loose from her braids. "When I was a little girl, my father took me to the port in Evalla. I wanted to stay forever, but we had to go home again and I thought it would break my heart."

The ship crested a wave and water splashed up over the rail, sending a thrill down Talia's spine as it drenched her to the bone.

Seawater dripped from her mother's chin. "I felt something then, calling out to me. It's even stronger now." She peered at Talia, an odd light in her eyes. "Are you sure you can't hear the waves singing?"

Talia looked back out over the water, and for an instant she imagined she *could* hear something, the haunted thread of an otherworldly music. But then she shook her head and it was gone again. "It's just the wind, Mama."

Her mother didn't seem to be listening, a secret smile on her lips. She shut her eyes and started humming.

Talia glanced uneasily between the sea and her mother. "Why don't we explore the rest of the ship?"

"Go ahead, dearest. I'll stay here. I need to understand what the sea is telling me."

"It's not telling you anything."

Her mother shrugged, the funny little smile back again. "You could hear it too, if you listen."

"Mama, there's nothing to hear!" She was beginning to fear that five days shut in a carriage with no food had addled her mother's wits.

"Just listen. Just listen." She started humming again.

Talia turned from the rail and strode away. She refused to think that her mother's strange melody was the very echo of the music she imagined hearing in her head.

She paced the main deck, watching the sailors hauling lines to adjust the sails, counting the bells that marked out watches every half hour. She scrambled up onto the smaller deck at the rear of the ship that formed the roof of the great cabin—she heard one of the sailors refer to it as the 'poop deck.'

The ship rolled beneath her, wood creaked, and lines snapped. A few of the sailors started singing, and their rough-sweet voices mingled perfectly with the wind and waves.

She looked back to where her mother still leaned against the port rail, purple dress bright against the sky. She told herself there was nothing wrong with her—a few solid days of food and sleep would set her right again.

"I've never seen anyone, man or woman, as enamored with the sea as she is. Except maybe you."

Talia jumped and turned to see Hanid climbing up beside her, his silver hair mussed from the wind. He gave her a wry smile. "It's like the sea is in your blood."

"I don't know what you're talking about," she snapped.

He shrugged. "Most people get horribly seasick their first time aboard ship. You and your mother seem entirely unaffected."

She didn't know why this line of questioning was making her so irritated. "I guess the sea air agrees with us."

"I guess it does." Hanid studied her a moment more, then shook his head and chuckled to himself. "Glad to have you sailing with us, in any case. Women are good luck aboard ship, you know. The Waves seem to prey mostly on the men."

"What do you mean?"

"You haven't heard the stories?" He spread his hands out toward the sea. "The Billow Maidens, singing in the storms to wreck the ships and drown the sailors. Their songs are so beautiful men can't resist, running their ships onto reefs or rocks, throwing themselves into the sea just to follow the music."

The wind flung a snatch of her mother's song into Talia's ears, and she cursed, which made Hanid laugh. "It's all superstition and nonsense."

"Maybe. But maybe not. I've been to the ends of the earth,

Miss Dahl-Saida—not everyone is as apathetic about religion as you Enduenans. I can't dismiss such stories entirely."

"Aren't you Enduenan?"

"My parents were. But I was born in Od and lived on Ryn. I served in the Emperor's army and was part of the failed campaign against Denlahn. I climbed the tallest mountain peak on Halda and saw millennia-old offerings to the god Tuer: wine and fruit and grains, as fresh as the day they were laid on his altar. I met a woman in Ita who kept a temple to the wind goddess—she swore the goddess spoke with her, and was teaching her how to weave the winds."

Talia shook her head in disgust. "That's absurd."

"She didn't seem to think so."

"Doesn't mean she was sane."

"Perhaps not." He smiled. "In any case, Miss Dahl-Saida, I didn't come up here to harass you. Captain sent me to ask if you needed anything."

She glanced once more toward her mother, who was still by the rail, staring transfixed into the waves. But Talia couldn't worry about her right now. "A proper tour of the ship would be nice. And ink and paper, if I may."

He saluted her smartly and quirked another smile. "At once, m'lady."

The sun slid into the sea, staining the water scarlet and the same fiery orange as Ayah's hair. Talia sat tucked up on the poop deck, her legs growing numb underneath her.

Dear Ayah, she scratched onto the paper Hanid had given her. She paused to glance west toward the sinking sun. She'd begun mentally composing a letter to her friend on the endless carriage ride, but now that it came time to pen it, she didn't know what to say. *I miss you,* perhaps, or, *I should have told you I am the Emperor's daughter.* Or, *I hope Eda didn't turn you out of the palace just because you're my friend.*

None of that seemed right. She rubbed one finger along the feather of her pen, and dipped the nib back in the inkwell.

There's a sailor called Hanid on this ship who's even more religious than you. He talked to a woman once who claimed she communed with the wind goddess and he believed her. But at least he's full of information, too. He told me all about our ship, the Lazy Jackal, *which hails from Evalla and is paid for on the Emperor's coin, but makes port all over the world. The Captain is part of Evalla's private navy, and one of the most esteemed sailors alive right now. Do you know, he's so renowned he's allowed to port in Denlahn without fear for his life? He's very polite to my mother and me, but there's no use trying to convince him to turn the ship around—Eda's gold is heavy in his pocket, and Hanid seems to think she's promised him land as well. Maybe even Irsa, though I try not to think about that.*

The Lazy Jackal *sails first to Ryn, and then on to Od and Ita before returning to Enduena. We're carrying figs and tea, cinnamon and other spices, mounds of cotton, and barrels upon barrels of rice (Hanid pointed them out to me when we were down in the cargo hold). There's also a half dozen pigs and one small goat to provide fresh meat and milk for the voyage, but so far all I've had is fish and biscuits. I expect I'll be heartily tired of them by the time we reach Ryn.*

My mother and I are not allowed to leave Ryn, not ever. I hope you will come and visit instead. The inhabitants swear the Tree was there once, which I hope will tempt you—you can investigate their claims and write them all down in a dusty book. I can laugh at you and all will very nearly be like it was before.

I do wonder why you never told me how beautiful the sea is— you were on a ship for months coming from Od. There are so many shades of green and gray. My mother thinks she hears it singing.

Her throat tightened, and she stilled her pen. The last of

the sunlight was just glancing off the water, and she turned to see her mother still perched by the rail. She hadn't moved an inch all day.

Chapter Six

TALIA WAS FAST ASLEEP IN THE CABIN belowdecks when the storm came. She started awake to the violent tilting of the floor beneath her and waves slamming against the sides of the ship, so hard she thought it might break apart. She climbed out of bed to look through the porthole, but the ship jerked her backward and sideways, throwing her in a heap against her mother's bunk. Somehow, her mother slept on.

She fought her way to her feet again, grabbing the edge of the porthole and digging her fingers into the wood around it. She peered through the glass.

The black sea leapt at the ship, clawing to get in. A flash of light exploded over the water, followed by a near-deafening crack of thunder. The vessel seemed to shake—the world seemed to shake.

She couldn't help but think of her mother's gods, and the stories she used to tell about them: Tuer of the mountain and Raiva of the trees. Mahl and Ahdairon, Lord and Lady of the air. Uerc of the beasts and Huen of the earth. Caida of the Stars and Hahld of the rivers. Aigir of the sea.

Watching the storm through the porthole, she could almost believe the stories were true. She was struck by her own helplessness, caught in the middle of the vast ocean at the mercy of the waves, or maybe even the gods.

Another flash of lightning, another *crrraaaack* of thunder. A wave hit the ship so hard it tipped sideways, throwing Talia against the door. Her bare foot caught on something sharp and she hissed in pain. The next moment she was tossed back toward the porthole. She touched it with one hand, and the icy coldness of the glass shot through her.

And then she saw something out there in the storm: a huge shape gleaming in the rain. Her thoughts tangled with images of sea monsters or gods come suddenly to life. She and her mother could die tonight. Drown in the black sea amidst the splintered remains of the ship.

Lightning slashed across the sky, illuminating the world for an instant, and there it was: a whale, nearly the size of the ship, swimming beside them in the storm. She stared, transfixed. Thunder crashed overhead, and once more the ship lurched, tipping her away from the porthole.

She scrambled back toward the glass, fighting the roll of the vessel, desperate for another glimpse of the whale. Just as she reached the porthole, lightning flashed again, but there was nothing out there anymore. The creature had vanished from sight like the sea had swallowed it whole. Like it had never existed at all.

Her mother awoke as the ship tipped again, and the porthole was suddenly on the ceiling. "Talia!"

"I'm here!"

"Talia!"

"Here." She grabbed her mother's hand in the dark, alarmed at the terror in her voice.

Her mother wept, sobs wracking her entire body and Talia clung to her, desperate to calm her down. The ship shuddered around them and the lightning roared. Any moment now Talia thought the vessel would break apart and they would all be devoured by the sea.

"She's angry. She can feel us here and she's so angry."

Her mother's words frightened Talia more than the storm. "What are you talking about?"

Another wave hit, knocking them both onto the floor. Talia heard something snap, and her mother screamed.

"Mama!"

Her mother screamed again. She couldn't seem to stop.

Talia wrestled to her feet, scrabbling in her pocket for a packet of matches. She lit the lamp on the ceiling. Orange light spun crazily through the cabin, illuminating her mother writhing on the floor with tears streaking down her cheeks. Her right wrist was bent almost entirely backwards against her arm.

Talia ran out into the storm to get the Captain.

Her mother wouldn't stop screaming.

Captain Oblaine came bolting down to their tiny cabin, hard on Talia's heels, and lifted her mother back into the bunk, careful not to knock her broken wrist.

"She's so angry!" her mother cried, writhing in the Captain's grasp. "She'll kill us all!"

The storm lashed the ship from side to side and lightning flared outside the porthole. Her mother kept screaming.

The Captain pinned her into the bunk while Talia watched, helpless and horrified.

"Find Hanid!" the Captain barked. "Ask him for the medical kit!"

And then Talia was running back up to the main deck, wrestling against the clawing wind and icy rain, shouting Hanid's name.

The ship lurched starboard, and Hanid was there, grasping her elbow.

She shouted into his ear so he could hear her: "My mother's hurt! We need the medical kit!"

He squeezed her arm and was gone, sliding across the deck.

She clung to a rope lashed about the main mast to keep herself upright and waited for him: one heartbeat. Two. Sailors swarmed the deck like frantic insects, hauling lines and trimming sails and fighting to keep the ship afloat. Their shouts and curses tangled with the memory of her mother's screams.

She counted to twelve and Hanid was back, lugging a large leather box with him. He pressed it into her arms. "Gods keep you!" he cried, then turned back to help his men.

Talia scrambled with the box back down into the hold, and Captain Oblaine took it from her, drawing out bandages and a glass bottle.

"She'll kill us all!" gasped her mother, over and over. Sweat and tears poured down her face.

Oblaine uncorked the bottle, and held it to her mother's lips. "Drink."

She did, coughing as she swallowed, her whole body trembling.

"What is that?" Talia demanded, kneeling on the floor beside him.

"Opium. It will ease her pain and calm her. Help her sleep through the night."

Sure enough her mother lay quiet now, her breathing steady again. The Captain bandaged her wrist with quiet efficiency.

He shook his head, his eyes finding Talia's. "Gods only know why I agreed to this commission. Catastrophe follows you."

"Why did you?"

He considered her. "It wasn't just for the money, if that's what you're thinking. If my daughter were here in your place, I would want someone to watch over her. Keep her safe."

She glanced at her mother's form in the bed, chest rising and falling in a steady rhythm. Her throat felt tight. "Thank you."

Oblaine nodded. "Call me if you need anything else."

He took the medical kit and went back up into the storm.

Talia stayed kneeling by her mother's bed, shuddering as the waves beat hard against the ship, trying to get in, trying to break them to pieces.

She fell asleep without meaning to and woke with the morning to find that the storm had passed. The sea once more ran calm.

Her mother woke, too, and her dark eyes were glassy with fever.

The Captain examined her mother, feeling her pulse and checking the bandage on her wrist. "Nothing to worry about," he told Talia gently. "It's just a fever, and will pass soon enough."

But Talia knew better. Her mother was stronger than the Emperor and as obdurate as a mountain. A mere fever would never incapacitate her like this.

She crouched by the bunk, taking her mother's good hand in her own and tenderly kissing her forehead. "Are you in pain, Mama?"

Tears leaked down her mother's cheeks. "The sea goddess saw us," she whispered. "She looked up from her Hall and saw us passing through her waters. So she sent a storm to break the ship, to snatch our souls down into her darkness. She'll kill us. She'll kill us!"

"Lie still, Mama," said Talia soothingly. "It was just a dream. We're safe now, the storm is over. Your wrist will heal, and we'll be together in Ryn very soon."

Her mother shuddered, eyes frantic. "She'll try again. She won't stop until she's satisfied! I have to go up. I have to watch the sea. I have to protect you!"

She tried to get out of bed, but Talia pressed her gently back onto the pillow. "Later, Mama. We can watch later. Sleep now."

And her mother sighed and shut her eyes. She fell into a fitful sleep, twisting in the bunk, sweat glistening on her forehead.

The day slipped slowly away, and her mother slid in and out of fretful dreams, writhing in the sheets, mumbling and crying in her sleep. Talia sat with her, holding her hand and wiping the sweat from her forehead. She pleaded with the gods she didn't believe in: *You took my father from me. You can't have my mother, too.*

Hanid came to see her in the midafternoon, carrying a battered tea tray. He set it on the floor under the porthole, and Talia's mouth watered at the scent of roasted pork, even though she didn't feel particularly hungry.

"How is she?"

Talia shook her head. "Sleeping, now. She keeps—she keeps talking about a sea goddess."

Hanid grabbed a bottle from off the tea tray—more opium—and uncorked it.

Her mother rustled uneasily in the tiny bunk, and Hanid tipped a few drops of the drug into her mouth. She swallowed automatically, and lay quieter.

"I wish you wouldn't do that," said Talia, eyeing the bottle with distaste.

"She'll do herself a harm, Miss Dahl-Saida. She needs to lay still."

Talia sat back against the side of the ship and took a plate of pork from the tray. She cut off a few bites and chewed, slowly. The meat was tasteless to her. "What's wrong with my mother?"

Hanid crouched on the floor across from her. "I think the sea is making her ill."

"She's not *seasick*," Talia objected.

"I didn't say she was."

Talia laid her plate down. "She keeps insisting the sea goddess is going to kill us, but in the stories . . . I thought it was Aigir who ruled the sea. Who is she talking about?"

"Rahn," said Hanid, black eyes meeting hers. "She tricked Aigir and took his throne. She collects all the souls of the drowned in her Hall at the bottom of the ocean."

Talia suppressed a shudder. "Lovely."

"Most sailors fear her on long voyages like this one."

"And you don't?"

Hanid shrugged. "She's just one goddess. I'm of the belief that the sea still protects Aigir's own. And the wind gods can be persuaded to kindness."

"Then you really do believe in the old stories."

His lips lifted in a half-smile. "Are you telling me you don't believe in anything at all, Miss Dahl-Saida?"

She winced. Suddenly she was eleven again, hearing her mother explain to her that her father had had an accident on the road. That he wasn't coming home. "If you believe in the gods, you believe in fate. I refuse to accept the philosophy that any part of my life is outside of my control. People spin those stories to try and make sense out of their own existence—I do fine on my own."

Hanid chuckled. "Says the girl banished from her homeland through no doing of her own."

"You think the gods brought me here?"

"I think you are limiting yourself to a rather narrow view of the world."

She ground her jaw. "Then you think the gods meant *this* for my mother?"

"I don't know. But there is certainly more going on with

her—with both of you—than either of us understands."

Talia didn't answer.

Hanid gave her a quiet smile. "Don't despair, Miss Dahl-Saida. She will be well again, I think."

And then he bowed and left the cabin.

Talia hugged her knees to her chest and screwed her eyes shut. *You took my father from me. You can't have my mother, too.*

You can't have her.

You can't.

The waves slapped against the side of the ship, and for a moment she thought she heard a thread of music curling out of the sea.

Chapter Seven

THE FEVER LATCHED TIGHT ONTO HER MOTHER, and wouldn't let go.

One week. Two. She slept poorly; she woke frantic. Captain Oblaine's opium supply dwindled—it was the only thing that made her easy again.

At the beginning of the third week, Talia got the Captain's permission to bring her mother to his private quarters, a small chamber adjoining the great cabin. There, at least, she could sit in bed and look out the windows to the sea. Oblaine's willingness to do so would have surprised Talia, if not for the marked pity in his eyes.

He felt sorry for the woman driven mad by her banishment.

He felt sorry for the girl clinging desperately to the idea that her mother would soon be perfectly well again. His pity made Talia angry, but she accepted it anyway.

Her mother was lucid, sometimes. She would wake in a quiet confusion, scoot up against her pillows and take Talia's hands in hers. She'd say she was sorry for bringing this upon them, but they would build a new life together in Ryn, take care of each other. She would smile at Talia, and then her eyes would slide over to the windows, a wild panic seizing her.

"I need to watch the sea! I need to protect the ship! If I'm not watching she will come—she will break us—she will drag our souls into the depths and there will be no rest—"

"Hush, Mama," Talia whispered, trying to soothe her even through her own fear. "All is well. There isn't any danger. Don't worry."

But her mother wept and wouldn't listen. Sometimes she wrested her way out of bed, stumbling through the Captain's quarters and out onto the deck toward the rail, toward the sea. Once, she made it all the way, and Talia was terrified she meant to throw herself overboard. But she didn't, she just stared into the water and crumpled to her knees. "She's so angry," she sobbed. "So angry."

Hanid and Captain Oblaine both appeared at Talia's elbow and helped half-carry her mother back to bed.

Her mother's wrist didn't heal. She was forever knocking it on something in her ravings, and Oblaine could do nothing but continue to bandage it, continue to knot a sling around her neck.

It was easiest when her mother slept. Those were the only times Talia left her side to wander listlessly about the deck, or climb up into the riggings and tuck herself against the main mast. She clung to the ropes and cried, shuddering in the icy wind. She ached with homesickness, and worry for her mother was eating her from the inside. She couldn't fix her mother, couldn't help her. She couldn't do *anything*, and she hated it.

One night, when her mother had been ill an entire month, Talia left her sleeping quietly in the captain's cabin and shimmied up the riggings to the crow's nest, her favorite spot. She wrapped herself in the blanket she'd brought and stared out at the stars, burning white and cold in the vast sky. They seemed close enough to touch, as if she could step from the mast and pluck them like oranges from the heavens.

The moon rose, round and silver, from out of the sea, and her mind jumped back to the night of her arrest, moonlight flooding into the ballroom. For a moment, she let herself long for the life Eda had stolen from her.

Hanid was right: This *was* outside of her control. She could no more crown herself Empress of Enduena, or shake the shadows from her mother's mind, than she could take a star from the sky. But that didn't mean she was helpless, either.

Her mother would get better when they landed in Ryn—Talia just needed to get her away from the sea. And they didn't have to stay with Eda's wretched Baron, they could scrape out a living of their own. Talia would find work somewhere, make enough money to give her mother all the comforts she deserved. They didn't *need* a grand life in Eddenahr to be happy.

The moon blurred a little before her eyes. *My mother is still here*, she told herself fiercely. *That hasn't changed.*

She sensed movement below her and peered down to see a lantern bobbing on the deck. "Your mother is asking for you, Miss Dahl-Saida!" came Hanid's voice.

She blinked the tears away and scrambled down in a hurry.

Her mother was sitting at the dining table in the great cabin, scribbling something on a piece of paper. She looked up and smiled. "There you are, dearest."

Talia settled into the chair across from her. "You're looking very well."

Another smile. "I'm feeling much better." *Scritch scritch scratch* went her pen. Moonlight poured in through the windows, illuminating her elegant handwriting.

"What are you doing?" Talia asked carefully.

"I'm transcribing the story my father told me when he took me to the seaside as a child. I just remembered it." She beamed at her paper, and kept writing.

The moon rose a little higher over the sea, and Talia saw sweat glimmering on her mother's brow. "Are you sure you wouldn't like to lie down again?"

"When I've finished." *Scritch scritch scratch.*

Talia wondered if she ought to go for Hanid or Captain Oblaine. "What's the story about?"

"You'll see. I'm so pleased I remembered! It explains everything." She paused to dip her pen in an inkwell.

The ship rolled beneath them, and the lantern swung back and forth from its hook in the ceiling, *creak creak, creak creak.*

Talia watched in silence as her mother wrote three more sentences across the paper. Then she laid the pen down, and blew on the ink to dry it. Her smile reached her ears as she handed the page over to her daughter.

Talia's eyes traveled across the words, so carefully and beautifully written.

"Well? Now do you understand?"

Talia bit her lip and met her mother's gaze, forcing herself to smile. "I do. Thank you for writing it down for me."

Her mother grinned, laughed, reached across the table to hug her. "I'd like to go on deck and watch for a while now."

"The captain and I have been watching in turns so you can get some rest, Mama. Don't worry, you can watch again soon."

Her mother nodded. "I can't watch all the time."

"Of course not. No one could. Now let's get you back to bed."

She allowed Talia to help her up from the table, leaning on her with her good arm. Talia led her through the door to the captain's bunk, and she climbed under the covers, pulling the blankets up to her chin.

"I'm glad you understand now," she whispered, her eyes drifting shut.

"Me too, Mama." Talia kissed her forehead and slipped back

out of the cabin. The moon was directly overhead now, flooding the whole deck in silver.

She thought she might be sick.

The story her mother had written for her was complete and utter nonsense.

Chapter Eight

TALIA'S MOTHER GOT BETTER AFTER THAT, IN body, at least. Her fever broke. She smiled again. Her wrist even started to heal. But she seemed very far away. Talia thought Captain Oblaine would make her move back belowdecks, but he didn't. The pity burned even darker in his eyes than before.

Because Talia's mother wasn't well. Not at all. She wandered about the ship, speaking nonsense, laughing for no reason, and standing straight as a pillar for hours on end as she stared into the sea. Watching, she said, always watching, or they would die.

The wind blew colder as the ship sailed further north. The sea grew choppy.

Talia spent her days with Hanid and the other men, learning how to work the lines and trim the sails, keeping them at the proper angle to the wind. If the sails were let out too far they flapped uselessly; if taken in too much they were equally ineffective. They required constant adjustment to keep the *Lazy Jackal* moving steadily on.

Hanid taught her how to understand the captain's sea charts and take readings with a compass or sightings of the sun and stars above the horizon with a sextant. She learned how to patch sails and tie knots. Hanid even persuaded Oblaine to let her take the ship's wheel a few times. She got the feeling Hanid was trying to distract her and she welcomed it, throwing herself headlong into his lessons. She tried to force away her worry for her mother and the continual ache of homesickness by exhausting herself.

But she couldn't shake her sense of dread. Every day the ship drew them further from Enduena and closer to Ryn. Every day her sense of foreboding intensified. What did Eda have in store for her there?

They had been three months at sea when another storm came, with little warning.

Hanid was teaching Talia how to tie a masthead knot, and an icy wind tore suddenly across the deck, ripping her hair from its braid. A wave crashed over the rail. She jerked her eyes up to see black clouds knotting tight across the sun.

They broke all at once.

"All hands!" came Captain Oblaine's sudden cry from farther down the deck. "All hands!"

Alarm bells clanged, and sailors shot up the riggings to furl the sails.

Hanid squeezed her arm. "With me."

A bolt of worry for her mother tore through her, but there wasn't time to think.

She and Hanid fought together through the raging wind and up the rigging to the fore topmast. They crawled out horizontally onto opposite sides of the topsail, clinging to the lines as they went. The rain nearly blinded her, bits of ice stinging her face and hands. Talia grabbed for the bottom of the sail and nearly lost her grip on the rigging. She gulped for breath and reached again. This time her fingers found the canvas. She pulled it up to the yard and scrambled to tie it in place, her hands so stiff and cold she could barely manage the slipknot. But she did, at last, and scooted backward to the mast, then down the rigging.

Hanid was already on deck again. "Many thanks!" he shouted to her above the storm. "Best get below now, m'lady."

"I have to find my mother!"

"It isn't safe!"

The ship lurched beneath them, the bow slanting nearly vertical into the ocean. Talia lost her footing and slid down the deck, choking on seawater, feet and hands scrambling for purchase.

She skidded toward the rail and barreled straight over as the ship jerked back up in the opposite direction. Somehow, she managed to grab the rail before the waves pulled the ship away. She screamed, forcing her fingers to hang on, struggling and failing to pull herself up. The sea grasped at her heels, yearning to drag her down into the depths. She thought she heard music.

And then: a strong hand closing around her arm, hauling her over the rail to safety. Hanid.

"Get below!" he bellowed.

But she couldn't. Her mother was alone in Captain Oblaine's cabin or, gods forbid, somewhere on deck.

Lightning split the sky in half, and the answering thunder seemed to crack directly over her head. The wind lashed ice at her face and it was so cold she could barely move. But she bent her head into the wind and doggedly clawed her way toward the great cabin, sickeningly certain she was already too late.

Ten steps. Eight. Another wave crashed over the ship, knocking Talia to her knees. Her hands grasped the deck. She pulled herself forward, crawling across the sea-drenched wood as wave after wave broke over her.

And then suddenly she'd made it, grasping the handle of the cabin door, pulling herself to her feet. She shoved the door open, and fell into the room.

She wrested it shut again, and turned to see her mother sitting calmly at the table. She was absurdly drinking tea, steam curling up from the spout of a cracked earthenware pot, while the green glass lantern burned bright overhead

Outside, the storm raged and the world wheeled. Here, everything seemed impossibly still.

Her mother raised the cup to her lips and drank, watching Talia with dark eyes. "I told you she was angry. She will never let us go."

Lightning flashed outside the windows.

"What do you mean?"

Her mother looked at Talia, her face wracked with impossible sadness. "It's because of what happened in the story I wrote down for you, the story of the youngest Wave. How could you forget?"

"Forgive me, Mama. I'm afraid I lost your paper. Won't you tell it to me now?"

Her mother rose from her chair and turned to look out over the raging sea. Tears dripped down her cheeks. She unlatched the window, rain lashing her face and her hair.

"Mama, come away from the window!"

But her mother opened it further, and stepped onto the sill. She teetered there precariously, the wind ripping through her purple skirt, waves and rain drenching her. "Listen, Talia, can't you hear it?"

"Get down from there!" Talia sprang around the table, but another wave slammed into the ship and knocked her to the floor.

"The Waves are singing!"

"Mama, what are you doing?" She scrabbled to get up again, the ship tilting and lurching beneath her.

Her mother looked back, a brilliant, dazzling smile touching her lips. "My darling girl. I'm saving you."

She turned once more to the sea, roaring and black beyond the ship.

And then she jumped.

"Mama!" Talia screamed, leaping toward the window,

lunging to grab her hand.

For an instant, she saw the silhouette of her mother against the storm—the edge of her dress, the tip of her shoe.

Talia reached, screaming, but her fingers grasped emptiness.

Her mother spiraled away into the darkness, the hem of her purple gown just out of reach.

She was six or seven when her mother first told her the story of how the world was made. Her father was in Eddenahr instead of at home in Irsa, so it was just the two of them.

It was winter, not cold enough for snow but cold enough to sit in front of the fire, wrapped in a blanket and sipping chocolate, rich and hot and sweet.

"In the beginning there wasn't anything," said her mother, sitting beside Talia. Her skirt pooled around her in a perfect circle of dark-green silk. "No light, no trees, no world. Just darkness."

Talia drank more chocolate and scooted closer, eyes wide, ears alert and listening.

"Then the One who was before everything, even the gods, shaped three Stars in the emptiness and set them swirling about a single point in the void. The Stars were the most powerful things in existence, because they were first, and closest to the One's heart."

The wind whistled outside of the windows. The fire popped, shooting hot embers out onto the stone floor. Talia watched them spark orange and then wink out, turning to ash.

"And in that point, as the Stars wheeled, the One who was before the gods made Endahr, the world. It was very beautiful, but it was empty, and so he made a Tree to fill it up, a huge white Tree formed from the dust of the Stars. He set it in the middle of Endahr, and it stretched its branches up to the heavens, but it still wasn't enough."

"What did he do then?" Talia whispered, the story pulsing sharp in her heart.

"He made the gods," said her mother, a smile touching her lips. *"Listen, and I will tell you their names:*

"Tuer was first, Lord of the Mountain, the most powerful of all the gods, and their leader. Raiva came after—she was born in the light of the Stars and woke already singing. She was made Lady of Trees and green growing things."

Talia squirmed happily and put her elbows down on her knees, forgetting about her chocolate.

"Huen was Lord of the Earth," her mother went on, *"and Caida the Guardian of Stars and Fire. Aigir was Lord of the Sea; Hahld his brother had charge of the rivers and streams. Ahdairon was the Lady of the Air—the birds obeyed her, and she dwelt with Mahl, Lord of Wind and Thunder. Last of all was Uerc, Lord of the Beasts. He rode a great black horse and wandered all of Endahr, naming the animals, and speaking to them."*

Talia pictured the gods as her mother talked about them, beautiful and mysterious and strong. Raiva had silver hair, she imagined, and Tuer looked a great deal like her father. Huen was like the Emperor, except he wore a brown coat, and Aigir and Hahld were vaguely green. Caida wore a gown made of fire, while Ahdairon had wings as bright as a parrot's. Mahl was always frowning. Uerc had a jaguar for a pet. She couldn't decide which one she liked best.

"The One who was before the gods charged them with the keeping of Endahr. He told them to guard it, to make it flourish and grow, and to guide and keep mankind when they awoke. So they were called the Nine Guardians."

"And did they guard Endahr?" asked Talia, tucking herself under her mother's arm.

Her mother smiled and kissed the top of her head, pulling her tight. *"For a time. The One created spirits to help them—beautiful beings a little less powerful than the gods, called the servants. Raiva taught them how to sing."*

"Is that the end of the story?" Talia said sleepily, yawning and leaning her head against her mother's chest.

"Almost. The gods and their servants dwelled happily on Endahr, eating fruit from the Tree and living in the shade of its branches. Birds and animals flourished. The Tree grew strong, the Stars burned bright. All was well until mankind awoke on Endahr."

"But where did mankind come from?"

"The One formed them from a Tree leaf and a spark of Starlight, then planted them in the earth until it was time for them to awake."

Talia listened to her mother's heartbeat, strong and steady beneath her ear. "What happened then?"

"Everything changed," her mother said. "But that is another story."

She fell asleep, then, in her mother's lap by the fire, filled with warmth and peace and love. The gods from the stories danced behind her eyes, and she wasn't afraid.

Part Two:

STAR AND TREE

And the gods rose up in their anger and as one plucked the Tree from the ground.

Chapter Nine

THE COACH RATTLED UP THE ROAD, ICY air leaking in through the crack under the door. Talia didn't think she would ever be warm again—the cold gnawed into her bones. She shuddered in the ratty blanket she had stolen from last night's flea-infested inn. She had no money to purchase any kind of coat, and no leisure to shop for one even if she did—the driver who had collected her from the seaport kept a strict schedule.

The landscape stretched out before her, endless low-rolling hills spotted with patches of purple heather. Clouds hung overhead, moody and dark, blotting out any hint of the morning sun.

She knew only two things about the Ruen-Dahr, the Baron's estate where she was headed; it stood on a bluff overlooking the sea, and the proprietor at the last inn thought it was haunted.

It had been four days since she left Captain Oblaine and Hanid at the seaport. Four days since she'd seen the ocean.

It had been two months and eleven days since she'd lost her mother.

They'd had a funeral of sorts on the ship. She'd tied a scrap of white sailcloth around her arm in lieu of proper mourning clothes. Captain Oblaine had spoken the formal words of burial, but Talia had stumbled over the traditional prayer: *May your spirit be gathered beyond the circles of the world, and your body rest quiet until the end of time, when the world is unmade.*

She didn't know the prayer for burial at sea.

She curled her body up tight on the carriage seat. Her mother's death was a constant, gnawing ache, as if her leg had been cut off but she still had phantom pains. Most days she did her best not to think about it, because when she did, when she really, truly *thought* about that night in the storm when her mother flung open the window, the world went black and she didn't know how she would ever go on, how she *could* ever go on. Because the truth was—the truth was—

The truth was she should have leapt up in time to pull her back.

She should have jumped out the window after her, grabbed her before the sea swallowed her up.

She should have done *something*.

But by the time she tore up on deck screaming for help it was already too late. Sailors threw ropes into the water below the spot where her mother had fallen. They shouted her name through the wind and the rain. One of them even dove into the raging waves to look for her.

But it was too late.

She was gone.

And Talia wished the sea would have claimed her, too.

She didn't know how to live with her mother's absence, with that phantom pain that would never go away.

The only solace she could find was in not thinking about it, and that was no comfort at all. It left her feeling numb and awful. Empty.

The coach lurched over a stone, shaking Talia from her thoughts. It turned onto a rutted path that wound steadily upward. She strained her eyes out across the hills, yearning to catch some glimpse of the sea. The wind blew harder, shaking the coach from side to side, and Talia pulled the awful blanket tighter around her shoulders. Where *had* Eda sent her?

The coach climbed higher, the road grew steeper. Talia thought she caught the sudden hint of salt in the air blowing under the door. Her heart slammed hard against her ribcage.

The carriage came over another ridge and then she did see it: the gleam of the sea off in the distance. A thrill went through her, and she hated herself—the sea had taken everything from her and yet here she was, as glad to see it again as a drowning man gasping a longed-for breath of air.

The coach turned and Talia lost the ocean behind a grassy bluff. She tried to swallow down her disappointment.

On and on they wound through the hills, her anxiety mounting with every moment.

And then—

A break in the road, the coach wheels clattering onto cobbled stones, a tall grim house rising above her, the sea gray and restless behind it.

She tamped down her nerves as the driver swept open the coach door and handed her out. She left the blanket on the seat in a burst of Enduenan pride, but she wasn't sure it mattered— she was still dressed in the cast-off trousers and shapeless, worn shirt Captain Oblaine had given her half a year ago. The lady she used to be had been left far behind in another life. She looked like what she was: an outcast, an orphan. A nobody.

She squared her shoulders and peered at the house, a sprawling old mansion that had clearly seen better days. The stones were weathered, the slate roofs crumbling, the windows smudged and dark. Several crooked towers stretched up into the sky, and from the highest one flew the Imperial banner: three stars on a blue field edged with gold. It flapped listlessly, its edges ragged and fraying. The scent of the sea wrapped all around her and she heard the waves pounding hard on the shore beyond the house. She longed to run down to the beach for a proper view, but she forced herself to stand there, waiting for some instruction from the driver.

She glanced back to see him wrestling a small leather chest from under his seat, and she heard the clink of coins as he tucked it under his arm.

"Well, m'lady," he said in a mocking tone, climbing down from the coach. "Let's be rid of you."

He strode up the cobbled drive to the house and Talia followed, anxious and jittery. She didn't precisely understand the conditions of her stay here, but, if Eda had anything to do with it, they couldn't possibly be pleasant.

The clouds broke, rain falling icy and cold, and they ran the rest of the way, darting up several steps to a tall brown door that was mercifully sheltered by the overhanging roof. The driver grasped the brass knocker and rapped three times.

Talia clamped her teeth down hard on the inside of her cheek to keep from shaking.

Footsteps sounded on the other side of the door, crisp shoes on hard stone, and a moment later the door creaked inward to reveal the plain face and starched cap of a middle-aged servingwoman. She peered at them with some annoyance, her eyes darting from the driver to Talia and then back again. "What is it? His Grace isn't expecting visitors today."

"Delivery from the Empress." The driver jerked his head in Talia's direction. "Miss Talia Dahl-Saida, erstwhile heiress of Irsa. Is the Baron at home?"

The servingwoman blinked a few times. "I'll fetch His Grace's steward." She shut the door in their faces.

The driver swore, glaring at Talia like everything was her fault.

She shifted from one foot to the other, in a dual attempt to generate warmth and dispel her nervous energy. The rain pounded hard at their backs—the driver would be soaked through on his trip back to the village. The thought gave her more pleasure than perhaps it should have.

The door opened again. A tall man stood there, dressed in a smart black coat and crisp cravat. He was somewhat past middle age, with the shockingly pale skin Talia was growing used to seeing in Ryn, and dark hair shot through with silver, tied back at the nape of his neck.

"Good afternoon," he said, addressing the driver, though his glance rested briefly on Talia. "You have word from the Empress? I'm Ahned, the Baron's steward."

The driver jabbed his thumb at Talia. "Was paid to deliver her here. You did receive notice of her arrival?"

"We were expecting two ladies. Weeks ago."

The driver shrugged. "There's just her. Ship was delayed on account of weather."

"I see."

Talia kept chewing on her cheek, trying not to feel like an unwanted horse at an auction.

"Well then." The driver handed Ahned the leather chest. "Payment, as promised. The annual installments will of course be forthcoming. You may inform the Baron."

"Of course." Ahned looked at Talia again. "Do you have trunks? Any luggage to bring in?"

She shook her head.

"Ah, well. Best get out of the wet." He opened the door wider.

The driver tipped his cap to Ahned and dashed back to the coach.

Talia took a deep breath and went into the house.

She stepped into a grand stone entrance hall, dim light slipping through the windows set high in the vaulted ceiling. It was just as cold in here as it was outside, if less damp. Talia shivered, dripping water on the floor like a half-drowned cat.

Ahned came in behind her and shut the door. "Welcome to the Ruen-Dahr, Miss Dahl-Saida. Give me a moment, and I'll see if your room is ready."

She nodded and he disappeared up the sweeping staircase on the far end of the foyer. Underneath the curve of the stairs was a large pair of double doors, the dark wood carved with shapes she couldn't distinguish from this distance. Across the room to her left an open doorway led into a carpeted hall.

As she stood there waiting for Ahned, she became gradually aware of a faint thread of music, winding its way from somewhere deep in the house. She'd never heard anything quite like it: soft and sad and beautiful, too. The rain pounded overhead and the music seemed to twist into the scattered rhythm, like the melody was just as natural as the weather.

Minutes ticked by and Ahned didn't return. Talia's toes and fingers grew numb with cold. She fidgeted, anxious, impatient, wanting just to sit down with a cup of tea or curl up by a warm fire or—gods above—take a hot bath. She wished Ayah were here—she'd have found some way to get into mischief already.

Talia cast an irritated eye up the stairs, but Ahned still didn't appear.

The music wound on as she waited, tugging at her strangely, and after a few more moments she couldn't stand it any longer. She had to find out what it was. With one last glance at the staircase, she crossed the foyer and stepped into the hall. The music grew a little louder. She passed a doorway that looked into a small dining room and kept going. The hall turned to the right, drawing her past a few more doors, all shut, and then at last to the source of the music—a room in the back of the house spilling light and melody into the corridor. She stopped in front of the door and peered in.

The room was small, but comfortable. A pair of armchairs were pulled up to a small fire; a window in the back wall looked out into the rain. Haphazardly-arranged shelves, overflowing with books and sheet music, lined the walls. Between them hung all kinds of instruments—viols and miniature harps, flutes and recorders of various sizes, a half dozen drums, and more that Talia had no names for.

Underneath the window stood another instrument she didn't know. It looked like a harpsichord—same shape and strings, same black-and-white keys marching up and down its widest part—but it had a completely different sound.

A young man sat behind the not-harpsichord, lost in creating the mesmerizing music that Talia had heard from the entrance hall. He looked to be about her age, with a wiry build and arms too long for his sleeves. He had light brown hair and skin paler than Ahned's. The inhabitants of Ryn clearly didn't spend much time in the sun, although—Talia glanced at the rain running down the window—maybe there wasn't much sun to spend time *in*.

She stood there and watched him play, his hands running so easily up and down the keys that she wondered whether he controlled the music or the music controlled him.

And then he lifted his head and saw her in the doorway. His fingers froze over the instrument and the music cut off abruptly. He blinked at her, his bright blue eyes owlish behind a pair of silver spectacles, and he seemed to grow paler than he already was.

He jerked to his feet, still staring, and slammed a cover down over the keys so hard it made Talia jump. "Who are you?" he demanded.

She suddenly wondered what she must look like to him: a half-drowned stranger who hadn't had a real bath in half a year.

"I'm Talia." Her voice came out in an undignified high squeak. "Talia Dahl-Saida," she added, more firmly, "heiress of Irsa."

"No, no, no." He shook his head, stepping around the instrument to come over to her. Up close he was several inches taller than Talia, his thatch of hair falling into his eyes and curling a little around his ears. He had a spattering of freckles across his nose and a cravat hung loose around his neck.

He grabbed her arms. "You can't be here. You have to leave." He turned her about and propelled her back into the hallway.

She jerked free. "I beg. Your. Pardon?"

He unhooked his spectacles and rubbed his eyes, pacing a few steps down the hall before coming back to her. He shoved his spectacles into his shirt pocket and swore, vehemently, by all nine gods and a handful of spirits Talia had never heard of before. "I don't *believe* this." He finally looked at her again.

She liked him a little better after all that swearing. "Who are *you*?"

He shrugged. "I'm Wen."

That was not exactly enlightening.

"But you really can't stay. You have to leave. Tonight, maybe. Tomorrow at the latest. It's not safe, do you understand?"

No. No, she *didn't* understand. She wanted to strangle him with his own cravat. "Do you have any idea what I've been through to get here? Of course you don't. How could you? In the last six months I was arrested, shoved onto a boat, and watched my mother *die*. I just got here and I am *not* leaving, *damn you!*"

His eyebrows lifted nearly to the top of his head and he took an involuntary step backward. "I'm so sor—" he began.

But then Ahned stepped up beside her and offered her his arm. "Ah," he said, his glance flicking between her and Wen, "I see you two have . . . met. Miss Dahl-Saida, your room is ready. So sorry for the delay."

Talia took his arm and allowed him to lead her down the hall, casting a baffled look at Wen over her shoulder as she went.

Chapter Ten

TALIA ALMOST DISSOLVED INTO GRATEFUL TEARS WHEN Ahned deposited her in her room—a bath was waiting there, steaming nicely.

The room itself was small and drab and colorless, a fire licking red behind the grate, a bed in one corner, and an old wooden wardrobe and dressing table opposite. Its best feature was the window looking north over the sea. Talia stared through it the whole time she was bathing, though there was little to see beyond the impenetrable rain running down the glass.

She had just climbed out of the bath and was toweling herself dry, her skin tingling with warmth and the delicious sensation of cleanliness, when there came a knock at her door. It opened a crack, and a woman in her late thirties peeked in, yellow curls spilling out from under her white maid's cap. "Beg pardon, Miss, but we've come to help you dress. Are you finished?"

Talia nodded, tugging the towel self-consciously around her, and the maid slipped into the room. A second maid who looked to be about Talia's age followed her, a gown draped over one arm. She had dark hair and wide eyes and was fidgeting nervously.

"I'm Lyna," said the first maid, "and this is Ro. We were told you brought nothing with you from Enduena. No gowns or shoes or undergarments or anything?"

The questions rankled. Talia didn't care to explain that she was completely penniless—not even a hairpin to her name, now. She thought of her mother, braiding her hair into a coronet down in the hold of the ship, and shook her head. "Nothing."

Lyna tutted and Ro, staring at Talia, fiddled with the fabric of the gown she'd brought. It was beautiful, a pale green silk with silver roses embroidered around the neckline and ribbons shimmering violet and dusky pink under the bodice.

"We've brought this for today," Lyna said, gesturing to the gown. "Dairon is gathering the rest. We'll bring them this evening."

"The rest?" Talia echoed. "Who's Dairon?"

"His Grace's housekeeper." Talia assumed Lyna was talking about the middle-aged woman who had first opened the front door. "Right now, we have to make you presentable. The Baron will be downstairs in half an hour."

Talia grimaced. She didn't want to meet the dusty old Baron.

Ro laid the gown on the bed, and Lyna pulled Talia's towel away, slipping her into a chemise that smelled strongly of lavender soap. The fabric was coarser than Talia had been used to in Enduena, but it was clean, and made her feel as exquisite as if she was dressed in hand-spun Itish silk.

Ro pulled something over her head and began tugging at the laces. Talia writhed out of her grasp, face hot. "I do not require a corset!"

The maid looked at her in confusion. Lyna frowned. "It will give you the proper shape for the gown, Miss. Are they not the fashion in Enduena?"

Talia's thundering pulse dulled a little. Was that all it was, here? A fashion? She really *had* come to the end of civilization. Only the prostitutes wore corsets at home. "No," she said. "No, they're not."

Ro's eyes grew even wider and Lyna shook her head, like

she thought *Talia* was the uncultured one. "Well, here they're required to make you look the proper lady," Ro said. "Now turn around."

Talia obeyed, wondering how the same garment could be the height of elegant society in one country and the lowest of base company in another. Her mother would have known how to talk her way out of it. She chewed on her lip as Ro cinched the corset tight. The boning dug sharply into her hips and across the top of her ribs.

The gown came next, falling in a cloud of silk and ribbons to Talia's ankles, and then she sat down on a stool while Lyna and Ro arranged her hair. They worked quickly, braiding and twisting and pulling and pinning, until the whole dark mass was swept up on top of Talia's head.

Last of all, Lyna set out a tray of little cosmetic jars on the dressing table. She brushed rouge on Talia's cheeks and indigo powder on her eyelids. She drew bold black lines around her eyes, and stained her lips a deep red. Talia blinked at herself in the mirror, and didn't recognize the person staring back.

Lyna nodded in satisfaction. "You're ready, Miss. Ahned will see you downstairs. Wendarien and the Baron are waiting."

"Wendarien . . .?" Talia began, wondering if she meant the rude young man from the music room.

But then the door opened and Ahned looked in.

Talia rose from the dressing table, uncomfortable in the corset and borrowed gown and feeling less like a lady than she ever had in her life.

She lifted her chin and went to take his arm.

Ahned escorted her down into the vestibule and led her under the sweep of the stair to the double doors, which were open a crack. He rapped on the left one and pushed it open further, nodding at her to go in.

She slipped through, and the door shut with a click behind her.

She found herself in a large, airy hall that might once have been a ballroom. Unlit chandeliers hung suspended from the ceiling, the crystal baubles tangled with dust and cobwebs, and sheets were draped over a few scattered pieces of furniture like ghosts in their mourning whites. Gray light streamed in through half a dozen arched windows on one wall, rain pouring against the glass. Two men—one young and one much older—were waiting for her there.

The young one stood facing the window, his back to the door. The old one was hunched in an ancient armchair, stuffing bursting out of the threadbare fabric.

Talia blinked at the scene, a little confused. She thought she was coming down for a late lunch. What was going on?

She paced toward them, dust swirling up from the floor. The old man lifted his head and the young man turned from the window. He was indeed the boy from the music room, dressed formally now in gray trousers and jacket, a white cravat stiff around his neck. His eyes followed her all the way from the door, but his body remained rigid.

She stopped a few feet away, resisting the urge to curtsy. Whatever her current status, she was the daughter of an Emperor, and therefore the Baron's superior.

"Miss Dahl-Saida," said the old man, his voice gravelly and rough, "you'll forgive me if I do not rise. The rain makes my bones ache."

Talia dipped her chin in acknowledgement. Up close, she realized that he wasn't as old as he seemed. He looked exhausted, his skin sagging and gray, like he was weighed down by some long, unshakeable illness.

"I am Baron Graimed Dacien-Tuer, Lord of the Ruen-Dahr, Governor of Ryn. I'm told you've met my son, Wendarien

Aidar-Holt."

Her glance slid over to Wen. He was still watching her intently, rain beating hard on the window behind him. His hands were curled into fists, tendons straining tight against his pale skin. "I have," she said.

The Baron nodded and looked up at his son. "Wendarien?"

Wen dug in his pocket and pulled out a small box made of dark wood inlaid with the emblem of a white tree. He opened it. Inside, on a square of red silk, lay an intricate silver ring set with a pale blue stone.

He picked up the ring and laid the box on the windowsill, then came a step nearer, took Talia's right hand in his left, and slid the ring onto her index finger. It fit perfectly.

She snatched her hand away and leapt backward, anger and mortification blazing hot within her. "What do you think you're doing?"

The Baron frowned. "Miss Dahl-Saida. Need I remind you that this betrothal was the first and foremost point in Her Imperial Majesty's contract?"

So, this is what Eda had planned. She was making sure, from thousands of miles across the sea, that Talia knew her place: heiress of nothing, Empress of no one. Eda wanted her to remember that fact every day for the rest of her life.

Rain beat against the glass. Wen watched her intently.

"If you refuse to accept the Empress's terms, I will expel you immediately from my house," said the Baron. "You will be as you are. Penniless. Friendless. Alone."

Once more she saw her mother, leaping into the storm, her purple gown filling up the square window.

"Wendarien," said the Baron, evidently taking her silence for acceptance.

Wen took her hand again, his jaw tight. This time she didn't pull away, just stared at him.

The Baron's voice came, horrible and obdurate as marble. "These two souls together pronounce their intention to be joined, as husband and as wife, and are hereafter marked only for each other, as signified by this ring."

The formal words of betrothal.

She looked at Wen and he looked back, and said nothing. His hand over hers was calloused and cold. Her mind wheeled.

"Do you agree to abide by the terms of this binding?" said the Baron.

Wen stared at her. The rain fell on and on.

"Wendarien," said the Baron, his tone dark and harsh.

"I—I agree."

"Miss Dahl-Saida?"

She didn't know what to do. For an eternal moment she said nothing, just stood there stupidly, motionless and numb. The wind howled outside, seeking some crack in the stones. The rain fell harder.

"Saving you," came her mother's voice in her mind. She watched her spiral out into darkness, watched the sea swallow her up.

"Miss Dahl-Saida?"

Talia jerked herself out of the memory and lifted her chin, channeling her mother's fierce elegance. She would tell these fools what they wanted to hear, and find a way to extricate herself afterward. That's what her mother would have done.

"I agree," she said. But her voice shook.

Wen dropped her hand and stepped back, his face tight with panic.

"Then it is done," said the Baron. "You will wed in the spring."

She faced the Baron, despising him, and curtsied low, as if he were an Emperor and she a slave.

And then she turned and swept out of the ballroom.

She made it all the way across the vestibule and out the front door before her resolve crumbled and the tears came.

Chapter Eleven

S HE WALKED OUT INTO THE RAIN AND was instantly soaked through, the gown clinging to her legs in a mess of silk and ribbons.

But she didn't care.

She crossed the drive and began to run, her shoes slapping hard against the flagstones as the cold rain stung her face and a chill crept down into her bones.

She ran faster, past a low outbuilding that was probably a stable, then down the slope of the hill and onto the shore. White sand stretched west as far as she could see, scattered with jagged black rocks that looked as though they had been thrown there in ancient times by a god. To the north there was nothing but ocean, waves crawling onto the shore and shrinking back again, yearning always for something they couldn't have.

She pulled off her shoes and dashed through the sand to the water's edge, letting the icy sea wash over her bare toes. She stood there, the rain biting hard into her skin, the waves lapping at her ankles and splashing up to her knees.

An eerie music whispered to her out of the storm. She could hear it, as clearly as she'd heard Wen playing in the back of the house: a song, tangled in the rain and wind and sea. It sounded to her like a lament. She shut her eyes and let it fill her up.

The waves crashed higher, breaking against her waist, crawling up to her shoulders, yearning to pull her down into the depths. She had the sudden sensation of fingers, like spots of ice against her neck, and she thought she heard a voice at her ear, whispering words in a language she didn't know. But she understood it anyway: *Come to us,* it seemed to say, *come to us.* The sand shifted beneath her feet and the waves battered her, knocking her to her knees and choking all her breath away. She fought through the water and scrambled up to the safety of the shore, her pulse erratic and too quick.

She stared, shuddering, out to sea, her mother's words echoing in her mind.

The waves are singing. Can't you hear it?

Had the sea called to her mother too? Is that why she'd jumped?

She gulped a breath and started running again, westward down the shore. She pushed herself faster and faster, trying to outrun her fear of the sea and her longing for it, the creeping dread that her mother's madness would become her own.

The ground began to rise steadily to her left, climbing up into sheer bluffs that blocked out half the sky, but the shoreline stayed true. She ran on, between the cliff and the sea, rain at her back and sand spraying up into her face.

She ran until she thought her lungs would burst, and then she dropped to her knees in the shadow of the cliff, sobbing for breath. The world tilted around her.

Only when she raised her head a few minutes later did she realize she'd run partway into a little cove, shells and bits of sea glass scattered over the wet sand. It had stopped raining, though the clouds still roiled uneasily in the sky. The respite wouldn't last.

Talia stood shakily and paced farther into the cove, hugging the cliff and grazing her hand gently across the rock. In the deepest part of the cove her fingers brushed over a tangle of seaweed and trailing vines that hung from the side of the cliff. Her hand passed through part of it, grasping empty air.

The wind whipped loose strands of hair into her face as she scrutinized the cliffside. There was a hollow cut into the rock, perfectly concealed from anyone who didn't know to look, and she tugged at the vines, trying to create a hole big enough to climb through.

But the plant was stubborn and impossibly knotted up. She wished Wen had given her a knife instead of a ring.

For the first time since fleeing the house, she glanced down at her right hand. In the moody gray light, the pale gem looked like a drop of the sea, caught just before dawn and bound in silver. She fought the urge to fling it into the ocean and went back to clawing at the vines, managing at last to pull enough foliage away to squeeze inside.

She stepped into a cave that burrowed deep into the cliff. It was much bigger than she had imagined: tall enough for her to stand upright, with room to spare, and wide enough to house two carriages. Fragments of light filtered through the vines and the hole she'd made, and Talia saw that she wasn't the cave's first visitor.

Something was half-buried in the center of the cavern, a curve of old wood poking up from the sand. She went to investigate, dropping to her knees and digging around the wooden thing until she could see what it was—the hull of a small boat, obviously old, but not rotten.

She stared at it awhile, rubbing off the dirt to try and make out what had once been written in red letters across the front. But the words were too faded. She felt a pang of ancient sorrow and loss, and she suddenly wished she hadn't come into this place. It was beginning to feel like a tomb.

Water lapped at her heels as the sea crept into the cove, and she pushed her way back through the tangle of vines before it was flooded entirely.

A thin line of shore was still visible between the cliff and the sea.

She ran back the way she'd come, racing against the rising tide.

The cliff fell gradually away as the shoreline rose to meet the bluff, and then she was dashing once more onto the white rock-strewn sand.

Her breath came shorter and cramps stabbed her sides. She dropped back to a walk.

The rain still held off, the clouds parting in places to show bits of ragged sky turning slowly orange and gold and scarlet. Away behind her, the sun was beginning to set.

She'd come a long way from the house. The gown was ruined, her shoes lost, her hair tumbled loose from its careful arrangement.

The ocean crashed beside her, and she stopped and stared out over the waves. She didn't let herself hear the distant strain of a song, shivering out there on the horizon, where sky met sea.

She tore her gaze away and saw someone running toward her across the sand.

It was Wen.

She clenched her hands into fists, the pale ring pressing into her palm, and strode forward to meet him.

He pulled up short five feet from her, breathing hard, his cravat flapping loose and his hair windblown. He stared at her. "You're—you're all right."

She thought of the cave and the boat, the sea creeping in, how she could have been trapped. The fear made her angry. "Are you following me?"

"Talia, I—"

"It's Miss Dahl-Saida!" she screeched at him.

He watched her guardedly and stuffed his hands in his

pockets. "Miss Dahl-Saida," he amended. "You're not allowed to walk down here. The Bar—my father has forbidden it."

Talia folded her arms across her chest. Wen's pale face glinted orange in the fractured light of the setting sun. "Forbidden it? Why?"

He shifted his feet, but didn't avert his gaze. "The sea is dangerous, Miss Dahl-Saida."

Distant music echoed in her ears. "What are you talking about?"

"Just come back to the house with me. I won't tell my father."

He reached to take her arm but she shook him off. The wind tore between them, whipping her dark hair into her eyes.

"I'll walk where I like, when I like. You can't tell me what to do. You don't own me."

His shoulders tensed. "Of course I don't. Why would you think that?"

"Why would you go along with *this*?" she demanded, shoving the ring into his face. "No hesitation, no objection, not even asking me how I feel about it?"

Over their heads, the light was beginning to fade, the last drops of gold swallowed up by the regathering clouds. The wind blew stronger, and she smelled rain.

"I'm sorry about that," he said, eyes serious. "I thought you knew. I thought you'd already agreed."

"Well I hadn't!" she said fiercely.

"I'm sorry. I didn't exactly have a choice either."

Tears burned behind her eyes and she fought them back, feeling so lost and frustrated and angry she didn't even know how to answer him.

The rain came all at once, driving and cold, and she jerked away from Wen and started briskly toward the house. He matched pace beside her, not saying anything.

She wished her mother were here. She would have been

able to convince the Baron and his awful son to let her out of the betrothal.

She glanced aside at Wen and he looked back at her, his face drenched with rain and shadow in the falling light. She hated how he stared at her, like if he looked long enough and deep enough he could see down into her soul. *She* didn't even know what was buried there—what gave him the right to try and uncover it?

"Miss Dahl-Saida. You're shivering."

And she was, though she hadn't realized it. He shrugged out of his jacket and draped it over her shoulders before she could protest. The inside of the coat was still dry, pulsing with the echo of his body heat. She pulled it tight, and warmth enveloped her.

"Thank you," she told him, reluctantly grateful.

They climbed the last little ways up to the house in the gathering dark, rain lashing icy against their skin. A lantern gleamed from the front door—Talia wondered if Ahned was looking out for them.

She walked faster, eager for the sanctuary of heat and dry clothes, and slipped on the flagstones, her arms windmilling. Wen grabbed her around the waist as she was about to go down, and for a moment she was caught in the circle of his arms, pressed up against his chest, his breath warm at her ear.

"Let me *go!*" she snapped.

He released her and leapt backward like he'd been holding a cobra. "Miss Dahl-Saida, I certainly didn't mean—"

But his words were lost in the sudden clamor of hooves coming up the drive. A horse and rider emerged from the rainy darkness. They clattered to a stop in front of the house, and the rider swung down.

The door opened and Ahned came out, a lantern in one hand. Yellow light slanted through the rain as he strode down the steps and took the horse's reins from the newcomer. Talia had the impression of a tall, strong form, a long coat, dark hair, the flash of a smile.

"Welcome home, my lord," said Ahned, with a little bow, then steered the horse back out into the rain, heading across the drive toward the stables. He passed Talia and Wen, the lantern swinging from one hand, and frowned. "Master Wendarien? What are you doing out here?"

Talia didn't hear Wen's answer, her eyes drawn to the rider who was just mounting the steps to the door, a dark silhouette against the light spilling out of the Ruen-Dahr.

"Get in out of the wet!" Ahned barked. Wen and Talia didn't have to be told twice. They ran the last few paces to the entrance, stumbling up the steps and through the door just behind the newcomer.

He turned at their arrival, black boots pooling rainwater on the stones, and her heart took up sudden residence in her ears. He looked about two or three years older than Talia, with dark hair and skin touched with bronze. He was soaked through, his long black coat plastered against his muscular body.

Talia realized she was staring.

He observed her with a kind of amused interest for a moment, and Talia's face flamed. Her feet were bare and muddy, her gown drenched with seawater and rain, and she was pretty sure there was sand in her hair. What must he think of her?

"Who's this, Wen?" he asked.

Talia glanced sideways. Wen stood completely rigid, every line in his body radiating tension. "Miss Talia Dahl-Saida of Enduena. My . . ." He swallowed, and set his jaw. "My fiancée."

She hated him for saying that.

The newcomer raised both eyebrows and grinned, his teeth flashing white. "Fiancée? How long was I gone?" Then: "Doesn't matter." And he turned to Talia. "Caiden Estahr-Sol, at your service."

He swept her a beautiful bow, and she tried to curtsy in return, but she was stiff with cold and didn't manage it very well.

He flashed her another smile anyway. "Very honored to meet you, Miss Dahl-Saida. Now if you'll excuse me, I've got to get out of these sopping clothes. I expect I'm not too late for dinner?" And he crossed the foyer and disappeared up the stairs without waiting for an answer.

Talia stared after him, blinking. "Who is *that*?" she asked Wen, who still hadn't moved from his place by the door.

"That," said Wen darkly, "is my brother."

Chapter Twelve

I DIDN'T KNOW YOU HAD A BROTHER!" Talia hissed, still staring after the newcomer in a state of complete bewilderment.

"Raiva's *tongue*," Wen cursed under his breath as he rubbed his eyes. "I didn't expect him home so soon. Excuse me."

And then he was gone up the stairs, too.

Talia stood there a few moments more, dripping water on the stones, and then went up to her own room and peeled off the ruined dress.

There wasn't time for another bath before dinner, but Lyna and Ro dug up a clean gown from somewhere and wrestled Talia into it. It was much plainer than the other one, made of a coarse burgundy with lace on the sleeves, and she wondered if it was one of theirs. They didn't have a second pair of shoes for her—she'd have to go barefoot.

"Dairon is still gathering things for you, Miss," Lyna explained as she tugged a comb through Talia's tangled hair. "Everything ought to be here before you go to bed. If we'd known you were going to go walking in the *rain* . . ." She shook her head disapprovingly and yanked at a knot so hard Talia's eyes started to tear.

She descended the staircase alone, anxious, though she

couldn't have said exactly why. Rain battered overhead on the domed roof, lanterns casting moody shadows around the vestibule. She padded across the cold stone and down the hallway, stopping just outside the dining room. Inside, a fire roared brightly on the hearth, and the Baron and Caiden sat at a long table underneath a many-paned window, rain glimmering on the glass. Wen was nowhere in sight.

Talia hovered in the doorway and waited for them to notice her, but they didn't. They sat with their heads bent together, talking animatedly about road conditions and taxes and the state of the harvest. She couldn't help staring at Caiden. He was sitting with his back to the door, so she couldn't see his face, but his straight, dark hair gleamed in the firelight, and the muscles in his arms were clearly outlined beneath the thin material of his shirt. He wore a gold ring on the smallest finger of his left hand, and she caught a glimpse of his jaw as he turned his face toward the Baron—it was strong and tan and cleanly shaven. His voice rose and fell as he talked, deep and smooth, it was tinged always with a hint of easy laughter.

And then suddenly he turned his head and saw her standing there. A surprised smile touched his lips as he pushed back his chair and stood at once, bowing politely. "Miss Dahl-Saida! Won't you join us?"

The Baron looked at Talia too, and frowned. "Oh. I'd forgotten you."

That was not exactly encouraging, but she stepped into the room anyway, sinking into a chair across from Caiden. She left an empty seat between herself and the Baron.

Caiden sat back down and smiled at her. "Forgive us for the dull conversation, Miss Dahl-Saida. I've just returned from my review of the province and I was telling my father about it."

"I see." She wondered how exactly Wen fit into this odd family hierarchy.

As if drawn by her thoughts, Wen appeared in the doorway, his damp hair curling over his ears, his cravat hastily and messily tied. The Baron glanced up in obvious irritation. "We've been waiting for you nearly a quarter of an hour, boy. Come and sit down."

Wen eyed Talia as he crossed the room, settling into the chair beside her. He smelled like rain and soap, with a slight hint of the sea, and he looked even more tense than he had in the vestibule. He fidgeted with the edge of the tablecloth.

Ro and the housekeeper, Dairon (who was indeed the middle-aged servingwoman who had first answered the door), brought in dinner on silver trays: rice with curried lamb, tea and wine, hot biscuits with honey. Talia realized she was ravenous. When was the last time she'd eaten? Had it really been this morning, at that flea-ridden inn? Thank gods for something other than fish.

She dug into the curry, forcing herself to eat slowly.

"I hear congratulations are in order," said Caiden to Wen, who wouldn't meet his eye. "Wendarien has found himself a bride."

The Baron spooned honey onto his biscuit and took a sip of wine. "I performed the betrothal ceremony myself this afternoon."

"And where did Wen find his lovely bride-to-be?" Caiden flashed another smile in Talia's direction, then looked at Wen again, his eyes hardening. "Did he pull her out of a mirror?"

The Baron choked on his wine and Wen gripped the edges of the table, his knuckles straining white against his skin. "The Empress sent her," he spat out.

Caiden raised an eyebrow. "We have an Empress now?"

"The former child Countess of Evalla, the Emperor's heir." The Baron carefully laid his wine glass back on the table.

Forty years ago, Evalla's army had been instrumental in the overthrow of Ryn. Talia wondered if the Baron was thinking of those days, back when he was royalty, and the Ruen-Dahr seemed suddenly very sad to her—the ghost of old glory, like the Baron was the ghost of a prince.

"I received a letter from Her Imperial Majesty two months ago, informing me of her imminent ascension to the throne and Miss Dahl-Saida's arrival."

Wen and Caiden locked eyes across the table. The tension between them seemed almost tangible, threads of hurt and hostility that Talia had no reference for.

"And why," Caiden continued, not breaking Wen's gaze, "would the new Empress of Enduena want to personally select a bride for my little brother?"

"It has nothing to do with him," Talia cut in, her own temper flaring. "I was banished here and the betrothal is part of my—" she couldn't finish.

"Part of your punishment," said Wen, so quietly Talia barely heard him.

She looked aside at him. What was he being punished for?

Caiden shook his head. "That's the most ludicrous thing I've heard in a long time."

"That the Empress banished me?"

His dark eyes met hers. "That you would agree to marry Wen."

"I didn't *agree* to—" she began, and then stopped herself. Because she absolutely had agreed to it a few hours ago. She felt sick.

For a few interminable moments, no one spoke. A clock ticked on the mantle. The rain lashed against the window. Wen rubbed his thumb around the base of his wine glass. The Baron chewed on a biscuit, honey clinging to his bony fingers.

And then Caiden let out a long breath, running his hands through his dark hair. "By the gods, Wendarien. I really don't understand why you're not on a ship to Od right now."

"It's a blessing he didn't go," said the Baron, "or we couldn't have fulfilled the Empress's terms."

Caiden shrugged, flashing a wicked grin. "I could have married her."

Talia flushed hot as the Baron frowned at Caiden and Wen clenched his jaw.

She glanced between the three men, obviously missing something. "Why would Wen go to Od?" She thought of Ayah, sobbing in the palace corridor. *What do you miss most?*

"University," said Caiden. "Wen is some kind of musical genius and they were ecstatic to have him. But he's not going, now. Do you want to tell her why, Wen?"

"Shut up," said Wen.

"Why? You don't want her to know that you stayed because the gods told you to? Because they gave you a vision, just like they gave your mother, and mine, before they *died*?"

"Shut up!" Wen cried.

"What, are you not sticking to that story anymore?" Caiden demanded.

"Enough!" said the Baron, shaking in his seat, wine sloshing over the rim of the glass he held tight in one hand. "We will not speak of this again."

"Gods' blood," Caiden swore, and sat back in his chair.

Wen shrank into himself.

The Baron set his wavering wine glass back on the table. He seemed more unnerved by the exchange than either of his sons.

Talia took a sip of tea, which had gone cold. What did Caiden mean, a vision from the gods?

Caiden gave her a wry smile. "Aren't we a merry bunch this evening. Forgive us, Miss Dahl-Saida."

She gave him a hesitant smile in return.

"Tell me about yourself," he went on, suddenly easy again. "You're from Enduena?"

"I am."

"What's it like?"

Talia blinked back images of riding with her father in the hills, of her mother telling stories by the fire. "It's beautiful. Very hot in the spring and summer, but the nights are filled with jasmine and stars. And the rains always come to wash the dust away."

He smiled again, and a chorus of starlings awoke in her chest. "It sounds magical."

"It is."

"What of your parents, Miss Dahl-Saida?" asked the Baron. "I was told to expect your mother as well as you. Did she not choose to join you?"

The air in the room seemed to close in around her. "My father has been gone nearly six years, now. My mother—my mother died on the sea crossing."

The Baron's face grew very pale, lines pressing deep into his forehead. "I didn't know—I didn't—realize. Your poor mother. You poor child." Moisture gleamed in the corners of his eyes. "How did she die?"

Talia hated the Baron for asking that question. She hated his affectation that her misery meant anything to him at all.

"Father," said Caiden sharply. "That's hardly an appropriate—"

"She drowned. She threw herself overboard in the middle of a storm and she drowned."

All three of them stared at her, shocked into silence.

Talia jerked up from her seat and accidentally knocked her wine glass over. The crystal hit the table with a delicate *tink,* and deep red liquid leaked across the polished wood. She stood staring at the spilled wine, her fingers digging hard into the back of her chair.

"I'm so sorry," came Wen's quiet voice.

She met his eyes, and saw a pain there that mirrored her own. Caiden gave her a tight smile. "How awful for you."

"Forgive me for my presumptuous questions," said the Baron. His voice shook.

The rain beat against the window and the fire burned too hot, and Talia felt like she was going to fracture into a thousand pieces. She couldn't stand it any longer.

She left the room without another word.

She sat in the window seat in her room, knees drawn up to her chin, staring down at the distant sea. The rain had stopped and the night was dark, but light from some downstairs window glinted on the water. The waves grasped fruitlessly for the rocky shore, and fell away again.

There was a knock at the door and Talia turned from the window. "What is it?" she called.

The door creaked open and Lyna and Ro came in, hefting a trunk between them. Dairon followed just behind.

"Good evening, Miss," said Dairon crisply. "I've brought your clothes. We would have had them ready earlier, but didn't know you would arrive without a stitch to your name." She frowned. "Lyna, Ro, set it down by the bed, please."

The maids did as she asked, plopping the trunk on the carpet in a cloud of dust and the sudden scent of cedar. Ro creaked the lid open, and Talia reluctantly left the window seat to come and see what all the fuss was about.

Lyna drew a gown out of the trunk that shimmered with blue and silver beading. She eyed Talia, then nodded and laid the dress on the bed. "The late Baroness seems to have been about your size, Miss. That's fortunate."

"Both late Baronesses, you mean," quipped Ro, pulling out a second gown. This one was dusty pink with long sleeves and a split skirt, for riding.

"Hold your tongue, girl," Dairon snapped at her.

Ro shrugged, and unearthed another dress. "My apologies, Miss."

Slowly, Lyna and Ro emptied the contents of the trunk, and Talia's bed was soon piled high with silk and velvet and satin. Dairon instructed the two maids to hang the dresses in the wardrobe while she took the empty trunk away and went to fetch something else. She stepped from the room and the mood lightened considerably.

The maids waved off Talia's offers to help, so she perched back in the window seat and watched them. "What did you mean 'both late Baronesses?'"

Ro quirked a grin at her, and slid a yellow gown onto a hanger. "The Baron was married twice." She leaned toward her conspiratorially. "Both of his wives died under mysterious circumstances."

"Utter nonsense," said Lyna, hanging a blue patterned dress in the wardrobe. "The Baron has just been very unlucky."

"Maybe," said Ro, putting the yellow gown by the blue one, "or maybe what they say about the house is true."

"What do they say?"

"That it's cursed." Ro fitted another gown onto a hanger and deposited it in the wardrobe. "That it was touched by the gods. They say the house is built on the same patch of land where the Tree lay for nine hundred years. That gods and men dwelled here together in the old days. Communed with heaven. That sort of thing."

Why did the old stories seem to be haunting her every step? "I have no interest in superstition."

"Oh, but it's *not* superstition. At least, the stuff about the house is not."

Talia snorted ungraciously. "You can prove the *Tree* used to lay under our feet?"

"Not that." Ro forgot all about the gowns and took a step

over to the window seat. "I mean about the Baron's wives. They were both happy, pretty things, and then they married the Baron, and came here, and went mad. One after the other."

Her heart jolted. "What did you say?"

"It's the house that changed them," said Ro, enjoying the effect her story was having. Her dark eyes sparkled. "It made them laugh and sing when nothing was there, made them talk nonsense all the time. Some rumors say they killed themselves." She whispered this last bit, eyes wide. "Some say the *Baron* killed them because he couldn't stand their insane laughing."

Talia felt herself go numb, her thoughts flashing back to her mother on the ship. Singing to the sea. Laughing into the storm. How could that have happened here, too?

"By the gods, Ro! There's no call for that kind of talk!"

Ro giggled and went back to hanging gowns. "In any case, it's what took a small part of the Baron's fortune, at least what hadn't already been claimed by the Empire. He spent nearly everything he had on doctors for the first Baroness, and he's not gone out in company once since the death of the second. He doesn't care about anything anymore and mismanages the province his family once ruled. All the real work falls to Caiden, of course. It's a wonder *he* hasn't gone mad yet."

"Don't listen to her, Miss," said Lyna. "It's all nonsense. Illness and a tragic accident took the Baron's wives away. Nothing more. He grieves for them still, stands all-night vigil at their graves every year on the anniversaries of their deaths. Their passing broke him."

"I don't care what you say," Ro grumbled. "This house is strange. Off." She sobered, fingering the material of a lilac dress. "I've heard whispers, sometimes, voices high in the tower. Laughter and crying, too. I think the Baron's wives are haunting this place, seeking revenge for their untimely deaths."

"Be *quiet*, girl," said Lyna. "If Dairon hears you talking like that she'll have you dismissed."

Ro gave a little shrug. "No, she won't. Not many people are willing to work in the Ruen-Dahr, and she's short-staffed as it is."

"Do you hear music?" Talia asked Ro carefully.

Ro gave her a strange look. "Music? No, Miss. Only Master Wendarien—"

"Ro!" said Lyna.

Ro tore her gaze away, suddenly uneasy. "I'm sorry, Miss. Lyna's right. I really shouldn't be talking about it. Just superstition."

Something clicked in Talia's mind. "Caiden and Wen have different mothers."

Ro nodded, pulling another dress off the bed. "Certainly they do—why else would they have different surnames? The first Baroness was Enduenan—that's where Lord Caiden's dark coloring comes from. She was the daughter of one of the Enduenan ambassadors who was stationed in Ryn after it was made part of the Empire. She died when he was two, and then Master Wendarien's mother—"

Lyna frowned. "Enough, you silly girl. Why must you prattle on so?"

Dairon returned just then, and Ro quickly snapped her mouth shut. The housekeeper had a smaller trunk with her, full of shoes and gloves. She made Talia try them all on, one after another, until she was satisfied Talia had enough variety. Then the maids packed those in the wardrobe, too, and all three bid her goodnight.

When they had gone, she went back to the window seat, Ro's words echoing in her mind.

They went mad. One after the other.

Some rumors say they killed themselves.

Chapter Thirteen

T ALIA WOKE JUST AFTER DAWN, HER MIND filled with a dread she couldn't explain, the raw edges of half-forgotten dreams nibbling at her consciousness. She went immediately to the window and pulled it open, sucking in a deep breath of salt-drenched air. The sky was heavy with clouds, but it wasn't raining. Away below her, the sea crept onto the shore, and once again she heard the distant strain of some unearthly music, whispering out there among the waves.

She blinked and saw her mother, drinking tea in the great cabin as the storm raged outside the ship. *Can't you hear it? The song of the waves.*

Talia cursed, jerking away from the window and latching it tight.

But the music lingered.

She stepped over to the wardrobe and flung open both doors, running her fingers along the smooth material of the Baronesses' gowns. They were all beautiful, though cut in the still-unfamiliar Ryn style. She pulled out a dress a shade of blue so dark it was nearly black, with long sleeves and tiny crystal beads sewn into the bodice and skirt. It shimmered in the gray light from the window, like a sky strewn with stars.

She put it on, struggling to fasten the back without help, but she managed it, finally. She tried not to dwell on the fact that the last woman who'd worn this gown was dead.

She tripped on the hem of the dress as she went downstairs and ran straight into Caiden—she would have fallen on her face if he hadn't grabbed her arm.

He let go and took a step back as she gaped, flushing so hard she couldn't even find her tongue to stammer out an apology.

He'd apparently been getting dressed *on the way down the stairs*, because his shirt flapped unbuttoned, giving her a full view of his muscled chest.

He laughed, white teeth flashing, and buttoned his shirt swiftly while she stared at him, her whole face on fire.

She scrambled for something witty to say, or anything to say at all.

He tucked in his shirttails. "I'm sorry about last night," he said, evidently past the awkwardness already. "That was the most uncomfortable dinner I've ever experienced, and I certainly didn't help much. I'm afraid I might have acted like a fool."

She couldn't help smiling. "None of us were at our best."

He laughed. "Definitely not. I was sorry to hear about your mother," he added, sobering. "I understand how hard that is, and if you ever need anything at all, just ask. I'm here."

His kindness touched her. "Thank you."

He gave her a sideways smile. "I really can't believe you're going to marry my brother."

The heat was back, rushing through her. "It wasn't my choice."

"That doesn't surprise me."

"You don't like Wen."

"Wen is . . . Wen is . . ." He shrugged. "Wen is Wen, I guess.

I'm not sure he's entirely sane. He claims he hears voices—our mothers' voices, haunting the tower, and an eerie music coming off the sea." Caiden grimaced and Talia tried to keep the discomfort from showing on her face. "My father and I thought it best for Wen to get away from here—he had the opportunity of a lifetime with University, and he threw it all away. I'll never understand why."

"You said something about the gods, too. About a vision. What did you mean?"

He shook his head. "Nothing. It's just . . . Wen puts too much stock in servants' rumors—he won't let our mothers' deaths alone, and my father is having a hard time forgiving him for it."

Some rumors say they killed themselves. Talia pushed Ro's voice away. "What about you?"

"I like to think I'm a fairly forgiving person."

She swallowed, losing herself in his piercing eyes. She suddenly never wanted to stop looking at him. Or him to stop looking at her.

And then she heard another step on the stair and turned to see Wen coming down, his glance torn between them. His jaw was clenched tight, dark shadows pressed under his eyes.

"Ah, Wen," said Caiden. "I was just telling your fiancée good morning."

Wen's jaw clenched tighter still. For an uncomfortable moment, the three of them just stood there in silence. Talia didn't know where to look.

And then Caiden flashed her another smile. "I'll see you later, Talia. My horse needs a run." He stepped past her, down the remaining stairs and across the entrance hall, disappearing out the front door.

She couldn't help staring after him.

"Miss Dahl-Saida."

Talia jerked her gaze toward Wen. "What?"

"Miss Dahl-Saida, I—" His forehead creased and he pulled his spectacles from his pocket, absently cleaning them on the tails of his shirt. "I'm sorry we didn't get off to a better start yesterday. I'm sorry you're so far from home and I'm sorry the Empress insisted on that . . . particular clause in her contract. I'm sorry about your mother—you can't imagine how much. And I'm sorry I'm not more—" He shrugged, clearly frustrated, his eyes wandering to the front door. "—dashing," he finished awkwardly.

She didn't attempt to persuade him otherwise. "What *is* it, between the two of you?"

"I don't want to talk about my brother."

"Well, I do." She crossed her arms, glaring at him.

He shifted his feet. "We've never had much in common. I think he despises me. Or is ashamed of me. Or both."

"Why?"

His owlish eyes bore into hers. "Because he can't see or hear the things I can. He thinks I'm mad, at best. Malicious, at worst."

"Are you?"

"No." He sighed. "I'm sorry, Miss Dahl-Saida. I get too caught up in my music sometimes, trying to capture the melodies in my head, the cadence of the sea. It can be somewhat of an obsession—my father and Caiden don't understand. I don't mean to be cryptic or rude—and I don't want you to hate me."

She considered that, trying to see things from his point of view. "Then what do you want?"

"To be your friend, I hope."

She didn't know how to respond. The betrothal might not be his fault, but he could have warned her or objected or *something*. And his continual niceness was almost grating—she'd liked him better yesterday when he'd cursed like a sailor. "I can't promise that right now."

"Fair enough." He slipped his spectacles back into his pocket. "In the meantime, how do you feel about breakfast?"

Talia and Wen ate alone in the dining hall. Caiden wasn't back from his ride yet (she tried to tell herself she wasn't disappointed), and the Baron remained upstairs. Wen told her that happened quite a lot.

Wen was quiet and fidgety and wouldn't stop looking at her, obviously wanting to talk more, but she had no desire to pick up the threads of their conversation. She was too restless for company—she needed to be alone.

She excused herself as politely as she could after her second cup of tea, and slipped back out into the vestibule, to the front door.

"Can I help you, Miss Dahl-Saida?"

The voice made her jump, and she wheeled around to see Ahned standing in the hall. The Baron's steward was dressed the same as yesterday—stern dark suit, black-and-silver hair tied back at the nape of his neck.

"I thought I'd go for a walk."

Ahned took a few paces toward her. "I can show you the garden."

"I'm going down to the shore."

Ahned raised an eyebrow. "The sea is forbidden, Miss Dahl-Saida."

"Why? Who forbids it?"

"The Baron."

"And why does the Baron care where I walk?"

"Because it is his house, Miss, and it is his rule."

"Am I just supposed to wander around inside for the rest of my life?"

"You may walk in the garden, or go to the stables, or follow the road down to the village. But the sea is forbidden."

She jutted out her chin, refusing to let him rattle her. "Why?"

"Miss Dahl-Saida, if you cannot be trusted to obey the rules, you will not be allowed out of the house at all. Is that understood?"

She glowered at him. "Perfectly."

"And can you be trusted?"

"Of course."

He wasn't convinced. "Swear by the gods you won't go down to the sea."

Why could she never seem to escape the gods she didn't want to believe in? She swallowed and forced herself to maintain eye contact. "I swear by the gods I won't go down to the sea."

He nodded. "What will it be then—garden or village or stables?"

"Garden."

Another jerk of his chin. "This way, Miss."

He walked back into the hallway, and Talia followed. They went past the empty dining room and through a door, into a short passageway that ended at another door. He stopped to unlock it, pulling a ring of keys from his belt. She eyed them with extreme irritation.

"I hope you have a lovely walk," he said, and went off down the hall.

Talia stepped into the garden, pushing the door shut behind her. She would have hardly called it a garden—it didn't deserve the name. It was merely a rambling rectangle of cold earth, enclosed on three sides by high stone walls overgrown with ivy. On one end marched several rows of bedraggled rosebushes sprouting knotted blossoms; on the other stood a willow tree overhanging a murky pool, limp leaves trailing in dirty water. There was a wooden hutch, which might have once housed birds, nailed into the side of the tree; now the carved doors sagged on their hinges, dirt and debris visible inside. Certainly a far cry from the Emperor's gardens, with their elaborate fountains and overflowing lily pools, macaws squawking at her from their aviary.

She thought of her father, taking her to see the tigers, of

her mother, promising she could have a parrot of her own. She thought of Ayah, wandering obliviously through the lily gardens with a book in her hand, spectacles pinching her freckled nose.

And she thought of Eda, mocking her for her dirty feet and ripped skirts after tumbling in the dust with a new litter of hounds.

Talia paced the grim square of earth, wandering through the knotted roses and over to the willow. It wasn't raining today, but the sky was still heavy with clouds. The wind blew up cool from the sea, bringing with it snatches of melody steeped in longing. She tried not to think about it.

There was an old stone bench by the pool, vines curling up its legs. Talia sank down on it and stared into the water. Lily pads floated on the surface of the pond. A hesitant white flower, just beginning to bloom, peeked up between the tangle of green; she caught a hint of its heady fragrance, and it reminded her of Eddenahr. This pond had once been beautiful, or at least someone had tried to make it so. She wondered which of the Baronesses had tended to it—Wen's mother, or Caiden's. She flushed, and scolded herself.

So Wen happened to have an incredibly handsome and intriguing and courteous brother. That didn't change anything.

Although Ayah would disagree. Talia grinned, imagining the lively discussion the two of them would have about Caiden's many admirable qualities—lingering of course on that morning's encounter on the stairs.

She threw a pebble into the pool, then got up and walked around the garden again. There was a gate in the front wall that looked out onto a graveyard, which she turned away from in a hurry. The back wall had a gate too, half-concealed with ivy, and she stopped to peer out toward the sea. She could feel it calling to her, a restless tugging at her heart.

The gate was locked, but she climbed the iron lattice and

hopped down to the other side. Her promise to Ahned made her uneasy, and she glanced back.

The house loomed above her, grim and dark, ivy creeping up the weatherworn stone. She could certainly understand why people thought it was haunted. But she didn't see anyone watching her, so she turned toward the sea again and started down the path winding away from the garden.

She'd only gone a few paces when she found a door set into the hill.

It was obviously ancient, made of carved stone. Two chains stretched across it, looping through iron rings on either side of the door and clasped tight in a heavy padlock that hung in the center.

She wondered what was inside. A temple? A crypt? She leaned forward to examine the carvings in the stone, worn by centuries of wind and weather and partially obscured by the padlock and chains. But she still recognized the Tree, huge and beautiful, its branches curling up into heaven. Around its base stood people wielding spears and battling the towering gods, who lashed lightning at them. A woman knelt at the very base of the carved door, her head bowed, weeping.

She could feel how ancient this place was, as if the power of the gods themselves was woven into the door, or bound tight behind it. She imagined she saw glints of light flying up from the carving like sparks from a smith's anvil.

The sudden thud of hooves in the sand shook her from her reverie. She looked down to see a lone horse and rider galloping along the shore: Caiden, his dark hair wild in the wind, stark against the mingled gray of sea and sky. The flock of starlings whirred inside of her. Why was he allowed to go down to the sea and she was not?

"Talia?"

She jerked around to see Wen standing on the path above

her, his spectacles perched precariously on his nose. There was ink on his fingers, and the top few buttons of his shirt were undone, his cravat absent.

She didn't snap at him for using her first name, or yell at him for following her, just nodded to the stone door. "What's down there?"

The muscles in his face clenched, and he shook his head. "Nothing."

"Nothing is shut away behind a heavy chain and an iron lock?"

"Leave it alone, Talia. Please."

"Why are there so many secrets here? Why won't anyone give me a straight answer?"

He considered her, his blue eyes huge behind his spectacles. "The Ruen-Dahr is centuries old. There used to be a temple here, and that door is a remnant of it. But it's in ruins now—it isn't safe to go inside. That's why it's locked up."

She doubted that was the whole truth. "A temple to the Tree?"

"Yes."

"Then people do believe the Tree was here, once."

Wind stirred through her hair, and she could still hear the echo of hoofbeats, away down by the ocean.

"You don't believe in the gods," said Wen, watching her. "Why would you care about the Tree?"

"How do you know I don't believe in them?"

He raised an eyebrow. "Do you?"

The challenge rankled her. "Not really." Her mind went back to her conversation with Hanid down in the ship's galley. "I want to be in control of my own fate."

He glanced at the door and she followed his gaze, staring at the weeping woman carved into the stone. The glints of light were gone. "You've never experienced anything that you can't rationally explain?"

She thought of the whale in the storm, the eerie music echoing among the waves, the feeling she'd gotten when she first saw the sea. Like it belonged to her. "No," she snapped.

He shrugged. "Well, I have."

She wished he would stop looking at her with such intensity. It was driving her crazy. She turned and started down the path again, but he grabbed her arm and pulled her back.

"Please don't go down there. The sea is unpredictable, and that makes it extremely dangerous."

For a moment longer she held his gaze, not challenging his half-answer. "Ahdairon choke you," she muttered, then pushed past him, walking back up the path. She scrambled over the gate and paced through the garden-that-wasn't-really-a-garden, and went inside, so frustrated with her situation she didn't know what to do with herself.

Gods above. It was hard to believe she'd only been in this awful place a *day*.

Chapter Fourteen

RESTLESS AND FIDGETY, SHE DECIDED TO EXPLORE the house. She paced through the back hallways, avoiding the music room in the event Wen might go there. She found the kitchen (Dairon ordered her out), the stairs to the cellar (Lyna did the same), and a small, vacant sitting room.

She climbed the stairs in the vestibule, not turning left to where she knew the boys' rooms and the Baron's suite were, but continuing on past her own room and to another, narrower staircase. This one twisted upward for a while, a worn, red runner curling down the center of it. The stairs spilled out onto a little alcove, with a window cut into the wall. It looked down over the garden, the sea glimmering beyond. From there, another staircase wound further upward to a green door at the top. She tried the handle—surprisingly unlocked—so she opened it and stepped through.

She found herself in the modest foyer of a dusty suite—a handsome private sitting room that led into a dressing room, with a bedchamber beyond. She paced through the sitting room first, peering at the portraits on the walls, all dusty, all faded. Several were of a dark-haired young woman with smooth brown skin; her eyes stared out of the painting and straight into Talia's.

In one she held a dark-haired baby, her lips curved into a smile, contentment radiating from her face. In another the baby was older, and the woman wasn't smiling anymore. Her expression looked strained, her eyes haunted.

The next series of portraits showed a blonde young woman, laughter in her bright blue eyes, a baby in her arms. In one of the paintings, a dark-haired little boy stood with her and her baby. The painter had depicted the boy smiling, but unhappiness came through in his eyes.

It was Caiden, Talia realized. Caiden and Wen and the second dead Baroness. The dark-haired woman had to be the first.

She felt like she was disturbing a mausoleum.

She walked quieter after that, passing through the dressing room and into the bedroom. Sheets were draped over the furniture, transforming couches and chairs, bookcases and mirrors into unearthly shapes. Cobwebs clung to bedposts and the corners of the walls. The whole place had a tinge of sadness to it and smelled like dead flowers.

Talia circled back to the dressing room, tugging open the doors of a large cedar wardrobe that stood in the corner by a tightly shuttered window. The wardrobe was empty, save for a bright blue gown she knew immediately was a wedding dress. She fingered the silk. There was silver stitching around the neckline, and a crown of dried flowers tied to the hanger with a ribbon. It seemed the servants had given Talia all the late Baronesses' gowns save one. This suite had clearly belonged to them, and she wondered if her own mother would have lived up here, too. Somehow, she didn't think so. These rooms ached with longing—things lost, but remembered always.

She was the only one left to remember her mother.

Talia shut the wardrobe in a hurry.

She left the suite, stepping back through the green door and onto the landing, then up a third set of even-narrower stairs, patches of bare stone showing through an ancient blue rug.

The air grew colder as she climbed, and she felt uneasy. She knew she shouldn't be up here.

At the top was another landing, another window. This one was small and round, the colored glass showing an image of the white Tree with three flaming Stars caught in its branches. Talia stared at it, her mouth going dry. The glass looked very old.

What was tucked away up here?

A plain door stood to the right of the stairs, and she pulled on the handle, pulse jumping.

But this door was locked tight.

Ro came to help her dress for dinner, cinching tight the laces of the despised corset, and buttoning the back of a pale yellow gown. The waistline was embroidered in green and studded with pearls; the sleeves were poufs of confectioner's cream, showing the length of Talia's brown arms. She wondered which Baroness the gown had belonged to—Caiden's mother, or Wen's.

She settled in front of the mirror while curly-headed Ro arranged her hair. "Have you worked at the Ruen-Dahr very long?"

"About a year," said Ro, twisting a strand of Talia's hair and pinning it up.

Talia grinned in what she hoped was a conspiratorial manner. "Then you know all the house's secrets, I imagine."

Ro laughed. "Not even the Baron knows *all* the house's secrets, Miss."

"But you know what happened to the Baronesses?"

In the mirror, Ro avoided her eyes. "I'm not supposed to talk about them. Lyna scolded me for what I said last night."

"I won't tell her," Talia promised.

Ro shook her head and grabbed another pin. "I'm sorry, Miss."

Talia chose her next words carefully. "What's at the top of the tower? I thought I might explore the house tomorrow, but I don't want to go places I'm not allowed."

Ro seemed relieved at this change in subject. "Nothing up there but the Baronesses' old suite, all dust and spiderwebs. There's the library too, of course, but it's locked up."

Now she was getting somewhere. "The library?"

The maid shrugged a little. "Some sort of tragedy, I don't know what. The Baron had it locked long before I came to work here."

Interesting. "What if I need something to read?"

"Master Wendarien keeps books in the music room. You could always ask him, Miss."

Talia grimaced—she'd take her chances with the locked door.

Ro slipped in a final pin, and stepped back, nodding in satisfaction. "You'll make a very pretty bride when the time comes, if you don't mind my saying so. It'll cheer up Master Wendarien, too."

Heat rushed through her, and she rose abruptly from the stool.

"Why does Wen need cheering up?"

"Because of the difficulty over University, of course. The Baron was so angry when he said he wasn't going after all, and then he had the audacity to claim he knew what had happened to the Baronesses and—" Ro cut herself off. "I'm sorry, Miss. I really shouldn't be talking about it."

Talia stamped down her frustration and tried a different tack. "Do you really hear voices from the tower?"

Ro caught her eye. "If I said I did, would you believe me?"

"Yes."

The maid's face grew tight. "Do you hear it, too?"

She didn't mean to say it, but the words spilled out anyway. "Not exactly. But my mother—my mother claimed the sea was singing to her. On the ship."

"I heard about her death, Miss Dahl-Saida. I'm very sorry for it."

She swallowed. "Thank you."

Ro regarded her with a shake of her head. "So much sadness in this house. I am sorry some of it has found you."

The wind whispered against the window, and Talia heard an unearthly melody coiling up from the sea. It sang of sorrow and danger and longing. It made her feel as if the waves had already swallowed her whole, and she was just taking a long time with the drowning.

Chapter Fifteen

CAIDEN AND WEN WERE WAITING FOR HER when she arrived in the dining hall, her skirts whispering about her knees. They both jerked their heads up and rose from their seats, bowing almost in unison, one light head and one dark. She felt exposed in the tight-waisted, short-sleeved gown, acutely aware of the brothers' gazes. She strode quickly to her chair from last evening, and sat down.

Wen and Caiden resumed their seats, and Lyna swept in carrying dinner: roasted fish with wild pears and a spicy-sweet sauce.

"Is the Baron not joining us?" Talia asked, in order to have something to say.

"My father is very tired," Caiden told her. "We've been holed up nearly since breakfast, going over the accounts from my review. He'll have his dinner upstairs in his rooms."

"Is he—" Talia cut herself off and glanced down at her plate, then back at Caiden. "Is the Baron ill?"

Wen fidgeted beside her and a hint of tension flicked across Caiden's face. "Our father has not been *well* since . . ."

"Since my mother died," said Wen quietly.

She looked at him. His face was open, his eyes seeking hers.

"Grief is not an illness," she said.

"Isn't it?"

"You are not ill. Caiden is not ill. I am not—" she swallowed and brought her hand up to her forehead "—ill."

Wen tapped his finger on the handle of his knife. "I think it's more to the point that our father does not wish to be well. And so he is not."

"He makes himself older than he is," Caiden agreed. His gaze locked with Wen's for a moment until Wen shifted uneasily and looked away.

For a while the three of them lapsed into silence, focusing solely on their plates. Talia kept stealing glances at Caiden, watching the way he cut his food or admiring his long fingers wrapped around his wine glass. He would fit in nicely at the Enduenan court, and she couldn't help wishing both of them were at the palace in Eddenahr, eating sherbet out of crystal glasses. They would dance at some elaborate party; he would ask her to go walking with him through the gardens in the starlight. She would marry *him* in the spring, diamonds in his hair and gold thread in hers.

She realized Caiden was talking to her, and she jerked her attention to the present. "I'm sorry?"

He quirked a grin. "I was just asking you why our esteemed Empress banished you to lowly Ryn. I can't imagine you having done anything to offend her."

Talia fiddled with her knife handle. "She found out that the Emperor intended to name me his heir, instead of her."

Caiden's eyebrows went to the top of his head. "Aigir's *bones.*"

"You were going to be Empress?" said Wen, shocked into speaking. "Why?"

"Because—well because I'm the Emperor's daughter." She stared at her plate, her food turning sour in her stomach. "The man I thought was my father nearly my whole life . . . it turns out he wasn't. My mother only told me a few days before Eda seized the Empire."

Wen shook his head and Caiden swore again. "Why don't you go back to Enduena? Raise an army of your own and take back the Empire? It's yours by birthright!"

The fire was making her too warm, and the neckline of her dress itched. "I have no money, no army, no support, no way to even make the return journey. Eda will kill me if I show my face there again."

Caiden leaned toward her across the table. "So find a way! Gather support, raise an army. Ryn would stand behind you."

"It's not that simple, Caiden. And besides—I'm not sure I even want to be Empress." She imagined sinking onto the Emperor's ivory throne, a crown on her head. She imagined Eda, groveling at her feet. But none of that would bring her mother back.

Caiden shrugged. "I just don't think you should dismiss the idea entirely. It's worth thinking about, anyway."

She tried to smile. "Perhaps." She scrambled for some way to change the subject. "I saw you out riding today. You have a very fine horse—is he of Enduenan stock?"

Caiden toasted her with his wine glass. "You have a good eye! He's half Enduenan, like me." He grinned. "Are you much of a rider?"

She nodded eagerly. "I won races back home. Beat all the boys. I wasn't technically supposed to even compete, but I did anyway." Two years ago she'd skipped out on a week of history and dancing lessons to attend the Festival of Uerc and ride in the desert races—with Ayah's help, of course. Traditionally, girls were not allowed to enter. Her mother had scolded her roundly afterward, but Talia could tell she was secretly proud. And there were more girls in the races the next year.

Caiden laughed. "You'll have to try my gelding. Fastest horse in Ryn—not many people can handle him."

"I could."

He grinned at her. "Come to the stables tomorrow and we'll see how good you really are."

Guilt and excitement tangled up inside of her, and she finally glanced over at Wen.

Caiden looked at him, too. "If it's all right with my little brother, of course."

It was a challenge, and Wen lifted his eyes to meet Caiden's. "You'll do whatever you wish, without regard to me, or anyone. Just like you always do."

Caiden held his gaze for a moment, and then laughed. "That's a rather harsh assessment of my character."

"But an accurate one."

Caiden shrugged. "We'll have to let Miss Dahl-Saida decide for herself." He rose from his seat and bowed, smiling at her. "Until tomorrow, then. I've more work to do this evening."

She smiled back. "Until tomorrow."

And then he was gone, and she was alone with her fiancé.

Wen didn't say anything to her, and she didn't say anything to him. She sipped wine for a few uncomfortable moments before excusing herself and retreating upstairs.

She opened the window in her room, leaning her arms on the sill and breathing in the cold, briny air.

Was there something to what Caiden had said? Should she really attempt to return to Enduena and reclaim her homeland? He'd said Ryn would stand behind her—did that mean him?

From the depths of the house she heard the distant threads of melody: Wen, playing in the music room. His song was less eerie than that of the sea, but it held more sorrow.

If Talia wanted to see what the Baron was hiding up in the library, she was going to have to get hold of Ahned's keys. She shadowed the Baron's steward all the next morning, a host of excuses ready if he caught her following him.

She used the first one when he came up from the wine cellar and spotted her in the hall: "I've been looking for Dairon or one of the maids. I need a cup of tea."

He frowned at her. "Breakfast will be served in half an hour, Miss Dahl-Saida. I expect you can wait until then." And then he continued down the corridor.

She counted to twenty, and followed.

He climbed the stairs to the Baron's tower suite, and Talia hid in an alcove, peering around the corner while he knocked on the door.

"My lord?"

She heard the Baron's muffled voice from inside the room. "How is the sea, today?"

"It runs very quiet, my lord."

"And the temple?"

Talia pressed her fingernails into the worn wood paneling, listening intently. Did he mean the door under the hill?

"Locked safe, my lord."

"Are you certain?"

"Yes, my lord. Shall I bring up your tea?"

"I'll take it with my son this morning."

"Then I shall send Master Caiden up at once, my lord."

Talia ducked into the alcove again, flattening herself against the wall and tensing as Ahned walked by. This time she counted to twenty-five before going after him.

The steward went down to the kitchen, where he began to prepare his master's tea. He filled a kettle and put it on the stove to boil, laid china out on a silver tray.

And then—to Talia's surprise and triumph—he took the ring of keys from his belt and hung it up on a little nail inside the china cupboard. She couldn't believe her luck.

Until Lyna appeared on the stairs with a basket of linens. "What are you doing here, Miss Dahl-Saida?" she inquired, far too loudly.

Ahned watched her suspiciously from the kitchen doorway, his arms folded across his chest.

She used another excuse: "I tore a seam in my gown—I didn't know if it could be mended, or . . .?"

Lyna frowned over the linens. "You have plenty of other gowns to wear."

"Oh. Well, yes, of course." She tried to accentuate how flustered she was. "I just didn't want it to show up unexplained in the laundry—"

Ahned shook his head as Lyna swept past her with the basket, her frown deepening. "It's nearly time for breakfast, Miss Dahl-Saida. You needn't worry about a ripped seam."

Talia gave her a relieved smile and went up to the dining room, hoping Ahned wouldn't need his keys again for a while.

She ate breakfast alone. Caiden was dining with the Baron, Ro told her, and Wen was working in the music room. "He often skips meals," said the dark-headed maid as she poured tea. "Gets so lost in his music, he forgets what day it is."

Talia kept herself from rudely remarking that Wen was perfectly free to go to Od any day he chose to pursue his dratted music. "Will the Baron and Caiden be long?"

"Oh yes, Miss. They're likely to remain upstairs until dinner." Ro gave her a bright smile and took her tray away.

Talia thought with a pang about Caiden's riding invitation. Had he forgotten? As an engaged woman it wasn't exactly appropriate for her to be alone with him for any length of time, but she doubted very much if the Baron would enforce those kinds of rules. Her conscience told her it was probably better this way—although her mental image of Ayah's laughing face disagreed.

When she'd eaten, she slipped once more down into the servants' domain, where she spotted Ro and Lyna busy in the laundry, and Ahned and Dairon chatting as they polished a mountain of silver. None of them saw her. She stepped into the kitchen, heart thundering, and opened the china cabinet.

There were the keys, still hanging on their hook.

She grabbed them, and hid the bundle of cold metal in the folds of her skirt.

Chapter Sixteen

TALIA CLIMBED THE STAIRS TO THE TOWER, her fingers sweaty around the key ring. She passed the door to the Baronesses' suite, and kept climbing up to the landing with the Tree and Stars in the stained glass window, and the locked door.

She tried the keys one by one. Some fit the lock, but didn't turn. Some didn't fit at all. She was halfway through the ring when she found the right one—it fit, turned, clicked.

She twisted the handle and opened the door.

She stepped into a round chamber bathed in gray light, dust motes rising from the floor. An oriel window on the far end of the room looked north; she could see the ocean down below, crashing white upon the unyielding sand. A few erratic raindrops blew against the glass.

A fireplace lay to her left, ashes scattered on the stones. The remaining wall space was covered—floor to ceiling—in bookshelves, built into the curvature of the room.

The whole place was in complete disarray.

Books were strewn across the floor, smashed ink bottles ground into the carpet, broken teacups and bits of charred paper scattered everywhere. Many of the shelves were empty, and

Talia's eyes went back to the fireplace; the ashes were mixed with fragments of burned pages.

The room enveloped her in strangeness. It smelled of dust and books, fire and flowers, and gave her a feeling similar to the one she'd had outside the stone temple—a sensation of power, bursting just below the surface. But she didn't see anything out of the ordinary.

She circled the chamber, tilting her head to read the titles of the books and brushing her fingers across their cracked leather spines.

There were books of history and politics. A few of poetry. Science and mapmaking and shipbuilding. She didn't understand why they were locked up here. What harm could be found in books?

But midway through the shelves, she began to understand.

Only half a dozen volumes remained in this section, all with titles like *The Binding of the Stars* and *The Death of Dia* and *The Coming of Man*. Books of myths—Ayah would be delighted.

She bent down and started scooping up books from the floor: *The Halls of Huen, Myths and Prophecies, The Words of the Gods.* Mixed with the many books of myths were even more volumes *about* the myths: scholarly criticisms, theories, and dissertations, one with the pompous title *The Key to the Mythologies.*

This had to be what the Baron was hiding.

But why? They were just stories.

A book lay facedown on the mantel, its spine broken. Talia picked it up and peered at the title. *One White Tree: Being the History of Mankind's Time Beneath Its Branches, Its Falling and Its Planting Anew.*

She rubbed her finger over the pages.

A pair of armchairs were pulled up next to the dead fire, burgundy cloth ripped in places, stuffing spilling out. She sank down into one of them, laying the book on her knees.

She didn't mean to. She didn't even want to.

But she did anyway.

She opened the book and began to read, a familiar story unfolding before her.

The summer was at its zenith, and Talia sat with her mother in their palace suite, eating sherbet with a silver spoon. She was nine, and they were in Eddenahr for a Court event neither of her parents could miss. A damp sheet hung in the window, providing some relief from the arid wind.

"Tell me about the Tree," said Talia, sherbet sweet on her tongue.

"I always tell you about the Tree. Wouldn't you prefer a different story, dearest?"

"I like the Tree best. Tell me everything."

Her mother smiled, and began:

"The Tree was vast and beautiful, shimmering with Starlight, and bearing blue and green leaves as long as a man's arm. Its canopy covered acres of land—maybe as much as this palace!"

"That big!" gasped Talia, like always.

"That big. All kinds of fruit grew on every silver branch, and it was food for the gods."

"I bet it was delicious."

"I bet so. Centuries passed, and the gods forgot that mankind was coming, that they were ever meant to guide anyone but themselves. And then mankind awoke in the shadow of the Tree, emerging from the earth where the One had planted them. Rais and Nira, the first man and woman on Endahr, opened their eyes in wonder, rejoicing in the Tree and the light of the Stars. They were companions for one another, and there was love in their eyes and their hearts, something the gods had never seen before.

"But the gods thought them small and without knowledge, and did not like that mankind had been given love and they had not. They did not understand how mankind could be content, when they knew nothing of the world and ruled nothing on it."

Talia's sherbet was melting into a little pool of pink and orange in her glass. She stirred it around with her spoon. "Rais and Nira had a lot of children and grandchildren," she prompted.

"Indeed. Mankind lived and loved and flourished under the Tree, soon numbering more than the gods. They ate freely of the Tree's fruit, like the gods and their servants, and this made the gods angrier than anything else. Men were inquisitive and clever, growing in strength and wisdom. They wanted to learn many things from the gods."

"But the gods didn't like them," said Talia. "They grew more and more afraid."

"Do you want to tell the story yourself?" There was quiet humor in her mother's voice.

"I just don't want you leaving out bits."

"I never do. The gods refused to teach mankind the ways of the world, fearing they would grow so strong in wisdom and knowledge they might challenge the gods and want to rule Endahr themselves. Tuer wouldn't teach them the ways of the mountains, and Huen wouldn't show them earth's secrets. Raiva wouldn't help them plant and harvest crops or learn music. Uerc wouldn't tell them how to tame animals. And on and on. None of the gods or servants would share their knowledge, so what did mankind do?" Her mother looked expectantly at Talia.

"They taught themselves how to build houses out of stone and wood, plant gardens, and make beautiful instruments and other things, out of silver and gold and jewels they dug from the earth."

"Yes. And they learned how to play these instruments and sing by listening to the Servants. When Raiva heard how beautiful mankind's music was, she silenced the servants, but the music lived on with mankind, beneath the Tree." Her mother paused and smiled at Talia. "What else did they do?"

"They tamed the animals. They bridled sixteen great silver horses for Rais and Nira's sixteen grandchildren."

"That's right. Their grandchildren had grown restless in the shadow of the Tree and desired to go west and explore the world. They believed they could live away from the gods and their servants, since they had grown great in strength and knowledge without their help. They wanted to take a seed from the Tree with them, so they could plant a new Tree wherever they decided to settle. They asked the gods to give them a seed, but the gods refused."

"They took one anyway."

"They did. Tahn, the youngest grandchild, stole a seed from the top branches of the Tree. When the gods found out, Tuer crushed the sacred seed rather than give it to mankind. So, Tahn cursed the gods: 'Your reign in Endahr will be broken as the seed has been broken. You will not always be immortal, you will one day taste death.'"

"Tuer was so angry, he killed Tahn. And mankind rebelled." Talia turned her eyes to the window. A sudden gust of wind tore through the sheet, nearly ripping it down. Dust rattled against the palace walls and bells sounded from the towers in the lower city—storm coming.

"They warred against the gods," said her mother. "They wanted the gods to leave Endahr, so they could rule it themselves. They took up a battle cry: 'Give us the Tree, give us the Tree, give us the Tree!'"

"And the gods gave it to them."

A faraway look came into her mother's eyes as the wind clawed at the sheet and the clamor of bells grew louder. "The gods plucked the Tree from the ground, and cast it down again. It fell with a terrible noise to the earth, and many men and women were crushed beneath it.

"'This is your Tree!' the gods said. 'Be content in its death, for now you must gather food for yourselves.' They were angry with mankind, and so they withdrew into their separate realms of mountain and wood, water and air. They ruled the world from afar and showed *themselves no more to men.*"

"*Blaidor wept,*" said Talia above the rising wind, "*Tahn's wife. She mourned for him, while the rest of the people mourned for the Tree.*"

Her mother smiled again. "*You know the stories better than I do, dearest. What happened next?*"

"*The Tree lay dead on the earth for three hundred years. Mankind did not flourish as they once had, now that they faced sickness and death. They no longer ate from the sacred Tree. No one dared to touch it.*"

"*And then?*" prompted her mother.

"*Mankind began to forget the gods and the glory of the Tree. They grew proud.*"

"*That's right. Only when the rain fell or the sea raged or the earth shook did mankind think of the gods, but their names seemed nothing more than ancient words in children's rhymes. Some men even doubted that gods ever existed and did not believe in the sacred Tree.*"

"*Haisar. He was arrogant and foolish.*"

"*Yes, Haisar. He wished to build a ship, great enough and strong enough to bear him to the ends of the earth and back, to win him fame and glory among mankind. He felled many trees and shaped them into ships, but they always failed to take him where he wanted to go. Nine times he nearly drowned. So he looked upon the great Tree and he didn't care that it was ancient and good and ought to be respected.*"

"*He struck it with his axe,*" said Talia. "*The earth swallowed him whole for his crime.*"

"*And how does this story end?*" her mother asked.

"*The gods didn't want to leave the sacred Tree to mankind anymore, and risk further dishonor. They fought each other for the keeping of it.*

"*Tuer wished to take the Tree to the tallest mountain. Raiva wished to plant it in her woods. Huen wished to take it under the earth, and Hahld to plant it where all the streams and rivers met. Mahl and Ahdairon wished to take the Tree with them to the air, and Caida to return it to the Stars. Uerc wished to take the Tree to the cliffs on the edge of the world."*

"But," said her mother.

"But Aigir wished to take the Tree with him into the depths of the sea, where no trees had ever grown."

"And he did. He had grown very strong, and so prevailed against the other gods. He took the Tree to the middle of the Northern Sea, and planted it there. The Tree thrust its roots down into the depths, and stretched its bare white branches up into the sky, and lived once more."

"And there it grows still."

Her mother smiled. "The end."

The storm broke all at once, rain and dust and wind slamming through the windows.

Up in the tower library in the Ruen-Dahr, the story of the Tree unfolded before Talia once again, sparking memories she'd long forgotten, making her miss her mother so much it hurt.

She gripped the book tightly, drinking in the words, forgetting that she needed to return Ahned's keys before he missed them.

Hours slipped away.

Rain beat against the window and she lost herself in reading, not lifting her head again until she had turned the very last page.

Chapter Seventeen

S HE WAS THE LAST TO ARRIVE AT dinner, hair still damp from her bath. Her rose-colored gown fell in graceful folds from the high waistline, a half dozen gray and pink silk flowers sewn into the center of the bodice.

The Baron was sitting at the head of the table. He looked up as she came in, while his sons both stood and bowed.

"You are very late this evening, Miss Dahl-Saida," said the Baron, his eyebrows drawing together.

She swept around to her usual chair and sat down. Wen and Caiden resumed their seats as well. "Apologies, sir. I lost track of the hour." She'd bolted from the library, slipping the keys back onto their nail a moment before Dairon found her in the kitchen. She'd used another excuse, inquiring about a bath. Dairon eyed her darkly and said she ought to learn to use her bell—didn't they have those in Enduena? But she'd kept the library key. It was tucked inside a dancing slipper, shoved in the deepest corner of the wardrobe. She hoped Ahned wouldn't notice it was gone.

The Baron grunted a little, and Lyna and Ro came in with dinner—more roasted fish, with hot, honeyed apricots, and a cold cucumber soup.

"Did you have a pleasant day, Miss Dahl-Saida?" asked

Caiden as she cut off a piece of meat.

"Tolerable. I—" she cast around for an explanation of what she'd been doing that had made her late. "I was out in the garden for much of it. Until it started raining, of course."

"Were you?" said Wen beside her, speaking for the first time. "I didn't see you there."

She eyed him coolly. "You must have been wrapped up in your music."

"On the contrary: I worked in the garden much of today."

Talia gave a careless shrug. "We must have missed each other. What about you, Caiden? How do you avoid boredom in the Ruen-Dahr?" She wanted to ask if he'd forgotten his promise to go riding with her, but she didn't quite dare.

Caiden laughed, his teeth flashing white. "Still going over the review with my father, I fear. Lots of things to sort through after three months on the road."

"What do you do other days?"

"I work on the accounts. I go riding—sometimes all the way to Wen's holding, sometimes to the village, sometimes just down to the beach."

She knew she shouldn't, but she said it anyway: "I thought the sea was forbidden."

Wen tensed beside her and Caiden's forehead furrowed. The Baron seemed to go even paler than usual.

Caiden tried to laugh it off. "I stay well away from the sea, of course. You know that, Father." He patted the Baron's arm.

"Why is the sea forbidden?" Talia looked straight into the Baron's gray face. "What are you all trying to hide from me?"

"Talia," said Wen.

"Why are there so many secrets in this gods-forsaken house? You can't lock everything away or dam up the sea and keep it from flowing. Why do you still live here if the Ruen-Dahr has caused you so much pain?"

Tears welled in the Baron's eyes and dripped down his cheeks.

She pitied him suddenly, but she didn't take back her words. "I was sent here against my will. I deserve to know what has happened in this house if I'm to be forced to stay here. There's so much you're not telling me, and I need to know why."

The Baron blinked at her, tears still falling.

Rain beat against the darkened window, the fire cracked and popped on the hearth. Caiden stared at his plate.

"My mother drowned," said Wen softly. "She tried to go sailing in a storm. The wind and the waves were too much for her to handle, and she barely made it away from the shore before her boat capsized. By the time they pulled her from the water, it was too late."

Talia stared at him, horrified.

"My father does not wish the sea to take anyone else."

She glanced back at the Baron, mortified that she'd upset him. "I'm so sorry, sir. Forgive me. I didn't know."

The Baron wouldn't look at her. He rose shakily from his seat, pushing his chair back. Caiden leapt up to help him, putting one arm under the old man's shoulders.

"I am very tired this evening," he whispered. "I will retire early."

As Caiden helped the Baron from the room, Wen jerked up from his seat. "Raiva's *heart*, Talia, what's wrong with you?"

"You wouldn't tell me anything. Why shouldn't I ask your father?"

"Because he can't handle it!" Wen paced over to the fire. "We don't—we don't *talk* about things like that. It upsets him too much."

"Your mother is *dead*!" Talia cried. "Why can't he accept it?"

Wen's face was hard. "Because it *hurts*. I would think you'd understand that."

"Of course it hurts," she choked out. "But that doesn't change the fact that it happened, that we all have to keep on living." She threw her napkin on the table and stood abruptly.

"Where were you today? You weren't in the garden. Did you go down to the beach again?"

"If I had, what would it matter?"

"Talia, you *can't*—"

"You don't own me," she spat at him. "You don't even know who I am. I can do whatever I want."

He shook his head. "No you can't—not here."

Her thoughts flashed to the betrothal, to the ring weighing heavy on her right hand.

"Tuer crush your bones," she said, and stormed from the room.

She dreamed she was sitting with her mother in the Emperor's aviary, the sun hot on her skin, a fountain burbling at her back.

"What happened to the Stars?" she asked her mother, closing her eyes to listen to the chattering parrots.

"The Stars, my darling?"

"There were three Stars in the beginning, wheeling about the earth. What happened to them?"

"The gods plucked them out of heaven. Well, two of them anyway."

She leaned her head on her mother's shoulder. "Tell me the story."

Her mother stroked Talia's hair. "When the gods withdrew into their separate realms, they no longer thought of mankind or Endahr. The gods forgot the tasks the One had appointed them at the beginning: They neglected to care for the earth, for the trees, for the animals and the waters and the wind. For the Stars. They forgot because they grew jealous of each other and were not content to rule in their realms alone. The gods quarreled for centuries, thunder and wind raging against the sea, beasts ravaging the earth. Mankind tilled the ground and tended the animals. But they could do nothing for the Stars. And so the Stars began to dim.

"The gods grew afraid, and decided to take the Stars for themselves before their power waned forever. But Tuer and Raiva had pity on mankind, and convinced the other seven gods to take only two of the Stars, and leave mankind one.

"So the gods warred over the keeping of the two Stars, which burned with greater power than they had ever imagined, for they retained still that first spark of life that the One had created at the beginning. Whoever wielded the Stars could give life, or take it, could break mountains and drain oceans. Whoever wielded the Stars could rule the gods, and the world.

"But as they fought, the earth trembled and the continents splintered into the sea, and mankind feared that the end had come."

"But it hadn't," said Talia.

"No. But night crept into Endahr, darkness covering all the world for half of every day, and when the last Star rose above the horizon, it shed hardly any light, and gave no heat at all. And mankind began to freeze in the darkness. So they cried out to the One who was before the gods to save them. He listened to their pleas, and made the remaining Star burn brighter and hotter than it had before, though it still did not equal the glory of the three. He made a mirror for the third Star, to reflect a shadow of its light in the darkness, and sprinkled lesser stars into the night sky."

"The sun and the moon and the stars," Talia mumbled into her mother's shoulder. The spray of the fountain touched her cheek. "What about the Stars the gods took?"

"They fought over them for centuries, but in the end Huen, the god of the earth, took the first Star. He bound it as a jewel into a ring made of gold, and brought it far beneath the earth. Aigir, god of the sea, took the second Star. He bound it in a band of silver and brought it into the ocean. With the power of the Star, he took dust and coral, weeds and shells, and formed them into a beautiful Hall at the base of the Immortal Tree."

"And that's what happened to the Stars," said Talia, sleep making her ears buzz.

"That's what happened to the Stars." Talia could hear the smile in her voice.

"I wonder how they made Stars into rings," she said, just before she fell asleep.

She thought she heard her mother reply: "With the Words of the gods," but she couldn't be certain. When she woke again, her mother had carried her back into her palace room, and a parrot of her very own was eyeing her from a brand new perch.

In her bed in the Ruen-Dahr, Talia twisted and shook. Her dream shifted.

She saw a ship in a dark sea, a woman laughing on a throne, a Tree that reached to heaven, a song that shook the world.

An army of Dead things rising out of the sea, clothed in shadows, every one of them screaming.

Chapter Eighteen

S HE HAD BREAKFAST ALONE IN HER ROOM the next morning, having no wish to run into Wen. The rain had stopped in the night, but there was still no hint of sunlight piercing the eternal clouds. A dreary grayness seemed to cling to the very stones of the Ruen-Dahr.

Talia sipped tea and ate sweet bread with raisins, staring down into the waves and trying to forget her dreams. What were the chances, she wondered, of being betrothed to a man whose mother had also drowned? She pushed the thought angrily away. There was no connection between them—her mother had taken her own life. Wen's had drowned by accident.

There was a knock at her door, and Ro poked her head in.

"I'm just finishing," Talia said, thinking the maid meant to take her breakfast tray.

"Lord Estahr-Sol is waiting for you in the stables, Miss. He said you'd arranged to have a ride?" The curiosity in Ro's eyes belied the casual tone of her words.

Talia swallowed down her tea and brushed the crumbs from her fingers, her pulse quickening with excitement. He *had* remembered! "His horse is half-Enduenan. Caiden thought I'd like to have a look at him."

Ro grinned. "I expect you would."

Talia flushed, but couldn't help smiling. "He's just being nice."

"Obviously." Ro's eyes sparkled. "Shall I do something with your hair?"

Twenty minutes later, Talia left the house and crossed the courtyard to the stable, wearing a deep-red gown with a split riding skirt, her hair pinned up in a coronet of elaborate braids. She toyed with the fingers of one of the late Baronesses' white gloves, and tried to ignore her nervousness.

She grasped the ring of the heavy wood door and slid it open.

The scent of hay and dust and horses assailed her senses, and she thought with a pang of home—she'd spent more time in the stable in Eddenahr than the palace, oftentimes with Ayah in tow. The Ruen-Dahr's stable was small, with a low roof, four stalls, and a short aisle running to a door in the back, which Talia assumed was the tack room. A single lantern hung from a beam in the middle of the ceiling, illuminating the whole space in a dim orange haze.

Caiden was lounging against the first stall, rubbing his gelding's black muzzle. He glanced toward the door at her approach, and flashed her a smile. "I was wondering if you were ever coming. I'll bring him out."

He clipped a lead to the horse's halter and unlatched the stall door, leading the gelding into the aisle. Talia approached the horse quietly so she wouldn't spook him. He eyed her under long black lashes but didn't shy away.

"I'll get his tack," Caiden told her, walking to the back room.

"Beautiful boy," Talia whispered into the horse's ear, stroking his tautly muscled neck. He was as magnificent as his master, and a thrill went through her at the thought of riding him—here was raw power, barely contained. In her mind, Ayah made an inappropriate remark that had nothing to do with horses.

"He likes you," Caiden noted, coming back with saddle and bridle.

"What's his name?"

"Avial."

"Where did you get him?" She kept petting the gelding as Caiden tacked him up, stroking his nose and velvety ears, tangling her fingers in his coarse mane.

"At the seaport last year. My father was angry at how much I spent on him, but I needed a good horse."

"And he is that."

Caiden grinned, cinching the saddle girth tight. "Well, Miss Dahl-Saida. Let's see if you're as good as you think you are."

They brought Avial out to the drive and down a winding path to the seashore. Talia eyed Caiden at this choice, but he just shook his head, the reins looped around one hand. "I always ride down here. Don't mind my father—he lives in a world of his own."

"How old were you, when the second Baroness died?" she asked him, as he stopped to adjust Avial's girth again.

He glanced up at her, patting the gelding's flank. "Nine."

"Do you remember much about her?"

He shortened Talia's stirrups. "She was musical, like Wen, and a dreamer like him, too."

She caught the implication in his tone. "You didn't like her." The wind blew her red skirt around her knees, its cold fingers seeking to tug her hair loose from its braided crown.

Caiden shrugged. "She wasn't my mother. She was very kind to me, but I suppose I resented her."

"And so you resented Wen, too?"

He raised one hand and brushed his windblown hair out

of his eyes. "We've always had our differences, but I've never resented him. I just wish he wouldn't let himself get so caught up in his mother's beliefs. He's convinced that the gods are real, that they inspire his music, that they had something to do with our mothers' deaths. He can't see the truth. He *won't* see it."

The words unnerved her. She felt a sudden affinity with Caiden; both of them were haunted by the shadows of things they couldn't control. "My mother—my mother believed in the myths and the gods, too, and—and it drove her mad."

He studied her, his dark eyes seeing deep. "I wish I could have met her."

She clamped down on her lip to keep back the sudden press of tears, but one slid down her cheek anyway.

"Talia." He turned to her, unexpectedly cupping one strong hand under her chin. His skin felt warm against her jaw, his thumb slightly rough as he brushed her tear away. "I'm so sorry," he told her softly. "You have lost so much."

She shuddered and leaned against him, and all at once he was wrapping his arms around her and she was crying hard into his chest. He held her tight, the wind wheeling about them and the black gelding lipping distractedly at Talia's braids. Caiden nudged him off.

"Hey," he said to Talia, not letting her go just yet. "Are you all right?"

She swallowed back another wave of tears, suddenly aware of his heartbeat just beneath her ear, of the strength in his encircling arms, the hardness of his chest. Of his scent: hay and earth and cedar. She jerked away and he released her, watching as she scrubbed the tears from her eyes.

"I'm sorry," she said, forcing her voice not to shake. "I don't normally sob on the shoulders of recent acquaintances."

He gave her a quiet smile. "Don't mention it."

She gulped a breath of air and smiled back.

"Well then," he said. "Enough stalling. Can you really ride this beast or was it all just talk?"

She laughed and he grinned at her.

He gave her a leg up and she settled comfortably into the saddle. "He's a lot of horse. If you give him his head he'll never stop running."

"I'd expect nothing less from Enduena's finest."

Caiden caught her eye. "I'm not sure Avial is Enduena's finest. Though you might be."

She laughed and bent over the gelding's neck, touching him with her heels. He leapt into motion and joy swept through her, cold wind singing past her ears. She urged Avial faster and faster, until his long strides matched the pace of her galloping heart.

She helped Caiden rub Avial down after his run, the lantern gleaming amber from the stable's ceiling. She was giddy with the sensation of speed and freedom—she could still taste it on her tongue, feel it on her skin. Oh, she'd missed that.

Caiden brushed the gelding's flank while Talia worked on his shoulder, Avial munching happily on some sugar cubes. He was as docile now as an old workhorse.

"I can't believe how fast you were going," said Caiden, shaking his head.

Talia glanced up to meet his eye. Her braids had shed their pins and tumbled free onto her shoulders. She tucked a few behind her ear. "Avial could almost match my Naia at home. I wish we could race them and see which one's faster."

"That would be grand." Caiden moved to the gelding's back, and Talia stepped around to the other side of him. "We'll have to try it out, when you're Empress and you've reclaimed everything that rightfully belongs to you."

Talia chewed on her lip.

"You must think about it sometimes. How grand it would be, half the known world at your fingertips. I could help you, you know. We could be racing in the desert by summer."

"You'd come with me?" she said in spite of herself.

"'Course I would! I'd be your trusted general, and when we'd won the Empire, you could make me a prince or something."

She had to smile. "I could do that."

He smiled back. "In the meantime, you can take Avial out whenever you like. I don't have the time to run him every day. With all that energy, he needs it."

"So do I."

He laughed.

They worked in silence for a few more minutes, and then shut Avial back in his stall.

"Are you really going to marry Wen?" Caiden blurted.

She looked up at him. His jaw was hard in the lamplight, rough stubble showing dark against his skin. "I don't want to, but the Empress has ordered it and your father said he'd throw me out of the house if I didn't agree."

"Damn the Empress—this is why we need to reclaim Enduena!" He softened. "And I would never let my father turn you out." He touched her cheek, brushing a stray strand of hair behind her ear.

She felt herself grow still at his touch—her breath, her pulse, her whole body. She stared into his eyes and wanted, very badly, to kiss him, to feel him wrap his arms tight around her like he'd done before her ride. *It would be wrong*, her brain told her, *you're engaged to his brother. But I was forced into it!* cried the other part of her. *It shouldn't even count!* And then Ayah's insistent voice: *Kiss him and find out, you ridiculous mongoose.*

He edged closer, his face only a few inches away. Her heartbeat thundered in every part of her.

"You're very beautiful, Talia of Enduena." His voice was quiet and rough.

"I'm betrothed to Wen," she said without conviction.

He touched her cheek and pulled her softly toward him. "I don't want to talk about Wen right now."

"Neither do I."

He pressed his lips against hers and she lost hold of everything, words and breath and even time, her whole being wrapped up in the sensation of kissing him, his warm fingers tangled in her hair.

Gray, midmorning light filtered in through the music room window, and Talia stood in the doorway, playing with the material of her patterned gown. Wen was sitting behind the not-harpsichord in the corner. He looked incredibly tired, dark smudges beneath his eyes, and she felt for him—she hadn't slept at all last night either. She flushed. She hated herself for being there, for what felt like her betrayal and the realization that it would hurt him, if he knew. But she couldn't regret the stolen kiss. She couldn't regret how she felt every time she thought about Caiden. It was a forced betrothal, she repeated over and over in her head—she wasn't betraying anyone, she wasn't breaking any trust. The words she'd spoken to the Baron in the dusty ballroom hardly counted.

"Wen?" she said after a moment.

He jerked his head up, startled. "What do you want?" he asked wearily.

"You weren't at breakfast."

He glanced out the window, then back at Talia. "I've been up most of the night. Hadn't realized the time. Come in, if you like." He stood and bowed politely, though it was clear his mind was far away.

She stepped into the room, glancing around at the crowded shelves, the haphazard collection of flutes and drums and viols, the long-dead fire. "Can you play all these instruments?"

Wen shrugged. "I made some of them."

She was impressed. "What's the one in the corner called?"

"A raina. It was my mother's. She sent for it all the way from Od. She almost attended University herself before she met my father."

Dozens of sheets of music were spread out on the instrument, and Talia realized, with interest, that Wen's fingers were covered in ink. "You're writing something."

"I'm always writing something."

She came closer. "Will you show me?"

He picked up one of the pages and handed it to her. She could read a little music, thanks to her extensive schooling in Eddenahr, but the staves and notes dancing before her eyes were too complex for her to properly comprehend. "Will you play a little?"

He took off his spectacles and rubbed at his eyes. "It won't sound right on the raina. It's written for a sixty-five piece ensemble."

"I'm sure you could play some of it. Please?"

He studied her with his owlish blue eyes, and looped the spectacles back around his ears. "Very well." He sat down at the raina and settled a few pages on the stand. Then he put his fingers on the keys, and began to play.

Music curled up from the instrument, profound and alive, intertwining melodies and counter melodies, with harmonies so intricate they made her ache. Layers of sound washed over her and crept into her. She'd never heard anything more beautiful, more haunting, in all her life, and she felt like she was glimpsing Wen's true self. Her guilt about kissing Caiden twisted deeper.

The music stopped, abruptly, Wen frowning and grabbing

the pen from a little table at his left elbow and scribbling furiously all over the page he'd been playing. For several long moments he crossed out notes and wrote new ones, until the music was absolutely incomprehensible—at least to Talia—and then he sighed, and laid the pen down again.

"Why did you *change* that?" she said. "It was—it was perfect."

Wen glanced up at her with a faraway expression in his eyes. "It's not the same as it is in my head."

She thought of the music whispering from the sea and wondered what that would sound like to him. Wondered if he ever heard it, too. "It was still beautiful," she said softly. She wanted him to play more, but she didn't feel like she had the right to ask.

He looked away from her, studying the raina's keys, the table with his pen and inkwells. "Miss Dahl-Saida, did you want something?"

His sudden distant formality made the guilt gnaw sharper. "I wondered if you knew where Caiden was. He said I could take Avial out any day I liked, but he's not in the stable, and—"

"He's gone to settle a dispute between two of my father's tenants. Some difficulty over a cow."

"Oh." She tried not to feel the disappointment crashing through her like a black wave.

A hard line came into Wen's face. "Was there anything else, Miss Dahl-Saida?"

She wanted to ask him how long Caiden would be gone and why he hadn't said goodbye. But she didn't. "Thank you for playing," she told him, and left the room.

She penned a letter to Ayah in the garden, sitting on the stone bench by the ruined pool and the drooping willow. She'd left the letters she'd written aboard ship with Hanid, who had promised to see them posted back to Enduena as quick as may be, though they wouldn't reach Ayah until the spring at least. She'd already given Ahned several new ones to post, and he'd frowned deeply but hadn't refused her.

She dipped her pen in the inkwell. *You'd probably love it here, it's dreary and dreadful and awful. Rains nearly every day.*

She scowled at the willow.

But I know you don't want to hear about the weather.

Ro says there's no telling how long Caiden will be gone—could be a day, could be three weeks. It's absolutely maddening. What if he forgets about me? What if yesterday didn't mean anything to him? What if he kisses every girl who turns up on his doorstep?

You always were the romantic, Ayah. If you were here, you'd convince me that I'm madly in love with Caiden and come up with some elaborate scheme to get me out of my betrothal to Wen. But I'm too sensible to imagine myself in love with a man I met five days ago.

At least I think I am.

But what do I owe Wen, anyway? What do I owe Eda? What's to keep me from leaving this wretched house, stowing away on a ship, and finding my way back to you?

Raindrops fell suddenly on her paper, smearing the ink. She didn't know the answer.

Chapter Nineteen

THE HOUSE SEEMED QUIETER WITHOUT CAIDEN. THE Baron stayed upstairs for meals. Wen spent hours in the music room. Talia tried not to let the boredom drive her mad.

And she tried not to listen to the constant, whispering music of the sea, drawing her toward something she didn't want to understand.

But the hours stretched on as relentlessly as the ocean, and on the third day of this insanity she went back up to the library.

It was just how she'd left it—in rampant disarray, smelling of books and smoke and long-dead flowers, a moment of time frozen in a drop of amber. She still caught that sensation of power, sparking somewhere just beyond her vision.

She didn't want to read, not really. Her eyes scanned the shelves and she felt the stories call to her, whispering in her mind to crack their spines and turn their pages and let the myths play out before her eyes. Wasn't that why she'd come up here?

She decided to clean the place, instead.

She picked up all the books and returned them to the shelves. She collected the pieces of broken teacups and shattered inkwells into a little pile on the hearth. Then she swept up the ashes and dumped them in the dustbin.

With nothing else to do she paced around the chamber, wanting and yet not wanting to read more myths, to understand the extent of her mother's madness and why she chose to take her own life. Why her mother left her to face the ghosts in this drafty old house all alone. Why the sea was now calling to her.

She grabbed a book at random off the shelf and dragged one of the armchairs over to the window, clouds still knotted gray above the sea. She sat down, and examined the book she'd chosen: *Song of the Sea: Of Rahn's Betrayal and the Doom of the Billow Maidens.*

Talia's mind went back to the long voyage, and Hanid's words to her on the deck: *You haven't heard the stories? The Billow Maidens, singing in the storms to wreck the ships and drown the sailors.*

The wind blew hard against the tower, and Talia opened the book.

She didn't remember ever hearing this story from her mother.

In the days when the Stars had been plucked from heaven and night had fallen over the world, there dwelt a lesser spirit on the shores of the sea, and her name was Rahn. Long ago she had lifted her voice to the Stars and was a servant to the goddess Raiva of the wood. But Rahn had long since parted ways with her fellow servants, many of whom chose to go to their rest beyond the circles of Endahr. But Rahn was not done with the world. She wished to become a goddess in her own right, and wield the power she felt herself born to.

Day and night, she strayed alone upon the shores of the great Northern Sea, for she knew Aigir had borne the second Star with him into the depths. She desired that Star above all things, and with it, the strength of the Tree.

So Rahn made a white ship with silver sails, bound together with the ancient Words of power she had learned from the gods. She cast the ship away from the shore and was seen no more upon the land.

Nine years she sailed upon the waters of the Northern Sea, for it is said the Hall of Aigir is hidden from those who might seek it. But Rahn did not despair.

She made an island rise up from the sea near the place she felt sure the Tree grew. She dwelt there three hundred years, and it is called the Isle of Rahn to this day, though few have ever seen it. There she spoke certain Words filled with darkness that she twisted to her purpose, and awoke a pair of sea serpents from the depths. Rahn bound them to her will and they obeyed her, and she sent them into the far reaches of the sea to await her call.

One day, Rahn lifted up her eyes and saw it at last—the great Tree that had been hidden from her for so long. She sat on the edge of the island and put her feet in the water. She raised her voice to the sky and sang the songs Raiva had taught her and her fellow servants at the beginning of the world.

She sang all day, and when the sun had set beyond the rim of the world and the moon had risen in the sky, Aigir ascended from the depths of the ocean. He looked on Rahn and he loved her, for she stirred in him memories of a time before the world had been broken.

"What is your name?" he asked her.

Rahn ceased her song, and smiled. "I am Rahn of the Stars. I lived beneath them at the beginning, and ate the fruit of this Tree."

"What do you do here, Rahn of the Stars?"

"I have come to see the Tree once more, and to speak with you, for my fellow spirits have deserted me and I am lonely."

"Did you not go to Huen?"

"The Lord of the Earth shut me out."

"Did you not go to Mahl?"

"The Lord of the Wind shut me out." Rahn sensed the light of the Star that Aigir wore on his finger, but she did not look at it. "Tell me,

Lord of the Sea, will you too shut me out?"

"I could never shut you out, daughter of light."

"Then may I go down into the depths and see the great Hall that you have made?"

Aigir considered her. "I know not. None have ever seen my Hall, save me alone."

"Then I shall wait," said Rahn. "I shall wait here until you know."

Aigir returned into the depths of the sea, but his heart had been struck, and he would never again be complete without her.

Three years Rahn sang to him under the sky, the songs that Raiva had taught her beneath the light of the Stars. Every morning Aigir came out of the waves to hear her, and every night he descended to his watery Hall.

He loved her, and there came a time when he could no longer bear to be parted from her.

One evening, when the stars shone cold above and the thread of a moon sat in the cradle of the sky, Aigir looked on Rahn and stretched out his hand. "Come, daughter of light," he said. "Bring your beauty and your song to fill my empty Hall, for it is cold as death without you. Come, and consent to be my wife."

Rahn smiled and took his hand, and he brought her down into the sea, to the great Hall that he had made with the power of the Star.

So Rahn wed Aigir, the god of the sea, and was counted a goddess among the Nine Guardians, and Aigir loved her and dwelt with her, and was content.

And Rahn bore to Aigir nine daughters who are the Waves, called by some the Billow Maidens. They were beautiful, the splendor of their mother and the strength of their father twined together. They were restless in the great empty Hall, but Aigir loved them, and made for them nine harps from a branch of the great Tree which had fallen.

So the Waves plied their fingers to the strings of the harps, and their music filled the Hall, and they too were content.

But Rahn was not content, though she smiled and pretended to love her husband. She had never loved him, and now that she was bound to him she began to hate him, and to resent the beauty of their nine daughters.

Many years Rahn had waited, and her patience could only endure so long. When the Billow Maidens had lived for a century, Rahn turned to her husband and spoke to him: "Will you not show me, oh lord of the sea, the depth and height and breadth of your realm? I have dwelt long with you and seen only this Hall. It is beautiful, but you rule the whole sea, and there is a great longing in my heart to see more of it."

Then Aigir was sad. "Are you not content in my Hall, that you should ask me this? There is much bitterness and evil in these wide waters, and those things cannot touch us in my Hall. Would you seek them out?"

"I would seek the marvels of the sea."

"All the marvels of the sea dwell here at the base of the Tree," said Aigir, and would speak of it no more.

But Rahn pressed him daily to show her his realm. It grieved him, for he saw her unhappiness, and knew she would not rest until he had granted her petition. He felt a great sense of unease, and the Star on his finger wavered a little in its eternal light.

Then Aigir at last relented, for he saw he should have no peace until he did so, and he could no longer bear to be the cause of Rahn's discontent. He formed a ship out of seawater, translucent as glass, and bound it together with the power of the Star. He set Rahn within it, and they said farewell to their nine daughters, bidding them to keep the Hall until their return.

And then they set off into the depths.

They sailed far, and the sea god showed his wife the many wonders of the deep waters. Rahn pressed Aigir ever further and deeper, and as they went Rahn called in her mind the blue and silver serpents she had raised so long ago.

One day, Rahn asked Aigir if they might seek the surface and look into the light of the sun, and he saw a spark of evil in her countenance. Dread cried out a warning in his heart, but he could not deny her.

So Aigir drove the ship upward, and they had gone so many fathoms deep it took them three days until they broke the surface of the water. Dawn showed rosy on the horizon, and there was a cold edge on the air.

Rahn looked up at the sky and laughed, and Aigir saw in her the darkness she had hidden from him all the years she dwelt with him under the sea.

And Aigir was afraid.

"Why have you brought me here, daughter of light?"

Her eyes were bright with triumph. "So that you would be too far from the Tree to draw upon its strength to save your own life." For Aigir had poured so much of his power into the Tree that when he was near it the Tree sustained him, and gave to him more might than he could have had alone. But this would be his undoing.

For Aigir saw in the dawning of the day the serpents which Rahn had awoken, and their scales flashed in the fire of the red sun. His heart broke, for he knew then that Rahn had never loved him. He wept, and the salt of his tears ran into the sea. "When you have slain me, oh daughter of light, what will you do?"

She smiled, and looked to him more beautiful than the night he first heard her song.

"When you are dead, oh lord of the sea, I will take the Star from your finger, and claim all your realms. I will rule the waters of the world in your stead, and one day perhaps the land as well."

He looked at her and smiled for the last time under the sun, but his smile was laced with sorrow. "I love you, Rahn of my heart. I would have given you the Star. You need only to have asked."

Then Rahn grew angry because of his compassion. She looked into the eyes of the blue and silver serpents and spoke one terrible Word, and it was Death.

And the serpents fell upon Aigir and rent him into pieces, and his blood stained the water, mingling red with the reflection of the rising sun.

Then Rahn took the Star from Aigir's hand and put it on her own, and she was glad.

And she bound the serpents to the ship that Aigir had made, and they bore her many leagues across the sea until she saw once more the Tree raising its branches to the heavens.

She dissolved the ship and set the serpents as guards about the Tree, that they might slay anyone who thought to descend into Aigir's Hall and take the Star from her finger.

Then Rahn gazed upon the glittering Hall and saw that she had no one to rule but her daughters, who wept over their harps. So she wove nets of seaweed and silver and moonlight, and drew to her all the dead of the sea.

And Rahn clothed the dead in silver garments and made them dance before her at the base of the great Immortal Tree, which had once borne food for the gods.

So the Hall of Aigir was filled with darkness, and what once had been good was made a mockery.

And she who wielded the Star sat upon her throne, and laughed.

Chapter Twenty

A SPATTERING OF RAIN RATTLED AGAINST the library window, and Talia jerked her head up from the book. Far below, the waters of the Northern Sea reached for the shore and shrank back again, a constant battle, a constant loss.

Why had her mother never told her this story?

She got up from the chair and paced around the library.

Can't you hear it? Her mother's voice echoed in her mind. *Can't you hear it? The Waves are singing.*

She ran to the window and wrestled it open, leaning out into the cold wind. She strained her ears and eyes down to the sea, listening with every part of her being.

There it was: the thread of a ghostly melody, out there in the cold waters.

She yanked the window shut again, heart jumping.

It couldn't be true. It *couldn't.*

She'd stopped believing in the gods the day her father had died. They'd failed to keep him safe. Her mother's belief in them had driven her to madness. And now—

Now the old stories were nibbling at the edges of her consciousness. Trying to lure her in. Trying to make her believe what she refused to even *consider—*

She shuddered, trying to shake the images from her head.

All the dead of the sea, drawn to Rahn's Hall in a glittering net. Talia's dreams made more sense now—the screaming shadows, the cruel woman laughing on her throne.

If the myths were true—

No. That was impossible.

She wouldn't let them be true. She *couldn't*.

But what if they were?

She could hear the music of the sea, even with the window latched tight. It sang to her of danger and sadness, of yearning and incredible, terrible power. Every snatch of unearthly melody sent a new pulse of horror through her heart.

If the myths were true, that meant her mother was down in Rahn's Hall right now, dancing before the goddess's throne, enduring a torment Talia couldn't imagine, though she had felt a sliver of it in her dreams. The memory of it crashed through her again, terror and pain fracturing every part of her.

She clamped her jaw shut to keep from screaming and shoved the dream away.

The dead don't feel, she told herself stubbornly. *The dead know nothing, when they're gone.*

Most people believed in paradise, a place beyond the circles of the world where there was no more sorrow or pain. It was the last remnant of religion in everyday society, and Talia wanted desperately to think of her mother there, at peace.

But if the stories were true and paradise existed, why not Rahn's Hall? Why not a place where souls were trapped and tormented by a wicked queen, unable to move on, unable to find rest?

Because it was too awful to think about. Because how could Talia go on, make a new life here, steal kisses with boys in stables if she really, truly *believed* that? How could she resign her mother to such a fate?

It's not true, she screamed inside her head. *It's not true, it* can't *be true!*

She forced herself to breathe, in and out, in and out. She couldn't stop shaking.

She tried to think rationally.

The stories said the Immortal Tree had lain dead on the earth for three hundred years. The inhabitants of Ryn claimed it had been *here*, underneath the very stones of the Ruen-Dahr itself.

Wen had said the chained door under the garden was an old temple to the Tree.

That, at least, she could investigate.

Maybe the myths would stop haunting her, if she could prove once and for all there was no truth to them. Lay all this to rest.

She told herself she didn't hear the music anymore, spooling up from the sea, twisting into her and not letting go.

But she did.

She stole Ahned's keys from their hook in the kitchen tea cupboard, then went out into the garden and hopped over the iron gate. She followed the path down the hill to the stone door, rain spattering cold on her face.

The door stood just as she remembered it, crossed with chains and secured in the center with a heavy iron lock. She tried the keys, one by one, but none of them fit. The wind whispered past her ears, and she dropped the key ring, running her fingers over the rough metal lock. If she hit it with something heavy enough, in just the right place, maybe she could break it open.

Thunder muttered in the distance. The rain bit colder.

She scanned the path, and her eyes landed on a large, vaguely square-shaped rock jutting partway out of the sand.

That would do.

She dug it out of the ground, sand grinding under her fingernails and scraping against her skin. She pulled the stone free and hefted it up, eyeing the lock. She threw it against the iron, yelping in surprise as it slipped from her hands and landed with a thud back in the sand. She grabbed it again and slammed it against the lock, this time keeping hold of it. The iron didn't yield.

Again and again Talia rammed the stone into the iron, sweat prickling between her shoulder blades despite the wind and spitting rain.

The stone slid and smashed her fingers against the door and she cried out, swallowing back a curse. She cradled her hand against her chest and waited for the pain to fade. She'd scraped the first finger of her right hand, just above the ring; spots of blood showed bright against her brown skin.

This wasn't working.

Desperate now, she eyed the door again, tracing the lines of the chains to where they ran into the hill. Those would be easier to break. She swung the rock at the metal links again and again. Gulls shrieked overhead and thunder growled louder among the knotted clouds. Her muscles strained.

Please, she thought, readying for another strike. *Please. I need to get in there. I need to know if the stories are true, why they're calling to me. I need to know if my mother—*

She bashed the stone once more against the iron.

The chain broke, springing free.

She stepped back, panting, and let the rock slide to the ground.

Now to actually open the door.

She traced the stone with her fingers, touching the carvings and looking for some kind of opening mechanism, but there wasn't one.

So she leaned her shoulder into the door and shoved, as hard as she could.

The stone creaked. She pushed again, and it slid slowly

sideways along a hidden groove in the ground. Dust rose choking into the air and she coughed, eyes blearing.

When it cleared, she took a deep breath and stepped across the threshold of the ancient temple.

A set of stairs led down from the door into the darkness and she followed them, her footsteps raising more dust as she went. She came to a dim archway and stopped to dig in her pockets for the candles and matches she'd brought from the library. She struck a match against the stone, then touched the flame to the wick. She held the candle high.

Through the arch lay a stone chamber, pillars carved into the walls, niches cut between them. What looked like a shrine rested in the center of the ancient room, dust and cobwebs clinging to the edges of a marble obelisk.

It smelled like deep earth down here, of flowers and honey and something else she couldn't name. But it was a fierce scent, wild and strong and good.

She paced around the chamber, shining the light of her candle at the walls, wincing as hot wax dripped onto her skin. There were dozens of old books piled into the niches, several silver goblets that still smelled of wine, a handful of little caskets filled with a curious assortment of earrings and cloak pins.

At the back of the room she found what once must have been a fountain—a statue of Blaidor kneeling over an empty basin, weeping for the husband the gods had killed. Talia brushed her fingers over the figure's stone head and went on.

On the other side of the room she found a glass jar containing some odd substance that pulsed with a faint golden light. It was warm to the touch, and smelled like fresh roses. She peered at the words cut into the stone just beneath the jar. It was a lengthy inscription, most of it worn away long ago. But she made out the phrase *Star-light*, and her mouth went dry. She set the jar down again in a hurry.

Could it be light from one of *the* Stars? Impossible. But she couldn't explain how else the substance in the glass could be glowing by itself, shut up for countless years down here in the dark.

She turned away, and went at last to the shrine in the middle of the quiet chamber.

The white marble obelisk ran from floor to ceiling, inscriptions carved into every surface. Partway up the pillar a hollow was cut into the stone, and a small glass-and-iron casket, bound in iron, rested inside. Talia touched the glass and jerked quickly away again at the sudden heat—it was much warmer than the pulsing jar.

She lifted her candle to illuminate the words cut into the marble.

There were many old-fashioned phrases and mythical references that she recognized from the book she'd read in the library and the stories her mother had told her so long ago.

May the gods remember us in our sorrow.

The Tree lies here in honor, once so disgraced.

The bite of Haisar's axe against what should never have been touched.

She circled slowly around the pillar, squinting in the flickering light from her candle.

A sliver fell free, a splinter forgotten by the gods.

The only piece left in Endahr.

Here entombed.

She chewed on her lip, the candle burning low.

The shard shall lie here in glory forever, and may whoever touch or remove it from this place be accursed, unless in greatest need.

Her fingers traced the words in the marble, and she felt intensely uneasy.

You shall know it by its light and its music.

You shall know it when you hold it.

That here lies the shard of the Immortal Tree.

May the gods remember us.
May the gods be with us.
May our sins be forgotten.

And then she was around at the front again, staring at the glass-and-iron casket.

You shall know it when you hold it, the shrine promised. *That here lies the shard of the Immortal Tree.*

She slid her fingers into the hollow and tugged the casket free.

Her hands shook as she knelt on the dusty stone floor and examined the casket. It had obviously once been sealed, but now the lock was broken. The lid opened easily.

The air seemed to tremble around her, like a host of invisible onlookers had all sucked in a breath.

A splinter of wood lay in the casket, no longer or wider than her own hand. It was white as bone and dry as dust but somehow it was beautiful. It smelled like honey and wine and blooming lilies in the sunlight.

You shall know it when you hold it, sang the shrine's promise in her head. *The shard of the Immortal Tree.*

Could it really be true? She reached out her hand, slowly, reverently. She had to know.

"Talia, don't!"

Chapter Twenty-One

SOMEONE GRABBED HER ARM AND PULLED HER away from the shrine, up the stairs and through the door and out onto the hill, rain spitting cold from the still-darkening sky. The sea rose black and wild beyond the shoreline.

It was Wen, his face white with terror. He grasped her shoulders, nearly shaking her. "Did you touch it? Did you touch it?"

She jerked away from him, breathing hard.

Gods above, it was real. The Star-light, the Tree. She'd *felt* it, they were *real.*

Gods above, *her mother.*

"Did you touch it?"

She took a breath, trying to reassemble her shattered nerves. "No," she managed. She was shaking violently. She couldn't seem to stop.

Wen caught hold of her shoulders, gently this time. "Talia. Talia, it's all right. It's all right."

She lifted one hand to her mouth, trying to focus on him. But her vision was fuzzy, the world spinning. She collapsed and he caught her, easing her to the ground. Rain dripped cold on her face.

He didn't let go and she didn't shake him off; his hands felt warm through the thin fabric of her dress; his presence tethered her to the earth. He looked at her intently. "Talia. Tell me what happened. Tell me what's wrong."

She stared at him, still shuddering. The rain fell harder but they didn't move, locked in that one unending moment. "My mother's dead," she whispered. "My mother's *dead*." Her voice cracked. "She drowned at sea. She drowned and Rahn caught her in a net and dragged her into the Hall—"

"Talia," he repeated, steady and serious. "You can't help your mother. She's gone. Rahn and the Hall of the Dead is just a story."

"I thought the Tree and the Stars were just stories." Her words were as shaky as the rest of her. "But—but down there— down there—" The sudden rush of tears choked her, and then she was sobbing on the hill, the rain churning the ground into mud beneath her dirty dress. She'd needed them to be just stories. But they weren't.

Wen wrapped his arm around her, then eased her to her feet. "Come on," he said, "let's get out of the cold."

She allowed him to lead her, stumbling, up through the garden and into the house. The tears wouldn't stop. All she could think about was her mother, leaping into the sea. Being dragged down into the shadowy Hall. Forced to dance before a goddess on a cold throne, always in pain. Forever dead, but not at rest, never allowed to find peace.

Wen brought her into the parlor, settled her into a chair by the fire, sat down across from her. The rain drummed against the window, running in rivulets down the glass. "Are you sure you didn't touch it?" he asked her softly.

Talia gnawed on her lip, desperately trying to get a hold of herself. "I'm sure," she choked out.

He breathed a sigh of relief.

"The Tree is real." She wanted him to deny it.

But he nodded, lines pressing into his forehead.

"Then why not Rahn's Hall?"

The question hung between them for a moment, Wen studying her, clearly trying to decide what to tell her. How much to tell her. "No one can ever know if the Hall is real," he said. "Not for sure. Because that would mean someone would have to go there, and live to come back and tell about it. And no one has."

She wanted to agree with him, but she couldn't. "How can some of the stories be real and not all of them?"

"No one knows what happens after death. So we tell stories about it."

Another shudder passed through her. "But—"

"The dead don't move," said Wen softly. "The dead don't feel. She's gone, Talia. You can't help her now."

An errant tear slid down her cheek. "I miss her so much."

Wen's eyes glimmered with moisture. "I know. I'm sorry."

"You miss your mother, too."

He nodded. "Every day."

She drew a breath, blinking back the imagined horrors that still crept through her brain. Wen was right. She could no more help her mother than he could help his. She met his gaze. "What—what would have happened if I touched it?"

"Caiden's mother touched it before she died. She contracted a mysterious illness, and we think—*I* think—it came from that sliver of wood. It isn't—it isn't supposed to be touched, or taken out of the temple."

The inscription from the obelisk flashed through her mind: *May whoever touch or remove it from this place be accursed.*

"That's why your father locked it up, instead of trying to get rid of it."

Wen nodded.

Talia stared into the flickering fire. "But why—why did she

go down there in the first place? Why didn't someone stop her?"

"No one knew the temple was there. She found it one day, dug away at the hill until she uncovered the door. And by the time anyone else read the inscription, it was too late."

"It could have been something else that made her ill. It wasn't necessarily that—that thing in the temple."

"Maybe," said Wen, uneasily. "I did some research a few years back, and the oldest records indicate that the temple predates the village by several centuries. I found a few stories that swear it was built by Haisar's brother, after the earth swallowed him for dishonoring the Tree. That would line up with the inscription's claim that the sliver was made by Haisar's axe."

Talia shivered. What would have happened if she'd touched it? "Thank you for stopping me." *Thank you for saving me*, she meant.

He nodded, the serious expression not leaving his face. "I'm glad I was there in time."

"Do you know anything about the jar of light down there? The . . . Star-light?" She could still feel the echo of its warmth on her skin where she'd touched it.

"Supposedly it was a spark that fell from the last Star when it was dying, after the gods stole the other two, before the One made it burn hotter and it became our sun. A child caught the spark in a glass and made an offering of it to the temple, so the story goes."

They looked at each other, and Talia suddenly saw in him a soul as lost as she was.

"Will you help me shut the temple up again?" he asked her.

Her skin crawled at the idea of going back in there, but she nodded.

Wen stood and offered Talia his hand. She took it carefully, and he pulled her up. He held her hand a moment too long, but when he let go she regretted the loss of his steadying warmth.

She followed him outside and back down to the ancient

170

chamber. Rain dripped over the door.

Talia lit another candle and held it up for Wen, hardly daring to breathe as he shut the lid of the glass-and-iron casket. He returned it to the hollow in the marble pillar, and then they stepped out into the rain. It took both of them to drag the stone door shut. They hammered the chains back into the hill, and Talia grabbed Ahned's keys from where she'd thrown them in the grass. The rain tapered off, dwindling to a few icy drops.

"Thanks," said Wen, as they trooped back into the house. "Ahned will never know."

She looked over and he was smiling at her, an unguarded, genuine smile.

The strangeness of the temple still pulsed through her, but her panic had faded. "Thank you for saving me," she said, brave enough now to tell him what she really wanted to.

In the vestibule, they heard the sudden clatter of wagon wheels on the stones in the courtyard. Talia's heart seized up— was it possible Caiden was coming back in a carriage?

The guardedness returned to Wen's face and he abruptly stepped away from Talia, bowed uncertainly, and disappeared down the hall, mumbling something about his symphony. She stared after him—she'd had a glimpse of what it might be like to be his friend, and she didn't quite want to let it go.

But every nerve was humming with the possibility of seeing Caiden again, of *kissing* Caiden again. She flushed and stepped out of the house, not even caring about her filthy dress.

She peered into the gathering twilight as the carriage drew near. It was made of light wood, with gold trim around the roof and the door, and was pulled by a handsome pair of matching grays. Avial was nowhere in sight, and Talia tried to shake off her disappointment—definitely not Caiden.

The carriage lurched to a stop in front of the house and

before the footman could even jump down, the door opened and a young woman stepped out. She adjusted her green felt hat, an ostentatious mess of ribbons and feathers finished with a large silver buckle. Talia thought it was extremely ugly.

The young woman herself was a tall, pale beauty, perfect yellow curls cascading out from underneath the horrible hat. She wore a bright-green gown, with a voluminous skirt, and delicate lace gloves.

Talia took all this in at a glance, staring at the newcomer and trying to make sense of her sudden presence.

The young woman saw Talia, too. She frowned, deeply, but didn't offer any comment.

A demure-looking maidservent stepped out of the carriage after her, and the footman hefted a trunk from off the roof. "Shall I start bringing these inside, my lady?" he asked, nodding at the remaining three trunks.

"Inform Lord Estahr-Sol of my arrival first," the young woman replied.

"At once, my lady." The footman set the trunk down beside the carriage and bowed smartly.

"Caiden isn't here," said Talia, folding her arms across her chest.

The footman, maidservent, and lady in the green dress all looked at her in surprise.

"Who are you?" said the young woman, frowning. "Did the Ruen-Dahr hire a new servant?"

Talia shoved down her flare of temper at the insinuation. "I'm a guest of the Baron's. Who are you?"

"Lady Blaive Nahm-Aina, of Shold. The Baron sent for me, and he certainly didn't say anything about *you*." Her words were clipped and cool. Her eyes were green, a perfect match for her gown—and that awful hat. "Where is Lord Estahr-Sol?"

"Gone to settle a dispute about a cow."

Blaive's frown seemed to have taken up permanent residence on her face. "When will he be back?"

"I don't know."

Blaive let out a little huff of breath, peering closer at Talia in the fading light. "Who did you say you were again?"

Talia didn't answer. "What do you want with Caiden?"

Blaive's eyes grew hard. "I'm his fiancée."

Chapter Twenty-Two

TALIA FELT HERSELF GROW VERY STILL, AN icy coldness
settling in the pit of her stomach. "His—his what?"
"Fiancée."

Talia glanced at Blaive's right hand—whatever her claims,
she wasn't wearing a ring. "Caiden never mentioned you."

The girl looked irritated. "I'm sure you're mistaken." She
turned toward the waiting maidservent and footman. "Take my
things inside. It seems I'll be welcoming Lord Estahr-Sol home
instead of the other way around."

The footman bowed and, liefting the trunk, brought it up the
front steps. He returned a few moments later and unstrapped a
second trunk from the carriage roof, carrying that inside as well.

The whole time Talia stood staring at Blaive, completely at
a loss for words, trying to figure out how she could possibly be
Caiden's fiancée.

When all four of Blaive's trunks had been taken inside, the
footman hopped back onto the carriage, and she dismissed both
him and the coachman with a regal nod. The driver turned the
carriage around, and it rumbled back down the road, disappearing
into the dusk.

A gust of wind blew suddenly over the stones, and Blaive

grabbed her hat to keep it from flying off. She gave Talia one last, fierce look and swept into the house without a word, her green skirts swishing, the maidservent at her heels.

Talia followed. She was halfway across the vestibule when the sound of hoofbeats sent her darting back onto the front steps again.

It was almost wholly dark now, but there was no mistaking Caiden's bold silhouette coming up the drive on Avial. He had another horse tied with a line to his saddle.

Her heart leapt. Suddenly she didn't care that she was still upset about him leaving without a word, or about the young woman inside claiming to be his fiancée. She practically ran down the steps to go and meet him.

"A welcome party!" he said, swinging down from his gelding and flashing a grin at her. "I figured you'd forgotten all about me by now."

She couldn't help but grin back. "As if I could."

"I bought you a horse." He waved at the extra mount behind his. "Only a quarter Enduenan, but it was the best I could do."

"You—you bought me a horse?"

He laughed. "Nothing but the finest for Enduena's next Empress—and I didn't think I'd ever get Avial back, otherwise."

She placed one hand on his chest, barely able to make out his face in the darkness. She breathed him in. "Thank you."

He wrapped his free hand in her hair. "I missed you," he murmured back as he pulled her face to his.

But she jerked away, Wen's guarded expression printed behind her eyes, Blaive's claim ringing in her ears. She couldn't kiss Caiden. Not here. Not like this. "I have to talk to you," she said, urgently.

His fingers found her neck, warm and smooth and wanting. "Talia—"

"Caiden?"

He quickly dropped his hand, and Talia turned to see Blaive standing on the steps, light from the house pooling around her. She'd taken off the hat and looked smaller without it. Younger, too. She couldn't be a day over eighteen.

Caiden stared at her, shock apparent on his face. "Bl—Blaive," he stammered, gathering himself enough to offer her a bow. "When did you—how long have you—" He looked at her helplessly, one hand still loosely holding his gelding's reins.

Talia stared, too. What had Blaive seen? What did she think had happened?

"I came to—I came to see you." Blaive's face was open, her chin trembling. "I've only just arrived."

Caiden gulped, still staring uselessly. He stood up a little straighter. "Well, I am—I am of course very—"

Ahned stepped into the drive behind Talia, his face impassive. "Shall I take the horses, my lord?"

"I uh—that is—" Caiden clenched his jaw. "Yes, Ahned. Thank you."

Caiden passed the reins over and Ahned led the horses away, shaking his head and muttering something under his breath about never having had such a full stable before.

For a moment, Caiden and Talia and Blaive just stood there, all looking at each other in abject confusion.

And then Caiden strode into the house without another word to either girl.

Talia ran after him, catching his arm halfway up the stairs, pulling him around to look at her. All of her forgiveness had evaporated. "What's going on? Who is she? What is she doing here?"

"Talia, not now."

She glanced down to see Blaive watching them from the vestibule. Talia clenched her jaw, and yanked Caiden on up the stairs to the first landing, out of Blaive's sight.

"Talia—"

"Who *is* she?"

Caiden grimaced, rubbing at his eyes. "She's an old family friend. We grew up together."

"Are you engaged?"

"What?"

"Blaive says you're engaged."

"Talia, I haven't seen her in two years."

"*Are you engaged?*" she repeated, practically shouting at him.

Caiden frowned. "No. No, of course not."

Talia took a steadying breath, nodded. "Do you love her?" She knew one kiss and one almost-kiss didn't give her any kind of claim on him, but she asked anyway.

Caiden shook his head, a frown pressed between his eyes. "I certainly thought I did, growing up. But I don't now." He smiled, a flash of white teeth against perfect lips. "Honestly, I haven't thought about her in a long time. A banished Empress from Enduena distracted me."

"Then you meant it."

"Meant what?"

"Kissing me."

He laughed. "Of course I meant it. I'm rather afraid I might be falling in love with you."

Her stomach dropped into her toes. "But what about Wen?"

Annoyance flicked across his face. "What *about* him?"

She thought about Wen pulling her out of the temple, sitting with her in the parlor until she'd calmed down, giving her that one unfettered smile. "We're betrothed."

Caiden smiled, reaching out to touch her face, brushing one finger against her cheek. "Then we'll have to remedy that."

Chapter Twenty-Three

UP IN HER ROOM, TALIA SCRUBBED THE dirt off her hands and changed into a fresh gown. It was silver, with elaborate beading at the high waistline and airy capped sleeves shaped to look like flower petals. She plaited her hair into a single braid that she wound around her head and pinned clumsily. Then she sat staring at herself in the mirror.

Everything tangled together in her brain: Wen pulling her out of the temple, Blaive claiming to be Caiden's fiancée, Caiden saying he was falling in love with her. Her mother, trapped and tormented beneath the sea, never at rest, never at peace. She couldn't quite shake that thought away, no matter what Wen said.

There came a sharp rap on the door, and Lyna poked her head in. "Forgive the intrusion, Miss Dahl-Saida, but the others are holding dinner for you."

"Thank you."

She rose slowly from the stool and went down to the dining room. Wen and Caiden scraped back their chairs and stood, bowing politely. Wen's eyes sought hers and she met them for a moment before glancing at Caiden. Had his taut frame relaxed a little at her arrival, or was she imagining it?

The boys resumed their seats, and Caiden looked at her with a hesitant smile.

Ro and Lyna came bustling in, pouring tea and wine and serving dinner: hot soup with a gamy meat, and sweet-nut bread.

Talia wasn't hungry. She was hyperaware of all three of them: Caiden's smoldering eyes, Wen's quiet grimace, Blaive's nervous energy. Talia sipped absently at her soup.

"You've grown, Wendarien," said Blaive suddenly, breaking the palpable silence. "I think you're taller than me, now."

"It is two years since we saw each other last, Lady Nahm-Aina," Wen returned, politely.

"Has it really been that long?" Blaive shook her head and forced a laugh. "I can't believe it. Caiden looks the same, anyway. Have I changed at all, Lord Estahr-Sol?"

Caiden glanced at Blaive, and Talia felt herself tense. He couldn't possibly be immune to her careful beauty. "I hadn't noticed, my lady."

Blaive wrapped one elegant hand around the stem of her wine glass. "I didn't quite catch your history, Miss—what was it?"

"Dahl-Saida," said Talia coolly. "And I did not catch yours."

Something in Blaive's glance wavered a little, but she simply lifted her chin higher and turned her attention back to Caiden. "My family has been friends with Caiden's ever since I was small. I spent nearly every summer here, and Caiden spent a few at Shold House on my father's estate. Do you remember that year my mother gave a party in our garden?" She smiled at Caiden, her eyes softening. "We spent days making paper lanterns, and then the dogs got into the house and spoiled them all. My mother was so upset but you just laughed, like it was the greatest joke in the world. Do you remember that?"

Caiden flicked his glance from Blaive to Talia, and back again. "I remember." He attempted a smile, but it came out more like a grimace.

Talia stamped down her discomfort. For a moment, her eyes met Wen's.

"We were happy then," said Blaive quietly.

Caiden set his jaw. "That was a long time ago. I hope I have long since learned the rules of propriety."

"You've always known the rules, Caiden. You just choose not to follow them."

They stared at each other, the thread of tension between them practically visible. Talia gripped her teacup unnecessarily tight.

Once more she found Blaive's green eyes fixed on her face. "But enough of my history, Miss Dahl-Saida. Tell me yours. I understand we are far from equals in regard to rank, but you need not be timid on that account."

Wen rose half out of his chair at that, and she could see Caiden scowling out of the corner of her eye.

But Talia just stared impassively back at Blaive, not showing that the jibe rankled her. "I'm from Enduena," she said, measuring each word. "I was banished to Ryn for the crime of being the Emperor's daughter, which puts me in precisely the same social sphere as the current Empress. But don't worry, Lady Nahm-Aina. I won't think less of you for having such a low rank."

Blaive opened and closed her mouth a few times, while Wen smiled down at his plate and Caiden blatantly grinned.

"I'm a little surprised that you're harboring a traitor in your house, Lord Estahr-Sol," said Blaive, trying another tack.

"It's not my house just yet. Talia is here on the Empress's order and the Empress's coin, and as for treachery—I think that quite depends on your point of view." Caiden caught Talia's eye and smiled at her.

Blaive frowned. "Well *I* should not like to be accused of treachery, whatever the point of view."

"Sometimes one gets caught on the wrong side of things despite the best of intentions," said Wen.

Talia thought of the temple, the strange Star-light, the sliver of the Tree he'd stopped her from touching.

"And sometimes one should just stay out of things altogether," Caiden told him darkly.

"Pardon me, my lord."

Talia looked up to see Ahned standing in the doorway.

"What is it?" said Caiden.

"There's a plan to ride out to the Ruen-Shained tomorrow—I've hired horses for the occasion. Do you and Lady Nahm-Aina wish to join the party?"

"Wen's holding?" said Blaive. "Why would we go there?"

"Miss Dahl-Saida has not yet seen the house, my lady," Ahned told her.

All of Talia's insecurities and discomfort about the forced betrothal came rushing back.

"Why would Miss Dahl-Saida care about Wen's house?"

Confusion lined the steward's face. "Because she's to live there come spring. Master Wendarien and Miss Dahl-Saida are betrothed."

Blaive's eyebrows arched to the top of her head. "Indeed?"

Talia looked at Wen but for once he didn't meet her eyes.

"Yes, my lady. Would you care to join the party?"

A smile spread across Blaive's face. "I would."

"And you, my lord?"

Caiden's gaze bore straight into Talia's. "I'll go."

The memory of that kiss in the stable nearly overwhelmed her.

"Very well. I'll have breakfast sent up to your rooms in the morning, and the horses will be ready just after." Ahned disappeared back into the hallway, and for a moment, no one spoke.

Then Blaive turned to Talia, her eyes filled with laughter. "Might I offer you my most heartfelt congratulations?"

Wen saved Talia the trouble of any reply. "How long might we expect your company at the Ruen-Dahr?" he asked Blaive pointedly.

Blaive turned to Caiden with undisguised regard. "However long the Lord Estahr-Sol wishes me to stay. Which I hope will be a very long time indeed."

Talia couldn't sleep.

Every time she shut her eyes she saw the Star-light pulsing in the temple, the piece of the Tree she'd almost touched.

Her mother, trapped beneath the crushing weight of the sea. No one to save her. No release. Just darkness and drowning for all eternity.

She gave up after a while, jerking out of bed and climbing the stairs to the tower library. She unlocked the door, stepped in, and lit a lamp to chase away the dark. The book she'd been reading that afternoon still lay in the chair by the window. She picked it up and settled into the chair, tucking her legs underneath her.

Outside the house, the wind whispered over the stones, and she heard the distant thread of a song spooling up from the sea.

She opened the book.

The Billow Maidens, who were the Waves, mourned the death of their father, and silenced their harps in the great Hall at the base of the Tree, which Rahn had made into a realm of the dead.

But Rahn wore the Star upon her finger, and had great power over them. She commanded the Waves to pick up their harps and let their music resound once more through the sea. Yet they would not.

And Rahn grew angry. She gave the Billow Maidens charge over the great nets she had woven. By the power of the Star she compelled them to go into the wide reaches of the sea every nine years to cast the nets and collect the dead, and bear them back to her Hall.

The Waves wept at their task, and their tears spilled into the sea as their father's had done, and all the waters of the ocean were mingled with the salt of their sorrow.

As the years slipped away, the Billow Maidens grew bitter and weary of their task, and they mourned for the dead souls who were made to dance in the dark of Rahn's Hall. The goddess delighted in torturing the dead, stripping away every ounce of their humanity until pain and fear were the only things left. The Waves could do nothing, and they began to hate the very sight of their mother.

They agreed they must take the Star from Rahn's hand, to end her power and her rule. The strength of Aigir flowed within them, and they were assured of their purpose.

So the Waves stole the Star from Rahn's hand while she was sleeping, and fled away out into the ocean. But the power of the Star was too great for them—they had not the strength or understanding to wield it, and they could not contain its fire. It burned them, and they feared they would die.

Then Rahn was filled with rage. She summoned her serpents and they pulled her swiftly through the sea to where the Waves were gathered, weeping, for they could not escape the fire of the Star.

And Rahn rebuked them, and took the Star and placed it again on her finger. The Billow Maidens wept all the more, for they feared their mother's wrath. They begged her forgiveness, but she would not heed them.

In her fury, Rahn lifted the Star high toward the heavens and cursed the Waves, binding them to sit silent nine hundred years in the Hall of the Dead, taking their power away from them and making it her own. There they must wait, unless some mortal braved death and life and the power of the goddess of the sea to come and free them.

But Endain, the youngest of the Billow Maidens, fell before her mother and groveled at her feet. "Please, please, oh Rahn our mother, must we never again see the sky? The darkness of your Hall will consume us, and we shall surely perish."

And Rahn looked at Endain and pitied her. "When the moon rises as a crescent in the night, you may go up to see it, and there you shall lift your voices to the sky, so that any who hear you may pity you and come down to the depths to seek your freedom. And that task which was so revolting is yet upon you: Every ninth year you shall gather the dead and bring them to my Hall."

The Waves wept, and descended once more into the Hall of the Dead, and Rahn compelled them take up again the harps that Aigir had made for them. So they plied the strings, and their music gave voice to their great sorrow.

And in the darkness of night, when the crescent moon showed the splinter of its face in the sky, the Billow Maidens rose up to the surface and sang, long and sad. Any man who sailed those waters and heard them singing was drawn to their voices. And whoever looked upon the Waves loved them and cast themselves into the sea and were drowned.

The Billow Maidens grew weary in their waiting, mourning the souls of the sailors they themselves called to their deaths.

But the Waves could not stop singing.

Up in the tower library, music slipped in through the window, a strange, haunting song that wrapped all around her.

Calling, calling.

Calling *her*.

Can't you hear it?

Hear what?

The Waves. They're singing.

They'd called her mother to her death—what were they

calling her to do?

Talia cursed and leapt up from the chair, hurling the book as hard as she could against the wall. A sense of helpless panic was rushing up to swallow her. She didn't want to die like her mother. She didn't want to throw her life away chasing after a story. But how could she go on living if all of this were real? Rahn and the Billow Maidens, the Star and the Tree. Her mother damned to the Hall of the Dead until the end of time.

She unlatched the window and flung it open wide, cold sea air rushing in to swallow her.

"I don't believe in you!" she shouted into the night. "I don't believe in you, *I don't believe in you!*"

But it wasn't true.

The music curled into her ears, wrapped around her heart.

The Waves. Singing.

Calling her to the sea, calling her to the Hall of the Dead.

"I'm sorry, Mama," she whispered, peering down into the dark waves. "I don't know how to help you. I'm sorry. I'm so sorry."

She closed her mind against the music. She latched the window shut again.

But the song wound on inside her.

Chapter Twenty-Four

S HE WAS LATE JOINING THE OTHERS THE next morning, her head fuzzy with too little sleep and the dreams that wouldn't release her.

The sun was unexpectedly shining, but the frigid wind bit at her ears as she stepped up to the knot of people and horses waiting in the courtyard. Blaive and Wen and Caiden stood with their mounts, Ahned holding the reins of a lovely chestnut mare with a gold-colored mane. The mare stamped impatiently, nostrils flaring. She was clearly ready for a run.

"This gal's a lot of horse, Miss Dahl-Saida," said Ahned as Talia came to take the reins from him, trying to force her thoughts to the present.

"Talia can handle her," said Caiden cheerfully, swinging up onto Avial.

Ahned frowned. "So you keep saying."

"I certainly wish you would have thought to hire more than one spirited mount, Caiden," said Blaive, frowning. She was dressed for the day in a nut-brown riding habit trimmed with fur, and was wearing another awful hat—this one seemed to be drowning in ostrich feathers and garish velvet ribbons.

"I had no idea of you coming when I hired her," Caiden

said lightly. "And anyway, Miss Dahl-Saida is an extremely accomplished rider."

Blaive pressed her lips together, a flush of color coming into her cheeks at the implication that *she* was *not*.

Ahned gave Talia a leg up into her saddle, and the mare danced underneath her like a spring tightly coiled.

"Up you go, my lady," said Ahned, hoisting Blaive onto the dappled gray.

Wen climbed into his saddle last of all, and Talia looked over at him. She found herself desperately wanting to talk to him more about the temple and the myths, and why he was so certain Rahn's Hall wasn't real.

Ahned checked the saddle girths for all four of them, and then nodded, though he cast another disapproving eye at Talia and the chestnut. "Anira knows to expect you," he said, addressing Caiden even though the riding party was ostensibly for Wen and Talia. "Take your time, but try and be back before dark. There'll be a man by to collect the horses."

"But not the chestnut," Caiden announced. "I bought her."

"Did you indeed," said Ahned, unimpressed. "Before dark, my lord."

Caiden flashed him an unabashed grin and let Avial out into a trot.

The rest followed—Wen, Blaive, and then Talia, bringing up the rear. They left the Ruen-Dahr and, despite Wen's objections, took the path that wound down to the shore. "It's faster this way, and Father won't know or care," Caiden told him.

"Uerc's beasts tear you to bits," Wen muttered not-quite-under his breath, and then relented.

The four of them cantered for a while along the coast, the waves bursting white against the shore and the gulls wheeling noisily overhead. Talia tried not to look at the sea as she crouched over her mount's neck, the mare a snarl of boundless energy beneath her. She could almost feel the horse laughing at their current pace, so she wrapped her fingers in the mare's gold mane and gave her her head.

They sprang away from the group in a flat-out gallop. Around them the world faded to a blur of sand and sea and sky. But they couldn't go fast enough to outrun the tangle of Talia's thoughts or the music rising suddenly from the sea.

And then there was another rider racing alongside her, matching her pace for pace: Caiden on Avial. "Is that all she's got?" he shouted over the wind, grinning like mad. He put his heels in Avial, and the black gelding lunged ahead.

Talia leaned even tighter against the chestnut's neck. "Run, lady," she whispered into the mare's ear. *"Run."*

The mare leapt forward like she'd been standing still. They caught up to Avial, and for a few delirious moments they raced evenly, side by side in the sand. Caiden shouted encouragingly at his gelding to keep up the mad pace, but the red mare didn't need any urging.

And then they were past Avial, running on alone. The wind sliced past Talia's cheeks, so swift and cold she could hardly catch a breath. All was rushing air and pounding hooves, motion and power and *speed*. She rode on the heels of the wind—she *was* the wind, no longer moored to the earth. It numbed her so much she could almost think clearly again, almost understand the things just beyond her grasp.

But not even the chestnut mare could run forever. She slowed bit by bit, and dropped finally back to a walk, her shoulders gleaming with sweat. Talia patted her neck, singing her praises.

"I didn't imagine she'd be *quite* that fast," said Caiden, riding up on Avial. "We won't go so easy on you next time."

She gave him a quiet smile, tugging her mind to the present with a considerable effort. Avial was blowing hard and had clearly reached his limit. She glanced behind her, and could barely see Blaive and Wen in the distance. She hadn't meant to leave them so far behind. She'd just needed to taste freedom for a while—maybe even more than the mare.

Caiden grinned at her. "Those two old women will catch up eventually. Don't worry about them."

"We should wait." She pulled the mare to a stop, and Caiden followed suit with Avial.

He was very close to her; she could see the beads of sweat on his forehead, the sand clinging to his jacket. His dark eyes met hers. "Why do you care so much about them?"

Not *them*. Certainly not Blaive. She considered telling Caiden about the temple, but decided against it. "I'm still betrothed to Wen."

Caiden gave a careless wave of one hand. "A technicality. I told you: We'll get you out of it. I'll talk to my father. Let him figure out how to appease the Empress."

She stared at him. "You'd do that?"

"Of course."

Did Caiden mean to imply that *he* would start courting her when the betrothal was called off? Caiden was the heir to the Ruen-Dahr. If she married him, she'd become Baroness, stay for the rest of her life on the edge of the world, the sea singing forever in her ears. How long before she couldn't resist anymore? How long before she went mad? Unless he was serious about going to Enduena with her and seizing the Empire.

"You nearly lost us back there!" came Blaive's airy voice.

Talia glanced back to see Wen and Blaive riding up to meet them. Blaive's cheeks were flushed with obvious annoyance, and her hat had shed a few of its feathers along the way.

Wen sat rigid in his saddle, looking carefully past Talia.

"Wen—" she began.

But Blaive cut her off. "We really ought to keep our party together, Lord Estahr-Sol," she admonished Caiden. "What would my father say if you lost me?" She smiled.

"I'm sure I don't know. Wen, do you want to lead the way from here?"

Wen shrugged. "If you like." He didn't meet Talia's eyes as he rode past her, and she felt uncomfortably exposed. She still wanted to talk to him, but she didn't know how to do it in front of Blaive and Caiden.

The group continued on in silence, riding inland away from the sea and into a long stretch of low, hilly ground. Patches of heather showed purple against crumbly gray dirt, and here and there white star-shaped flowers struggled up toward the sky. The riding party followed a narrow track that wound through the moorlands, Talia bringing up the rear. She twisted in her saddle for a last glimpse at the ocean, and the haunted thread of music fell away from her. She felt a strange twinge of loss.

The track led them southwest for several miles, widening a little as it went, and then all at once the four of them were riding down a hill to the Ruen-Shained. Wen's holding was a simple two-story stone cottage with a low outbuilding on one end and a fenced pasture between. A cow snoozed in the field, and a half dozen sheep grazed in the hills beyond the house.

"Here it is," said Blaive, far too brightly. "The future home of Master and Mistress Aidar-Holt."

Wen didn't say anything, a hard line pressed between his eyes. Caiden scowled, like he'd forgotten the entire pretense of their outing. Talia watched them both, feeling entirely helpless.

"Shabbier than I remembered," Blaive added to no one in particular.

They rode into a gravel yard, and a black-coated servant and a blond-headed boy came up to take their horses. Talia dismounted, her legs wobbling beneath her, and handed the mare's reins to the servant.

"Welcome to the Ruen-Shained," he said in a voice that

sounded so much like Ahned's Talia had to wonder if they were brothers. He took Wen's reins as well, leaving the boy to collect Avial and Blaive's mount. "Anira has lunch in the garden for you when you're ready, sir," he said to Wen. "I know you'll want to show Miss Dahl-Saida about."

And then he and the boy led the horses down to the outbuilding, leaving Talia, Wen, Caiden, and Blaive to stand staring at each other in silence. The wind rustled through Blaive's hat feathers. "Well?" she said.

Caiden cast a scornful eye at Wen. "The tour is yours to give, brother dear," he said dryly.

"Why did you even come?" Wen snapped at him in a sudden flare of temper. "Never mind. I know why. This is all a game to you, just like everything else."

"If you'd gone to Od you wouldn't have to participate in this one."

Is that what Caiden thought Talia was? A game?

"Should we go in?" said Blaive smoothly. Her glance flicked anxiously between them.

"If you wish," said Wen.

He paced up to the house and the other three followed, Caiden dropping back to walk beside Talia. "Aren't you glad I'm here?" he said in an overly loud whisper. "How bored would you be if I hadn't come?"

Wen's shoulders tightened, and Talia's gut clenched. "Stop making jokes at his expense," she told Caiden in an undertone.

He gave her a confused look, but didn't say anything more.

For all its modesty—and it was quite modest, even for a second son—the cottage looked cozy and inviting. It had a bright blue door with a brass knocker, and a white cat was curled up on one of the windowsills inside. Talia found herself wanting to take a nap.

The door opened without them knocking, and an old woman

in a serving cap ushered them inside. "Master Wendarien, so nice to see you!" she said, pulling him into a hug and kissing his cheek. Her voice was shaky and soft. "Lord Caiden, Lady Blaive, what a pleasant surprise! It's been too long since you came to visit."

Caiden ducked his head and looked embarrassed, while Blaive apologized for not coming sooner.

The servingwoman turned to Talia with a warm smile. "*This* must be the young lady."

And then there was Wen at her elbow, lending her strength, his fingers lightly touching her sleeve. "Anira, may I present Miss Talia Dahl-Saida, of Enduena. "

"The future mistress of this house! Oh, you are very welcome, my dear." And she pulled Talia into an embrace as well, crushing her against her bony shoulder. She smelled like cinnamon. "I won't delay you," Anira went on, releasing Talia, "I know you must be eager to see the Ruen-Shained."

Talia managed a smile.

"This way." Wen took her arm, steering her past the overexuberant servingwoman. Talia was intently aware of his proximity—the hard muscle of his forearm beneath her hand, his tight way of walking, like he was doing his best to keep himself from falling to pieces and raging at the world. For all that, his presence steadied her.

But she was conscious of Caiden, too, walking just behind. Blaive trailed in the rear.

They passed from the low entranceway, which was carpeted with elaborate rugs much faded from their original glory, and up a creaky stair. Wen let go of her arm and she shrunk a little without his steady warmth. But she wasn't brave enough to reach for him again.

The house was small, the tour brief. Wen spooled out a short history of how it was the last of a number of modest holdings his family had once awarded to faithful lords, back when they were royalty. The other holdings had been surrendered to Enduena, when Ryn was absorbed into the Empire.

Talia peeked into four upstairs bedrooms, a downstairs sitting room, and a tiny parlor.

"Where will your music room be?" she asked Wen as the four of them trooped through the back of the house and out toward the garden.

"What do you mean?"

"The music room. Where will you put your raina and the other instruments?"

He studied her. "I hadn't thought about it."

"Perhaps the sitting room? There's just enough space, I would think."

"Even more space at the University," said Caiden, his voice dripping sarcasm. She wished he would leave Wen alone.

"Lovely idea," put in Blaive, not to be outdone. "We can hire a cart from the village and start moving everything over today!"

They ate lunch in the garden, a pleasant terrace at the back of the house that looked out toward the distant sea. Anira had laid out a little picnic for them: cold chicken, cider, fresh apples, and coffee. Talia laced her fingers around her coffee mug and drank deeply, shuddering in the wind.

The majority of the meal passed in an uneasy silence. Wen didn't say anything at all, while Caiden made various attempts at humor and Blaive tried to flirt with him. Caiden's attitude toward Wen was making Talia increasingly uncomfortable. She caught Wen's eyes across the way and smiled at him, but he didn't smile back, just studied her. Would he be content, she wondered, spinning out his life in this little house, watching sheep and composing music no one else would ever hear?

No one except for her, if she stayed with him.

The thought startled her—when had she considered, even for a moment, that she would actually marry him?

She dropped her gaze from Wen's and took a drink of cider.

The wind bit colder and colder as the afternoon went on, and dark clouds began to roll in from the south. Talia was relieved when Anira appeared and said apologetically that they should head back if they wanted to outrun the weather.

The rain caught up with them halfway to the Ruen-Dahr, and the four of them arrived drenched and shuddering just before dinner, a lantern gleaming bright at the door.

Chapter Twenty-Five

S IIE WAS EXHAUSTED ENOUGH TO SLEEP THE whole night through, images of Stars and Waves and screaming dead shadows haunting her dreams. She awoke to find the rain had frozen overnight, snow tracing delicate patterns on her window. Her room was completely frigid. She wrapped herself in a blanket and settled on the window seat.

All the world below her, save the sea, was shrouded in white, snow clinging to the rocks and the sand and the hills to the south, blanketing everything in soft winter quilts. The beauty of the landscape took her breath away. It had snowed only rarely in Irsa, a light dusting a handful of times throughout her childhood, and not at all in Eddenahr. The capital was far too warm for anything but an occasional cold rain in the early spring months.

Ro came in with a breakfast tray, and when she'd laid it on the dressing table, she knelt to coax life back into Talia's fire. "It hasn't been snowing long enough to close the roads, so the seamstress ought to be here presently," she said, sweeping away yesterday's ashes.

"Seamstress?" said Talia, leaving the window nook to pour herself some tea.

"The Baron sent for her last week. You're to have a few

dresses of your own, and a bridal gown, of course, Miss."

She clenched her teeth. "A bridal gown?"

Ro glanced at Talia over her shoulder. "It's unlucky to get married in another woman's dress, you know." She quirked a grin. "Especially if she's dead."

"Don't joke about that," Talia snapped, her voice coming out louder than she'd intended.

Ro turned back to the fire. "Sorry, Miss."

Flames sparked on the stones, and Ro got up and left the room.

Talia nibbled fitfully at her breakfast, staring out at the snow and trying not to think about the sea goddess and her Star, the nine Waves playing music for the dead.

The seamstress barged in when Talia was only halfway through her pot of tea, a wide flat box tucked under one arm, a wooden stool dangling from the other. She was young, no older than Talia herself, and was angular and tall. She wore her brown hair pulled into a rigid knot at the back of her head.

"Up you go then," she said, plopping down the stool and waving Talia onto it. Then she set the box on the bed and opened it, revealing half a dozen unfinished gowns.

Talia laid down her teacup and obligingly stepped onto the stool.

The seamstress made her try on all of the half-sewn gowns, one after the other, circling her with a critical eye and a fist full of pins. She took measurements and made notes in a little green book, pausing now and then to pin the open seams.

Talia tried on the bridal gown last of all. It was a deep blue, as brilliant as the Enduenan summer sky, with the beginnings of delicate silver embroidery around the neckline. It was beautiful.

The seamstress kept circling like a shrewd hawk, an intense frown of concentration on her face. She slipped a few pins in under Talia's shoulders, and more around her waist. Then she stood back

to scrutinize her work. "That will do, I think. The Baron's requested
he see you in the gown. Shall I wait while you go and show him?"

Talia chewed her lip. What if Caiden had already spoken to
him? "I wouldn't think the Baron would care about a wedding
dress."

The seamstress shrugged. "He's paying for it. Go on up,
Miss. Make sure he approves."

Talia grimaced, but acquiesced, gathering her skirt in both
hands to keep it from dragging across the floor. She stepped out
into the hall, and started up the flight of stairs that led to the
Baron's suite. She had little wish for a private interview with
him, but she supposed she'd better get it over with.

The Baron answered her quiet knock with a call of admittance
and she swept into his study, immediately oppressed with a wall
of heat. He was sitting in an armchair pulled close to a roaring
fire, a patchwork quilt laying over his knees. He looked more
shrunken and old and ill than the last time she'd seen him.

"What is it?" he asked in some confusion.

"The seamstress is here. I came to show you my . . . the . . .
the bridal gown."

He glanced at the dress without seeing it, tears creeping into
the corners of his eyes. "I miss them, you know," he whispered.
"Every day. But the gods took them from me, and I cannot get
them back." He put his head in his hands and wept, his thin
shoulders shaking.

Talia's heart wrenched. She crossed the room and knelt
beside his chair. "I'm very sorry, sir," she said softly. "I will never
stop missing my mother, not ever. It hurts too much, so I try not
to think about it. But I do anyway. Part of me is always thinking
about it. Remembering how she died. Remembering how she
lived. Remembering *her*, because I'm the only one left to do it."
She tried not to think about where her mother was now, but
she couldn't help it—water choking into her lungs, an agony of

darkness and pain that never ended.

The Baron lifted his head, his eyes meeting hers. "That's it exactly. The boys—the boys miss them, too, but not like me."

She felt a deep twist of compassion and kinship for this poor, wasted man. She leaned over and kissed his papery cheek.

"I wish I could bring them back," he whispered.

She jerked away from him. "What did you say?"

Tears slid down his pale face. "I wish I could bring them back."

Shouldn't she be wishing that for her mother? Drowning for eternity. No escape. No release.

"Gone forever," the Baron muttered to the fire, his chin dropping forward onto his chest. He sighed and fell asleep, his breaths coming in rattling rasps.

Talia crept from the room, dread knotted tight around her heart.

What if she *could* bring her mother back? What if there was a way to free her? What if—

She ran right into Wen, who was coming up the stairs the other way.

She stopped short and he did too, staring at her with his mouth hanging open. She struggled to keep control of herself, digging her fingers into the skirt of her dress. "Why did Caiden's mother go down to the temple? How did your mother drown?" She took a steadying breath. "There's something you're not telling me. I want to know what it is."

He looked at her, the muscles tight in his jaw. "I can't tell you."

She opened her mouth to argue, but he held up his hand.

"I have to show you."

She blinked at him. "All right."

He studied her, and it felt like he was looking deep down to her core. "Is that a wedding gown?" he said softly.

"Yes."

A quiet smile touched his lips. "I think it's bad luck for me to see you. Though I'm glad I have."

She gave him a hesitant smile back, and he flushed a little. "Meet me in the library," he told her. "I know you have a key."

Despite everything, she almost laughed. He bowed and strode on up the stairs.

She went back to her room, slipping out of the unfinished bridal gown and into a patterned gray dress.

"Did the Baron approve?" the seamstress inquired, laying the gown in the box with the rest.

"He did," said Talia.

But she wasn't thinking about the Baron.

Chapter Twenty-Six

WEN WAS WAITING FOR HER WHEN SHE stepped into the library, his tall form dark against the window. His expression was serious, his eyes hard. "Do you know about the Words of the gods?"

"They're mentioned in the myths," she said after a few moments of uneasy silence. She felt again that hidden power she'd sensed so strongly when she'd first discovered the library. "Words of power, given to the gods at the beginning of the world. The spirits learned them, too, and taught them to a few mortals, or so the story goes."

Wen nodded. "The Words were written down in books. Kept hidden. Kept secret. Some say they can be found in any great library in the world. I found one of them. And I think my mother—and Caiden's—found it, too."

He turned to look at the left wall of the tower, and spoke three words in a language she had never heard before. The words sounded more like music than speaking; she could feel their power.

A doorway appeared in the wall, shimmering and black.

Talia drew a sharp breath.

"The Words of opening," he said, answering her unspoken question. Intensity burned in his blue eyes. "You have to promise me something."

Her throat constricted. "What's that?"

"When you see—when you see what I'm about to show you, don't do anything rash."

Gooseflesh prickled up and down her skin. "I'll try not to."

He gave her a tight smile, and held out his hand. "Are you ready?"

She took his hand, and his fingers folded warm around hers, steady and certain. "Yes."

They stepped side by side through the doorway.

She found herself in a cool, dim chamber that smelled of wine and honey, dust swirling up from the floor. The ceiling and walls disappeared into shadowy darkness, so Talia couldn't tell how big the space really was. Tall mirrors the color of obsidian filled the room, too many for her to count. They seemed eerie, and she realized it was because they didn't reflect anything at all.

"What is this place?" she asked in a hushed voice.

"Look in the mirrors and you'll see."

She stepped up to the nearest mirror.

The black glass stared back at her, impenetrable, and she held her breath. Then it wavered, and began to change.

Inside the mirror she saw the void, or rather, she *felt* it, an impossible darkness where no life could possibly exist. Three Stars appeared, wheeling in that darkness, and she knew somehow she was witnessing the making of the world. She couldn't even comprehend it, but it was beautiful, and it made her ache.

She heard Wen's voice as if from a great distance, felt him tugging her hand. "Come. You must not look too long."

And she allowed him to pull her away from the mirror.

The coldness of the chamber crept into her. She stepped up to a second obsidian glass.

The mirror stared blankly back at her for a few moments before the surface began to ripple, and an image shuddered into being. She saw the Tree growing beautiful and good out of the earth, its branches spread wide, fruit bursting amidst its leaves. She could smell the Tree, touch it, *hear* it. She thought it was singing to her. But no, those were the gods, raising their voices in the shelter of the Tree, making music to the three blazing Stars.

And then, Wen's voice in her ear, his hand pulling her away: "You must not look too long."

She looked in a third mirror, and saw mankind's rebellion against the gods playing out before her eyes. She watched the gods uproot the Tree and fling it to the ground in their great anger. She saw men and women die, saw Blaidor weeping bitterly. Talia felt the ancient woman's sorrow like it was her own; fiery tears dripped down her cheeks.

Wen tugged her away.

She looked into a fourth mirror, and saw the gods warring over the fallen Tree. She watched Aigir claim the victory and plant the Tree anew in the midst of the ocean.

In the fifth mirror, the gods plucked two of the Stars from heaven, and Huen of the Earth and Aigir of the Sea bound them like jewels in bands of gold and silver.

On and on around the room, Talia gazed into the mirrors. In every one she saw the myths live and burn and *be*. But she never got to look her fill—Wen was always tugging her away, on to the next glass, the next bit of history.

Time fell away and the cold seeped into her bones. She forgot herself. Forgot Wen and her mother and everything else. There were only the mirrors. Only the stories unfolding before her eyes, the stories that had shaped the world. She felt them and knew them. She became them. She lived a thousand lives and bore a thousand sorrows. She felt the weight of time, resting wholly upon her.

And always, far away, a voice speaking her name, a hand pulling her from the living memories of what once had been. It hurt more and more every time, a dagger twisting sharp.

And then, a deep breath, a tired focusing of her eyes.

Wen, standing before her, urgency in his gaze.

There was only one mirror left that she hadn't looked into.

She could feel his fingers, interlaced in hers, his skin grown icy.

"This mirror is different from the others," he said, his voice rough and hoarse. "As far as I can tell, it shows the future."

She felt impossibly weary.

"But you must take care, Talia. The future isn't written yet."

There were no words—she didn't know if she could even form any. But she nodded, her throat dry and her breaths short.

She turned to the last mirror, and looked in.

She saw a white ship on a stormy sea, a patchwork sail torn to shreds, a girl clinging to the mast, icy hail stinging her cheeks. Wind roared in her ears, and she could feel the rough mast, splinters digging into her palms. Lightning seared across the sky, blinding her. A scream tore raw from her throat.

The mirror changed, and she saw the white Tree stretching bony branches into the sky, black waves crashing against its scarred trunk. Two serpents swam around the Tree, their lithe bodies shifting shades of blue and silver. They rushed toward her, and she knew she would be torn to shreds.

But then the mirror changed again.

She looked into a watery Hall filled with shadows, and she saw the shadows were the dead. They danced in endless rows before a goddess on a high throne. There was darkness in the goddess's beautiful face, and on one hand she wore a shining Star.

One of the dead broke away from the dance, and Talia saw it was her mother, though her face was gray, her eyes empty. Her mouth was open, frozen in inaudible screams.

Talia, came her mother's voice, slithering through her head. *You have come for me at last! I cannot bear it. Take me away. Take me back to the light. The light! The light! The light!*

And Talia reached out to take her mother's hand. *I will save you, Mama. I will save you.*

The scene changed once more, and Talia saw her mother standing at the foot of the goddess's throne, weeping for the pain that wracked her ruined body.

Where is the other? seethed the goddess. *The one you tried to protect, the one you continue to hide from me?*

There is no one, said her mother, shuddering but strong.

You lie! The sea whispers to me of her, and I will not rest until she is mine.

There is no one!

I will find her when I rise, and I will chain her with you in the depths.

She heard her mother's scream inside her own head, and then she felt the pain, splintering through every part of her. She wanted to let it rip her into a million fragments, wanted the release it would bring. But she could not break, for her soul was bound forever to the darkness.

From somewhere outside of herself she heard Wen's voice, felt his strong hands wrap around her arm. He tore her from the vision like an arrow from a wound.

She was screaming, hitting him with her fists, clawing at him with her fingers, but he didn't let her go. He held tight as she collapsed onto the floor of the library, crying uncontrollably.

"It may not be true," he told her, over and over. "Whatever it is you saw, the future isn't written yet. It may not be true. It may not be true."

But she sobbed on his shoulder because she knew that it was.

Part Three:

SONG AND WAVES

Aigir took the remaining Star and bound it in a band of silver. He bore it with him into the depths of the ocean, and wrought a beautiful Hall at the roots of the Tree.

Chapter Twenty-Seven

DUSK WAS FALLING OUTSIDE THE LIBRARY WINDOW, and Talia and Wen sat across from each other in chairs pulled up to the hearth. Wen had built a fire and the flames licked thirstily on the stones, but the heat did nothing to dispel the chill in the deepest parts of her. He'd brought her tea, as well—the laden tray lay untouched at her elbow.

"We were in there nearly a day," said Talia quietly, glancing at the window. Snow clung white to the pane.

"Almost two. I spoke to Ahned on the stairs. And don't worry. I saw him before we went up, asked him to tell everyone we were both ill, caught a cold on the ride back from the Ruen-Shained."

Talia swallowed past the lump in her throat, and looked up at Wen. "Explain."

He studied her for a moment without speaking, and then turned his gaze to the fire. "I came up to the library last year. I stole Ahned's keys and made myself a copy, and I snuck in every day, pouring through the books that my mother had loved so much, angry at my father for locking them away from me. I had always believed in the gods, but the stories came alive as I was reading them, and I *felt* their truth."

His eyes flicked momentarily to Talia's before returning to

the fire. She swallowed and twisted her fingers in her lap, not saying anything.

"I knew there were things about my mother's death that my father wasn't telling me. I knew they had something to do with the myths. And then I found a bundle of Caiden's mother's notes stuffed into a corner bookshelf, the pages half burnt. She wrote very vividly about visions she'd seen, about a temple under the garden, about a sliver of the Tree. She seemed convinced it was her destiny to use the piece of the Tree to defend against some coming evil."

"And she found it," said Talia, "but it killed her."

Wen nodded. "Yes."

"What about your mother?"

"I found a few scattered pages of her notes, too. She wrote in great detail about the sea, and how she felt it was imperative to find a creature called 'Endain's Whale,' also to guard against an unnamed threat."

That made Talia uneasy.

"I didn't understand where their information was coming from, what visions Caiden's mother was referring to, or why they both seemed convinced something terrible was going to happen. I still don't."

Talia studied his profile in the firelight. "And then you found a book of Words."

"It was strange. I could have sworn I had paged through every book in the library. But one day, there it was: a thin, green volume tucked into a corner shelf. It was obviously old, the leather cracked, a white tree stamped into the cover. I'd never seen the language it was written in before. The Words looked more like—more like musical notation than letters. It's hard to explain."

"Could you read them?"

"Not at first. I poured through every page, feeling the power caught in paper and ink, desperate to make sense of it. And then I found my mother's handwriting on the back cover—she'd evidently started translating the book. She'd transcribed three Words, and I said them aloud and the mirror room opened, just as it did today."

"So you think your mother—and Caiden's—both went into the mirror room?"

"I do. Caiden's mother went missing without explanation for thirteen days before turning up in the forgotten temple. My mother disappeared for ten, and then decided to go sailing." There was a grim edge to his voice. "Where else could they have gone?"

"And you think the visions they saw in the last mirror—"

"Led to their deaths." He met her eyes, his jaw a hard line.

"How long did you go missing?"

"Five days." He looked back into the fire.

"What did you tell your father?"

"I told him the truth. Caiden too."

She understood what he wasn't saying. "They didn't believe you."

Wen jerked up from his chair and paced over to the window, every line in his body taut.

Talia followed.

"I told them everything. What I'd seen in the mirrors. What I suspected had happened to our mothers. I even convinced them to come up to the library, to look in the mirrors with me. I spoke the Words, the room appeared, I led them inside."

"Then why—"

"They couldn't see it," said Wen roughly. He turned to Talia. "The Ruen-Dahr seems to choose the people it lets in on its secrets. I don't understand why. It chose me, and evidently my mother and Caiden's, but not him or my father. They thought I was making it up. Mocking them both. Making light of the dead and my father's suffering. They were furious. I'd told them before that I'd heard voices from the tower room, whispers of music from the sea, but they never believed me—they thought I was going mad. This just made it worse. Much worse."

Talia put her hand on Wen's arm. He shut his eyes, leaning against the wall.

"Is that when you told them you didn't want to go to University after all?" Talia asked softly.

He opened his eyes again, staring at her, tracing every line of her face. "Yes."

"Why, Wen?"

"I stayed to change my fate."

Understanding dawned on her. "You saw something in the mirror that made you stay."

He looked back out the window.

"What did you see?"

He didn't answer. Somehow, she hadn't expected him to. "It hasn't killed you," she said. "Whatever you saw, it hasn't killed you. Maybe it was a fluke, what happened to the Baronesses. Maybe they misinterpreted the things they saw—"

"It hasn't happened yet." He went over to the fire and stood staring into the flames. "What I saw hasn't happened yet."

This time, Talia didn't follow. She watched him, pondering this new depth to his character she hadn't even guessed at before.

"What are you going to do?" Wen said, without looking at her. "About the things *you* saw in the mirror."

She blinked and saw her mother, reaching out to her, desperate and screaming. *Take me back to the light! Take me back to the light!*

"I don't know."

He caught her eye, and she knew he could see she was lying.

Chapter Twenty-Eight

S HE CAME DOWN FROM THE LIBRARY ALONE.
Now she was certain.

She wouldn't leave her mother for Rahn to torment. She couldn't. She was going to save her. Set her free.

How, she didn't quite know yet. But that had to be what the Waves were calling her to do, and the mirrors proved she would make it that far. Beyond that—

She knew one thing: She couldn't tell Wen what she'd seen, couldn't tell him the plans forming slowly in her mind.

He would try and stop her.

And she was afraid she'd let him. Because Rahn had been looking for *her*, and if the goddess ever found her—

"Talia?"

She jerked around. Caiden stood there in his shirtsleeves, hair wet from a bath.

His face relaxed at the sight of her, and he laid a hand on her arm. "I'm so glad to see you. Are you feeling better?"

She blinked at him in confusion before she remembered Wen saying something about explaining their two-day absence with illness. "Oh, um . . . yes. Much better." She smiled thinly.

He smiled back, the lamp in the hall glimmering on his

smooth skin. He slid his arm around her waist and she breathed him in, soap and ink and cedar. "The mare missed you," he said softly. "I took her out yesterday, but she didn't run as well for me. What do you think you'll name her?"

Talia was suddenly hyperaware of her heartbeat, pulsing harder where Caiden's skin touched her own. She wanted to forget everything and melt into him, but the images she'd seen in the mirror were too recent. Too real. "Ahdairon," she said quietly. "After the wind goddess."

He laughed a little into her hair. "Fitting."

And then he was kissing her forehead, her cheek, her—

"Stealing your brother's betrothed is not exactly honorable, Caiden," came a sudden voice. "I wouldn't have thought it your style."

Caiden jolted away from her, and Talia turned to see Blaive dressed for dinner. Her curls glinted in the lamplight. The neckline of her blush-pink gown was cut low, showing off her pale shoulders, her perfect collarbones, the emerald glittering on her breast.

"What do you *want*, Blaive?" Caiden demanded.

Talia sagged back against her bedroom door. She hadn't meant to let him kiss her. It wasn't fair to Wen, or herself, or Caiden either.

"Your father would never approve, you know," said Blaive, not quailing under his gaze.

"Of what?" said Caiden.

A humorless smile touched Blaive's face. "Of *her*."

Talia bristled. "There's nothing—"

"Nothing going on? No kissing in the hall when you think no one's looking, no purchasing of extravagant horses, no making a mockery of your future with Wen? Don't you dare claim there's nothing going on."

"You have *no right* to address me like that."

"I have every right, Miss Dahl-Saida." Blaive shifted her glance to Caiden, though she kept talking to Talia. "I am Caiden's oldest friend. His dearest friend. It's you who has no right." Her curls trembled around her temples. "My father's growing old, as well as yours. I'll inherit soon. I won't be able to manage everything myself."

Caiden stared at her. "Blaive—"

"I wouldn't need to stay there," she continued, cutting him off. "I'll only need to hire a competent steward, and visit once or twice a year, to make sure they're handling it properly." Her green eyes caught his brown ones, and Talia felt something rippling between them, a connection that was broken now, and mostly forgotten, but had once been strong.

His face grew taut, sharpening the angle of his jaw.

"Your father wrote to me last month," she said softly. "Told me to come, hinted that the Ruen-Dahr needed a new mistress. Make him proud, Caiden. Let me stay here with you. It's what we always planned, after all."

Rage hardened every line of Caiden's frame. "My father had no *right* to invite you here. You might as well pack your bags and leave this evening, Blaive. It will save you future disappointment."

She smiled. "Does your father know? About Talia?"

"There's nothing to know," Talia objected, but neither of them was paying attention to her.

"If you think for one second that I would *dream* of marrying *you*—"

"You'll do what your father tells you to," Blaive snapped, "like you always have."

He shut his mouth, eyes blazing fire.

"Now, if you'll excuse me," said Blaive, gathering her taffeta skirts. "I believe I'm late for dinner." And she swept down the stairs in a haze of righteous fury.

Talia stared after her, shocked. She disliked Blaive more

than she thought possible, but she was also a little awed by the girl's tenacity.

Caiden was obviously rattled. He stood there vacantly staring for a solid minute, before at last bowing vaguely in Talia's direction and retreating upstairs.

Talia took a breath and went into her room, collapsing in the window seat and ringing for one of the maids to bring her dinner. She had no wish to encounter Blaive again.

She dreamed of the boat from the hidden cove, upright and whole, adrift in a dark sea. A patchwork sail swelled to catch the wind. She was standing at the tiller, guiding the boat through the black waves.

The sea began to groan, and a host of shadows rose from beneath the water. They were clothed in gray and bound in chains and every one of them was screaming, though they made no sound. At their head a goddess rode on the back of a sea serpent. She wore a crown of bones and fire, and the Star shone bright from her finger.

A wave crashed against Talia's boat, and black water enveloped her. Chains wrapped around her ankles, dragging her down and down and down. No matter how she fought, she couldn't get free.

The goddess's laughter rang in her ears, and she could see nothing before her but shadows, and death.

Talia jerked from sleep, skin drenched in sweat. She got out of bed, lit a candle, and changed into a fresh nightgown, splashing water on her face and willing her pulse to return to normal.

Outside the window the clouds had ebbed away, stars showing white in the fathomless dark. She unlatched the casement and leaned out into the night. Icy air raced into her lungs, and away out over the sea, she heard music. It was filled with longing, and danger, and impossible sorrow. She tried not to listen.

The boat from the hidden cove. How had she not remembered that yesterday—no, two days ago—in the mirror room? Was it possible she was meant to use that boat to sail to Rahn's Hall and free her mother? She couldn't think about the other part of her dream—the dead rising from the sea, chains around her ankles. Death.

She shivered in the frigid wind, but didn't pull the window shut.

She could feel her fate like an inescapable noose, every moment cinching tighter. The gods were giving her all the pieces. She just had to figure out how to put them together.

Chapter Twenty-Nine

CAIDEN WASN'T AT DINNER.

Talia hadn't seen him all day. She was the first to arrive in the dining room, still thinking about the boat in the hidden cove, trying to figure out what she should do first. The boat needed repair—she wouldn't know how much until she dug it out of the sand. Somehow, she had to figure out how to even *find* Rahn's Hall—it wasn't like it'd be marked in ink on a map. And in the event she actually made it, she'd need some kind of plan to dive into the sea and pull her mother out from among the dead.

It sounded like nonsense, when she thought about it like that, and yet—

She knew it wasn't.

Blaive breezed in a few moments later with a smile on her face, settling into her chair in a pouf of powder-pink skirts. Wen came in just after, his spectacles pinched tight on his nose, ink spattered all over his hands and even a few black stains on his shirt. He smiled at Talia and she smiled back, her guilt at the things she wasn't telling him gnawing deep.

"Caiden's not coming," Blaive explained smoothly to no one in particular, as the maids brought in dinner. "He's upstairs with the Baron."

"Oh?" Talia wondered faintly if Caiden was talking to him about the betrothal. Not that it mattered anymore, really—she would be gone by the spring. She swallowed past the lump in her throat.

"I saw the Baron myself this morning," Blaive continued, unfolding her napkin on her lap. "We had quite a chat over tea."

Wen frowned, clearly more in tune with this conversation than Talia. "What did you chat about?"

Her smile deepened to dangerous dimensions. "Responsibility. Contracts. Propriety. Honoring one's commitments."

"What did you do?" said Talia.

Blaive locked eyes with her. "I simply pointed out a few things going on under the Baron's nose that he was unaware of."

"Such as?" Talia prodded, grinding her jaw.

Blaive gave a dimpled smile. "The particulars aren't important." She saluted Talia with her wine glass.

Caiden wasn't at breakfast either.

Sausages and porridge and dried winter pears were spread out on the table, with hot tea and cider. Exhausted, Talia barely touched any of it. She'd been up late reading, trying to gather as much information as she could about Rahn's Hall. But it wasn't like there were any charts helpfully pointing the way. Just stories, and not very many of them at that.

Blaive sat, primly stirring cream and sugar into her porridge, her fitted orange gown a bold splash of color in the dull room. Flames danced hot on the hearth, living echoes of her brilliance.

Wen sat scratching at a piece of music paper, the tea at his elbow untouched.

"What are you doing?" Talia asked him, tired of silence and loath to speak to Blaive.

He glanced up at her briefly then back at his music. "Working on my symphony. It comes in bits and pieces, and if I don't write it down immediately, I can't get it back again. It's been exploding in my mind since . . . since the other day."

Since the mirror room, Talia thought, and suppressed a shudder. She watched the quick movement of his pen across the paper and wondered what horrible thing he'd seen in the last mirror that hadn't happened yet.

"Caiden's out riding, in case anyone wanted to know," said Blaive, smugness rolling off of her in waves. "He left quite early this morning."

Talia sipped her tea without tasting it. She shouldn't care about Caiden's whereabouts, not with everything else that was going on, but she did. "Do you know where he went?"

Blaive shrugged her pretty, orange-clad shoulders, a smile playing about her lips. "I'm afraid I don't."

Wen's pen scribbled rapidly over his paper, black notes marching up and down the staff lines. Talia wondered what it sounded like in his head.

"I suppose," said Blaive, her tone overbright, "we'll just have to wait and ask him when he comes back."

Talia went riding after breakfast, ostensibly to exercise Ahdairon—she was really just hoping to find Caiden. The air was freezing despite her warm cloak, but at least it wasn't snowing.

He was nowhere to be seen. His absence and Blaive's flippancy gnawed at her. She rode along the empty shoreline for a while, music whispering to her from the waves, and she felt incredibly guilty. Her mother was waiting for her, tortured endlessly by a malicious goddess, while she worried about a *boy*.

And yet, she couldn't shake him from her head.

Two hours later, she shut Ahdairon back into the stable, Avial's stall still empty. Where had Caiden gone? What was Blaive not telling her?

She had a cup of tea in the parlor and tried to read a book titled *The Words of the Gods,* but she couldn't concentrate, sentences blurring uselessly before her eyes. Her thoughts jumped from her mother to Caiden and back again, and at last she snapped the book shut in frustration. She stood outside the music room, listening as Wen pounded out a haunted counterpoint on his raina, wondering what he would say if he knew what she was planning. She paced around the cold garden, peering through the wrought iron gate at the uneasy sea, its unearthly music tangling with Wen's melodies.

But Caiden still didn't come back.

The fire jumped and sparked in the dining hall, the wind howling just beyond the glass. The lamp on the table burned low, the supplemental candles in their silver holders dripping wax on freshly ironed linen.

Talia and Wen were dining alone, both Caiden *and* Blaive failing to appear. Wen hadn't brought his music with him this time. He looked tired and far away, but vaguely contented.

"Did you finish it?" she asked him, looking across the wavering candle flames. "Your symphony?"

"Not yet." A smile tugged at his lips. "But I have the first movement mostly down."

His happiness was infectious, and she smiled back. "I'm glad for you." She cut off a piece of roast venison and chewed it slowly.

"Are you doing all right?" he asked, his eyes growing serious. "I didn't know if you wanted to be left alone, or if you wanted to talk about . . . about the mirror room. I know it . . . changed some things for me, the first time I went in there."

She swallowed her meat, grasping awkwardly for a lie. "I'm fine. Really."

"You promised me you wouldn't do anything crazy."

She pushed down her guilt. "I won't."

And then they both heard hoofbeats ringing distantly on the stones in front of the house. She felt herself go rigid.

Wen's face closed a little.

"Wen—"

"You don't have to hide it from me," he said. "I know you care for him. I don't blame you."

She sat there, staring at Wen, as the fire popped and the wind shrieked outside the Ruen-Dahr. Bright spots of snow showed white against the window. Yes, she did care for Caiden, but she cared about Wen, too. And now she'd hurt him.

"I'm sorry," she said, entirely miserable.

"Don't be." He shrugged, affecting carelessness. Then added gently, "Go and see him, then."

She chewed on her lip and got up from the table, wishing she could erase the pain from his eyes. "I'll be right back."

"I'll be here."

Out on the flagstone drive the snow was falling thick and fast. It clung to her hair and gown, and she hugged her chest, shuddering in the freezing wind. She'd hurt Wen, and she didn't know how to fix it.

But wasn't it better this way? She was leaving soon. It would hurt him more, if he knew she considered him her friend and wasn't planning on telling him her secret. Or even saying goodbye.

And then she saw them coming back from the stables and she forgot about everything else.

Caiden and Blaive, walking close together, her arm around his waist, her face radiant. His face, dazed.

They stopped short when they saw her, perched on the steps like a ghost, her skirt whirling about her knees.

"Caiden?" said Talia hesitantly.

His glance was fierce and cold in the orange light spilling out of the Ruen-Dahr's windows.

And then Blaive stepped forward, lifting her right hand so Talia was sure to see the ring gleaming on her first finger: an amethyst bound intricately in gold.

Talia stared, too shocked to quite understand.

"Caiden has asked me to marry him!" Blaive's face split in a brilliant smile, and her expression held no malice—only joy. "He rode into the village today to set my ring. Isn't it beautiful?"

But Talia was staring at Caiden. What did he *mean*, asking Blaive to marry him? He'd kissed *her*. He'd practically promised her the world. She'd thought—she'd thought—

He stood rigid, the muscles jumping in his jaw. "It was my mother's ring," he said, not taking his eyes from Talia's. "Rather, my mother's stone. It took time to find the proper setting."

Somewhere in his distant face Talia thought she saw something else—that under different circumstances the ring would have been given to her.

"We're to be married before the month is out," Blaive went on. "In three weeks, if everything can be arranged."

She was suddenly aware of Caiden's arm, resting easily on Blaive's shoulders. Of Blaive's perfume, which smelled of honey and blackberries.

Snow fell wet against her face, the cold numbing her skin.

Caiden's eyes numbed every other part of her.

Chapter Thirty

TALIA?"
She didn't know how Wen had found her up here, tucked into a corner of the dead Baronesses' forgotten suite, her knees hugged to her chin. It was freezing and dark—she hadn't brought a lamp.

"Talia?" His voice was softer this time.

She saw his silhouette against the door, hair tousled and cravat flapping loose around his neck. She hated this—the feeling of helpless, weightless falling, when she'd thought the ground underneath her stood firm. But it was almost a relief to see Wen.

"I'm in here."

He stepped into the room, and she heard the scrape of a match against metal. Light flared in the dark as Wen lit a lamp.

She'd squeezed into the tightest space she could find, between a sheet-shrouded armchair and the Baronesses' empty wardrobe, the wall cold and hard against her back.

Wen sat across from her, studying her with his deep-seeing eyes. The lamp flame wavered on the table, and shadows played across his face.

"My father threatened to disinherit him."

She stared past his shoulder at the flowered wallpaper. It was faded, stripped away in places.

"Talia. Listen to me. He would have lost everything—the Ruen-Dahr, the land, the title."

She forced her glance back to Wen, trying to focus on his words. She felt tight and strange and empty. "What do you mean?"

Wen swallowed, lacing his hands together. "Blaive told my father that she'd seen you and my brother . . . together." He flushed in the lamplight, but didn't look away.

She wished the earth would open and swallow her up.

"My father was—my father was angry."

She chewed on the inside of her cheek. "He wanted more for Caiden than me."

Wen's brow creased. "He's wanted the two of them to marry all their lives. It wasn't about you."

But it was, and they both knew it. Blaive had lands and wealth and social status. Talia had nothing.

Wen shifted where he sat. "He asked her to come here with that specific end in mind."

Talia leaned her head back against the wall, staring up at the shadowed ceiling. Everything seemed far away, now. Her mother. Rahn's Hall. The cursed Billow Maidens.

She shut her eyes, listening to the wind roaring outside the Ruen-Dahr and blowing snow over the stones. If it weren't so cold, if the ship were repaired, if she had the right supplies—if only it wouldn't take time to prepare everything, she could leave tonight and never have to see Caiden again.

"You would have inherited in his place. You would have become Baron."

Wen shook his head. "I've never wanted that. I don't want it now. To be tied to the Ruen-Dahr and my father's sorrow—I couldn't handle it. Caiden was born to govern Ryn, and it suits him, far, far better than it would suit me. But I'm sorry, Talia.

I'm so sorry." He sounded miserable.

Talia opened her eyes. "Why?" She saw in his face the boy who had pulled her from the temple, the boy who had showed her the answers in the mirror room and asked for nothing in return. The boy who heard music in his head, like she heard it in the waves.

For a moment he didn't say anything, the muscles in his jaw tightening and then relaxing again. "Because it isn't fair for you not to be happy. You deserve happiness, after everything you've gone through."

She could see in his eyes that there was more he could have said, but he didn't.

"Are they—are they really getting married in three weeks?" Wen nodded.

"And did—did Caiden . . . tell you all this?"

"I spoke to my father."

"I see." Talia watched the lamp on the table, the light soft and flickering. She traced a pattern in the dust on the floor. Her throat hurt. "Thanks for telling me. Thanks for showing me the mirror room and saving me from the temple and—" She looked up into his face, saw his steadiness, his strength. "Thank you for caring."

"Always." He scooted a little closer to her, and she shifted out from between the chair and wardrobe, leaning her head on his shoulder. His breath was warm at her ear. Comforting. She almost told him everything, but she held back, screwing her eyes shut and trying to hold tight to the last frail threads mooring her to the earth.

She stood outside Caiden's door and knocked, three times. There were things she had to say to him. Things she needed him to hear. Light from the hall lamp pooled on the crimson carpet, and her breaths came quick and short.

Talia knocked again.

She thought she heard steps from inside of the room, but they didn't draw any closer. The door didn't open.

"Caiden?"

No answer.

"Miss Dahl-Saida?"

Talia jerked around to see Ahned standing in the hall, an oil lamp in one hand. He frowned. "You shouldn't be here."

"I came to speak with Caiden."

The steward's frown deepened. "Miss Dahl-Saida, please return to your room."

She stood straight and still, clenching the skirt of her violet gown. "Will you tell him something for me?"

"If you wish."

Talia jutted her chin out. "Tell him congratulations," she said viciously.

She swept down the hall, not turning her head even when she heard Caiden's door open, his tread on the carpet, his voice speaking quietly to Ahned.

Chapter Thirty-One

CAIDEN STOOD WITH HIS BACK TO HER at the window of the dusty ballroom, his shoulders rigid, the muscles in his neck taut. He held a goblet of wine, but did not raise it to his lips.

She'd followed him in here from the dining room, her mind bursting with the things she had to say before tomorrow.

Before he was married and she couldn't in good conscience say them at all.

The three weeks had passed swiftly, the wedding everywhere: Blaive, handwriting invitations in the dining room, expensive cream paper and bottles of blue ink strewn all across the table. Meetings with a chef, a team of seamstresses, a florist who kept a hot house for just such winter flower emergencies. Caiden, riding back and forth to Shold to discuss arrangements with Blaive's father.

Talia had hidden upstairs between meals, scouring the library for books on shipbuilding and sailing, and any references she could find to Rahn or the Hall of the Dead. She wanted to be ready when the weather grew warm enough, and she had no desire to go blindly into the sea goddess's domain. She was close to uncovering something she felt sure was important—the dates of the myths and the Billow Maidens' nine-hundred-year curse. She even found a handful of prophecies predicting Rahn's return from the sea to rule the world that the goddess believed was rightfully hers. But Talia hadn't found everything she needed to pin down the timeline completely.

And none of that had distracted her wholly from Caiden.

"You've been avoiding me," said Talia, stepping up beside him at the window in the ballroom.

The snow had stopped for the time being, and a pale sun was sinking westward through ragged clouds. Out over the sea the sky was edged with liquid gold.

He fiddled with the rim of the goblet. "I have nothing to say."

She wasn't about to be put off so easily. "Yes, you do."

His jaw tightened. The sun slid from view beyond the western hills.

"Do you want me to apologize?"

He still wouldn't look at her, but she didn't take her eyes from his face. "I want you to explain."

"I'm going to marry Blaive," he said to the window.

"Why?"

"Because I love her."

The words fell flat and Talia felt empty. "No, you don't."

"I didn't make you any promises, Talia. I was flirting with you. That's all."

"That isn't all," she said fiercely. "And you know it!"

He jerked away from the window, wine sloshing over the rim of his cup. "You were betrothed to Wen from the beginning. I was always meant for Blaive. There never could have been anything between us."

"You said you'd talk to your father. Get him to call off my engagement to Wen."

"It was nothing more than a meaningless dalliance. I was

angry with Wen, and I wanted to hurt him. Anything that happened after that—*gods.*" He cut himself off. "I'm sorry if you took it for something more than that, but that's all the apology I can offer."

"You bought me Ahdairon. You kissed me. You promised to help me reclaim the gods-damned Empire. You told me you *loved me*—"

"I never loved you."

"You said—"

"I. Never. Loved you." Every word was hard as flint. "I love *Blaive*, and I'm marrying her in the morning. That's the end of it."

She set her jaw. "Blaive was right, Caiden Estahr-Sol. You always do what your father tells you."

His eyes burned holes straight through her.

"I wish you much happiness," she choked out. "Both of you."

And then she left him alone by the window in the swiftly gathering dark.

It was freezing in the stone building on the top of the hill, the relative warmth of the Ruen-Dahr seeming far away. Candles filled the niches in the walls, flames dancing bright, but there was no fire to combat the harsh winter wind seeping in under the door.

This place had once been a temple—the walls were carved with scenes from mythology, and there was an ancient stone altar at the back of the room. It reminded Talia of the forgotten temple beneath the garden, but there were no mythical relics here. Sometime in the last century hard wooden benches had been brought in, two rows of four arranged on either side of a short center aisle. Unaccountably, the whole place smelled like summer and heady wine. It overflowed with flowers: snowdrops and primroses, daisies and lavender and heather. There were even bundles of cabbage roses from the florist's hothouse.

Talia sat stiff on one of the benches, clamping her teeth together to keep from shivering. Wen was sitting on her right, a few handbreadths away. His cravat was neatly tied, his jaw shaved smooth. But she still glimpsed ink stains on his fingers. They hadn't spoken much since the night in the old Baronesses' suite, but the sight of him always relieved her, a breath of fresh air in the stuffy confines of the Ruen-Dahr.

Blaive's father and her two younger sisters sat across the aisle, while the Baron and Caiden stood near the old altar. The wedding had been planned too suddenly for any of Ryn's aristocracy to arrange travel in the dead of winter, and, from Ro's account, the Baron hadn't spoken to any of them in a decade, anyway. Still, it seemed almost a somber affair, despite the flowers.

The Baron was shaky on his feet, leaning heavily on a gold-headed cane shaped like a bird. He looked incredibly ill—the carriage ride couldn't possibly have been good for him.

She didn't want to look at Caiden, but she forced herself to. He was dressed formally, in a crisp midnight-blue suit and cravat, his hair meticulously trimmed. He stood rigid, his eyes staring away beyond her to the door, waiting for his bride.

Waiting for Blaive.

Talia hadn't wanted to come, but she'd allowed herself to be woken early and handed into the hired carriage with Wen and the Baron. She should have hidden up in the library.

Bells rang bright outside the old temple's door, and Talia rose to her feet, along with Wen and Blaive's father and sisters. Suddenly she wasn't thinking about the cold anymore.

The door burst open and Blaive came in, snow clinging to her golden hair despite the canopy her maidservant was dutifully holding over her head. The maid tugged the door shut again and

Blaive swept slowly up the aisle, regal as the Empress, radiant as the sun. She was wearing a bright-blue gown, trimmed with white fur and silver beading, a cascade of snowdrops woven into her hair.

Blaive went to join Caiden at the front of the room, joy alive in her eyes. He regarded her with a distant smile, and took her hand. They knelt together before the altar while the Baron spoke the formal words of binding. His voice was as shuddery as he was, but echoed clearly in the stone chamber:

"As the Stars shone with one light, may you be one. As the Tree flourished upon the earth, may you flourish. Until the last Star falls from heaven, may your love endure. Until death parts you, may you be true. Until time itself is ended, may you be of one mind and one heart and one soul."

The images from the mirrors unfolded behind Talia's eyes, and she tried not to shudder.

"Caiden Estahr-Sol, heir of Ryn. Do you bind yourself to this lady? To guard her and keep her for all of time?"

Talia felt the sudden touch of warm fingers against her cold ones, and she glanced down to find that Wen had taken her hand.

"I bind myself," said Caiden, his eyes boring straight into Blaive's, "for all of time."

"Blaive Nahm-Aina, heiress of Shold. Do you bind yourself to this man? To guard him and keep him for all of time?"

Wen didn't let go, and Talia held tight to him, glad he was standing there with her. He smiled at her, a soft, sad smile, and squeezed her hand. She squeezed back.

"I bind myself," said Blaive, her quavery words echoing among the stones, "for all of time."

"Then by the will of the gods and the One who created them, let it be so."

"By the will of the gods," Caiden said.

"Let it be so," Blaive whispered.

Caiden drew her to her feet again, and they stared at each other, something strong and almost tangible rippling between them: a thread, once broken, knotted together again.

Then Caiden bent his head and kissed his bride on the lips. And Wen didn't let go of Talia's hand.

They had an early luncheon in the village inn to celebrate the marriage—Talia and Wen, the Baron, Blaive's father and sisters, Caiden and his new bride. A modest affair to be sure, Ro had gossiped to Talia earlier, but with the Baron's debts it was all he could really afford.

Flowers overwhelmed the small common room; they spilled over the fireplace mantel, wound around the cast-iron lamps in the ceiling, draped across the long wooden tables.

The eight of them sat around one table, dining on soup and pheasant and roasted mushrooms, savory pies and fresh greens. They sipped rose wine and currant tea, nibbling on little cakes dusted with powdered sugar.

Talia ate everything without tasting it. She tried not to stare at the heavy gold ring on Caiden's right hand, or his left hand either, brown fingers interlaced with Blaive's pale ones. She tried not to look when Blaive's sisters teased the new couple into kissing in front of everyone, multiple times. She tried not to see the light in Caiden's eyes as he smiled at his new bride. They would be leaving on their honeymoon today, traveling to the seaport on the other side of Ryn, three weeks in a luxurious inn looking out over the sea.

She didn't want to think about it, but she couldn't seem to think about anything else. The heat of the roaring fire and the heady scent of flowers felt oppressive, the room closing in around her.

She caught movement out of the corner of her eye, and

glanced sideways to see Wen shrugging into his coat. He jerked his chin at the door, and relief blossomed in her chest—he was offering her a chance at escape.

She murmured something to the Baron, which he probably didn't hear, and left the table, grabbing her cloak from the wall. She settled it onto her shoulders and followed Wen out into the street.

It was quieter outside the inn, a hush fallen around the tiny village. She pulled the hood of the cloak up over her hair, blinking snow out of her eyes.

Wen smiled a little. "Impossible to breathe in there. I hate to think how many flowers Blaive would have gotten if she'd had more than three weeks to order them."

She couldn't quite laugh yet, but she cracked a smile for him. "We would have drowned in primroses and snowdrops." She drew a breath of icy air that cut deep into her lungs.

"Walk back with me?" he said.

"Five miles in all this snow?"

He shrugged, another smile playing about his lips. "Better than waiting out that interminable dinner." He waved one hand at the inn behind him.

"True." She looked at the blanketed road, winding its slow white way up to the Ruen-Dahr. Her heart felt quieter with Wen there.

"Shall we?" He offered her his arm.

She rested her fingers lightly on his sleeve; she'd forgotten her gloves inside, but she wasn't about to go back and retrieve them.

They walked awhile in silence, snow catching white in Wen's hair and caking the hood of Talia's cloak. The world was hushed and still around them.

"Thank you," she said softly, leaning into him as they went.

His eyes were bright in the winter storm. "At our wedding," he said, his tone mild and teasing, "let's skip the luncheon."

At that, she did laugh.

Chapter Thirty-Two

LOSING CAIDEN WASN'T AS HARD AS SHE thought it would be. She didn't feel like she would die, or that there was a knife twisting in her heart, or anything melodramatic enough for one of Ayah's stories.

She simply felt empty.

A ship without a course.

A bird without wings.

But she refused to stoop to pining for him like a neglected hound.

Winter settled heavily over the house, the snow there to stay. It was too cold to go riding. Too cold to do anything but scour the library for answers she was unsure existed, plot out her repairs for the ship, and try not to think about everything she'd lost.

Sometimes she sat with Wen in the music room or had tea with him in the parlor. His presence relaxed her, his easy smile warming her from the inside. But then he would ask what she was reading about in the library, and she had to lie to him. He knew it, too—she could see it in his eyes. But he never pressed her.

One evening, halfway through Caiden and Blaive's honeymoon, Talia went up to the library as usual and peered again at the titles on the shelves. There were hardly any books of myths left that she hadn't read, but she grabbed one of them and settled by the fire, pulling a blanket over her knees.

She was scarcely two pages in when she realized it was the story she had been searching for without realizing it—the story that would save her, or damn her. Or both.

Long ago there lived a maiden called Lida in the land of Od. She dwelt with her father and sister in a tiny village on the edge of the sea and her father, a painter, was very poor.

Both Lida and her sister, Dahna, were beautiful: Lida had hair the color of light, while Dahna's was black as the void.

And Lida loved Cyne, the governor's son, for he was kindhearted and handsome and never seemed to stop smiling. She cherished him a long while, mourning because she had no dowry. But her heart was full of laughter and goodness, and Cyne saw it and came to love her in return, though he kept it to himself.

On a cloudy day in spring, Cyne saw Lida walking alone upon the seashore, and his heart was pricked, for she wept into the wind. He came up to her and took her hand, and asked her the cause of her sadness.

"Oh, my lord," she said. "I love a man who is above me, and I can offer him no dowry, for my father is poor."

Then Cyne wiped away her tears. "A strange tale indeed," he said, "for I love a lady whose father is poor, and I care not for any dowry."

And Lida looked into his eyes and saw the love he had for her, and she smiled.

Then Cyne gathered her into his arms and kissed her, and they pledged their troth as the sea crashed upon the shore.

But Dahna saw Cyne kiss her sister and was filled with rage, for she had loved Cyne many years. The wind rose up and her hair blew wildly about her, a crown for her head, raven black.

Preparations began at once, for Lida and Cyne were to be married with the autumn. All the village women aided Lida in sewing linens, tailoring the bridal gown, and readying the house she was to share with her husband.

And Lida was filled with joy, her radiance increasing as the wedding day drew near. But the blackness in Dahna's heart grew until it had consumed her, and she knew only jealousy and hatred.

On the eve of the marriage, Dahna clothed herself in false smiles, and asked Lida to walk with her on the beach, that they might share one last evening together before her husband took her away.

And Lida was glad and consented, and the sisters wandered together over the sand as the Sun sank westward in a blaze of yellow fire.

They walked very far, and Lida began to grow fearful of the coming night and exhaustion in the morning. "Come, sister," she said. "Let us go back."

"It is not yet night. Come with me, just a little further." And Dahna pulled her on.

The sun dropped out of sight over the rim of the world.

"Please, Dahna," said Lida, touching her sister's arm. "We must go back now. We have walked too far and I am very tired."

Then Dahna turned in a rage, and, seizing her sister with a grip of iron, dragged her into the sea.

Lida cried out in fear, for the waves grasped at her, choking her breath away, and her sister was strong. She struggled and looked up into Dahna's face and saw that she was laughing.

"You shall not have him!" cried Dahna. "If I cannot have him, neither shall you!" Then Dahna pushed Lida's head under the water and would not let her up, no matter how Lida writhed in her grasp. She held her there until Lida grew weaker and weaker, and her body was at last limp and still.

Then Dahna looked up into the sky and felt very cold, but she did not regret what she had done.

She did not return to the village, not that night nor any night after, and no tale tells what happened to her.

It was three days before an old fisherman found the body of Lida, and sent her to rest beneath the waves, as was his custom. When Cyne heard it his heart broke, for the sea had robbed him of even one last glance at his bride. He mourned and raged, longing for death to claim him too, that he and his love might be together for eternity.

He wandered often along the shores of the sea, staring out into its endless waves. He remembered the stories he had heard in his childhood—tales of the Immortal Tree, of Rahn and the Hall where she sat enthroned, the dead of the sea dancing before her. He thought of Lida alone in the faceless masses in the Hall of the Dead, and he determined not to resign her to such a bitter fate.

So Cyne built a ship with the wood of a few scarce trees that grew on the shore of Od, and he strengthened it with the ancient Words of power and set off into the deep waters, on a night that burned with stars.

Long years he sailed on the Northern Sea, and his love for Lida made him strong.

One morning, he lifted his eyes and at last saw the Tree, reaching up from the depths, the blue-and-silver serpents circling it. But Cyne was not afraid, for he bore his father's sword. It burned with white fire, and was said to have been made in the days when mankind dwelt under the shadow of that selfsame Tree.

The serpents feared the sword, and let him pass.

Then speaking aloud the Words he had long studied in his father's library, Cyne turned himself into a sea-dragon, and dove into the water.

He followed the trunk of the Tree many fathoms down, and his love for Lida and the Words that guarded him made him strong.

At last he came into Rahn's Hall, and, shedding the sea-dragon form, he held his sword high. He beheld the dead, and Lida among them, weeping for the pain of her torment. He gave a cry, and, springing to her side, he seized her hand and led her to the dais, where Rahn sat enthroned, the Star bright on her finger.

Then Rahn looked upon him and was surprised, for she had seen no living man for many centuries. "What do you do here, son of the dust? You are not among the dead: I see the life that burns still in your eyes. Why have you come to my Hall?"

And Cyne answered, "I come here for the great love I bear this maiden, who was drowned on the eve of our wedding. Release her soul from your Hall and let her return with me—let her still be my bride. She should not yet dwell among the dead."

And Rahn saw the fire in his eyes and the flame of the sword which the sea could not quench. Never had such a thing been asked of her, and never before had she seen such love in the face of a man.

"Let her return to the light," said Cyne.

Then Rahn looked into his heart and saw that it was pure, and she almost repented of the murder of Aigir, wishing suddenly for the love he had once borne her. She lifted her hand so the Star blazed brighter. "Take her, son of the dust. It will not matter in the end, when I rule the earth as well as the sea and all mankind are in chains. Take her, and leave my Hall, and return here no more."

And Cyne rejoiced, and bore Lida up with him to the surface of the sea, setting her within his ship.

Then Lida stirred and woke and lived, and he kissed her under the sky and wept long. They sailed together many months upon the sea, returning at last to Od where they were met with much rejoicing, and were at last wed.

Long and happily they lived beneath the sun, and when they died they died together, and the One who was before the gods gathered them beyond the circles of Endahr, and there they dwell in peace for all eternity. But their children set a watch over the sea, lest Rahn come ever to the shores of the earth and sought to claim it. And they watch still.

It was possible, then.

Dread prickled down her spine and she closed the book, staring blankly into the fire. Could she really hang her entire future on such an absurd story? A sword that burned in the ocean. A man changing into a sea-dragon. A dead bride brought back to life.

But wasn't that what she wanted for her mother? Wasn't that what the gods were calling her to do, with their dreams and their mirrors and their ships in hidden coves? She didn't want to think about Rahn leaving the sea, or that the gods might want her to do something about it. Saving her mother was hopeless enough. She refused to worry about the fate of the whole world as well.

She gnawed on her lip, frustrated, and got up from her chair. "Talia?"

She wheeled around to see Wen standing in the doorway. His face was white as marble, every freckle standing out in stark relief.

"Wen! What's wrong?"

For a moment he just stared at her, jaw working but no words coming out. He blinked. Swallowed. "The Baron's dead," he said. Then, voice cracking, "My father's dead."

"What?" she whispered, reaching out to touch his arm.

"I don't know what to do. Ahned's gone to the village for a priest and to send word to Caiden and I—I don't know what to do." His face twisted.

"Oh, Wen." She put her arm around him and he sagged against her, heavy and cold. "Do you want to . . . do you want to sit with him? Until Ahned comes back?"

He nodded, and they walked together down from the library and into the Baron's bedchamber, Wen stumbling and dazed, Talia supporting him as much as she could. Flames burned weakly in the hearth, and a pair of heavy drapes were pulled tight over the window, blocking out the winter snow. A lamp glowed, flickering orange over the Baron's still form.

Wen stared at his dead father, and Talia ached for him.

"He was ill yesterday," Wen said. "Ahned and I took turns sitting up with him. He was coughing, struggling to breathe, and then he just . . . he just . . . stopped."

"Oh, Wen."

"I don't think he ever forgave me for what I told him about the mirror room. About my mother. I always disappointed him, from the moment I was born. I don't think he ever fell out of love with Caiden's mother. I don't think he ever fully loved mine."

Or me, his unspoken words echoed after him.

Talia blinked back the sudden press of tears and slid her hand into Wen's. "I'm sure he loved you very much."

They stood together looking down at the Baron for a long while, as the fire turned to ash and the wind moaned outside the house. Talia didn't let go of his hand. This time it was her being strong, her being steady. But she stared at the Baron's gray skin and saw her mother, clothed in death, drowning forever beneath the haunting sea.

Chapter Thirty-Three

THEY CAME BACK FROM THEIR HONEYMOON IN the middle of a blizzard, the horses tugging the carriage through the quickly drifting snow. Wen braved the cold to go out and meet them, while Talia watched from the window.

He unfolded a canopy and held it over his new sister-in-law's head to shield her from the worst of the snow during the short walk to the house. His shoulders were slumped, his frame weighed down with grief.

As the trio approached the door, Talia hid behind the curve of the stair like a coward.

Wen and Blaive came in first, the new bride's cheeks flushed and her eyes sparking fire. Caiden followed just after, shaking the snow from his coat and his dark hair, glancing once over his shoulder to shout instructions to Ahned regarding the trunks.

Wen folded the canopy and Blaive shrugged out of her cloak. Lyna took both cloak and canopy and disappeared down the hall.

"You got the message, then," said Wen, all stiffness and fettered sorrow.

Caiden rubbed a hand over his eyes. He looked exhausted. "Last evening. We came as quickly as we could. We'll hold the funeral today?"

Wen nodded. "This afternoon."

Blaive hovered near Caiden, her cheeks pink with delicate worry. "Darling, I'm so sorry."

He waved her off, rubbing at his forehead.

Darling. Even now, the careless endearment made Talia's face heat. She should leave her hiding place, offer her condolences. But she just stayed in the shelter of the stair.

"Shall we go and change?" Blaive's fingers whispered across Caiden's sleeve.

"You go ahead. I'm fine as I am."

"But we should wear our mourning whites. Show proper respect to your poor father."

"*Later,*" Caiden snapped.

Her face colored. "All right." She swept upstairs, her gown brushing over the carpet.

Talia still didn't move. She heard the clatter of wheels over stone in the courtyard, the carriage heading back to the village.

"How is she?" said Caiden, turning his glance to Wen.

Talia drew a sharp breath.

Wen looked his brother square in the face, anger hard in his eyes. "Are you so indifferent to our father's death that you *dare* ask me that?"

"Please tell me. Is she . . . well?"

"If you're asking whether she's made herself sick for the love of you, I can assure you she has not."

"Don't mock me, Wen."

"Mock you?" Wen's jaw ground hard. "You threw her away like she was nothing."

"You don't understand!" Caiden slammed the heel of his right hand against the wall, making Talia jump. "Father would have disinherited me, cut me off from everything—"

Wen shook his head. "I realize that. I know, Caiden. I do.

But Father is dead, now. How can you not even *care?*"

Caiden's eyes flashed, wild and angry. "If he'd died two weeks earlier, I wouldn't have had to marry Blaive!"

Wen cursed and punched Caiden in the face so hard he stumbled backward, blood springing bright on his lip.

Caiden swore at him and walked away up the stairs, his boots ringing loud.

Talia felt strange and confused and awful, to her core. Wen looked over and caught her eye. Had he known she was there the whole time?

He was shaking, and there was blood on his knuckles. "I can't believe he doesn't care."

Talia swallowed and left her hiding place to go over to him. "He shouldn't have said that. Any of it." It hurt to see the tears brimming in his eyes. She lightly touched his arm. "He cares, Wen. Of course he does. He just doesn't realize it yet."

They laid Baron Graimed Dacien-Tuer to rest on the hill outside the garden, between his two wives, the headstones of his ancestors in scattered rows behind them. Wen and Caiden lowered their father's casket into the grave, while an ancient priest from the village intoned the benediction in his dust-dry voice, and Talia and Blaive and Ahned looked on. Snow settled heavily on Talia's shoulders, catching on her eyelashes, blurring her vision with white.

Caiden dropped a handful of earth into the grave, his face as expressionless as stone, his jaw swollen where Wen had hit him. Wen threw another handful, dirt falling and skittering like ice across the wood of his father's casket. His shoulders were stiff, his eyes wet.

"May your spirit be gathered beyond the circles of the

world," said the priest, "and your body rest quiet until the end of time, when the world is unmade."

The wind whirled the words around her, the same ones she'd said in the ship for her mother. The only eulogy she knew.

"Until the end of time," they all echoed together around the grave, pale ghosts in mourning whites to match the snow. Talia couldn't help but think that the Baron was at peace now, and her mother was not. Her throat caught, and she could barely finish with the others: "When the world is unmade."

And then it was over. Ahned and the priest set to work filling in the grave as Caiden led the way back into the house.

The servants had tea and a roaring fire waiting for them in the parlor, but no one seemed particularly hungry.

Blaive settled into a chair near the fire and poured tea that she didn't touch, while Caiden took up a post by the window, his back to the room. Talia sat down across from Blaive. Wen leaned against the fireplace mantel, fidgeting with the hem of his white jacket.

Snow fell on outside the window. No one spoke.

Talia willed Wen to look at her, but he just stared at the floor.

Blaive cleared her throat and curled her fingers around her teacup. "A very sad day," she said, the silence evidently making her uncomfortable.

"It isn't sad for him," said Caiden from the window. "This is all he ever wanted. To be with them again."

"Shut up," said Wen.

But Caiden wasn't finished. "He's been dying for ten years. We ought to congratulate him on his success at last."

"Shut *up!*" Wen cried.

Caiden jerked away from the window, rage hard in his eyes. "Or *what*, little brother?"

"Father deserves our respect."

"Why? He certainly never respected *you*."

Wen ground his jaw. "Because he's our father, and whatever his faults, he loved us."

"After his own fashion," Caiden sneered.

Blaive twisted her hands in her lap, clearly out of her depth. "It's unlucky to speak ill of the dead," she said quietly.

"Don't pretend *you* had any great love for my father," Caiden snapped at her. "You used him. Manipulated him into forcing this marriage on me."

Her face tightened. "You're just a boy used to obeying his father. Now he's gone and you haven't any idea what to do."

"Stars' fire take you," Caiden spat, and strode abruptly from the room. Blaive looked after him, gnawing on her lip, and then got up and followed, white skirts skimming over the floor in her wake.

Talia looked at Wen, who paced over to the window and stood staring out at the snow.

"I watched my mother drown," he said quietly. "Did I ever tell you that? I ran out onto the beach that day in the storm. I saw her boat cast off from the shore and the wind catch her sail, tearing it to pieces. I saw her capsize, struggling in the water. I ran down the shore, tried to reach her, but I was too late—and too small to help her. I didn't understand why she would leave us like that. She was my whole world, and then she was gone. It took both my father and Ahned to drag her body back to shore." He shuddered.

Talia went over to him, laying one hand on his shoulder. Tears pressed behind her eyes. "I'm sorry, Wen. You don't know how much."

"We buried her on the hill, like we did my father, just now. I stood there at her grave and hated everything. My father. My brother. The earth, the gods. Because I didn't understand. But I do, now." He turned from the window, his blue gaze focused on her. "I understand that you should never throw your life away. Not when you're leaving the ones you love behind. Life is precious. No matter what Caiden says, my father—my father shouldn't have sought out death. Shouldn't have wished for it. Shouldn't have welcomed it when it came."

Her stomach wrenched. "But what if the ones you love go ahead of you? What if you could bring them back?" It was unfair of her to ask him that, but she couldn't help herself.

He blinked, and she was shocked to see a tear sliding down his cheek. "The dead are the dead, Talia Dahl-Saida. There's no changing that. You can't bring them back."

But she thought about her dreams, about the myths and the visions she'd seen in the mirror, and she knew he was wrong.

Chapter Thirty-Four

"TALIA?"

Someone caught her arm in the hall just outside her room, and she turned to see Caiden standing there, his dark hair hanging limp in his eyes, his white cravat loose at his neck.

She stepped back and he released her, but his gaze never left her face. "What do you want?" she asked him, wary. Outside the Ruen-Dahr it was full night, the Baron several hours in his grave. Inside, lamplight flickered orange from its wall sconce.

A muscle jumped in Caiden's jaw. He was nervous. "I haven't stopped thinking about you since I left."

She dug her fingernails into her palm. "I don't want to talk to you, Caiden."

"I know, but—" He took a step toward her. "I have to tell you that—that I'm sorry. That I miss you. That I—that I love you—"

"Get away from me!" she snapped angrily. "You made it very clear that you never loved me." She stalked away from him, heading toward the stairs and the meal waiting in the dining room, but he followed, grabbing for her hand. She shook him off. "Leave me alone!"

"Talia, listen. Please. I *do* love you. You have to understand. It was just my father. And now that he's gone—well, that changes everything." He stared at her, willing her to hear him. He licked his lips, another nervous tic.

"Stay with me. I'll find a lawyer to dissolve my marriage with Blaive, I'll make *you* my wife, in name as well as in truth. Please, Talia. Please." His voice was rough with tears.

She recoiled, like she'd stepped into a pit of snakes. "I could never stay with you after everything you've done—not as your wife and *certainly* not as your mistress! If you let go of your selfishness for half a moment, you might make something of your situation—of yourself—and be the better for it. But there's no future for us."

"Please, Talia—"

"Goodbye, Caiden."

She left him in the hallway and swept downstairs, every nerve on fire.

Talia stepped into the dining room and found Blaive there, alone, her head in her hands. She looked up, and Talia saw that her soft face was streaked with tears. "I thought I could make him forget you, but I was wrong. He doesn't want me. He wants you."

Talia's skin was still crawling at Caiden's words. "No, he doesn't. Or he won't for very long." She looked into the other girl's eyes. "He wants what he can't have. What he'll never have."

Blaive bit her lip, chin trembling. "He barely speaks to me. He hardly *looks* at me. He can't forgive me for manipulating his father—"

"He shouldn't treat you like that no matter what you did. It was *his* choice to marry you. No one forced him to do it."

"But the Baron—"

"It doesn't matter," said Talia, gently.

Fresh tears slid down Blaive's pale cheeks. "He loved me, once." Her voice cracked. "Two years ago, now. He teased me and I laughed at him and we were so happy."

"What happened?"

"We quarreled. It was foolish, but I was sixteen and I wanted my way and he wanted his and—I went home and he didn't come after me. I was too proud to write him, and so I didn't. But I forgave him. I thought he would appear at Shold House one day, and we'd both apologize, and be married. Live out our lives together. Be impossibly happy." She wiped her face with the back of her hand, curls sticking to her damp face. "But he didn't. And then the Baron wrote me, inviting me back to the Ruen-Dahr, implying that Caiden was ready to marry, but I didn't know he'd written without Caiden's consent. I didn't know Caiden had really forgotten all about me."

Talia swallowed past her tight throat. "I'm so sorry."

Blaive caught her eye and smiled sadly. "It wasn't your doing."

"Even so." She had the sudden realization that the two of them could have been friends, perhaps, in another lifetime, in some other story. She smiled back.

Talia went directly to the music room, praying she wouldn't bump into Caiden again on her way. Wen was sitting at the raina, mourning clothes hanging too-loose on his thin frame.

"Wen?"

He looked up, eyes unfocused behind his spectacles, and practically leapt from his seat to come over to her. "What's wrong?" He folded his hand around hers.

"I—I have a favor to ask."

"Anything. Anything at all."

"I need to go away for a while. I thought—I thought maybe

you would let me stay at your holding for a few weeks—for the rest of the winter, perhaps." It would be easier, when she was away from here. Away from Caiden and the sea and her fate. She'd be able to *think* again.

"Of course you may stay at the Ruen-Shained, for as long as you wish," he said, his eyes dark with concern. "What's happened?"

"I just—I need to—I can't see Caiden again."

Anger hardened his face. "What did he do to you?"

"Nothing." She tried to smile. "Nothing, Wen. I promise. I just need to go away."

He studied her a moment more. "When would you like to leave?"

"Tonight. At once, if possible."

Wen glanced out the window and nodded. It had stopped snowing. "Give me half an hour to arrange everything."

There was only time for one trip up to the library—she grabbed as many books off the shelves as she could carry and brought them down to her room. She packed quickly, stuffing the books and an assortment of the dead Baronesses' gowns into two ragged carpetbags she unearthed from the wardrobe. Then she settled her fur-lined cloak around her shoulders, and she was ready.

Wen appeared at her door and offered to carry the bags for her, but she only gave him one, hefting the other herself. She followed him downstairs, across the foyer, and out into the snowy drive. Ahned was waiting with Avial and Ahdairon, and he quickly loaded Talia's bags onto the saddles.

It was freezing; the horses' breath fogged in front of them, and Talia's toes were already going numb. She swung up onto Ahdairon, and Wen mounted Avial, taking the lantern Ahned handed him.

Wen nudged the gelding into a trot, and Talia followed on the mare, the wind sharp and icy on her skin. The lantern bobbed from Wen's saddle, a wayward star in the dark.

They arrived almost before she was ready to, trotting up to the house, light spilling from the windows like liquid gold onto the snow-covered drive. Wen swung down and handed his reins to Talia while he went to speak with the housekeeper. She sat and waited for him, staring up at the hesitant winter stars peeking through a patch of cloud.

Wen and Anira came out a few minutes later, the housekeeper all hugs and smiles, Wen solemn and steady beside her.

"Miss Dahl-Saida," said Anira, helping Talia off Ahdairon. "I was so sorry to hear about the Baron's passing. A little peace and quiet will do you good, I'm sure of it."

Wen untied the bags, and the tall servant who reminded Talia so strongly of Ahned took them inside. "If you need anything, just send word. I'll come as quickly as I can."

She looked at Wen, standing there in the drive with his hands stuffed into his pockets, and she wished suddenly that he would stay with her. "Are you going to be all right?"

He shrugged. "I'm always all right."

"No, you're not." She brushed her fingers briefly across his sleeve. "I'm sorry about your father."

He caught her hand with his own, pressed it tight. "I'm a ride away if you need anything. Goodbye, Talia."

And then he swung back up onto the gelding and rode away into the winter darkness, leaving her with a faint sensation of loss that didn't quite fade with his hoofbeats.

Chapter Thirty-Five

I N THE MORNING, TALIA PULLED ON A worn gown and slipped downstairs, nearly colliding with Anira and a laden breakfast tray.

"I was just about to bring this up for you, Miss."

"I fear I'm not hungry just yet. I actually wanted to ask if I could borrow a shovel."

"A shovel?"

Talia shoved her hands in her pockets and tried to look innocent. "I thought I'd do some gardening."

The old servingwoman raised her eyebrows, laughter lines crinkling her papery cheeks. "While it's still winter? Dearie, you aren't going to be gardening."

Talia opened her mouth to protest, but Anira held up one hand. "Master Wendarien left instructions that you need quiet and peace. We're not to interfere with any . . . gardening . . . you might wish to do." She winked. "I'll find you that shovel."

And that was that.

She slogged through the snow down to the hidden cove, the shovel slung over her shoulder, a lantern dangling from one hand.

She set to work, beginning the long job of digging the

ship out of the sand. It was harder than she thought, and she regretted skipping breakfast. She dug and dug, until her hands started to blister and the sea crept in at her heels, knocking over the lantern. The light snuffed out.

Talia yelped, and scrambled out onto the shore again.

This was going to take much longer than a day.

She trudged back to the Ruen-Shained, vowing to be better prepared tomorrow.

For the rest of the day she poured through the books she'd brought from the library, searching for further mentions of journeying to Rahn's Hall. Anira brought her tea. The white cat curled up on her feet and fell asleep, but Talia didn't notice.

She read a book about Ryn's history, and found an interesting tidbit about the Ruen-Dahr: It was reportedly built by a sailor nearly four centuries earlier in order to "set a watch on the sea." Talia found the phrasing intriguing, especially considering how similar it was to the end of the myth about Lida and Cyne. Their children had "set a watch" because of Rahn. Was that the purpose of the Ruen-Dahr?

Talia didn't want to think about that. She shut the book and switched to one about ship repair.

When night came, she left her books in the parlor and went upstairs to the cozy room Anira had given her. A white moon looked in through her window as she pulled the dead Baronesses' gowns from the carpetbags and took them apart, seam by seam.

It was very late when she'd finished, but sleep was awhile coming. Even here, a mile away from the sea, she could hear the music, twisting in her mind, burrowing into her heart. Calling her down to Rahn's Hall. When at last she slept, the haunting melodies followed her into her dreams.

Her days settled into a pattern, and gradually her plans started to take shape.

In the mornings, she went out to the cove and dug until the

tide drove her away, slowly uncovering the boat. It turned out to be bigger than she imagined: a dinghy over twenty feet long, with a fitting for a mast that must have long since rotted away.

In the afternoons she read and read, as much as she could about the gods. She'd found a whole book about their Words, fascinating accounts of men and women who used them to transform into various creatures and move mountains. But it wasn't the book Wen had told her about, filled with the actual Words themselves, and turned out to be vastly less helpful than she'd hoped.

She found a story about a girl called Dia, who sailed to the Hall of the Dead to rescue her brother. When Rahn wouldn't let him go, Dia chose to stay in his place among the dancers so her brother could be free. That wasn't quite the solution Talia was looking for, but at least it gave her more proof that the Hall could be found.

She read about sailing and ship repair, grateful for all the things Hanid had taught her so many months ago. She hunted through the Ruen-Shained's disused study and found half a dozen crackly old charts of the Northern Sea, a tarnished but functioning sextant, and an ancient compass in perfect working order.

In the evenings, Talia sewed together her patchwork sail with the material from the dismantled gowns. It grew before her, billowing over her knees like a multicolored wave.

And at night, when she fell asleep, she dreamed of the sea, of herself tormented in her mother's place, black water crushing her into oblivion.

It took her almost a week to fully uncover the boat, her hands blistering against the rough wood of the shovel. But she managed it at last and was pleased to see that the ship was in remarkable shape. No cracks in the hull or the stern. A workable rudder, even an ancient oar lying in the bottom. She'd need to find a mast, somehow, and seal the outside of the ship with pitch and work up all the riggings. But the little ship seemed to be as sound as if the gods themselves had bound it with Words of protection. Maybe they had.

The afternoon she freed the ship, Talia trudged back to the Ruen-Shained to find Wen perched on the front steps, his long legs stretched out in front of him. He leapt to his feet when he caught sight of her.

"Thought I'd come visit, see how you were. If you don't mind, of course," he added hurriedly.

"Not at all. It's good to see you." She smiled, glad she'd washed most of the grime off her hands in the ocean before coming back—though there was no hiding the mud on her hem.

If Wen noticed, he didn't say anything. He smiled in return, and they walked into the house, shutting the door against the cold wind. The snow had melted over the last few days, but it wasn't warm enough to stand around outside for very long.

"Tell me all the news," said Talia.

Wen leaned back against the door. "Blaive's decided to redecorate. Dairon is all in a huff, and Ahned's frowning deeply at the amount of money she's spending. No one's told him about the party she's planning yet."

Talia laughed. "She's gotten bored."

He grinned at her, a dimple pressing into his cheek. "Indeed."

"What about you?"

He sobered a little, and scratched at his ear. "Same as always. Writing too much. Spending too many hours in the music room."

It was only then that Talia noticed the dark circles under his eyes. "You haven't been sleeping," she said with concern.

"I've been worried about you."

"You came to check up on me." She said it gently, so he'd

know she wasn't angry.

"I'm glad you haven't slipped off anywhere," he admitted.

She poked him in the arm. "I promised I wouldn't do anything crazy, remember?"

"I'm not sure you are entirely trustworthy, Miss Dahl-Saida."

They had tea in the parlor, Talia shoving her books off the table before Wen could look at the titles too closely. She pulled up an extra chair by the fire and they sat, sipping their tea and eating cake and playing with the white cat, who kept trying to sneak his head into the cream.

It felt strangely comfortable, being there with him.

Suddenly she was aware of the ring on her right hand, dirt ground into the silver whorls from her work digging out the ship. For the first time since the day Wen had put it on her finger, she didn't mind it so much.

Wen sensed the change in her. "Talia?"

"What about our wedding?" The words tumbled from her lips without her permission, but she didn't regret them.

He studied her for a moment without replying, absently petting the cat who had curled up on his knees. "I'm not going to make you do something you don't want to do," he said at last. "My—my father isn't here anymore to press the issue. And as the new Baron, Caiden . . . well, Caiden won't either. We . . ." Wen's lips twitched a little. " . . . discussed it," he finished vaguely, waving one hand.

Talia wondered if Wen's fist had found Caiden's face again. She wouldn't mind if it had. "And the Empress's contract?"

"Caiden and I discussed that, too. We have it handled."

She didn't press him, and he turned his gaze to the white cat, who was purring loudly.

She fiddled with the ring, twisting it off her finger and holding it out to him. "You'll be wanting this back, then."

He shook his head. "I want you to have it."

"But it's your mother's—"

He pressed the ring back into her hand. "It's yours now."

Another week slipped by. Then two. Then three. The days began to grow hesitantly warmer, the snow seemingly gone for good, and Talia thought she smelled a hint of spring in the air. But with the improving weather, her anxiety about what she was planning to do sharpened.

Every morning, she walked out to the hidden cove, slowly making the ship seaworthy. She scoured the beach, miraculously finding a sturdy pole that would make a suitable mast. She rode out to the village to order rope and twine and pitch. When the issue of payment came up, the shopkeeper informed her that he'd had word from the Ruen-Dahr to provide her with anything she required, and the bill would be sent to the Baron. That made Talia guilty, but it was far too serendipitous to pass up.

And every few days, Wen came to see her.

He would be waiting when she came back from the cove—lounging on the front steps, or perched on the pasture fence, legs dangling, or playing with the cat in the parlor.

He told her all the gossip from the Ruen-Dahr. Blaive's remodeling project and party plans had the whole house in an uproar. Artisans and chefs and seamstresses were tramping through at all hours of the day, disrupting Dairon's careful routine, demanding payment that wasn't strictly available. The housekeeper grew so agitated Ahned had to send her off on holiday, and, meanwhile, Lyna and Ro were quarreling with Blaive's maid to a ridiculous degree.

Wen's stories made her laugh and she enjoyed his company more than she admitted to herself, even though it made her progress with the boat slower than it could have been.

The days he didn't come, she tore through the rest of the books she'd brought from the Ruen-Dahr's library, always searching for more accounts of Rahn's Hall.

One afternoon, her hands cracked and bleeding from her work on the ship, she stepped into the parlor to find Wen conversing with an unfamiliar, black-coated man. They both stood as she entered, bowing solemnly, and she hastily attempted to clean her hands on her filthy skirt to no avail. She curtsied in confusion, not missing the panicked look on Wen's face.

The black-coated man had Enduenan coloring and was perhaps thirty, his face narrow and his brows etched in an eternal frown. "Mrs. Aidar-Holt? I'm Nalin Den-Erras, Her Imperial Majesty's ambassador to Ryn. I've just been speaking to your husband, and it appears everything is in order."

She balked. "My hus—" But Wen caught her eye and shook his head, so she echoed faintly, "In order?"

The ambassador nodded, drawing a sheaf of paper from his breast pocket. "It seems the terms of Her Imperial Majesty's contract have been carried out as instructed. Wendarien assures me you have, in fact, wed?"

Understanding dawned on her.

"Just a month ago," said Wen.

Talia nodded, holding out her right hand so the ambassador could see the ring. She thanked the gods Wen had insisted she keep it.

Den-Erras frowned. "What *have* you been doing to your hands, Mrs. Aidar-Holt?"

She smiled brightly. "Gardening."

He grimaced. "All I need is your marriage papers, then, and I shall return them to Her Imperial Majesty as proof."

"We don't have—"

"Here they are," Wen interrupted, drawing a few sheets of cream paper from a narrow drawer in the sideboard.

Talia had to force herself to not look astonished.

The ambassador glanced over them, frowning all the while, then at last nodded and folded them up. "There is one other thing." From his other pocket, he drew out a stack of letters tied with string, and plopped them in Talia's hands.

She recognized them with a sinking heart—every single letter she'd ever written to Ayah.

"Contact with Enduena is forbidden, Mrs. Aidar-Holt. You are lucky I intercepted your correspondence before Her Imperial Majesty learned of them. She would not be so lenient."

"Huen swallow your liver," Talia muttered under her breath.

Wen choked off a startled laugh.

The ambassador just kept frowning. "I'll wish you good day, then."

Talia stared slack-jawed at Wen, waiting until she heard the front door click shut and hoofbeats fading away from the house before she collapsed onto the floor, laughing so hard her eyes began to stream.

Wen sat beside her, grinning wider than she'd ever seen him. "Well *that* was a narrow escape."

He gave her a handkerchief and she wiped her eyes, still giggling. "What would he have done if he thought we *weren't* married? Frowned severely and thrown us into the sea?"

Wen snorted, which made Talia laugh even harder.

"Seriously, though. How in Endahr did you have marriage papers in the sideboard?"

"I found them in my father's things when we were shutting up his office. They weren't signed, of course, but he had them ready for us. I forged your signature and brought them here a while back, just in case something like this were to happen."

Talia leaned back against the sofa, absently petting the white cat who came to rub against her knee. "I'm glad you did."

He nodded at the letters. "Who are those for?"

"My friend Ayah. She's apprenticed to a palace librarian, always knee-deep in dusty books, and she's originally from Od. You two would have a lot to talk about." Talia sobered. "She'll never know what really happened."

"Maybe I can write to her. Explain things, tuck one of your letters inside of mine. Our wretched ambassador can't have anything to say about that, especially if I send Ahned to see it personally onto a ship."

Talia brushed her finger over the crackly envelopes. "I'd like that."

"Den Arras did have one good question." Wen scooted closer to her, laid gentle fingers on her arm. "What *have* you done to your hands? They're the worst I've ever seen. And don't give me that nonsense about gardening. I've spoken with Anira—you disappear down to the beach every morning."

So he had been paying attention. She didn't know what to say—she just shrugged and shook her head.

He didn't press her. Instead, he cleaned her hands, gently washing the dirt and blood away, bandaging the cuts in strips of white linen. "I wish you'd let me help you, with whatever it is you're doing."

She didn't want to lie to him anymore. "I have to do it alone, Wen. I'm sorry."

He sighed, like that was the answer he'd expected. "Then for the gods' sake, Talia, be careful."

But she couldn't promise that.

Chapter Thirty-Six

I T WAS RAINING AGAIN, FAT DROPS AGAINST the windows. Talia sat reading in the parlor in her usual chair, pouring over stories about Rahn's Hall for the hundredth time, while the white cat purred by her feet. A sudden spattering of hail rattled the glass and she started, knocking her pen off the end table with one elbow. The white cat pounced on it and batted it behind the bookcase, ink splattering all across the carpet.

"Caida's teeth," said Talia, sighing, and she got out of her chair to retrieve the pen. She scrabbled behind the bookcase with one arm, straining to reach, and hit something wedged tight against the wall. It came loose and slid to the floor in a swirl of dust. She sneezed, loudly. The cat leapt up onto her chair.

She sat back on her heels and pulled the object out: a sheaf of yellowed pages, pressed between two loose covers and bound with a length of dirty leather cord. She stared at it for a moment, brushing off the dust and wondering how long ago it had fallen behind the shelf and been forgotten. Or perhaps someone had hidden it. The edges of the cover glimmered with remnants of gold leaf. For some reason, it reminded her of the temple under the hill at the Ruen-Dahr.

She untied the leather cord, taking off the top cover with

care. The pages, creased and brittle with age, were written out by hand in a tight, elegant script.

At the top was written: *The Sorrow of Endain, as told by Ahna Groy-Aild, penned in the seven hundredth year of the Billow Maidens' curse.*

Talia's heart began to race. She grabbed the lamp and rested it beside her, bowing her head over the ancient writing.

But Endain, the youngest Billow Maiden, grew weary in her binding. The power of the sea god flowed stronger in her than her older sisters, and she felt the weight of Rahn's curse more acutely than the rest.

Every month she resisted the pull of the moon, staying at the base of the Tree when the other Waves had already swum to the surface. But the struggle cost her dearly. She could feel the curse writhing within her, stilling her heart, sucking her breath away.

And then her mouth would open of its own accord, and the sea would pull her swiftly upward. Helpless, she joined her sisters' haunted chorus, and sang the sailors to their doom.

Every nine years she and the other Billow Maidens gathered the dead in Rahn's enchanted nets, and dragged them down to the Hall. There, Endain plied the strings of her harp, waiting for the turn of the month and the rising of the crescent moon to call her up again.

She was death.

She was doom.

And she could never break free.

One night, when Endain had bowed under the yoke of her mother's curse for five hundred years, the crescent moon rose out of the sea and she obeyed its bidding. She swam a little apart from her sisters, for she wished to sing in solitude. Their united voices drew the ships in droves; Endain alone sometimes drew no one. If the ships did not come, the sailors did not drown—it was her small rebellion.

But on that evening, the moon rippling silver in the water, a ship bobbed helplessly in the sea very near her. The curse tore the song from her lips, making it echo between moon and waves, louder with every note. She saw that the ship was ruined; its masts were cracked and the sails were sagging, water seeping into the fractured hull. The vessel was slowly sinking.

Only one sailor had survived the wreck, a dark-eyed man with skin that shone like polished copper and hair as black as ink. He was weak and ragged; he had fought hard against the storm that had already doomed his shipmates.

He heard her song and lifted his weary head and saw her there, watching him from the waves. He sat very still.

The curse drove her to swim nearer, and the sailor put his hands upon the rail and dragged himself upright. The ship shuddered and groaned, the water crept higher.

The song wrested itself out of her, and she stared at him and wished she could stop.

"Lady," he said, his eyes fixed on her, "I know what you are. Would you think me a beggar if I asked you to spare me?"

And she found she could answer him, cutting off her music for a time. "I am a slave, sir. It is not within my power to spare you."

"Surely a slave can go against her mistress's bidding if she wishes it."

"I cannot."

The wind stirred through her long hair, and she could hear her sisters in the distance, their music twisting like shards of bone in her heart.

"Spare me, lady," said the sailor. "Deny the will of your mother."

"If I leave you be, the sea will claim you."

"Then take me to shore. I will show you the way."

"You do not wish to descend with me into my mother's Hall?"

"There is no life for me in Rahn's Hall."

"You do not wish to save me then. You think only of yourself."

The sailor's eyes looked long into hers, and she was troubled.

"You are the daughter of the sea god, and I am only a man,"

he said. "What could I hope to do for you that you cannot do for yourself?"

The ship tipped into the water, the waves lapping at the sailor's heels.

His arrogance angered her. "You do not understand the nature of the bond laid upon me."

"Then tell me, that I might understand."

"I must rise to the surface with every crescent moon and sing to the ships. I must gather the dead every nine years, and bring them to my mother. It is my doom, and I cannot disobey."

"Does the curse say you must go down to the Hall again when you have sung?" the sailor objected. "Does the curse forbid you from going where you will the other eight years? Does it deny you the ability to visit the shores of the world?"

She did not answer. She did not know how.

The ship shuddered, sinking below the surface of the sea. The sailor clung to the rail, watching her. "Perhaps you are stronger than you think, Daughter of Aigir. Can you not draw on the power that is your birthright?" Sorrow came into his face. "If you do not save me, save yourself. Do not let her rule you. Do not let her win."

And then a wave crashed over his head, and he was lost from sight.

Endain dove into the sea and caught his arm, dragging him to the surface again. His body was heavy and cold, but she held onto him. He coughed and sputtered in the air that brought his kind life. She was relieved. She didn't want him to be dead. She didn't want him to join the mass before her mother's throne.

"I will bear you to land," she told him. "I will spare your life, if I am able."

She swam with him a little ways, and knew she could not carry him. So she reached deep into herself and caught the thread of the sea god's power, and with it called down a lesser star from heaven. Endain knew nothing of ships, so she shaped the star into a whale, huge and mighty. She climbed onto the whale's back and laid the sailor

down beside her. He stirred, and opened his eyes, and began to weep.
"Why are you weeping?" she asked him. He hadn't wept before.
She didn't understand why he did now.

"I am overwhelmed by your mercy, lady."

"Do not thank me yet," said Endain. "The moon still shines in
heaven. My mother has not called me back down into her hellish Hall."

"Perhaps she has no charge to call you," said the sailor. "Not until
you must bear the nets."

"We must hope that that is so."

The whale bore them south through the cold sea. The crescent moon
slid slowly down the rim of the sky, until it disappeared altogether.

Nothing happened. Endain was not seized by the curse. The wind
blew through her hair and she looked at the sailor and was undone by
his wisdom, and her own foolishness.

"All these centuries I have acted the slave without claiming the
scant bit of freedom allowed me."

"You did not know," the sailor told her. "And neither did I. It was
only a guess. A wish."

"Then it has been granted." Endain smiled at him.

He smiled back. She felt it, pricking at her heart.

So the whale carried them long through the waters of the sea, and
at every crescent moon Endain did her duty, singing to the night. But
the sailor bound a cloth about her mouth and plugged his ears, so her
music did him no harm.

At last they reached the shores of Endahr, and Endain sent the
whale out into the sea, bidding him to return when she called him
back to her.

Then Endain stood with the sailor on the shore, the wind clawing
at her hair and the sea lapping at her heels. "You are saved," she told
him. "What will you do now?" And her heart trembled, for she loved
him, and feared he would leave her.

But the sailor raised one hand to touch the face of the sea god's
daughter. "Would you think me a beggar if I asked you to be my wife?"

Endain was filled up with joy. "If you are a beggar, then I am a thief, for I've stolen you away from the sea."

And he laughed and kissed her under the wide sky, and she went with him to his village, where they were wed with the music of bells.

Endain was content, though she was seized sometimes with a sharp longing for her home. On those days, she strode down to the sea and wept awhile upon the sand, stirring her feet into the water, drawing on the strength of her father. But when she had quenched her longing, she turned to see the sailor waiting for her, his hand outstretched, a question in his eyes.

"I thought I had lost you," he would say, as she left the sea and stepped once more into his arms.

"I would never leave you of my own accord," she would answer. "I love you far too much for that."

The sailor dreaded the day when the sea would take her back from him, but he never spoke of it to her.

Every month, when the crescent moon rose into the sky, Endain would sing in the tiny house she shared with the sailor. She bound her own mouth willingly. She stuffed cotton into his ears. And he held her as she sang, tears streaming down his face and hers, for the power of her music moved them both.

A year passed in this manner, and Endain and the sailor lived in happiness, sorrow touching them only rarely. It happened that one month, when the moon had risen and set and Endain ceased her singing, that she wept more than usual, and the sailor looked into her eyes and asked what ailed her.

Then she wiped the tears from her face. "Oh, my heart, the ninth year is approaching, and already I feel the pull of the sea. I must return to the doom that my mother put upon me, and I know she will bind me tighter than before. I know I will not be able to come back to you."

The sailor looked at her, and knew there was yet something more.

"I must leave you, and the child growing within me."

Then the sailor's heart broke, because he had not known about the child, and because he knew she spoke the truth. He had counted the years, too. He had hoped he counted wrong, but he had not. "Perhaps she has forgotten you. Perhaps she will leave you in peace."

"Perhaps," said Endain, but she did not believe it.

The crescent moons waxed and waned, and on the eve of the ninth year, when Endain would be called upon to man the nets with her sisters, she bore the sailor a daughter in their little house. The child had her father's dark eyes and her mother's hair, the frothy pale color of seafoam.

A moment only, Endain held her daughter with the sailor beside her, before she felt the pull of the curse, stronger than ever before. She kissed her daughter, and laid her in the sailor's arms. And then she kissed him too, passionate and long.

"I love you, oh my heart, but the sea is calling me now. I must answer, or my mother will come, and find me here, and kill you both. Four hundred more years of my curse I can bear, but your deaths I cannot. Keep her. Hide her from the sea and from her birthright. Hide her from my mother, lest her and those after her be bound by my fate. Promise me."

"I promise," said the sailor, his face wracked with grief.

Endain's heart broke, but she left the little house, her husband and her daughter, and strode down to the shore of the sea.

Rahn waited for her there, the Star white-hot on her finger, fury blazing in her eyes. Then Rahn grasped her daughter by the hair, and forced her to look deep into the Star, so that Endain was blinded. And she dragged Endain through the sea, back down into the Hall of the Dead, and cursed her anew. Endain alone of all the Waves was bound for the remainder of the nine hundred years to sit at the base of the Tree, forever plying the strings of her harp. And there she sits still, in darkness and sorrow, dreaming of her dark-eyed daughter.

But the sailor kept his promise, raising his daughter in laughter and light, far from the shores of the sea. Sometimes, the longing would take her, as it had taken her mother, but he did not explain that longing to her or what it meant.

Not until she was married, and had borne a child of her own, and that child had borne a child, did the sailor call her to him, for he was dying and could not let Endain's story die with him. So he told her the truth—that in her veins flowed the power of Aigir and that part of her would always wish for the sea. But she must never go there, or Rahn would take her life. He had built a house on the shore where Endain first brought him, a house called the Ruen-Dahr, and he had appointed there a guardian to watch for Rahn and to be the last defense against her. He wove the house with the Words of the gods to strengthen it and choose for itself future guardians. He told his daughter that as long as she stayed away from the sea, she would be protected. One day, the house or its guardian might call her back again, but only in the greatest need. In the end, it could be that only Endain's descendant and the guardian together would have the power to stand against Rahn.

So the sailor died at last, having lived a century alone on Endahr, without his Wave beside him. His daughter mourned and buried him, and passed on the knowledge of her heritage and the Ruen-Dahr to her own child. In time, her child told it to his children and so on down the years, until it was just a story claimed by a single bloodline, a story they swore to be true.

I am of that bloodline, and I feel the pull of the sea too strongly to dwell here on its shore. I came to see the house for myself, and the Words yet bind it with great power. We are protected still, but I do not know for how long. Rahn is returning, and I do not think a guardian alone will be enough to stop her.

I have penned the tale as best as I remember hearing it from my own grandfather. He is the fifth great-grandchild of Endain and the sailor, if my figures are correct, making me the seventh. I do not know where I will go. Perhaps to Enduena, if I can bear to make the voyage. I will have to be locked in chains belowdecks, for I do not trust myself not to leap into the sea.

I only pray to the gods that the yearning lessens for any who follow in my bloodline.

Chapter Thirty-Seven

I T ENDED THERE.

Talia looked up from the pages, a roaring in her ears. For a moment, she couldn't breathe.

She jerked to her feet and dashed outside into the rain, leaving the papers where she'd dropped them. She ran out onto the moor behind the house, feet smacking hard against the soggy ground. Cold rain blurred her vision.

She felt the story in her bones, in her blood, in every stride she took barreling headlong a mile and a half over the moor to the sea.

It wasn't true. It couldn't possibly be true.

But she knew that it was.

She slowed her pace when she reached the bluff, following a worn track that wound down to the shore. There, the cliff sheltered her a little from the wind and the rain. But the mad pulse of her heart didn't diminish.

She tore off her shoes and stepped up to the edge of the water, letting the sea lap over her bare feet and soak the hem of her dress. Music echoed out over the waves, louder than ever before, a cacophony of longing, of certainty, of power. It raced through her. Filled her up.

All at once she felt herself ripped out of time and space, the sky tilting above her, the sea roaring below. She blinked and she was looking through a different pair of eyes at a face she knew was dear to her: a dark-haired man holding a child. He was weeping, and the anguish in her soul almost made her turn back but she couldn't. She had to protect him. She opened her mouth and sang to the sea, the song she shared with her sisters, the music that called men to their deaths. She would remember him forever, but she must leave him now.

The sea became her, and she became the sea, and the leagues of distance between her and her love were gone in an instant. She stood once more before her mother in the Hall of the Dead. She feared her more than anything, but she did not regret what she had done. Rahn did not rail at her, did not curse or scream, and that was the worst of all, for it meant her anger ran deeper than Endain had ever seen it.

"Bow before me," came her mother's voice, in her mind. She knelt in the dust, and the sea whispered over her shoulders. She stared into the Star as Rahn raised it to her face. She sang as Rahn blinded her, as the fire shot through her and burned down to her soul. And she thought only of her sailor and the daughter she had left behind.

The vision jolted Talia sideways, and she blinked up at a shoreline she knew: the bluff where the Ruen-Dahr stood, only it was not built yet. Broad-shouldered men were laying the foundation with newly hewn stone, sweating though the day was cold. The dark-haired sailor stood among them, speaking or singing—she couldn't tell which—Words of power spooling from his lips in little glints of gold. They seeped into the stones, wrapped around them. Strengthened them.

She blinked and the house was whole, a woman dressed in blue kneeling before the sailor. A little dark-haired girl clung to his knees.

"Do you accept the charge?" said the sailor, wind flapping through his long cloak.

"I do," returned the woman. "I will guard the house, and watch the sea until the end of my days."

Then the sailor hung a gold medallion around her neck and gave her a ring of keys, and he and the little girl strode away.

Suddenly, the sailor stood in the cove where Talia was, though the sun was shining in his dark hair and he was alone. He seemed to be staring straight into her eyes. "I know you will come back one day," he said. "My descendant, and hers. I want you to know you are strong, strong enough to find Rahn's Hall, strong enough to defeat her. And I want you to tell Endain, when you find her again, that I love her, that I never stopped loving her, that though I am dead and gone I think of her still, and I'm waiting for her beyond the circles of the world. Break Rahn's curse. Stop her before she comes to rule the world. Set Endain free. Set yourself free." And then the sailor smiled, and vanished.

Talia staggered backward and almost fell into the sea, but she grabbed hold of the cliff and kept herself upright. Waves lashed against her and rain bit at her face.

If she'd denied it before, she couldn't any longer.

She understood now why she could hear the music in the waves. Understood why the gods had burdened her with this fate and why her mother had leapt into the sea—she'd known about their heritage. She'd known Rahn sensed her and Talia's presence. She'd cast herself into the storm so Rahn would take her instead of Talia. And Rahn had. But she sensed Talia still, and was tormenting her mother because of it. Talia was part Wave, part sea god. She could never escape that.

The realization overwhelmed her, horrified her. It thrilled her somehow, too.

But there was still one more thing she had to know.

She was soaked through by the time she arrived at the Ruen-Dahr, breathless and shaking the water from her hair. She bolted past a confused Ahned, and nearly ran headlong into a man carrying a bucket of fresh plaster. She jerked sideways to avoid him, and dashed up the stairs to the room she hadn't seen in weeks, praying they were still there, that they hadn't been thrown out.

She tore through the gowns in her wardrobe and there they were—the clothes she had worn aboard the *Lazy Jackal* half a year ago, balled in the corner underneath a pair of dirty riding boots.

She pulled them out, scrabbling in the pockets of the baggy pants. The right one was empty, and her panic redoubled.

In the left pocket she found the piece of paper, crumpled and creased and stiff with seawater.

She crouched back on her heels, hardly daring to breathe, and unfolded it.

Her mother's handwriting marched in front of her eyes, the words Talia had thought the ravings of a madwoman all at once perfectly clear:

The sea runs in my veins, as it does in yours, my darling girl. My father told me when I was young. We are the heritage of the sea god, we are Endain's children, and so only we can strike the goddess down from her throne. Endain rode the Whale here, and we must ride it back again. The Whale will save us. We must take the Star from Rahn's hand, we must turn her own power against her, we must set the dead free. The time has come. The nine hundred years are nearly ended, and when they are she will rise with her dead and fill all the world with shadows. I have felt it. I have heard it in the song of the Waves. We must stop her, before it is too late. We must return to our birthright. The sea made us, and the sea will take us back again. Come, my dearest Talia. I will be waiting for you there.

The paper tore between Talia's fingers. She started to shake.

She left her room almost without realizing it, and her feet took her up to the library. The door was unlocked but the tower was empty, the hearth swept clean. She felt the power of the mirror room, dancing just behind her eyes—she could almost see the sparks of light glimmering where the door ought to be. She didn't know the Words Wen had used to open it, but she realized she didn't need them.

"I am Endain's daughter," she whispered to the air. "I belong here. Let me in."

The wall shimmered and the door appeared. She stepped through.

With an effort she passed by mirror after mirror until she came to the last one. "What will happen if I do not go?" she asked. It seemed a question the mirror was meant to answer. She steeled herself for the things she didn't want to see, and looked in.

The black glass wavered. She felt suddenly very cold.

Water pressed in all around her, but she could see nothing. Fire burned in her eyes; she knew it would never stop. Her fingers whispered past her harp strings and she played a lament for the bond laid on herself and her sisters, for the loss of the man she had loved, for the dead souls bound forever in the shadows that moved beyond her blind eyes.

The mirror twisted and changed, flashing images in quick succession. Talia once more saw her mother, screaming before Rahn's throne, the pain twisting in and in and in. She heard the clank of chains, saw sparks fly from a hammer somewhere in the dark. She heard the Billow Maidens singing, and their music was *danger* and *sorrow* and *pain never ending.*

She saw the image from her dream, a wide black sea and the dead rising out of it, silent and screaming. They were bound in iron around their necks and wrists and ankles, all chained together in a grotesque, clanking horde. Rahn led them, riding on the back of a blue-and-silver serpent. Her woven crown was made of fire and human finger bones, and the Star gleamed from her hand. Behind her came the Billow Maidens, and they were collared in gold and bound with chains between them, like the dead.

No! Talia tried to scream, but the mirror wasn't finished.

She blinked and saw the shore of the Ruen-Dahr, a lone figure standing with one arm outstretched. He held a sword that pulsed with the power of the Words. He trembled as he waited, and Talia knew him to be the guardian, the last defense for the land against the sea goddess.

But more than that: It was Wen. He looked solemn and strange; there were silver threads in his hair.

Rahn came toward him with the Waves and the dead at her back. She stepped from the sea onto the shore, and Wen did not waver. "Go back," he said. "Go back to the deep."

But the goddess laughed. "Whatever power was woven into this shore is ended now." She lifted her hand and the Ruen-Dahr crumbled to dust behind him. But still he did not back down.

"Go back to the deep!"

Rahn smiled and raised the Star. "You cannot stop me."

"But I will try anyway." And he leapt at her with a fierce cry, the sword flashing before him.

Rahn shouted a Word Talia knew was *Death*, and raised the Star, knocking him backward against a jutting rock. Talia both heard and felt the snap of his bones as he fell limp and dead onto the shore.

Rahn trod over his lifeless body without a glance, her terrible army surging just behind.

Talia's heart cried out, but she couldn't tear her eyes away. The mirror wasn't finished.

She saw Rahn striding across all the continents of the world, crowning herself queen, making the living worship her along with the dead. Rivers and forests were choked with shadows. Palaces were knocked down and rebuilt with human bones. All the gods remaining on Endahr crept out of their corners of the earth: Tuer and Raiva, Hahld and Ahdairon and Mahl. But they were not strong enough anymore to defeat her. Rahn killed them, one by one, and then clapped them in chains.

No more, Talia thought. *Please, no more.*

But the mirror changed again. She blinked and was astonished to see the throne room in Eddenahr, with its huge, arched hall, hidden fountains burbling in the alcoves, and jasmine twining through the window lattice. The two thrones on a dais in the center of the hall were made of bone and iron. Rahn sat in one of the thrones, the Star bright on her finger. In the other throne, Talia saw herself.

She was clothed in robes woven of sea glass and water, a coral crown on her head, strands of blue and green in her hair. Her skin was strange, speckled like river stones. Her mouth was twisted into a cruel smile.

And at her feet knelt the shadow of the Empress, gray and dead, bound in chains. "Please," Eda moaned, weeping with pain, "let me free. Let me go."

But Talia shook her head. "In life you tormented me, took from me everything I had ever known. Now you will be tormented until the end of time."

"Please," she begged. "Please!"

Talia waved her hand and a pair of dead guards came forward and dragged the Empress away.

Rahn looked at Talia on her throne, and smiled. "You do very well, my daughter."

The scene changed again, and Talia wrestled with Rahn in a field of bones, clawing for the Star on the goddess's finger. They fought for centuries as the world wheeled around them, and at last Talia was triumphant and claimed the Star as her own. She struck Rahn with its cold fire, and when the goddess fell dead to the ground Talia slid it onto her own hand. She felt the power surge through her, and she knew no one would ever take anything from her ever again.

Beyond the field of bones, the sea lapped upon the shore, and suddenly, she saw the shadow of someone she had once known: a boy, weighed down with chains. He looked very sad.

"Talia," he said, coming near her. "You have to let it go."

But she would not relinquish the Star, not even for this boy. She could do only one thing for him. "Be at peace," she whispered, and touched the Star gently to his forehead. "Goodbye, Wen."

He smiled at her and dissolved like smoke into the air, going at last to his rest beyond the world.

And then she was wholly alone.

Chapter Thirty-Eight

TALIA. TALIA. TALIA."

She took a breath and opened her eyes. She was crouched in the hallway outside of her room, her throat raw from screaming, her face wet with tears. She had no memory of leaving the library.

Wen knelt beside her, his face wracked with worry. "Talia," he repeated softly. "It's okay. You're okay."

She focused on breathing, in and out and in again, willing herself to regain her calm. But she couldn't seem to stop shaking.

He folded his hand around hers, rubbed his thumb over her skin. "What's wrong? What did you see?"

"Nothing," she sobbed. "Nothing." He was alive. Wen was still alive. Whatever awful future the mirror had shown her hadn't happened yet.

He studied her, serious, alarmed. "Please, Talia. You've been missing three days from the Ruen-Shained. I know you went into the mirror room."

She felt numb and weak and impossibly thirsty. She scooted back from him and leaned against the wall, hugging her knees to her chest.

"I could help you, you know," Wen said when she still didn't answer. "With the things you saw. With whatever it is you mean to do about them."

She saw him falling dead to the sand, Rahn and her army striding over his body.

She saw him fade into nothing as she stood on the field of bones, an all-powerful goddess.

Alone.

She couldn't tell Wen the truth about the Ruen-Dahr—how it chose guardians, how it had chosen him—not if she wanted to save him. He would try to stop her. Aigir's tears, he would take his role as guardian too seriously and try to *help* her. And then her visions would come true.

"Talia?" His eyes pierced through her.

By all the gods who ever walked the earth, she wanted to save him. "You could still go to University," she said, forcing her voice steady. "It isn't too late. You deserve a chance to share your music with the world. A chance at happiness." The words hurt, and she didn't know why.

"Gods," he swore softly. "You don't understand at all, do you?"

"Understand what?"

The intensity in his gaze was hard to bear. "I could never be happy anywhere without you."

The admission startled her so much she almost told him everything. But instead she asked him, "Did you see me in the mirror?"

He looked away.

"What did you see?"

Wen put his head in his hands. His voice came rough and ragged, and she knew what he would say before he said it: "I saw you sailing from the coast of the Ruen-Dahr in a ship with patchwork sails."

"What happens?"

For a moment he was silent, and the world seemed to suck

in a breath, waiting for his answer.

He lifted his face and his eyes were wet. "You drown. Just like my mother."

"You said the future isn't written yet," she said fiercely.

"Then don't go. Stay here. Change your fate."

He didn't understand—how could he? The gods themselves had woven together the threads of her fate and were pulling them tight. She was the descendant of the sea god Aigir, the only one who could even attempt to confront Rahn and free the dead. If Wen's vision was true she would fail. But if she stayed Wen would die, and all the world with him.

There wasn't even a choice for her to make.

Wen was still waiting for her answer.

"I'll stay," she promised.

She went back to the Ruen-Shained, her mother's note burning a hole in her pocket, Wen's knowing gaze burning a hole in her heart.

Chapter Thirty-Nine

SHE STOOD ON THE FRONT STEPS OF the Ruen-Dahr and looked out into the night, a cool wind rushing past her face. Clouds were knotting over the stars, but there was still enough moonlight to see by. It shouldn't delay her.

Music drifted from inside the house, fiddles and drums, a flute and the faint sweet notes of a harp—Blaive's party was just getting started.

She ought to be on her way. She'd gotten what she came for, the two items tucked safely in the leather knapsack slung across her shoulder. The rest of her supplies were waiting in the cove: books and sea charts, the compass and sextant, a knife and matches and a waterproof tarp, rope and fishing equipment, salted meat and dried fruit.

She'd been busy the last few weeks, plotting out her course through the sea, reading and rereading the myths, making all the necessary preparations. She'd cross-checked the dates of the myths with her ancestor's account, coming to the same conclusion over and over again. Nearly nine hundred years ago, Rahn had cursed the Billow Maidens to sing their haunted melodies and gather the dead in their terrible nets. That's why the Waves were calling her now: Talia was the only one of Endain's bloodline left to stand against Rahn, before the goddess used the power of the Star to curse them anew.

It was the final piece of the puzzle, the last knot in the weave of her fate.

The Waves were calling, and it was time to answer, time to save her mother and Wen and the world. To save herself.

But the thought of Wen kept her standing there.

He'd only visited her once at the Ruen-Shained after she'd lied to him. He told her the date of Blaive's party. Asked her if she would come.

Now she was here.

She'd likely never see him again, and she realized she couldn't go without saying goodbye.

Talia shrugged out of the knapsack, tucked it safe under the stair, and slipped into the house.

He was standing alone, just outside the huge doorway to the ballroom, dressed in a gray waistcoat and jacket, his cravat neatly tied. Hundreds of candles danced in the glittering chandeliers, the scent of beeswax and roses and spiced wine drifting out into the vestibule. Couples danced in glittering pairs, and Talia was thrown back to a year ago in Eddenahr, when Eda had burst into the Emperor's ballroom and changed everything.

"Wen?" she said softly.

He turned from the door, and she felt her heart constrict as his eyes brightened at the sight of her. "You're here," he said. "You came."

"Wen—"

"You look so beautiful." He held out his hand. "Would you care for a dance?"

"I'm not dressed for dancing." She was wearing a plain gray-

and-rose gown, the sturdiest garment in her wardrobe.

"Of course you are," he said, and folded his fingers around hers.

He drew her close, one hand pressing against the small of her back, the other resting lightly on her shoulder. She didn't pull away. They danced together quietly, easily, out of time with the quick-stepping jig that poured from the ballroom. She felt her resolve crumbling. Why was it so hard to leave him? It shouldn't be.

She pulled suddenly away and he did too, a careful distance in his expression. "Are you all right, Talia?"

She scrambled for an answer. "I thought—I thought perhaps I'd change into something better for dancing in. Would you wait for me?"

His smile started in his eyes and spread to his lips. "I would like nothing better, Miss Dahl-Saida."

"Ten minutes, and I'll be back."

For an instant more she studied him, the freckles on his nose and the stubble on his chin and the lines pressed into his forehead. And then she turned away and went upstairs to her room, pausing briefly to leave two letters on her bed— one for Ayah, one for Wen. She passed quickly through the hall and down the servants' stairs, then out a side door into the night.

The wind sang through her hair as she galloped along the shoreline toward the hidden cove, Ahdairon's hoofbeats thudding in the sand. Her knapsack thumped heavy against her waist, its contents making her uneasy. She thought of Wen, waiting for her to come back downstairs to dance with him, not knowing she was already gone.

But there was no turning back.

When she reached the cove, Talia reined in the mare and

swung down. She took off the bridle and tied it to the saddle so the reins wouldn't drag. "Off home you go now," she told Ahdairon, smacking her flank. The horse eyed her with confusion, but started obediently down the coast the way they'd come. She should get back to the Ruen-Dahr without any trouble.

The ship was waiting for her, its bow poking through the trailing vines, water lapping quietly at the hull. Moonlight illuminated the words she'd painted on the bow only yesterday, her name for the ship: *Endain's Heart*. The tide was rising. She loosed the boat from the driftwood post where she'd moored it, then wrapped the rope securely around her shoulder and tugged it out of the hidden cove. She felt calm. Steady. Certain.

She climbed into the ship, raised the mast and lashed it securely in place, her patchwork sail furled and ready. She double-checked the knapsack and secured it with her other supplies in the bottom of the boat, before covering everything with the waterproof tarp.

Everything was in order.

There was nothing left to do but set sail.

She scrambled back onto the shore, putting her shoulder to the stern of *Endain's Heart*, and shoving it out into deeper water. The waves caught the boat and her final decision was made for her—all at once she was fighting through the water, grabbing the side of the ship and pulling herself into it.

She caught her breath and checked the sail and rudder, then cast one last glance back to the shore.

Someone was standing there in the moonlight, arms windmilling. Shouting at her, though the words were lost in the sound of the surf.

It was Wen.

Part Four:

SHIP AND SEA

So Rahn made a white ship with silver sails, and she cast it away from the shore and was seen no more upon the land.

Chapter Forty

S HE TORE HER EYES AWAY FROM THE figure on the shore, steeling herself against the sound of his voice. She couldn't go back. He'd die if she did.

She fumbled with the knots keeping the sail lashed tight around the mast, and it unfurled all at once, a hodgepodge of color in the fractured light of the moon. The wind caught it, filled it. The ship cut through the rising waves.

"Talia!"

She glanced back to shore just in time to see him rip off his jacket and plunge into the sea.

"No!" she screamed. "Wen, go back!"

A wave crashed over his head but he wrestled to the surface again, fighting the current. He swam toward the ship.

The water was rough and choppy away from the shore. The wind was rising.

Wen would drown.

She cursed and grabbed for the sail, wrestling with the patchwork fabric to furl it once more. She adjusted the tiller and grabbed the oar stowed in the bottom of the boat, paddling desperately back in the direction she had come. Wen's head poked up above the water.

Just a little closer.

A wave crashed into the ship, drenching her through, but she hardly noticed. Wen disappeared from sight. She dug the oar in harder, praying to every god she knew that he wasn't lost forever.

And then there he was, bursting back to the surface again, close enough to touch.

Talia cried out, leaning over the side to grab his arm. She hauled him up into the boat, which rocked alarmingly at the sudden addition of his weight, more water splashing in.

He coughed and choked and sputtered, and she stared at him, shaking so hard her eyes could barely focus. "What are you *doing*?" she demanded, her voice high and tight. "You could have drowned!"

"What are *you* doing?" he shot back.

"Following my fate!"

"Do you mean killing yourself?"

Another wave crashed over the side of the boat, the sea churning beneath them. The wind rose stronger, whipping Talia's hair loose from its braid. Thunder growled, and the ship lurched. It grew suddenly dark, knotted clouds blocking out the moonlight.

"We have to get back to shore before the storm hits!"

"I'm not going back!" she told him fiercely.

A sudden gust of wind slammed into her, nearly knocking her into the ocean, but Wen caught her wrist and held her back. They both fell to their knees. The sail unfurled as the wind loosened the knots, and Talia leapt up to wrestle it down again before it was torn apart. Wen helped, steady hands beside her in the dark.

"Talia, we *have* to go back."

"I'm prepared for storms."

"A fisherman wouldn't dare go out in this old tub on a sunny day—what makes you think you can cross the ocean in it?"

"I'm not a fisherman!" she shouted above the wind. "The sea is in my blood and I'm not going to die." *At least not yet,* she thought.

"This is madness!"

The rain hit like a wall of ice, and any chance for conversation was lost.

No matter what Wen wanted, they were too far out to sea now to turn around in this squall. And she *was* prepared, even if she hadn't thought she'd face adverse weather so soon.

She tugged a coil of rope out from under the tarp in the stern of the boat and lashed herself and Wen to the mast. Wen helped, understanding her purpose. Her nerves hummed as she huddled close to him, pulling the waterproof cloak over their knees. She wasn't scared now that he was safe in the boat.

The storm, the sea—it thrilled her. She had never felt more alive. For an instant she was thrown back into her vision of Endain; she became the sea, and the sea became her.

Lightning flashed and thunder growled and the ship tilted, but didn't capsize. Talia shut her eyes, the rain washing cold over her. Wen grabbed her hand, their fingers tangling tight together.

Melody shimmered suddenly around them, rich and strong and beautiful, and she opened her eyes to see Wen singing. She didn't understand the language, but she recognized the Words of the gods, spooling from his lips and wrapping around them— Words of power and protection that glinted in the dark. She blinked at him through the rain, startled but somehow not surprised. He must have studied the book he'd found more than he let on.

The storm began to diminish and the wind slowly dropped. In another hour the rain stopped altogether and moonlight broke through the clouds—they'd survived.

Talia let out a breath, working with Wen to untie themselves from the mast. She let the sail loose, her heart thrilling as it caught the wind. She dug her compass out of her pocket and took a reading; the storm had blown them a little too far west, but that was easily corrected. She put her hand to the tiller and nudged the ship north again, on into the open sea.

On into the unknown.

Chapter Forty-One

THE SUN ROSE SOFT OVER THE SEA, gold light refracting off the water, wind swelling in the patchwork sail. Talia stood at the stern of the ship, hand steady on the tiller, while Wen slept up near the bow, the waterproof cloak draped over him. The sea seemed content, now that she was on her way. It sang to her, of *freedom* and *power* and *peace*.

Wen stirred and opened his eyes, stretching and blinking up at her. She left the rudder and knelt down in the boat, handing him a small packet wrapped in oilcloth.

"Breakfast," she said. "I hope you like salted beef. There's water, too, but we'll have to use it sparingly." She hadn't brought enough food for both of them, but they could always try fishing when the dried meat ran out. Water was the real problem—she should have rigged something up to collect the rain last night. Next time.

Wen took the packet without a word, unwrapping the beef and tearing off a piece. He chewed slowly.

Talia untangled her hair with her fingers and rebraided it, tying off the end with a bit of twine.

"So . . . what's your plan then?" Wen asked her.

She glanced over at him. The rising sun shone scarlet on his skin. His hair was matted on one side where he'd slept on it, and stubble showed dark along his jaw. "The plan was for you to go to University and forget about me."

He scratched his chin, his eyes not leaving hers. "You lied to me."

She didn't apologize. "It was the only way I could say goodbye and still slip away without you knowing. Though it didn't exactly work. I left you a letter."

"I found it." He leaned back against the mast, watching her. "You said you were leaving, you said you were sorry. That was all."

She took a breath. "I'm going to the Hall of the Dead, to save my mother and free the dead, to defeat Rahn, if I can. I thought it would sound insane. Even to you." She glanced out over the waves, more certain of her purpose than ever. The sea seemed to hum with anticipation.

Wen just studied her, waiting, the packet of dried meat forgotten in his hands.

"I'm a descendant of Endain—of Aigir and Rahn herself. Journeying to the Hall of the Dead, destroying Rahn—it's what I was meant to do."

She told him about her mother's story and the handwritten account she'd found in the library, about the vision she'd seen of Endain and the sailor, about the boat the gods had left her in the hidden cove. But she didn't tell him about the Ruen-Dahr or the guardians who were supposed to watch for Rahn's return. She didn't want him to know that's what he was. Wen listened thoughtfully.

The sun rose a little higher in the sky. The ship creaked, and the waves slapped quietly against it.

"And you really think you can find it? The Hall of the Dead is just a story."

"No, it's not. I saw it in the last mirror. And I don't know if I can find it, but I have to try."

He frowned. "What did you see, exactly?"

"I saw myself crossing the sea. Finding the white Tree, standing in Rahn's Hall. Speaking with my mother."

"What about the second time you went to the mirror room? What did you see then?"

She shook her head and lied: "Nothing."

His lips pressed together in a grim line. "Why won't you tell me?"

"Because there's more at stake than you know, because—" She grimaced, and cut herself off. "Do you think I'm mad?"

"No. But I think you're going to kill yourself without reason."

"I've planned it out," she said. "I've made all the calculations, I have a pretty good guess where to look for the Tree—"

"Talia, even if you find a place that is supposed to be impossible to find, even if you somehow manage to reach the Hall of the Dead without drowning, how do you expect to go up against a goddess who wields the power of the Star and Tree together? Why would you even *want* to?"

"Did your vision come true?" she snapped, anger racing through her.

"What?" He looked bewildered.

"You said you saw me sailing away, alone. You said you saw me drowning in a storm. Did it come true?"

He clenched and then unclenched his jaw. "No."

"Then we've already averted fate."

"There has to be something else. Something we're missing, something you're not telling me."

"Clearly fate can be changed. It isn't written in stone."

He scooted forward, and took hold of her arm. "It can't be that simple, Talia. Maybe the gods gave us a second chance. If we turn the ship around, we could be home by dinner. Please. Let's go back."

She pulled away. "I'm not going back. Even if—even if I never find the Hall or the Tree. I'm part Billow Maiden. Maybe there's something for me out here—I don't think I'm supposed to go back." She shrugged a little at how nonsensical that all sounded.

Wen sighed and rubbed his forehead. "What *is* your plan then? Where are we going?"

Talia pulled out the charts, and showed him. "North," she said, pointing, "and a little west. Everything I read about the Hall and the Tree reference them being 'in the middle of the sea,' so we're sailing to the exact midpoint between all six continents. Or at least as close as I can calculate."

"The stories also say the Tree is hidden and can't be seen by mortal eyes," Wen pointed out.

Talia scrutinized him. "I'm banking on the fact that I have Aigir's blood running through me. And in any case, you might be able to help with that."

The sun rose higher, and Talia and Wen shared half a bottle of water between them. Talia adjusted the sail for the hundredth time, then took a sight with the sextant. Wen took another look at her charts. Then they both sat down again and stared at each other.

"You studied the book of Words you found, didn't you?" said Talia.

"Before I even went into the mirror room," he admitted. "I picked up the translation where my mother had left off. The Words are like music—they make sense to me, like they've been burning in my head since I was born."

"And you can . . . do things with them?"

Wen shrugged. "I haven't really tried. My father would have lost his *mind* if he knew."

"You tried last night."

"I'm not sure it helped."

"I'm not sure it didn't. What kind of Words did you study?"

He met her eyes. "As many as I could, though some of them seem more impossible than others."

"Like what?"

He looked out across the sea. "There are Words of protection and destruction. Words to change your shape and to drive someone else mad. Words to make things grow. Words to move mountains."

"Do you think they're all possible?"

"I don't know. Maybe."

She considered this, watching the play of light in the waves. "What were the Words you sang into the storm? Can you teach them to me?"

Wen met her eyes. "Words of protection," he said. "And I can try."

So he did, as the hours passed and *Endain's Heart* slid through the gray waters of the Northern Sea. He sounded out the Words for her and explained what they meant. Talia was impressed by how many he remembered. She couldn't hold onto a single Word; when she tried to say one it slipped away from her, just beyond her reach.

But he kept trying, his fingers brushing gently against her face, teaching her mouth the proper shape.

By the afternoon, the impromptu lesson had run its course, and they settled on opposite ends of the boat—Talia by the tiller, Wen leaning back against the mast. Her head felt clearer, away from him.

Light dazzled off the water in the afternoon sun, a cool wind whispering past Talia's face.

"Tell me about your mother," Wen said unexpectedly.

She glanced at him. "My mother was—my mother was

strong, and kind. She demanded respect, and you had to earn her praise. She took things very seriously, but she laughed louder than anyone."

"And she loved you," said Wen, watching her.

Talia thought of the stories by the fireplace, the vigil in her palace room when she was so ill, the gift of the red horse for her birthday. Leaping into the sea to save her from Rahn's anger. Talia took a steadying breath. "Very much."

"Do you really think you can bring her back to life?"

The question twisted into her and she looked away, out into the iron sea. She didn't know. How could she? "It's been done before. In the old stories. But at the very least I mean to free her soul from Rahn's Hall. She deserves to be at peace."

He had no answer for that.

She drew a breath. "Tell me about University."

"What do you want to know?"

"Everything you gave up to stop me sailing off in this ship."

A smile touched his lips. "There are dozens of libraries, rooms filled with instruments, masters to tutor you and refine your skills, trained musicians to play your pieces. The best students tour the world, bringing their music to every continent. They do nothing but make music, all day, every day." He fell silent again, but his eyes didn't leave her face.

"You could have had all that."

His intense gaze caught her, held her. "None of that matters more than this."

She heard the echo of his unspoken words: *more than you.* She tried not to see Wen falling limp to the shore, Rahn's Star blazing in his eyes.

"You shouldn't have come," she said quietly. "I can't protect you."

"You don't have to protect me. We can protect each other."

The ship rocked gently beneath them, and Talia was suddenly, profoundly glad that she wasn't alone out here.

Chapter Forty-Two

D AYS SLIPPED BY, AND TALIA AND WEN settled into a quiet rhythm. At night, they slept in turns, holding the ship on a steady course and keeping an eye out for storms. During the day, they fished, and, if the sea was still enough, they roasted their catch in the coals of a small cooking pot. The weather was mostly fair, with a squall or two some evenings, but none as bad as the storm the night they'd left the coast. Talia rigged up the tarp to catch the rain and refill their water bottles, which eased her mind.

They spent long hours in silence—the comfortable kind that didn't demand anything. Most often, Talia sat in the stern, her hand at the tiller, while Wen sat in the hull with his legs stretched out and his head tipped against the mast, lips moving silently. She figured out after a few days of this that he was composing music in his head, and she offered him the backs of her charts and the margins of her books so he could write it down. After that, he was constantly scribbling notes.

The hardest part was Wen being there with her. His company made her happier than she really understood, but she still hadn't told him about the things she'd seen in the mirror room. Every time she closed her eyes she saw the image of his death playing out in endless repetition.

She was afraid that if she said it out loud, it would come true.

Late afternoon sunlight danced across the water, bathing the little ship in liquid gold. Talia sat, laughing, at her usual place in the stern, waving her hands around as she told Wen about one of her and Ayah's escapades. "We snuck off into the hills without telling anyone and camped out for three *days* in the desert, waiting for Ayah's dratted constellation to line up with the moon. She swore up and down that it had been prophesied in one of her ancient books, but I didn't believe her. It did, of course, that third night. I'd never seen anything more beautiful, though I refused to admit to Ayah that it had anything to do with the old stories."

"You are marvelously stubborn," Wen teased.

Talia stuck out her tongue at him. "When we got back—*gods*, was my mother angry! She wouldn't let me out of the palace for a week, and made me copy out an entire book of horrendously dull lists: household accounts, provincial taxes, shipping reports. I would have died of boredom if Ayah hadn't helped me."

Wen laughed, shaking his head. "You weren't at all the well-behaved young lady I took you for."

"What gave you the idea I was ever well-behaved?" Talia grinned. "I was in trouble with every single person in the palace at one time or another."

He grinned too, scratching at his nose. The sunburn he'd gotten their first few days at sea had faded into a slight tan and an explosion of new freckles, and there were cuts on his chin from his most recent attempt at shaving with Talia's knife. She realized suddenly that he was rather handsome.

She shaded her eyes with her hand and peered ahead of them into the never-ending ocean. "I should check our readings again." They'd been sailing nearly four weeks now, and she'd thought they were making good progress, but something felt off.

She unrolled the charts and Wen took out the compass. He read off the degrees for her and she marked them on the chart, frowning. It was the wrong time of day to take a sight on the sextant—she'd taken one at noon and would take another at midnight. "We should be getting close. At least, I think so. Maybe I miscalculated." She sighed, letting the chart roll back up again.

"What happens when we do get close?"

Talia laid her hand on the tiller again. "The Billow Maidens' curse is over."

He looked at her, waiting for her to go on.

"Rahn cursed them for nine hundred years, and as far as I can figure out, their enchantment ends this year. In another week or two. The Billow Maidens know—that's why they've been calling me. It's too big of a coincidence to ignore."

"And you think they'll help you—help us—defeat Rahn?"

Talia nodded. "They won't be bound to her anymore. Their power will return. And Endain should feel enough kinship with me to want to help. At least I hope so. Rahn plans to bind the Waves again when their curse is over. She means to renew her hold on their power, to join it with hers and rise from the sea and conquer the world." She chewed on her lip and told him part of the truth: "That's what I saw the second time I looked in the mirror."

He clenched his jaw. "There's still more."

She rubbed her thumb against the edge of the crackly chart. "There's a reason you found the mirror room, why you saw me in your vision, why we're both here now."

"And what's that?" he asked her quietly.

"Remember how you said you thought the house chose you? It—it did. The sailor—my ancestor—built the Ruen-Dahr, wove

Words into the stones so it would never lack for a guardian. Only the knowledge was lost and the mirrors forgotten—"

"A guardian against what?"

"Against the sea. Against Rahn's return. Your mother sensed her coming, Caiden's too. I think they were meant to be Guardians. But they didn't know why and they couldn't stop her. The not understanding—I think that's what drove them mad."

His face tightened. "Why didn't you tell me this before?"

"I didn't want you to feel more responsible for me than you already did. You've been trying to protect me this whole time—you, the last guardian, me, the last of Endain's bloodline. Everything's come full circle and we're here. Together. Against her."

"What makes you think you can stop her?"

The sea sang to her of *eternity* and *rest* and *release*. "I was born to it. Every moment of my life has brought me to this point and I can't—I won't—shirk from the fate the gods have led me to. It's the reason for everything, don't you see?"

He looked at her unhappily. "What's your plan, Talia? Please tell me you have a plan."

She quirked a smile at him. "I do, in fact." She stowed the chart and dug her leather knapsack out from under the rest of the supplies. "I read a lot about Rahn. She was strong once, but now she draws on the Tree and the Star to give her power, like Aigir did before her. Some historians believe that only the Tree and the Star could ever defeat her."

Wen raised an eyebrow, listening.

And then she told him. "I stole something from the temple under the garden."

"What did you steal?"

She undid the knapsack, drawing out a jar that pulsed with unnatural light, and a sliver of wood bound in a glass-and-iron casket.

Wen yelped and scrabbled backward making the ship lurch and water splash over the side. "Gods' *bones*, Talia!"

"It's all right," she said, cradling the jar in one hand and the casket in the other. "Honestly. They don't seem to do anything bad to me."

He came warily closer again. "That killed Caiden's mother."

"I haven't opened it, haven't touched it. I won't, not until we need to use it."

He rubbed at his temples. "You shouldn't have taken the risk."

"I had to, Wen. I couldn't come empty-handed—this isn't a suicide mission. Now we have a piece of the Star and the Tree. Maybe—maybe it will be enough to turn Rahn's power against her. We can do this—the daughter of the sea, and the last guardian." She tucked the jar and the casket back into the knapsack, and fastened it again. "We can do this," she repeated firmly.

He shook his head, a smile quirking at his lips. "You are full of surprises, Talia Dahl-Saida."

She smiled back at him, struck by the softness in his eyes. "I just hope it's enough."

Wen took a breath. "Me too."

"Talia! Talia! Wake up!"

She felt Wen shaking her shoulder, and she stirred foggily from restless dreams to find him leaning over her, his face drawn and scared.

"Storm's coming."

That was enough to jerk her fully awake. She looked up at the sky, the noonday sun blotted out, angry clouds tumbling in from all directions. A cold wind ripped at her hair and the waves were already rising, smashing hard against the side of the boat.

Together, they furled the sail and lashed it to the mast. They secured their belongings underneath the tarp, Talia at the last minute grabbing the knapsack and slinging it over her shoulder. She could feel the pulse of the Star-light, warm beneath the leather. Then she and Wen sat down and tied themselves to the mast as well, the ropes tight around their chests and their backs pressed into the wood, leaving their arms free.

They'd been through a half dozen storms already, but this one felt different. Darker. More dangerous.

The black clouds swallowed the last piece of the sky, and all at once it was wholly dark. Wen caught her hand in his. She could feel his pulse in his wrist, nervous, quick.

A wave crashed over the side of the ship. Lightning flared to the north. Thunder crashed, so loud and close it seemed to shake the world.

She'd run out of time. Oh gods, she'd run out of time! Billow Maiden heritage or not, they were too far away from land to weather a storm that could easily sink a much bigger boat. She was going to die here—*Wen* was going to die here, and it was all her fault.

She looked over at him as he braced himself for the coming onslaught.

The clouds broke and the rain came, roaring and dark. Lightning seared the sky, so near and bright it momentarily blinded her. The answering thunderclap was deafening. Wen's hand held tight to hers, and she felt the ship tilt beneath them, then the tug of ropes around her waist as gravity tried to pull them down. A wave slammed into the mast; she choked on seawater.

She craned her neck to the right, her vision clearing enough to see Wen through the rain in another flash of lightning. He shouted something, but the wind tore his words away. He pulled something out of his pocket and Talia squinted to make out what it was: a knife, to cut themselves free from the mast if the ship capsized. She nodded, to show she understood. It would only buy them a little time, but it would be better than drowning in the dark, unable to even move.

Wen yelled into the storm, and she caught snatches of his Words tangling up with the rain; she could feel their power encircling her.

But nothing else happened. The wind didn't lessen, the waves didn't recede. The Words weren't enough.

Water poured into the ship, seething over the sides. Talia glanced at Wen, and he was the one who nodded this time. He started sawing at the ropes while she grabbed a bucket and began fruitlessly bailing water, straining against the cords around her chest.

Hail stung her cheeks. Above them and around them and beneath them the storm wheeled. The sea tossed the ship about like a child tossing a stone.

Beside her, Wen was working frantically with the knife. He was only about halfway through.

Another wave rammed into them and the ship tilted sideways, almost capsizing.

"Wen!"

One cord snapped, then another. He dropped the knife and she grabbed the blade as it slid by, ignoring the sudden bite of pain. She grasped the handle, furiously sawing at the rope.

He was nearly free.

She was so intent on her task she didn't feel the ship tilting beneath her.

And then dark water closed over her head.

For a moment she wasn't afraid, her hand steady on the knife, sawing through the last rope binding Wen. She felt the cord break, felt him kicking with his legs and propelling himself upward.

And then, numbing panic.

Her eyes were open, but she saw only blackness. She felt the rope beneath her fingers, but she couldn't get the knife at the right angle to keep cutting. She couldn't breathe. The water pressed over her head, heavy and dark, killing her slowly.

She jerked her body against the rope, but it wouldn't give way and the knife slid from her palm. She found the knot, fumbling with it uselessly. She could distinguish the dark shape of the ship in the water now, but it didn't matter.

And then Wen was beside her, tugging at the rope. She saw the flash of his white face, felt the pressure of his hand on her shoulder.

The rope broke free.

Talia fought upward, bursting above the surface of the water, choking and gasping for air. She spotted Wen, but he was too far away from her. She tried to cry out but another wave hit, and her mouth filled up with seawater.

She clawed through the waves, breaking the surface again, gulping another desperate breath of air. Somehow she managed to grab hold of a splintered piece of wood that had broken off the ship, and she clung to it as the sea tossed her about and hail burned her skin. She couldn't see Wen anymore—there was nothing but the rain and the sea, swirling and dark. The knapsack was still hanging from her shoulder, the Star-light and Tree-sliver safe inside. But she didn't know how to use their power to save them.

She screamed into the storm, a single Word, over and over and over—her failsafe, one last plan she hadn't told Wen.

But no one answered.

Nothing came.

A wave slammed over her head, and she lost her grip on the piece of wood. The sea pulled her under, her fingers grasping at nothing.

Her lungs screamed for air, but she had no strength left.

Water crept into her nose and her mouth and dragged her down, down, down, away from the storm and the ship and Wen.

In another moment she would be lost. She would sleep as the sea creatures slept, and perhaps she would come to the Hall of the Dead after all, caught in the Billow Maidens' terrible nets.

Her consciousness blurred. She had one fleeting thought of deep sorrow: Wen shouldn't have followed her out here. He belonged with the artisans and craftsmen on Od, filling the world with his beautiful music. Now he was lost forever.

Despair and darkness closed around her, and she could feel herself slipping away.

In another moment, she would be gone.

Chapter Forty-Three

A VOICE ECHOED INSIDE OF HER, ALL STONE and storm and boundless power. She thought the strength of it would kill her—if she'd had breath, she would have screamed.

The sea heard too. It shivered around her and let her go.

Suddenly she was hurtling up, up, up beyond the grasping fingers of the waves, back into the storm and the rain and the life-giving air. She gulped for breath, coughing up the water in her lungs. She scrubbed the salt from her stinging eyes.

Something moved beneath her, vast and dark. Something alive. It lifted her partially from the water and gleamed in the white flashes of lightning: a huge rippling shape, more than twice as long as her shattered ship. Waves washed over it—over *her*—but the thing didn't heed them.

"Endain's daughter." That voice again—as strong as the earth, searing through her whole body.

She did scream then, and leapt back into the ocean. She glimpsed the fan of a wide, flat tail, the curve of a broad back. Waves clawed at her hair and pulled at her heels, trying to drag her down into the darkness. She struggled to stay above the surface of the water.

"The sea means you harm."

Lightning ripped across the sky and for an instant she saw all of it—a massive creature, with long, powerful flippers and a huge mouth and the gleam of a great black eye. It propelled itself easily through the angry sea, like it didn't even notice the storm.

"The sea will destroy you."

Terror writhed cold in her mind, of the creature or the waves—she didn't know.

Another spear of lightning slashed the sky, illuminating all at once the wreckage of her ship and the ragged figure clinging to the fractured mast. Gods above, he was still alive. Joy warred with her fear.

"Wen!"

She tried to swim toward him but the sea wouldn't let her. Waves slammed over her head and choked her breath away. He was alive, and she couldn't reach him. She clawed her way back to the surface.

His voice cut through the wind, Words of power spilling out of him like music and twisting into the storm. But then he was screaming, screaming and screaming, as if he endured unimaginable pain. In a flash of lightning she saw his body twisting, writhing. *Changing.*

"Wen!"

She wasn't close enough. The sea was toying with her, keeping them apart. And somewhere behind her the creature waited.

"Wen!"

White-hot light, the crackle of electricity in her ears. His arms spreading out, shivering and shifting until they were wings, wide and white. His head jerking back, feathers crawling up his neck. Claws curling out where his legs should have been, clothes shedding off of him like so many torn shadows.

And then he wasn't Wen anymore, but a huge, white seabird. He spread his wings and flew toward her.

But the storm wasn't finished. The wind caught him, wheeled him about in the rain, and slammed him hard against the broken mast.

She heard the *snap* of bone and the bird's sharp cry. Waves crashed over her, water creeping into her nose and mouth. She'd found him and lost him in the same moment, and now both of them would die.

"Endain's daughter," thundered the powerful voice all around her. "The sea means you harm."

Once again she was lifted out of the water, beyond the grasp of the waves. The creature swam steady beneath her, a leviathan of the deep, strength rippling beneath its skin. It could crush her in a moment, it could swallow her whole. But it didn't.

Her fear of the creature was outweighed by her desperation for Wen. "We have to save him," she begged. "Please."

She heard the low rumble of the Whale's deep voice. "Then save him."

Lightning streaked the sky and there he was, clinging to a scrap of wood with both clawed feet, one wing dragging limp. She slid into the water and swam to him, wrapping her arm around his strange feathered body, pulling him back onto the Whale. The bird shuddered and shook and she held onto him, not understanding what he had done, or why he had done it. Not understanding how everything had gone so wrong.

"He spoke the Words to change his form," said the Whale, deep and dangerous. "He thought he could save you."

Tears stung her eyes. "Can't you change him back?"

"Only he could do that."

"Then why doesn't he?"

"I do not think he knows how."

The bird huddled close to her, his broken wing hanging awkwardly away from his body. She tore strips of cloth from her soaked skirt and bandaged the wing as best as she was able. When it was done, the bird gave a shuddering sigh and laid his head in Talia's lap. She stroked his feathers, tears dripping down her chin.

The storm seemed a little less wild now, the waves not as high. But her fear was deeper than before, the reality of what she was doing stark and awful.

Lightning flashed, and the sea devoured the remaining fragments of her ship. The rain dwindled to a few icy drops, and the wind stopped roaring. A slice of moon cut through the clouds.

"Why are you here, daughter of Endain?" asked the Whale.

She blinked out over the sea, her fear of the creature tying her in knots. "I'm going to the Hall of the Dead." Her voice sounded ragged and rough to her own ears.

The Whale made a low *hmmmm* sound beneath her, vibrations rippling through his skin. The wind wrapped around Talia, the scent of roses mingling unaccountably with the lingering rain. Silence stretched into the darkness.

"Do you so despair of your life, that you seek Rahn's Hall?" he said at last. "Do you not wish for a future?"

She screwed her eyes shut and saw before her the Ruen-Shained, the white cat curled purring in the corner, the spot in the sitting room where Wen's raina would go. Wen, sitting at the instrument, scribbling notes on paper, ink spots all over his hands. Talia, coming in with a tea tray, Wen looking up with a smile.

The realization unfolded inside of her like jasmine flowers drinking in moonlight. How cruel to understand she wished for that future, just as all hope for it was gone. She looked down at Wen's white head, an immense sorrow weighing heavy. "My future can't matter, not now. I'm going to destroy Rahn. To end her rule and free my mother's soul. Will you take me to the Tree, Whale? Will you take me back the way you once carried Endain?"

Stars gleamed suddenly through the remnant of the clouds; the scent of roses bit sharper. "That is why you called me, is it not?"

Chapter Forty-Four

NIGHT TURNED TO DAY, THE SUN BURNING gold behind the torn threads of clouds, and the Whale didn't say anything more. Talia sat tense and afraid on his broad back with the seabird sleeping beside her. She felt lost. Alone. Powerless. She was at the mercy of a creature from a story, adrift in a dark sea.

She hadn't expected him to answer her call.

There was a footnote in the account of Endain that her many-greats-grandmother had written—an explanation of how Endain meant to call the Whale back to her, and a Word spelled out phonetically that was supposed to mean "Come to my aid."

That's what she'd shouted over and over into the storm.

Now a Whale made of Starlight four centuries ago was carrying her through the sea, and Wen wasn't Wen anymore. The Words of the gods were more powerful than she had thought possible.

How could Wen have done this to himself? To save her, the Whale had said.

She wished to the gods he hadn't followed her. And yet what was left for him at home if she failed?

"You have the power to heal him," came the Whale's earth-rending voice, shocking after such an extended silence.

Talia jerked her head up. "I can change him back?"

"You can heal his wing."

"Oh." For a moment, she'd thought everything could be well again. "How?"

"Use the Words," said the Whale.

"I don't know the Words. Wen tried to teach me, but I couldn't—"

"You called me with a Word, Endain's daughter. Do not fear. I will tell you which ones to say."

His voice calmed her. Water lapped over her knees and she stroked Wen's feathers, taking a deep breath. The Whale spoke a Word that sounded like a deep, brassy note, strong enough to shake the stars from the sky. She shut her eyes and let the Word sink into her until she felt it belonged to her somehow, even though it still didn't make sense. It was different from the Words Wen had tried to teach her—she could hold onto this one without it slipping away.

She opened her eyes and looked down at Wen. She mimicked the Whale's voice, and the Word left her lips, piercing and clear. The bird stirred in his sleep. Talia caught a breath of sweet summer air.

"Is it done?" she asked the Whale.

"Look and see."

She eased the bandage gently from Wen's wing, and saw that it was healed, the bone knit straight and any trace of blood entirely gone.

The bird ruffled his feathers, experimentally spreading his wings. He flexed them and leapt suddenly into the air, flying in a wide circle above Talia and the Whale.

She stared up at the white bird, afraid he would fly away and leave her alone with the Whale. She was scarcely able to breathe until he landed again and settled beside her.

The day passed, slowly and quickly at once. Without the ship to sail or her charts to study, there was nothing for Talia to do but stare into the waves, tangled up in her own mad thoughts.

Her knapsack was still miraculously slung over her shoulder, the pouch fastened tight. The faint pulse of Star-light behind the leather comforted her, and for a while her worries fled away.

Night spread over the ocean, a clear black sky blazing with more stars than she had seen in all her life. The Whale swam on through the Northern Sea and Wen flew above them, a flash of white in the dark.

She had no desire to sleep, but she felt hazy around the edges, like she was caught somewhere in the space between dreams and waking. The sea ran calm, its music sad and aching in her ears.

"What is your name, daughter of Endain?" Once again, the Whale's voice startled her.

"Talia Dahl-Saida."

"A strong name."

"I have never felt strong."

"And yet you are here."

A sickle moon rose up out of the waves.

"What are you?" asked Talia quietly.

"I am the Whale."

"I think you're more than that. You're not at all what I thought from reading my ancestor's account. I didn't even know if you were real."

The Whale's laugh hummed up and down his spine, reminding her of a purring lion—content but not entirely harmless. "What did you think I was?"

"A fable. A story. A colorful addition to a myth."

"It's a wonder you took the trouble to call me, then."

A fair point. Talia changed tack. "Why didn't you help Endain, when Rahn dragged her back to the Hall?"

"Because she did not ask me."

"And you've been waiting in the sea ever since?"

Another hum of that dangerous laughter. "I come and go as I please, Talia Endain. I am not bound to one place, or one form."

"But Endain made you. She created you out of Starlight."

"Endain did not make me. She called me, just as you called me. I simply chose to take the form most helpful for her."

"And you did the same for me?"

"You had need of me, so I came."

This was not quite an answer, but she didn't know how to phrase her question any better.

"Why did *you* come, Talia Endain?" he asked her, his voice *hmmmm*-ing quieter than before.

She studied her hands in the moonlight, twisting them in her lap. "Because the gods and the Waves called me. Because my mother needs me. Because—" Once more she saw Wen falling limp and dead into the sand. "Because there was nothing else left."

"Nothing at all?"

The Ruen-Shained appeared again in her mind, followed by Caiden asking her to stay with him and Blaive crying in the dining room. "I gave my heart to a fool and I ruined Wen's life—and maybe Blaive's, too—and I can't—I *won't*—leave my mother's soul trapped in torment for eternity." She clenched her jaw, a tear racing down her cheek.

Waves slapped against the Whale's sides, sliding over the hem of her dress. "It is never foolish to love," he rumbled. "Love is the noblest of all things, and the most powerful."

Talia looked down at her right hand where Wen's ring glimmered on her first finger. "Love has broken me."

"To love is to be broken. That is the very definition of the word."

Wen flew on far above them, his wings catching the moonlight and scattering the stars. She studied him intently, her heart tight.

"He loves you. Did you know that?"

"Yes," she whispered. But that was not the knowledge that tormented her. "Can't you change him back?"

"It was his own doing," the Whale told her gently, "and so it must be his undoing."

"But you said yourself he can't do it!"

The Whale *hmmmm*'d and she took a deep breath, tearing her eyes away from the white seabird.

"Perhaps the Words he used to change his form have not yet ended. He wanted to protect you. To save you. Maybe he hasn't done it yet."

"He shouldn't be here. He shouldn't have followed me."

"You do not want him here, Talia Endain?"

"I don't want him to get hurt."

"Ah," said the Whale. "That is not quite the same thing."

Chapter Forty-Five

I N THE MORNING, TALIA WOKE TO FIND Wen beside her, his wings folded and his head on her knee. He stirred at her movement and looked up at her, unblinking.

"Wen," she said, "you have to go home." She'd decided it last night, just before sleep had finally claimed her. If she failed in her quest, nothing could save him, but if she succeeded—she wanted him far from here, far from Rahn and any repercussions.

The seabird tilted his head to the side, the rising sun glinting amber on his feathers. He looked fierce and wild, but somehow not unlike himself.

Beneath them, the Whale swam on and the sea lapped cold at his sides, splashing Talia's knees.

"Fly home, Wen," she whispered. "Please fly home. It's my fault you're here. I want to save you. Please."

But the seabird just stared at her with his strange black eyes, his answer as clear as if he'd said it aloud: *I will not leave you.*

"You have to go home," she cried, her fear for him so sharp she could taste it. "You have to!" She shoved him off the back of the Whale but he caught himself before he hit the water, wings flapping to regain his balance. He flew back to her side.

She pushed him off again, and again he flew back to her.

The third time, Wen leapt into the air before she could shove him, the wind from his wings whipping through her hair. *"Fly home, Wen!"* she screamed. *"You have to fly home!"*

And the Whale rumbled quietly beneath her: "Talia Endain, I do not think he will go."

She dropped to her knees on the Whale's back and swiped angrily at the tears that broke through her defenses.

The white seabird watched her for a while from the air and she stared up at him. "I don't want you to die," she said. "I can't lose you, too. That's what I saw, the second time I looked in the mirror. I saw you die. I can't bear it. Please go home. *Please.*"

But Wen flew down and settled across from her, his wild eyes staring into hers. He folded his wings and she could almost hear his voice. *I will not leave you.*

This time, she didn't try and push him away. Dread enveloped her, but it was tangled tight with relief.

"Will you teach me the Words of the gods?" Talia said to the Whale in the afternoon, staring down toward his great gray head. "I'll need them when I go down to Rahn's Hall. To shield me from the weight of the water. To give me the strength to defeat her."

The Whale rumbled beneath her. "I will teach you, Talia Endain, but you cannot defeat her with Words alone."

She brushed her fingers over the knapsack containing the Star-light and the sliver of the Tree. "I don't intend to."

He rumbled again, this time with that lion-purr laughter. "That is very well."

Talia pulled herself to a sitting position.

"The Words I speak in your hearing must not be uttered

until the time you have need of them, or their power will wane. They were given to the gods at the making of the world, to help them shape it, but they are not as strong as they once were. Do you understand?"

She nodded. "I think so."

"Then tune your ears and listen. I will sing to you in the language of the Stars themselves, that the Words might burn stronger in the music of their original tongue."

And then the Whale began to sing.

It was a terrible, beautiful song, and it echoed all around her, slipping into her mind and her soul, making her ache.

The knapsack at her hip grew hot as fire—the Star-light, awakening to the song. She had to take it off her shoulder, scramble away from it, up toward the Whale's broad head. If she hadn't, she felt the heat might have consumed her.

The Whale sang all day, and she sat staring over the sea, listening with every ounce of her being. The sun passed over the arc of the sky and sank down again in a blaze of yellow flame.

When night fell over the world and the round disc of the moon awoke out of the waves, the Whale stopped singing. Talia caught a sharp breath—the sudden absence of his music disturbed her.

Wen settled beside her, and she put one hand on his wing.

And then the Whale taught her the Words she would need: Words to change her form, like Wen had done; Words to protect her from the weight of the water; Words to give her a voice in the depths of Rahn's Hall. They sank into her heart, as the Words Wen tried to teach her had not.

The moon slipped back into the sea and the lesser stars faded in the light of the rising sun, and the Whale at last stopped speaking. The Words burned on in Talia's mind, and she knew she would be able to use them when she needed to. They made so much more sense to her after the Whale's song, and she understood what Wen had meant: the Words came easy to him, because they were like music. She glanced at the white bird, his feathers ruffling in the night wind.

"How long will the Words last, down in Rahn's Hall?" Talia asked the Whale.

"Long enough, I hope, for your purpose."

She stared out over the sea. "What happens when their power fades? When the Words unravel? Will the blood of Aigir save me then?"

"No, daughter of Endain. There is not enough sea god blood in your veins for that. When the Words unravel, you will drown."

Chapter Forty-Six

TIME DID NOT SEEM TO PASS IN the normal way, riding on the back of the Whale through the deep waters of the Northern Sea. Talia slept sometimes, but not often. She was rarely tired. She didn't feel hungry or thirsty, and so had no need to eat or drink. She wondered if it had anything to do with the Star-light and Tree-sliver tucked into her knapsack. The Tree had fed the gods once. Maybe that's what it was doing for her. Or perhaps the sea sustained her, feeding the descendant of Aigir with life and health in a way she couldn't understand. She felt stronger than she ever had. Her thoughts were clearer. And the music of the waves ceased to bother her, like the sea understood she was coming and had no need to call her anymore.

She spent many long hours in silence, staring out over the sea or lying on her back and gazing up at the wide sky. Wen sat with her sometimes, but more often he flew behind them, always watchful. The lack of hunger didn't seem to extend to him. He went hunting every day, snatching up glimmering silver fish from the water and eating them when he thought Talia wasn't looking. She wished he was home, but was also immeasurably glad that he'd stayed with her.

Every morning she reviewed her plans for when she reached Rahn's Hall. And every night she shut her eyes and let the Words the Whale had taught her burn fresh through her mind, powerful and certain, ready to be uttered. But she didn't let herself speak them yet.

Sometimes, the Whale would tell her to hold her breath, and he would dive suddenly deep into the ocean, water folding around her heavy and cold. The Whale would feast on krill while she watched fish darting through the sea, or studied the coral formations that looked to her like strange miniature palaces. She saw huge sea turtles and the occasional octopus, and stingrays with wings wider than Wen's. And just when she felt her lungs would burst from the lack of air, the Whale swam to the surface again.

Once, when they were deep below the sea, she heard the sound of iron against iron, saw sparks glinting red somewhere among the waves. The Whale swam nearer, and Talia felt the heat of an impossible forge. A shadowy monster crouched over an anvil—he had the body of a man with the spine of a sea dragon and the head of a lion. He pounded on a curve of iron, sparks glinting off his hammer, Words of power twisting into the metal. He wept as he worked, and a school of yellow fish swam past his face to drink the tears away.

"It is the god Hahld," the Whale told her when they breached the surface again. "Rahn trapped him and bound him, and now he makes collars for the dead."

She couldn't stop shuddering.

A few days later, when the sun burned bright in a wide sky, Talia saw a white ship in the distance, with tall masts and silver sails. It drew slowly nearer, its shining prow carved in the shape of a beautiful woman with jewels caught in her long hair. Sailors in loose-fitting clothing and smart green caps manned the riggings with rapid efficiency, their rough voices caught up in a sea chantey. They drew close enough for Talia to see the bright flash of their eyes and the deft movements of their hands. But they didn't seem to notice her, or the Whale.

A banner snapped out in a sudden breeze, three Stars on a field of white with red edges: the crest of Denlahn, long-time enemy of the Enduenan Empire. But this wasn't a warship; it carried no guns, and the sails were not painted red.

A young man came up to the rail and stared out over the water. He had dark brown eyes and darker skin, and he wore red silk robes with a velvet cap. Talia caught the glint of a sword hilt at his side. He was almost near enough to touch, but he stared right through her, away out to sea.

"He can't see or hear you," said the Whale.

"Why not?"

"We sail in different waters. They go to the living; we go to the dead."

The words sent a chill down her spine. Talia turned to look after the ship as it drew away from her, the sailors' chantey growing faint on the wind. "I wonder where they're headed."

"To Enduena," said the Whale. "The young man is a Prince of Denlahn, an offering of peace to the Empress."

"To Eda?"

"Indeed. She has been threatening war with Denlahn since she was crowned."

The ship grew tiny on the distant horizon, and for an instant Talia saw a different future: herself, Empress of Enduena, standing on the quay in Evalla as the white ship landed and the solemn Denlahn Prince came to take her hand. "And will Eda marry him?"

"Yes. But the prince will not be content to bring peace, for much bitterness and anger dwell hot in his heart."

"What will happen?"

"The Empire will fall."

She blinked, and that alternate future vanished with the ship, swallowed by the horizon. "Whale, how do you know all that?"

She felt his sigh, reverberating through his long body. "I know many things, Talia Endain."

"Do all of them make you sad?"

"Many," he returned, "but not all."

Rain streamed cold from an iron sky and waves churned angrily, large and black and crested with foam. But the Whale's heat warmed her, and he swam close enough to the surface that she could always keep her head above the greedy fingers of the water. Wen huddled close, and she folded her hands in his warm wings.

A light appeared ahead of her in the darkness, bright enough to pierce through the storm.

"What is it?" she asked the Whale.

"The lamps from the lighthouse on the island of Shyd."

"That must be a very lonely task."

"A man called Dain keeps the lights. He lives on Shyd all alone, waiting for the bride promised him by the Empress as a reward for his seven years' service. But the Empress will not send her. Dain will wait ten years, and his bride will not come. He will grow weary in his loneliness and anger, and he will douse the lamps. A ship will break on the rocks and there will be war. Dain will die alone and forgotten on the sea."

Talia held tighter to Wen. "I don't like that at all."

"And yet it is so."

"But if he doesn't douse the light," said Talia, "what then? If I were to go to Shyd and say to him, 'Keep the light always burning,' and tell him what will happen if he does not, would all be well?"

"It is not for mankind to know what lies in their future."

Talia looked at Wen, thinking of the visions in the mirrors, the unshakeable grip of her fate. "If I die here, if I die in Rahn's Hall—I never had a choice. It was always going to happen."

"You had many choices, Talia Endain, and your choices led you here. Dain has the choice to douse the lamps, or not."

"But you know which he will choose."

"But it is still his choice."

Talia stamped down her frustration, ice stinging her cheeks. "Do you know what lies in my future?"

"I do."

"Can you tell me?"

"If I could," said the Whale, "would you want me to?"

She looked back at the lighthouse as they drew away from it, strong and shining through the rain. She thought of the last vision she'd seen in the mirror: herself standing in a field of bones, the Star shining bright on her finger. If that was her future, she'd like to keep thinking she had the power to change it. "No," she answered.

Wen unfolded one of his wings and wrapped it around her.

"That is as it should be," said the Whale.

She woke to the damp breath of wind on her face, and the absence of Wen's warm wing. Waves slapped hard against the Whale, seawater splashing like ice on her skin. For the first time since the Whale had rescued her, she felt truly cold. She fumbled around for her knapsack and slipped her hands inside. But not even the Star-light could warm her.

Mist hung heavy in the air, and she couldn't tell the time of day. Peering through it, she saw Wen perched near the Whale's head, listening intently. She felt the rumble of the Whale's voice, but could not distinguish his words. She realized they were not meant for her.

The Whale spoke a long while and Talia stayed shivering by his tail, wondering what he was saying to Wen.

At last the great seabird bowed his head, and the rumbling of the Whale's voice ceased. It started raining, driving the mist back into the sea, and Wen leapt suddenly into the air with a rush of white wings. Talia quickly lost sight of him.

The minutes stretched on and Wen didn't come back. Worry gnawed her, and she crawled up the Whale's rippling back as he swam, waves breaking over her. She settled near the great creature's head, so that if she looked down she could see his black eyes and his enormous mouth.

"What did you say to Wen?" she asked.

"I told him what lies ahead of him."

"And what is that?"

Lightning showed jagged against the horizon, and the black waves were crested with white. The Whale rose with them, adopting the rhythm of the sea.

"That is not for you to know, Talia Endain."

"I know you can't tell me my own future, but why can't you tell me Wen's?"

The Whale sighed, and she felt the shiver of it pass beneath her. "It would grieve you to hear."

She hugged her knees to her chest, waves splashing up over the Whale's head and soaking her to the skin. "Tell me. Please. I have to know."

"Talia Endain, he will die for the love of you."

"Is that what you told him?" she demanded. "Is that why he's flying up there in the storm? Why don't you send him home and save his life? I don't want him to die. He *can't* die. *Why won't you send him away?*"

"Hush," said the Whale gently, "I have told you what will be."

She pounded her fists into the Whale's skin and screamed at the sky.

"Talia," said the Whale, a note of command in his voice.

Tears coursed freely down her cheeks, mingling with the rain. She bit her lip and tasted blood.

"There is still time left, you know."

"Time for what?" she choked out.

"To tell him that you love him."

Chapter Forty-Seven

S HE DIDN'T KNOW HOW LONG SHE HAD been riding on the Whale. A week, perhaps, a year, half a century—it didn't matter. Every day she sensed they drew nearer to the Tree, and every day she tried to prepare herself for what awaited her in the Hall of the Dead. Her hand slipped often into the leather knapsack, folding around the pulsing Star-light. She didn't dare touch the casket containing the Tree, or try out the Words the Whale had taught her. Not yet.

Wen rarely came to perch beside her anymore, choosing to fly above, sunlight drenching his white wings. She missed his steady presence, and the Whale's words were never far from her mind.

But she didn't know how to save him.

One bright afternoon, a speck of green appeared in the sea ahead of them. As the Whale drew nearer, Talia saw it was an island, no larger than the bottom floor of the Ruen-Dahr. It was covered with trees and the distant glimmer of water, and on the shore stood seven goats.

They appeared to be very old, with long beards and yellowed horns and ragged coats of white and gray. Around each of their necks hung a gold medallion on a scarlet cord, the metal flashing bright in the sun. The goats looked past Talia, just as the boy on the ship had.

"The Isle of Rahn," said the Whale. "It has drifted some ways from where she set it at first. She did not bother to bind it in place."

"Then we're close," said Talia, suddenly afraid. She glanced up at Wen, who kept pace above them. "Who are the goats?"

"The Watchers, the Wonderers, the Fearful. They were once great lords of mankind, and they sought the Tree and the power at its base. But they were too afraid to go further than the Isle of Rahn. So they sit, waiting an eternity for the courage to continue or the cowardice to turn back. Rahn found them a few centuries ago and turned them into goats, to mock them."

The island slid past, and was soon lost in the distance. "Do you fear Rahn?"

"Fear her?" Laughter rippled through the Whale's skin. "No. I do not fear her. Rahn is a spirit, and she has grown very strong. But she has forgotten that she has not always been strong, and that her strength cannot last forever. All things must fall, in the end, and return to dust. I do not fear her. I pity her."

"She's stronger than I am," said Talia quietly.

"You knew that from the beginning, and yet you are here. But you do not come empty-handed."

Talia brushed her fingers against the leather knapsack. "Why is Endain the only one who knew to call you? Why do the other stories not speak of you?"

His voice was sad and deep and filled with memory. "I am written into every line of the old histories, for those who have the heart to see it."

The wind wrapped around her and she caught the sudden aroma of roses and fire, deep earth and sweet rain. "What is that?"

"The Tree," said the Whale. "We are very close."

Two days later, Talia saw it.

At first it was nothing but a tiny white scar in the distance, rising out of the sea, but it still made her heart pound and her mouth go dry. The Immortal Tree, formed at the beginning of all things—it was *real*.

The Tree's scent grew wilder and stronger as the Whale swam closer, until Talia felt almost drunk with it. She had to remind herself to breathe, in and out, in and out.

Wen flew lower in the sky, just a few feet above her; she could feel the rush of air from his wings and looked up to find him watching her. She wished again that he was safe at home, far away from here. Far away from her.

But his presence gave her courage.

The Tree loomed near, bone-white in the sun, its leafless branches clawing some forty feet up into the sky. Talia could feel its strength, and the immensity of its age. Its trunk was nicked with countless scars, and she held tight to the leather knapsack, wondering which one her splinter had come from.

Strong sorrow gripped her. The Tree wasn't meant to be here, stripped of its glory and original purpose. This was all wrong.

And then she saw the serpents, lunging toward her through the sea, their bodies rising and falling in sinuous arcs, fins flashing green.

"Don't be afraid," came the Whale's steady voice beneath her.

The serpents slammed into his side and one of them sprang up at her, roaring, its mouth open wide, its teeth as long as spearheads. She screamed and tried to kick at it, but the serpent latched onto her leg, biting deep. White-hot agony burst behind her eyes.

She scrabbled in the knapsack, seizing hold of the Star-light. "Let go!" she cried through gritted teeth. "By the power of the

Star I command you to let me go!"

The serpent shrank away, teeth ripping out of her leg, and she screamed again, the pain unbearable.

And then Wen was there, in a rush of white wings, diving straight at the serpent. The sea-snake turned on him, lunging with its knife-blade teeth.

"Wen!" Talia shrieked, but he jerked himself up into the air—just missing the serpent's jaws.

The serpents turned to the Whale, leaping at him, tearing at his skin. The Whale rammed his body sideways and shook them back into the sea. "Go, daughter of Endain. It is time."

She leapt into the water, the knapsack slapping against her hip, and swam toward the Tree.

Behind her, the Whale bellowed in anger and pain, the serpents screeched with the noise of a thousand tormented souls.

But she couldn't turn back.

Wen's claws dug into her shoulder, sudden and sharp, and his wings whirred as he half-lifted her out of the sea.

"Wen!" she cried, trying to wrench out of his grasp. "You have to let me go. You have to let me do this!"

The waves crashed hard and cold over both of them. He didn't let go.

She looked back at the Whale and the serpents, who were locked in an impossible battle, the serpents sinking their shining teeth into the Whale's sides, the Whale violently twisting his great body and shaking them off, lashing them hard with his tail. The Whale was strong but the serpents were lithe, coming at him from every side.

The Whale's bellowing cries and the serpents' screams echoed all around her until it seemed the world would crack in half because of the noise.

And then the Whale started singing.

He sang as the serpents wailed and flung themselves at him

with renewed fury.

He sang as they stripped away his flesh and the sea ran red with his blood.

His voice overpowered theirs, but he was not winning the battle.

"Whale!" Talia screamed, tears running down her face.

Wen was tugging her away, away, but she wouldn't go. At last he released her, hovering just above her head. She treaded water, ice seeping into her bones.

Over and over the serpents lunged at the Whale, again and again he shook them off. But Talia could see he grew weaker with every attack. She could not bear to watch, and she could not bear to look away.

The serpents drew back once more, torn and bloodied, their scales dripping red. For an instant Talia thought it was over, that the Whale had won.

But then they coiled themselves and sprang at the Whale one last time. He turned to meet them full on.

There came a noise like water breaking on stone, then the notes of the Whale's song wavered, and went out. The white Tree shuddered like a knife had gone into its heart.

"No!" Talia roared. *"No!"*

But the Whale lay dead in the midst of the sea, the serpents' broken bodies beside him. Their mingled blood stained the water.

Wen's claws bit into her shoulder again, but she couldn't tear her eyes from the Whale's body.

The sea washed over her, and she felt its anger creeping into her.

The Words the Whale had taught her resounded strong in her mind, and she turned her eyes to the Tree. She would not let the Whale's death be in vain.

It was time to do what she had come all this way to do.

Once more she shook Wen off her shoulder and he let her go, but he did not fly away.

She looked up at him, fear and grief raw inside her. "Please go home, Wen. *Please*. Don't follow me. You can't help me now."

And then she took a deep breath, and finally, finally, spoke aloud four of the Words the Whale had taught her.

Pain exploded in her body and she knew she was screaming, but the sound seemed to come from outside of herself. She felt her skin fall away, felt her bones crack and change. Her muscles broke and her lungs burned and she saw her hair lying loose and dark in the water beside her. Fire coursed through her veins, and the sea closed over her head and choked her breath away.

Chapter Forty-Eight

THE NEXT MOMENT THE PAIN VANISHED AND she could breathe again, even though she was still under water.

The Whale had told her how to turn herself into a fish. He'd also taught her Words to bind and protect her in her human form beneath the sea, but they would only hold a little while.

She could see everything now, the delicate shifting shades of the water, the colors of the algae drifting by, an odd lumpy shape she felt sure was important, the red stain of the Whale's blood—or was it her own blood? She shuddered, and swam toward the Tree.

The water parted easily, and she drew close enough she could have touched the Tree if she still had hands. There were tiny patterns in the bark, swirled and notched like fingerprints. She stared at the trunk, dread weighing heavy.

There was no turning back.

She dove into the sea, down and down and down. Glancing back, she saw the silhouette of a huge seabird swimming after her. *He will die for the love of you*, she heard the Whale say. *Die for the love of you.*

But she didn't know how to save him.

She followed the Tree as she swam downward, a gleaming white road to the bottom of the sea. The girth of the trunk grew rapidly as she went, and after a while she could no longer see all the way around it.

The water was murky and dull, and the muffled weight of an impenetrable silence echoed all around.

A ghostly face appeared before her, translucent and green, its dead mouth open in a silent cry. She jerked herself away from it and nearly collided with another face, twisted in agony, it too soundlessly screaming.

And then there were faces everywhere, crowding around her as she swam: wavering images of men and women and children, all of them in anguish, all of them shrieking without voices. They had no bodies, no hands to reach for her—they were just the echo of people, faces pressed up against a window.

She tried not to look into their eyes. She tried not to be caught in their despair. She tried not to shudder as she swam on—through them—ghostly mist clinging to her scales.

Music sprang suddenly into being, eerie and awful and filled with fear, nearly deafening her after the long silence. It was the opposite of the Whale's song—it made her want to hide from watching eyes and crawling worms. It filled her with shame, every dark thing she'd ever done rushing into her consciousness. She wanted to die, because only death could free her from the music, the darkness, the regret.

Screams mingled with the song, the haunted cries of the ghostly faces all at once magnified beyond bearing. She could not shut them out.

But something drove her onward, downward, deeper and deeper and deeper into the sea.

She wouldn't turn back, not if the faces grew hands and ripped her flesh from her body.

On and on, down and down, the music and the screams and

the ghostly faces howling around her. She didn't know how long she'd been here. A year. A century. The torment was unending.

She forgot she was once human, she forgot her mother and the Ruen-Dahr and Wen. The memories of what had happened to her, long ago on the shores of the sea, slipped away. There was only water and darkness, only agony and screaming and the awful, shrieking music.

She thought it would swallow her whole.

The last piece of her soul unraveled.

And then she reached the base of the Tree.

The images and music and screams ceased. Her memory came rushing back: her journey, the storm, the Whale being torn apart by the serpents.

Wen.

She twisted around to look back the way she had come and saw him still following her, his wings pressed tight against his sides—the power of the Words that bound him into his bird form must be protecting him, allowing him to breathe even down here.

The Words that the Whale had taught her burned once more in her mind, and just as Wen touched the ocean floor with one of his clawed feet, dust and ground seashells swirling up around him, she let those Words spill out of her.

Pain fractured her. She felt herself unfolding, out and out, stretching, tearing, growing. The Words burned through her and she shouted more of them as she changed, Words of protection and strength, for Wen as well as herself.

The pain pulsed, and faded. Her vision cleared. She looked down at her hands—her skin was once more her own. It felt impossibly strange down here, caught in the sea's hand but not crushed into oblivion. Her hair pooled around her in the water, her gown whispering at her ankles as though stirred by some quiet wind. Everything moved slowly, the drifting tendrils of a dream.

She turned and saw Wen standing beside her, *human* Wen, his feet bare in the powdery sand. They were both wearing white, their clothing shimmering with the power of the Words that bound them.

"Wen." His name slipped from her mouth and spun out like honey. The knapsack hung over Wen's shoulder.

He smiled. "Thought you might need this," he said, brushing his hand against the leather.

She stepped to his side and wrapped her arms around his neck, wildly glad he was here with her. And terrified about what might happen to him because he was.

He hugged her back, solid and warm. Strong. She didn't ever want to let go.

But the weight of the sea pressed heavy on her body, the faint threads of music echoed in her ears.

She pulled away.

He looked at her, his eyes, as always, seeing deep. "Don't worry about me," he said, shrugging out of the knapsack and handing it to her. She slipped it over her head. "I'll be all right." He brushed his finger across her cheek, and her stomach wrenched. Then he took her hand. She could feel his heartbeat, pulsing with hers, in their joined palms.

Together, they paced around the Tree.

Chapter Forty-Nine

THEY STOOD ON THE VERY OUTSKIRTS OF the Hall of the Dead, a space so strange and immense Talia couldn't properly comprehend it. On the far end of the Hall, hundreds of feet away from them, a dais jutted forty feet into the air. A point of light shone so brightly from it her eyes teared when she tried to look at it: Rahn's Star.

Between them and the dais, a dark river poured, silent and raging.

Tree roots coiled beneath the powdery ocean floor like huge burrowing snakes, winding around the Hall to form its boundaries. Here and there the roots twisted up above the sand to form beautiful arched doorways that looked into inky darkness.

Away to her right sat the Billow Maidens all in a row, their hair pouring to the ground in brilliant shades of cerulean and coral, vermillion and stone. From this distance they all seemed to blend into one another, haunted music spilling from their harps. Their presence unnerved her. Even after all this time and every impossible thing she'd already seen, Talia hadn't quite believed they were real.

She glanced over at Wen. "We have to talk to the Waves."

Slowly, they stepped further into the Hall, chalky dust

swirling up from their feet.

That's when she noticed that the river in front of the dais wasn't a river at all.

She recoiled, dragging Wen to a stop.

Scores of gray shrouded figures danced in a torrent, moving in endless formation to the sighing of the Billow Maidens' harps. They were clothed in shadows, slippery gray garments that ate up the light. They did not speak as they danced, following the everlasting steps with quiet solemnity.

To get to the Billow Maidens, Talia and Wen would have to pass through them.

And they would have to do it quickly, before Rahn noticed them.

They stepped into the ranks of the dead, the embodiment of the ghostly faces that had haunted her during her long descent to the Hall: men and women, children and babies, queens and princes and sailors alike. Patches of gleaming bones showed through their cold, dead skin. Every face was twisted into soundless torment, every pair of eyes unblinking, unseeing, unknowing.

All were intent on their dancing, wholly silent.

Talia and Wen wound through them, fighting against the tide to reach the edge of the Hall where the Billow Maidens sat. The dance flowed the other way, but the shadows let them pass, bony fingers whispering through Talia's hair as they went. She held tight to Wen with one hand, and the pulsing Star-light with the other.

They drew close enough to the Billow Maidens that Talia could distinguish them from one another.

Their faces were various shapes, some round, others thin, some sharp and birdlike, some sleek, almost feline. They had long, lithe fingers, and their skin was speckled like stones. Shells and sea stars and threads of gold were woven into their hair, but they, like the dead, were clothed in gray. Their harps were intricately carved, each resembling a different creature: a winged horse, a lion, a griffin, a bird. The instruments seemed to be strung with strands of their own hair.

The Wave in the center of the sisters had seafoam hair and a harp carved like a dragon. There were burn marks on her face, and her eyes stared out into nothing, as blank and unseeing as the dead: Endain, blinded by Rahn for her rebellion, trapped in darkness for four hundred years, cut off from the man she loved. Her fingers slipped along her harp strings, and the saddest notes of the music seemed to come from her.

Talia's heart broke for her many-times-great-grandmother. Her hand moved from the Star-light to the glass-and-iron casket containing the sliver of the Tree. She fiddled with the latch, undoing it and brushing her fingers across the wood. A blaze of power seared through her, and she clamped her teeth together to keep from crying out. The splinter felt the nearness of the Tree as her Star-light sensed the glory of Rahn's Star, as a small part of her felt she belonged here, in the depths of the shadowy sea.

She and Wen were only a few paces from the Waves now—they had almost reached them. And then a tremor passed through the dead, and the light from the high dais grew so bright Talia had to screw her eyes shut against it.

A voice seethed through the Hall, and it sounded like iron and wind and raging sea. *"There are trespassers in my Hall. Bring them to me."*

And then suddenly the dead were shrieking, skeletal fingers sliding over Talia's shoulders, pulling at her arms, wrapping around her waist, propelling her toward the dais and that high, terrible throne.

They ripped Wen away from her.

"Wen!"

He craned his head around to hers, his eyes wide with terror.

She grabbed the Star-light from the knapsack and hurled it at him, light wheeling in the darkness. He reached out a hand to catch it—

And then the dead crawled over her, obscuring her vision, hurtling her on as if she was a stone caught in a horrible gray sea. She tasted shadow. The music of the Billow Maidens twisted into her, in and in and in, until she thought she would go mad.

And then a strong hand closed around her wrist, yanking her out of the mass of dead, beyond the reach of the unstoppable tide. She stood, shaking, and looked straight into the eyes of her mother.

Or the thing that once had been her mother.

Her face was waxen and gray, her mouth twisted into a soundless scream. Her skin was translucent as tracing paper, her hair white and ragged, hung through with brown weeds and bits of jagged seashells. She was clothed, like the other dead, in a shapeless garment the color of despair.

But her eyes were almost alive, and she was staring at her as if Talia were the ghost, and she the one being haunted.

"Mama," Talia whispered. "Thank the gods. I've come to save you. Bring you back to the light."

Her mother said nothing, just stared and stared, seawater rippling through her colorless hair.

A voice came from the thing that was her mother, but her lips remained frozen, her eyes unblinking. "What are you?"

She laid a hand on her mother's arm, trying not to shudder at the feel of her skin, cold and dead beneath the tremulous sleeve. "I'm your daughter. I'm Talia."

"Talia," whispered her mother. This time her lips did move, half a breath after she spoke. The dead thing lifted her hand and brushed hesitant fingers across Talia's face. "Talia. Talia."

"Yes. We're going home, Mama."

And then her mother blinked, and a single silver tear slid

down her ashen cheek. "But I am . . . but I am dead."

"You saved me, Mama, that night on the ship. Now I'm here to save you."

More silver tears ran down her mother's cheeks. "I cannot go with you. I cannot be free. I am bound here for all of time, until the dead rise from the sea. But even then I will belong to her."

"The stories say I can save you. The stories say I can bring you back to life."

"The stories are wrong. I cannot be free. You must go or she will make you join the dance, too. Even now she compels me to draw you into the figures, to teach you the steps and hold you here until your life flees away and you become one of the dead. Please, Talia. You must go. You can't help me."

"I won't leave you," said Talia fiercely. "I won't lose you forever. I can help you!"

She saw the change fold over her mother, the blankness crawl back into her face. "Dance with me," her mother moaned, the words cold and dead and far away, the spark of life in her eyes entirely extinguished. "You must dance with me."

And then she seized Talia's arm and jerked her into the shadowy throng.

Chapter Fifty

THE MUSIC BURNED IN HER EARS AND the dead teemed all around, and her mother would not release her. Dead fingers bit sharp and cold into her arm. "Let go of me! You can come back. You can live again."

But her mother didn't hear. "It isn't so bad," she said, her mouth frozen once more into a silent, agonized scream. "Once you learn the steps, it is easy to be dead."

Talia slipped her free hand into the knapsack still hanging at her hip, and took the Tree-sliver from its casket. "*Let go of me*," she commanded, holding the shard up into her dead mother's face. Power coursed through her, so strong it scared her.

Her mother screamed and released her, scrabbling desperately away from the Tree-shard. An instant more and she was lost in the tide of the dead, teeming dark, before Rahn's throne.

Talia scrambled backward. The sea roared in her ears and the power of the Words pulsed in her skin, fading from her bit by bit. The Whale's voice echoed in her mind: *When the Words unravel, you will drown.*

She curled her fingers around the Tree-shard and willed the Words to stay. Another surge of power flashed through her body. She lifted her head, still holding tight to the Tree, and walked toward the river of the dead.

She stepped into the dance, shouldering her way past scores of empty faces, frozen screams, hopeless shadows. They danced and spun in their endless rows, but they didn't touch her, seeming to fear the Tree-shard in her hand.

And then she saw, coming toward her through the dead, a steady, unwavering light. The shadows parted and there was Wen, his skin torn and his clothes in tatters, his jaw tight with determination. The Star-light shone strong in his hand.

She met him in the midst of the dancers, her free hand tangling in his. "Thank the gods. I thought I'd lost you."

He squeezed her hand, his blue eyes locking onto hers. His face was taut with concentration, or maybe pain. The Words of protection were fading from him, too. "She's watching us, Talia. She knows we're here."

"Then it's time," said Talia grimly. She stared at him a moment, studying every line of his face, carving it into her memory. "But Wen, before we do this, there's something I have to tell you—"

"Tell me later," he said softly. "When we're safe at home again."

He smiled at her.

It hurt. It hurt so much. But she forced herself to smile back. "Let's finish this," she said. "Together."

"Together," he agreed.

He let go of her hand and she tore her glance away from him. They both started scaling the dais, one on either side of the tangled tower of seaweed and bone.

She climbed as quickly as she could, grabbing bones and roots and coral, the weight of the water trying to crush her into oblivion. Pearls skittered down like pebbles around her and the coral sliced her fingers, but she almost didn't feel the pain. Around the dais, Wen kept pace with her, the Star-light in one hand.

Unbidden, the Whale's words coiled through her head: *He will die for the love of you.*

The Billow Maidens' music rose to a horrid, keening wail, and she looked down to find them staring at her. Watching. Listening. Even Endain's blind eyes were raised toward her.

And then Talia was grasping the top of the dais, her eyes level with Rahn's feet, bare and white beneath the wavering hem of her dress.

"You are very bold, worm of the earth," came the goddess's voice above her, jagged lightning and wind and waves twined together. "Come. Let me have a look at you."

Talia scrambled onto the dais, her skin crawling, and came face-to-face with Rahn.

For a moment, she found herself transfixed by the goddess's beauty: hair the color of finely spun gold, shot through with veins of silver; skin as pale as the Tree; eyes as blue as the deepest part of the sea, filled with hatred and sorrow, wisdom and laughter and, above all, an immense, terrible strength. Tendrils from the seaweed that made up her throne curled through her hair and twined about her shoulders, caresses for their cold queen.

The goddess eyed Talia coolly, almost disinterestedly. "Very few of the race of mankind have ever dared come to my Hall. Why have you?"

Talia stared the goddess down. "I have come to destroy you." Her words cut strong and clear through the Hall, but her knees shook. She could feel the Words peeling themselves from her skin, bit by bit.

The goddess looked at her, her expression a mixture of amusement and annoyance. The Star on her hand glittered and flashed. "What nonsense do you speak before me?"

Below them, the Billow Maidens' music faded to the barest whisper, and Talia knew they were listening.

"I am a daughter of Endain. The strength of mankind and

the power of the sea flow through my veins. Your evil won't endure, and when you are gone the dead will at last find peace. Your rule is at an end."

"Fool! There is no power on earth or sea or heaven that can stand against the Star and the Tree! I will rule the world until the end of time itself, and you will dance with the other *worms* at my feet, and worship me."

"I will *never* worship you. And you're wrong. There are powers that stand against you. *I* stand against you, bound with the very Words that spoke you into existence. And I am not alone." Talia peered down below the dais to where the Waves were watching, fingers slipping slower over their harp strings. "Daughters of Aigir, there is no bond set upon you anymore! The nine centuries of your curse are ended—you need not play for your mother and her dead any longer if you do not wish it."

"Silence! You will speak no more in this Hall. My daughters will do my bidding, now and forever, bond or no." Rahn's voice writhed through the sea, impenetrable, unmovable.

But below the dais, the Waves silenced their harp strings, one by one.

The dead moaned before the throne, confused, faltering in their dance without the Waves' music to guide them.

The hand that bore the Star began to shake. The goddess rose from her throne, towering above Talia with majesty and rage. The sea slipped about her shoulders like a robe for an Empress, blue and green, white and silver. "Do not think you will defeat me!" Rahn thundered. "Many have tried and all have failed, and the ranks of my dead only swell."

"The birthrights of the daughters of Aigir were not yours to take. You stole their power for nine hundred years—now it has returned to them, every drop."

"And they're rather angry with you," added Wen, choosing that moment to leap onto the dais opposite Talia.

A split-second glance passed between them, and as one, Talia and Wen flung themselves at Rahn, a Word of *Death* echoing on their lips.

Talia seized one of Rahn's arms and Wen the other. She had time only to reflect that the goddess's arm was surprisingly human-feeling before she and Wen yanked her backward, tumbling with her down the side of the dais. Rahn raged as she fell, shrieking Words into the sea, but Wen and Talia didn't let go.

They hit the ground in a rain of bone shards and pearls, and in the same instant Talia's fingers closed around the Star. She yanked it from the goddess's hand.

Fire shot through her.

She screamed, for the Star was drawing her into its heart and she couldn't bear the pain. She would splinter into a thousand pieces; she would turn to dust, the fragments of her soul broken and scattered for all eternity.

But then she felt a change inside herself, the blood of Aigir crying out. She had a right to the Star. She could contain its power, control it just as he once had. She would destroy Rahn, save Wen and her mother, free the dead. And then—then she could do anything she wanted. Return to Eddenahr and execute Eda for her crimes. Take Wen to Od where he belonged. Crown herself Empress of all the world, never again have to endure pain or heartbreak or sorrow.

She wanted that, more fiercely than she had ever wanted anything. The power of the Star flooded through her. She welcomed it, let it in.

But then she felt fingers tightening around her wrist, biting sharp and cold, a cuff of bone. "Don't," hissed a voice.

She blinked and found her dead mother beside her, a spark of life in her eyes. "You'll become like her."

Talia gasped and dropped the Star. The fire winked out. She stared at it, relief and regret warring inside of her.

Rahn rose to her feet, shaking Wen off her like an annoying insect. Rage writhed in her beautiful face, but her hand looked frail without the Star.

The goddess lifted her hands above her head, and began to speak, Words of power falling fast from her lips.

They were dark Words. Evil Words, full of shadows and decay.

Talia felt them coiling toward her, circling her neck, choking her life away.

The Star blazed white where it had fallen in the sand, but Rahn didn't reach for it. The earth shook beneath Talia's feet, and a piercing wail sounded behind her. Then came the noise of cracking wood, so loud it nearly deafened her. The wail went on and on, and Talia realized it was coming from the Tree. The shard in her knapsack seemed to shudder.

"Do you think I need the Star to defeat you?" the goddess bellowed. "Do you think I need the Star, when I command the power of the Tree?"

Gnarled, bony roots rose up from the ground like sea serpents, twining around Talia's ankles, yanking her down into the dust. *Let me go*, Talia whispered in her mind, scrabbling for the Tree-shard. *Let me go, and I will free you.* The roots loosened, but did not withdraw.

"The sea is mine," cried Rahn, triumphant. "The *world* is mine. You will bow before me, and you will dance forever!"

From the corner of her eye, Talia saw Wen untangle himself from where Rahn had thrown him, and creep back toward the goddess, the Star-light pulsing in his hands.

He lunged at her, seizing her arm and yanking her down onto the ocean floor. Words poured from his lips, as powerful as Rahn's but filled with music instead of fear. The Star-light pulsed as he spoke, giving him strength.

But Rahn knocked the Star-light from his hand. She shrieked a terrible Word and he was flung suddenly backward, landing in the dust with the crack of bones, his neck bent at a wrong angle.

Talia screamed, twisting her foot from the Tree root and yanking the splinter from her pack.

She looked up to see the shadow of her mother standing beside her. For an instant death faded away, and her mother's skin grew brown and warm again, threads of black shimmering in her ethereal white hair. Her mother's hand wrapped around her own, and holding the Tree-shard they leapt toward the fallen goddess.

Light seared at the edges of Talia's vision—her mother had grabbed hold of the Star. It burned and burned, but it could not hurt her because she was already dead.

They hovered over Rahn, Star and Tree-shard held high, and Talia looked deep into the goddess's eyes. "Your strength is ended. Your throne is broken. Now *we* command the power of the Star and the Tree."

And then Talia and her mother drove the Tree-shard into Rahn's heart.

Chapter Fifty-One

THE TREE STOPPED SCREAMING.

The Hall grew still.

Rahn stared up at them, eyes clouding over, pain creasing her beautiful face.

And then she was still, too.

Talia let go of the Tree-splinter, her arm numb and her body shaking. Her mother looked at her, a smile touching her lips. Then she sighed and dropped the Star, collapsing beside it.

Wen didn't move in the dust where Rahn had flung him. He lay as still as her mother, as still as Rahn herself, nothing but shadows in the dark.

Die for the love of you, die for the love of you.

She turned to see the Waves striding toward the Star, their hair streaming over their shoulders, their bodies twisting and changing as they came. They shifted into the forms of nine horses, their nostrils blowing fire, manes rippling cerulean and pearl, coral and stone and seafoam.

They reached the Star, seething with flame, and fell upon it, striking it with their hooves. *"We break the Star in pieces,"* they spoke in unison. *"We divide its light, we scatter it about the sea, that its true power may never again be wielded by one alone."*

Talia's arm seared with pain from stabbing Rahn, and the weight of water suddenly overwhelmed her. She couldn't breathe.

The last of the Words protecting her were gone.

Across the Hall, the Tree groaned and shook, and with a mighty crack of thunder, it split in two.

Around her, the ground gave way and the sea began to boil.

The dead wept, stumbling into one another and falling to the ground, no longer compelled to dance. They cried out in horror and fear.

And then the Billow Maidens turned to the dead, gathering them up into one swirling, shadowed mass. *"We will bear you to your peace. We will bear you beyond the circles of the world, that you might find your rest at last."*

And in the wheel of the Waves' music a vast chariot wavered into being, shining with the light of the fractured Star. The dead stepped into the chariot one by one, disappearing into its depths, and Talia watched them, spots of white-hot agony sparking behind her eyes. She could feel herself dying. Falling. Fading.

The shadow that was her mother got up from the ground, trembling and tenuous, fainter than mist. She climbed into the chariot, and for the space of three heartbeats, glanced back. She smiled, and Talia reached out for her, unable to bear being parted from her, here at the end of everything. *Thank you,* whispered her mother's voice inside her head. *Thank you for saving me.*

"Wait! Mama, please wait."

But with one final smile, her mother turned and disappeared into the ranks of the dead.

The chariot was full, the dead all accounted for. The Waves in their horse forms harnessed themselves to the chariot, and began to pull it away.

Endain looked back at her, and Talia saw she was whole again, her eyesight restored.

"Your sailor is waiting for you," said Talia, the grief and the pain shaking her to pieces. "Beyond the circles of the world. He never forgot you."

Endain smiled. "Thank you, my daughter. I go to him, now."

Talia blinked, and the chariot vanished from sight.

And then she was slipping, sliding into the boiling ground, the sea overwhelming her.

Words poured from her mouth, Words of strength and protection. Words of healing and transformation.

She collapsed onto the ocean floor and the dark waters of the sea folded over her.

The Hall of the Dead fell into the depths of the earth, and was swallowed whole.

Chapter Fifty-Two

S O THE HALL OF THE DEAD SLIPPED *into the earth, and the Tree shuddered and the sea moaned.*

A young woman lay in the dust of bones and coral, half-transformed into a fish, a shining tail where her legs should have been. The waves whispered over her, caressing her face, as if mourning for a fallen queen.

Three paces from her a white seabird who had once been a man lifted his head and saw her laying there. She hadn't had enough Words to save herself, but she had said enough to heal him, to change his form before hers.

The bird curled his claws around her shoulders, spreading his wings and straining upward with all his strength. Slowly, he rose with her through the water, the earth groaning and shaking beneath them.

Fear pressed black in his mind, for he could feel her fading, the last spark of life in her heart nearly gone out. So he beat his wings, yearning for the sunlight and the air, and he drew the woman with the silver tail up and up, away from the horrors of the broken Hall.

A crack of thunder shook the sea, and the bird who was once a man felt the heat of a terrible light. The Tree turned black before his eyes, charred with the fire of the splintered Star, and it too began to sink into the ground. Dead branches reached out to pull the bird and the woman down with it, but he jerked them away, ever upward, ever onward.

She was dying, his strength was fading, and he could see no end to the bitter gray waves dividing them from air. From life.

On he drove himself through the water, his claws holding tight to the woman's shoulders; beneath them the sea shook, and the Tree was swallowed up by the earth.

The last of his strength gave out. He resigned himself to the inevitability of her death, and his, and then all at once they broke through the surface, and air rushed into his lungs.

He pulled her head out of the water, but she didn't breathe. She lay still as stone in his grasp, not moving or speaking or opening her eyes. But he could still feel that faint spark in her heart, and he knew she wasn't beyond all hope.

The sky was dark with knotted clouds. The wind bit sharp and cold, and the waves beat against him, iron gray capped with white. There was no sign that the Tree had ever been there. He mourned its passing: the last good thing from the beginning of the world, gone.

Once more he spread his great wings, and, strengthening his grasp on the young woman's shoulders, he rose with her into the sky. The Words gave him the power to lift her, but even her slight weight was too much for him. His wings felt like they were being torn from his body.

He screamed in pain, but he did not let her go. He would never let her go, even if it meant falling with her back into the sea.

Words burned in his mind and spilled from his beak, Words to give him the strength to carry her, away from the boiling waves and the last resting place of the Immortal Tree.

All day he carried her over the sea, his muscles straining with every beat of his wings.

Night fell, and he flew on, because there was nowhere for them to stop and rest. Stars appeared over the water. Half a moon climbed the arc of the sky and sank back down. Dawn burned red on the horizon, and he didn't stop.

Day turned to night and night to day, again and again and again. Still he flew, finding no end to the black water. Still the woman in his claws did not wake.

But he didn't regret his task. His love for her and the power of the ancient Words drove him on.

The seabird bore her many leagues across the wide reaches of the Northern Sea, through searing days and bitter nights. Icy rain stung his wings. Raging winds lashed him about in the sky, tearing at his feathers, trying to rip her away from him.

But he didn't let her go.

He flew on, coming after countless days to a chain of brilliant green islands, jagged cliffs crashing down into the sea. He had wished for land since pulling her out of the Hall, but he didn't stop now. He knew that once he laid her down he wouldn't have the strength to bear her up again.

On a night alive with white stars, as the round moon dipped low near the horizon and the sea lay black and glittering beneath, a song rose on the air, a song he knew. He looked down and saw a great Whale, passing through the waters, his body scored with many wounds, healed and faded into scars. The bird listened, and felt new strength rushing into his weary body. When he looked again, the Whale was gone, but the song echoed in his ears, buoying him up.

On and on he flew, the power of the Words and the song fading slowly away. His bones weakened and his sinews tore. Every day he flew a little lower in the sky, because his wings began to fail him.

There came a day when the seabird who had once been a man felt the last of his strength slip away from him. He knew he had only moments before exhaustion claimed him, and he plummeted like a stone into the sea.

But then he saw the line of the shore he had yearned so long to see. It rushed up toward him almost before he understood—a long stretch of sand, jagged black rocks, waves falling cold upon the beach. The towers of a stone house, a ragged banner snapping in the breeze.

And on the shore where Talia Dahl-Saida had once stood, staring out into the sea, the white seabird who had once been Wendarien Aidar-Holt laid her gently down, resting her head in the sand.

Exhaustion overwhelmed him and he collapsed beside her, laying one protective wing over her body. He fell into the sweet nothingness of sleep, and dreamed of ships with silver sails and a great white Tree swallowed up by the waves.

Chapter Fifty-Three

S HE DREAMED OF FLYING OVER THE WIDE, dark sea, of wind rushing through her hair and tugging at her tail. She saw tall ships and green islands; she brushed her fingertips against the freezing stars; she flew into the pathways of the sun. And all the while she heard the whir of wings and felt the jab of thorns in her shoulders. She tried to pry them out but she couldn't. It was the only thing about her dream she didn't like.

And then one day she laid her head on a cloud of white feathers, and fell asleep.

Chapter Fifty-Four

T ALIA WOKE TO THE GENTLE TOUCH OF snow on her skin, and the sound of the sea washing endlessly over the shore. She felt sad, and old, and impossibly tired.

Something prickled at the edge of her consciousness, something she should remember, but didn't. She tried to pin down her thoughts like insects on a board, arrange them into a coherent order. She glanced down the length of her body, and was confused to see a pair of bare brown feet peeking out from beneath the hem of a ragged white dress. Didn't she have a tail?

Her memory came rushing back: sailing with Wen on the Northern Sea, the storm that had wrecked the ship, the Whale. Wen, in the form of a bird, refusing to leave her. The serpents cutting the Whale to shreds, the shadowy ghost of her mother, Wen rushing at Rahn, the Star-light held high.

Wen flying backward in the Hall of the Dead, his bones snapping, his neck bent at the wrong angle.

He will die for the love of you.

All the breath rushed out of her body. She wheeled around to see him lying pale and still beside her amid the wreck of a great white bird. Feathers clung to his arms and hands, his eyes were shut tight, and he wasn't breathing. Snow gathered soft in his hair.

She cried out and folded his hand in hers, but it was cold. It was so, so, cold. She couldn't feel anything. No pulse. No faint hope of life. "No," she whispered, tears slipping down her cheeks. "Wen, no. Please, please, no." And she cradled his head in her arms and rocked him back and forth, sobbing. She loved him. She loved him so deeply, and she'd realized it too late. She hadn't ever told him.

She wept into his hair, entirely broken.

"Daughter of Endain," came a voice, as strong as the sea, "why are you weeping?"

She lifted her head and saw the Whale, swimming a short distance from the shore, one black eye fixed upon her. "Whale," she breathed.

"I am here," he rumbled. His voice sounded as if it was coming to her through all the weight of water and time, down from the beginning of the world, and on past its ending.

"But you were dead." Snow swirled around her, diaphanous and white.

"And so I was, for a while."

"I don't understand."

The Whale *hmmmm'*d, low and long. "Rahn's power was broken when she was destroyed. The wicked things she and her servants did are now undone forever."

"Can you save Wen?" Her fingers curled tight around his pale, cold hand, willing herself to feel a heartbeat. But there was nothing.

"You already did," said the Whale. "And now he has saved you. He was the only one who could."

She thought of her dream, flying so long, thorns digging into her shoulders. Not thorns—claws. "He carried me here. All the way from Rahn's Hall." Her voice broke. "You said he would die for the love of me."

"And so he has," said the Whale, gently.

She bowed over Wen, clinging to him, grief overwhelming her.

"Do not despair, daughter of Endain. Love can change many things. Even fate."

She lifted her head and the Whale was gone, like he had never been there at all, nothing but the endless iron sea stretching into the horizon.

She glanced back into Wen's pale face, memorizing the freckles scattered across his nose, his half-grown beard and the snow clinging to his eyelashes.

"I love you," she said softly. "Forgive me, Wen. Forgive me for waiting too long. For not understanding sooner."

And she bent her head and softly kissed his lips.

His mouth was cold and smooth, but it warmed faintly against hers. Her heart seized. She didn't draw away. Slowly, impossibly slowly, she felt life and breath come whispering into him. Beneath her hand, splayed across his chest, his heart began to pulse, steady and strong.

She raised her head, a cry choking out of her, and Wen's eyes flew open. He gasped for breath, gulping it in like a drowning man. He sat up, chest rising and falling, drinking the air. Alive. Whole. Well.

She stared at him, her hand going to her mouth. She was crying again. She couldn't stop.

His eyes found her face, and held there. "Talia?" he whispered, his voice hoarse, like he hadn't used it in a long time.

"I thought you were dead," she sobbed. "I thought you were dead."

His jaw worked, tears sparking in his own eyes. He reached out one hand, and smoothed his fingers over her cheek, wiping the tears away. He touched her eyelashes, gentle as a whisper. "I'm not dead."

A sob choked her, and Wen leaned closer, fingers trembling over her chin, caressing the curve of her neck. "I'm not dead." He lifted his other hand and wrapped both around her face.

She stared into him, her joy hot and bright.

He kissed her forehead, her eyelids, one and then the other. He kissed her cheek and her neck, and his lips were soft as the snow, but infinitely warmer.

She wrapped her arms around his shoulders and leaned into him, crushing him so tight against her she could feel his heartbeat.

And then his mouth found hers. Light sparked through her body, her heart pulsing hot. He tasted like fire and storm and music; she could feel his strength, and his softness, too.

Snow swirled around them, thick and wet, but she didn't feel it, swallowed up in the fierceness of their kiss. She never wanted to let him go.

He drew back before she was ready, looking at her with bright eyes, his smile overwhelming her.

"I love you," she told him, her mouth mere breaths from his. "I have since the day you showed me the mirror room. Since before. But I didn't know it, not then."

He rubbed his thumb over her cheek, the smile not straying from his lips. "I'm afraid I've loved you a little longer than that."

She laughed, and he grinned and then kissed her again, lingering and long.

When he pulled away, he put his arm around her and drew her close. She lay her head on his shoulder.

"Will you stay with me?" he asked her.

She stared out into the sea, snowflakes vanishing into the silver-gray waves. "Gods, Wen," she whispered into his neck. "I could never be happy anywhere without you."

Chapter Fifty-Five

THEY WALKED UP TO THE HOUSE THE back way, and found that the garden had collapsed into the temple. Slabs of stone poked up through dead roses at odd angles; dust swirled strangely with the snow. The door was broken in half, unable to bear the weight of the hill, and the air smelled of roses, and fire.

They stood and stared at it awhile, Wen's hand caught fast in hers. "The Tree is gone from the world," he said. "I guess it doesn't need temples anymore."

Ahned met them at the front door, peering at them strangely. He didn't ask any questions, just led them up to the tower library. Shards of black glass littered the floor, remnants of the mirror room. No need for a guardian anymore, either, since Rahn was destroyed.

They had tea with Ahned in the parlor. Talia felt like a stranger, her eyes darting constantly to Wen's, wondering when they could be gone. "Where are Blaive and Caiden?" she asked.

The steward stirred sugar into his tea, but didn't drink any. "They've gone together to review the province. They took it very hard when you disappeared. Blamed themselves."

"But are they well? Are they happy?"

Ahned smiled. "They always were a tumultuous pair, but they seem to have mended whatever breach lay between them. They're to have a child in the spring."

A weight lifted from her shoulders.

He sobered again, studying her and Wen in turn. "Two months after you disappeared, the wreck of a boat washed up on shore. We thought for certain you were both dead. Then, nine days ago, you appeared on the beach in the ruins of a great feathered creature, caught in some enchanted sleep. We couldn't wake you. We didn't dare move you. You had the look of ones who were gods-touched."

"And so we were," said Wen, his eyes far away. "We went to the ends of the earth, but the gods saw fit to bring us back again."

Ahned shook his head, bewildered.

They stayed only long enough, after that, to pack up Wen's music and a few changes of clothes for each of them. Ahned found them wool coats, and they shrugged them on in the vestibule, snow falling thicker outside the windows. The steward eyed them unhappily. "Are you sure you don't want to wait until the Baron and Baroness return? Or at least until I can hire you a carriage from the village?"

"Thanks, Ahned, but no." Wen glanced at Talia.

"We're meant to be moving on," she agreed.

Ahned sighed. "You're unlikely to find a ship to take you until spring, in any case."

"We'll find one," said Wen.

"The Baron won't like it."

Wen smiled ruefully. "Caiden will be fine. We'll write to him when we reach Od. Explain everything."

"Letters!" said Ahned. "I almost forgot, Miss Dahl-Saida—this came for you while you were away." He drew an envelope from his breast pocket and handed it to her.

It was from Enduena, postmarked a year past, and she

instantly recognized Ayah's handwriting. She broke the seal, drinking in every word; her friend was safe, and was returning to Od—she'd taken a position as a librarian at the University. She read it over twice before folding it up again and tucking it into her own coat pocket.

"Are you ready?" said Wen, his fingers warm around hers.

She squeezed his hand. "I am now."

And they went out into the snow.

Chapter Fifty-Six

THE SUN SANK INTO THE SEA, A globe of scarlet fire, and Talia shut her eyes and drank in the tangy air, the last tendrils of light caressing her face. She brushed her fingers across the ship's rail, listening to the creak of wood, the slap of waves, the sound of the wind filling up the wide sails.

It was a long way to Od: four thousand miles northwest of Ryn, a voyage as lengthy as the one from Enduena. But she could never be too long out here, caught between the sky and the sea and the last ragged remnants of her fate.

It was strange to be leaving Ryn, to be leaving the Ruen-Dahr and what she'd once thought would be her future.

She didn't hear Wen's step, and she started a little when she felt him wrap his arms around her from behind. He nestled his chin on her shoulder, and she sighed and leaned into him.

"You're going to miss it, aren't you?"

She knew he meant the sea. "I'll always belong out here, among the waves. I think part of me went away with them—my mother, the Billow Maidens. I don't hear their music anymore. It makes me ache."

"Every time I fall asleep I dream I'm flying," he told her softly.

She turned to look up at him, touching the patch of white hair that fell across his forehead. It matched the threads of white running through her own dark hair. Half a year had spun away while they journeyed to Rahn's Hall and back again. Neither of them had come away unscathed.

"We'll visit the ocean," he said. "As often as we can. As often as you like."

"It won't be the same."

"I know."

She thought about everything awaiting them in Od: Wen would pursue his music; she would study myth and history, joining Ayah if she could, and write down the Words fading fast from her memory. She wanted to preserve them. But she couldn't quite shake away her sorrow at having to leave the sea. She laid her head on Wen's shoulder and he held her tight, the fragrant wind wrapping around them. "The Whale told me you were going to die," she said, voicing the thought that had been bothering her.

"The mirrors told me you would drown."

"Then why are we still here?"

He laced his fingers through hers. "We changed our fates, you and I."

She nestled tighter against him, blinking out into the darkening sky.

They watched together as night unfolded over the sea, Wen's arms wrapped warm around her, waves lapping quiet against the ship.

Epilogue

STARS SPRAWLED WHITE AND COLD ABOVE THE little valley where the musicians waited, rosining bows and moistening reeds and tightening strings. Pages fluttered on stands, illuminated by the torches that ringed the ensemble in bright flares of orange. Up on the hill an audience waited too, pulling shawls and coats tighter around them in the chilly autumn wind.

Talia stood with the rest of the crowd on the hill, but she didn't feel the cold. Away to the east she could see the silver shimmer of the sea, and even from this distance it filled her up, made her strong.

Below her, Wen stepped up to the ensemble, his silhouette bold against the torchlight.

"Your husband certainly is a solemn fellow," said Ayah beside her, her wild orange hair escaping out from underneath her hood. "I don't know what you see in him."

"*Gods*, Ayah!" Talia punched her in the arm.

Her friend just laughed. "You know I'm teasing."

She did. Ayah had stood witness at their wedding—three years ago, now—and she often dined with them in their little cottage on the outskirts of the University. She'd listened in awe to their story, asked them to repeat it over and over as she wrote it all down in a book. Talia thought of that book gathering dust on a library shelf one day, forgotten with the other impossible stories. It made her sad.

Sometimes, it all still felt like a dream. But when she shut her eyes and heard the waves whispering, when she saw the way Wen walked, stooped slightly like he carried an impossible weight he could never be free of, when she felt the fire of the Star, burning forever in the palm of her hand—she knew it had been real.

Her heart felt quieter when Wen turned to the hill, looked up at her through the haze of torchlight. Smiled.

Then he faced the ensemble again, and lifted his baton.

Music filled the valley, and Talia staggered backward, gasping.

Below her, Wen's symphony spooled out the music of the waves, a perfect replication of the song she'd heard every day from the Ruen-Dahr, calling her to the sea. Melody poured into her, washed over her. Sparks of gold flew up from the instruments like fireflies in summer—echoes of the Words woven into the music.

She left Ayah, slipped down the hill to stand near Wen. She drank in the song of the sea, let it overwhelm her. Tears dripped down her cheeks.

She could have stood there listening for a lifetime, but the symphony ended before she was ready, the last firefly notes quavering on strings.

For a moment, there was only stunned silence from the listeners on the hill, but then they broke into wild applause.

Wen didn't acknowledge them, just turned to Talia, seeking her approval.

"Beautiful," she whispered, wrapping her arm around his waist.

He kissed her forehead and drew her close.

"Did you know that's what it sounded like? The music of the sea?"

"It's how it sounded to me, in my head—I kept trying to capture it, back at the Ruen-Dahr. I always heard it more strongly when you were near. Now it's finally finished."

She breathed him in, ink and soap and the faint tinge of wildness that had clung to him ever since that day on the beach.

"We won't stay in Od forever," he murmured into her hair. "If the sea calls you again—when it does—we'll follow."

"I know. But not yet."

"Not yet." He laced his fingers in hers, and they turned together to the still-cheering crowd on the hill.

Not yet, she thought. *But soon.* She caught the sudden faint scent of the sea on the wind, and it made her smile. Somewhere far away she thought she heard the Whale, singing down the stars.

ACKNOWLEDGMENTS

THIS BOOK HAS BEEN A LONG TIME in the making—over eleven years from the time I first penned it to publication day! I have grown so much as a writer and a human being since then, and this little book has grown and changed with me, but somehow turned out to be more itself than it was in the beginning. That is due vastly to all the amazing people who have influenced me and my writing and helped to shape *Beneath the Haunting Sea* along the way.

First of all, a huge, HUGE thank you to my agent, Sarah Davies, who I still can't believe signed me, and who I'm pretty sure is secretly a wizard. Thanks for taking a chance on me, for inspiring me to tear my manuscript apart and put it back together again, and draw things out of it that were always meant to be there. You're tenacious and amazing and wonderful, and I'm so, so grateful to have you in my corner.

Thank you to Alyssa Raymond, my fairy god–editor, without whom *Sea* would have never seen the light of day. Thank you for believing in me and this book, for pushing me to dig deeper into my world and characters, and polishing *Sea* until it gleamed.

Thank you to the entire team at Page Street Publishing, for making my lifelong dream of publication a reality!

Thank you to the fantastic people who've run National Novel Writing Month over the years—NaNoWriMo inspired me to complete my first novel after graduating college, and many of my first drafts were penned during NaNo, including *Sea*, in November 2006. In fact, a random writing dare from that year actually still exists in this book—the island of goats that Talia observes as she's riding the Whale came from that dare!

Thank you to all the agents who replied with encouraging words whilst I was querying, including Diana Fox, who once responded to an early version of this manuscript with a detailed, helpful critique, and referred to my myths as "really good Silmarillion fan fiction." (I still think this is the greatest compliment ever.) Huge thanks also to Valerie Noble, whose enthusiasm on a certain day in March 2015 made me squawk with such excitement I frightened the cat.

To my best friend in the whole world, Jenny Downer, for the many, many hours of coffee shop writing sessions, deep conversations, and even hugs (but of course only when I most needed them). You're hilarious and inspiring and have the best taste in everything, and please don't leave me and move away to Canada (unless I can come, too!!).

To my dear, dear friend Esther LaFay, aka Future Me, who many years ago claimed the title of Number One Fan. Thanks for your wise advice (like, "Joanna, you should definitely go on a second date with that boy" which worked out well, as I married him), always understanding how I feel, basically sharing a brain with me, and knowing the difficulty of being a sensitive INFP soul in a world that never quite aligns with our deeply felt ideals.

To my critique partner Jen Fulmer—I'm so glad we found each other!! I would never have gotten *Sea* ready for querying if it wasn't for you, and you're also the one who sent me the tweet about Sarah being open to queries again! Your encouragement, brainstorming sessions, and virtual hugs have meant more to me than I can possibly express. Thank you for sharing your heart and your words and your time with me!

To my critique partner Laura Weymouth, for epic group chats, making me jealous 'cause you basically live in Narnia, hashing out plot details, thoughtful critiques, believing in me and my story, and just generally being all-around awesome. You're still wrong about one thing, though—Éowyn and (book) Faramir foreverrrrrrrr!

To my INFP soul-sister Hanna Howard—you've been a constant source of encouragement and inspiration, and I don't know what I'd do without our long text chats filled with so many exclamation points and emojis they would probably give our agents heart attacks. I can't wait for the day when our dream of traipsing across the Scottish Highlands together, and our other possibly-more-realistic dream of a joint book tour tea party, become reality. Deep breaths! More tea!

To all the writing friends I've made along the way, including Joi Weaver, Amy Trueblood, Ashley Carlson, the NaNoWriMo Viddler group, the AZ YA writing group, and so many others.

To the band Keane, for their album *Under the Iron Sea*, which inspired much of the mood (and a few scenes) in my book, and which I listened to constantly whilst drafting, once upon a time in 2006 when both book and album were new. To the singer-songwriter Loreena McKennitt, another huge source of inspiration whilst plotting and drafting *Sea*, for her haunting melodies and lyrics steeped in longing. And to the band Of Monsters and Men, whose albums *My Head is an Animal* and *Beneath the Skin* got me through round after round of revision with my sanity mostly intact.

To Megan Whalen Turner and her phenomenal *Queen's Thief* series, which sparked the concept of integrating myths into an overarching storyline. I aspire to one day write a book as masterfully plotted as hers.

To my fellow *The Lord of the Rings* enthusiast Taleah Greve, for freaking out with me over the *Fellowship* trailer our freshman year of college, and for letting me borrow your awesome name.

To my fantastic friends for all their encouragement and enthusiasm: Bethany Brownholtz, Deanna Reynolds, Jessica Fox, Seth and Emily Higgins, LeeAnn and Josh Reynolds, Grace Hart, Danielle Pajak, Renee Ferguson, Lauren Brauchie, Brian and Meghan Gonzales, and Michelle Bastian.

To my parents, for their overwhelming support over the years. My dad, for always letting me rope him into ridiculous writing projects growing up, and for the many wonderful photoshoots. My mom, for her many writing cheers and hugs, for letting me get her addicted to tea, and always being willing to meet up for fro-yo. I love you guys!

To my siblings: Daniel, Corrie, and Andrew, for the many adventures growing up, and the now-that-we're-grown-up adventures, too.

And to my amazing husband, Aaron, for sticking with me during the glacial, arduous, and often excruciating querying and submission process. You give fantastic hugs, always know when I need ice cream, and don't seem to mind me sobbing on your shoulder from time to time. You are so encouraging and supportive, and I love you more than I could ever properly express. I'm so glad we finally found each other. Thanks for being the bestest life buddy of all time—I can't wait to see what's in store for us next!

ABOUT THE AUTHOR

J OANNA RUTH MEYER WROTE her very first story at the age of seven—it starred four female "mystery-solvers" and a villain in a gorilla suit, and remains unfinished to this day.

Since then, she's grown up (reluctantly), earned a Bachelor of Music in Piano Performance, taught approximately one billion piano lessons, and written eight novels, many of them during National Novel Writing Month. *Beneath the Haunting Sea* was first drafted during NaNoWriMo in 2006.

Joanna hails from Mesa, Arizona, where she lives with her dear husband and son, a rascally feline, and an enormous grand piano. When she's not writing, she's trying to convince her students that Bach is actually awesome, or plotting her escape from the desert. She loves good music, thick books, loose-leaf tea, rainstorms, and staring out of windows. One day, she aspires to own an old Victorian house with creaky wooden floors and a tower (for writing in, of course!).